Hard Left

by
Bruce Kirkpatrick

HARD LEFT
By
Bruce Kirkpatrick

This novel is a work of fiction. Names, characters, places and incidents either are the products of the author's imagination or are used fictitiously, and any resemblance to actual persons, living or dead, events or locales is entirely coincidental.

ISBN: 978-1-4303-2191-0
First Printing: June 2007; Second printing: August 2007.
Published by Lulu

ACKNOWLEDGEMENTS

Thanks to all of you who encouraged me to put this story to paper. You know who you are. A special thanks always to Nancy Anderson for being a tour guide on the discovery of my life's work, my passion. (Read her book, *Work with Passion: How to Do What You Love for a Living*). Thanks to Shadd Williams for the first read, great ideas and all those lunchtime conversations. To John Jaeger, those light bulb bombs were a great idea, but I don't want to know how you know that. To Joy Crough, for keeping me balanced. A very special thanks to my wife, Nancy, who is quite simply the best wife in the whole wide world and much better than I deserve. I thank God for her everyday.

Cover design by Alan Crisp, alancrisp.com.

For Conor and Kelley –
do what you love and the rest will follow

THE PAIN TRAIN

The needle looked more like a huge number two pencil as the orthopedic doctor turned toward Cody Calhoun.

"This may hurt a little, better grab hold of something," he warned as he began to prep Cody's left knee.

Cody was only 15 years old but knew enough that if a doctor told you it was going to hurt and to hold on for dear life, it was really going to hurt. He didn't fool anyone by sugarcoating it.

Cody grabbed the steel bars that run the length of the hospital bed and gritted his teeth. The doctor already had the syringe poised when Cody noticed the huge compartment at the end of the needle. That's where the fluid was going to go when he drained it from the damaged knee. It looked like one of those 12-inch beakers with the white hash marks every inch or so that were used in chemistry class. It was without a doubt the single, biggest needle Cody Calhoun had ever seen in his entire life.

The next thing he knew it punctured his knee. Then he sort of lost track of time and everything else except the direct line of searing pain that was on a fast track directly from his kneecap to his brain. Do not pass go, do not collect $200, just heat the tracks up, baby, you're riding the railroad of pain now.

The only thing that brought Cody back to reality was when Dr. Kervorkian (not his real name) moved the needle to find a new well to tap. This immediately opened up a new main line and the railroad hit top speed. This was a high speed, direct line, 200 mile per hour, turbo train delivering the goods, a train full of pain, to the depot, the brain pain center. Pain received, the depot is open for the next shipment. Yessir, no waiting, our doors are always open. Got another train coming in, clear the tracks, direct line to the depot.

This non-stop railroad was illuminated in bright reds and yellows. None of the drab colors of grays, browns, and blacks mostly associated with your everyday cargo trains.

Cody surfaced from this maze of colors and railroads just as the doctor was examining the contents of his beaker-needle. The color was a deep red, swirled with a milky yellow substance that looked something like honey that was ready to crystallize.

"Never thought I'd get more than a pint, but that son a of gun was full, wasn't it?" he asked as he brought the beaker-needle close to the boy's face.

"Did you want to take a look at it, son?"

"Uh…uh…nah," Cody managed to mutter, as his mouth was just then beginning to unclench. In fact, his whole body had pretty much gone rigid.

"How do you feel? Better I bet, right."

As the teenager surveyed the damage, he had to admit to himself that he felt better, but considering he had just gotten off a moving 200 mile-per-hour pain train with white-hot tracks, he figured almost anything would feel better.

He looked down at his knee and noticed that it was now about half the size it had been just minutes (or was it hours?) ago, but it had a rather large hole just to the right of the kneecap. About the size of a dime, he estimated, but then again, everything was a bit exaggerated right at the moment.

He barely observed the next few minutes. He told himself he was just catching his breath. Actually, it was more like he had started to breathe again. Funny how the body stops functioning in certain areas, like breathing, when it's battling on other fronts. The doctor was talking to the nurse, they tidied up a bit, chuckled some to each other and talked to Cody's mom, who had stepped out of the emergency room just after the good doctor had produced the Amazonian needle.

It was just as Cody was regaining some semblance of time and space that he noticed how the doctor was dressed. Since it was sometime after ten o'clock at night, Dr. Kalvasian (his real name) looked a bit disheveled. His white lab coat barely hid the clothes of a man who had been aroused in mid-evening from a comfortable night of woodworking. He had sawdust sprinkled on his hiking boots and lightly coating his cream colored painter's pants. He hadn't bothered to change when he had been called to the emergency room by the nurse, saying that the Calhoun family had another injury that he should probably look at right away. He had only run his fingers through his thinning gray hair, changed from his prescription safety goggles to his bifocals, and brushed the sawdust from his salt and pepper goatee in the rearview mirror. His light blue chambray shirt looked frayed at the cuffs and collar and about 20 shades lighter than when he had purchased it.

Then Dr. Kalvasian turned to Cody.

"That knee was damaged pretty good, son. Your ligaments were stretched and I wouldn't be surprised if there were some minute tears in there, maybe even cartilage damage. Not enough to require surgery, but enough to make sure that knee won't be 100% for a long while. I recommend we keep it in the cast for two to three weeks and then examine it again. No activity, stay off it, use your crutches."

"How long's a long time," Cody managed.

"I'd say two or three months minimum. If you're smart…"

"Meaning what?" Cody blurted.

"Listen, I've seen you play hoops on the high school team. My grandson's a big fan of the game and we make almost every home game, " the doctor began. "You're good, you have a nice game, maybe even a shot at playing at the next level. Mind you, I'm no tremendous judge of talent, but anyone can tell you have a little something extra when it comes to enthusiasm. And that often makes up for what your body can't do. But now your body is going to be able to do less. You damaged the internal and the external lateral ligaments. Those are the ones that hold your knee stable as you move laterally, from side to side. And ligaments are like rubber bands, they stretch, they're elastic in some regards, but they don't always go back to their original state. It looks like you've damaged this particular knee before…"

"At least twice that he will admit to," Sarah Calhoun interjected.

Cody's mom wasn't usually the type to interrupt. Mostly she was quiet and shy, only speaking out when it concerned her son or when she was backed into a corner. Raising a 15 year old boy wasn't an easy job for a single mom, especially one who had been spoiled to death as a child by doting, well-to-do parents who couldn't figure out in the first place why she had married Thomas Calhoun. She had been taught to speak when spoken to and to keep your tone civil and obedient. But at the moment she was a little scared and battling a queasy stomach. She hated hospitals, the smell of antiseptic filling the tiny room, and she hated the fact that her only boy was white as a sheet.

"All the more reason to stay off it for an extended period of time. You might also want to try another sport."

Basketball was Cody's life. Not even Laurel Luckinbill, who was perhaps the finest looking woman in the entire high school, took precedence over basketball and she was enough to turn any young boy's head away from almost anything. This man was talking nonsense here! Cody kept silent. He was good at that.

Dr. Kalvasian felt obligated to press on. "You see, son, the knee is an intricate piece of work. Most people think of it as a hinge type joint, but it's more than that. A hinge basically has only one moving part, the hinge, which moves two parts back and forth. But the knee is much, much more than that. It's got three major bone groups meeting there, 11 separate ligaments, all the intricacies of the kneecap, various membranes and cartilage all combining in this one very delicate part of the body that takes way more stress than it was meant to."

Cody was envisioning the inside of his left knee. He could see each and every ligament as the doctor described it. Except he saw them as frayed and dangling, like rubber bands that had been stretched too far and had snapped. He felt like the only thing keeping his lower leg from separating completely and smashing to the white linoleum floor was the skin surrounding the damaged knee. He swore the skin felt like it had been stretched, too. Maybe those ligaments were shot. He dreaded the thought.

"God didn't make the knee to play basketball. Or sports at all for that matter. He designed it to run away from wild beasts," the doctor explained.

"Wanna run that by me again, " Cody mumbled.

" No, really, stay with me here. The knee is pretty well

made to run in short sprints in one direction, like away from a wooly mammoth or a saber toothed tiger, but it's not made to do what you've been doing to it for the past few years. Back and forth, up and down, sideways, and this way and that way. Son, if you continue to abuse it, now that it's had some fairly major damage, it's going to give you trouble for the rest of your life. Is basketball worth a lifetime of pain?"

Cody didn't particularly want to answer that question at the moment. Considering the pain he was now in and the pain that locomotive had just delivered, he considered it an unfair question. Just give me time to get my head together, Cody thought, and I can better take a crack at that question. He did, however, keep visualizing his left knee. Ligaments, membranes, cartilage - all in lockdown mode, shivering from the recent damage, trying to recoup, shaking from the pain locomotive. All right troops, let's assess the casualties. Anybody able to function in here?

"Cody, the doctor asked you a question," mom insisted.

He hated it when she repeated the obvious. Like I didn't hear the question, Cody thought. No, he heard it, he just didn't know how to answer it.

"I don't know if I can answer that question right now. Are we done here? Are you going to put a band aid on that and send me home now or are we going to continue to plod through Gray's Anatomy?"

Cody didn't mean to sound disrespectful although he knew he had. All he wanted to do was interject a bit of humor in what had turned out to be a rather depressing evening all the way around. He was tired, he was in pain, he was hot and sweaty. The lecture was over as far as he was concerned. How come adults always seem to push the point just beyond what was necessary? Did they think teenagers were stupid or something?

Dr. Kalvasian gave a knowing smile and a slight nod of his head to indicate he knew the message had been received, at least as much as possible on this particular evening.

"See you in a week in my office," he said.

"I'll count the days," Cody replied.

IN MY ROOM

Later that night Cody lay on his bed surveying the damage. He knee throbbed and he knew sleep was not going to be easy. He was depressed as he lay back on his pillow and put his hands over his face.

He recalled the exact moment only hours before that his knee had failed him--this time. As a sophomore on the Mountain View Bobcats basketball team, he had seen decent playing time through the first 12 games of the year. Not too many sophomores got time at the varsity level and this year Cody was the only 10th grader on the team. Coach always said with his speed and hustle, Cody just couldn't be denied a shot to play with the big boys. Relentless was the word coach often used to describe him.

Cody was jumping for a rebound in the second quarter of the game when the opposing forward had knocked him away with a well-hidden hip check. Cody remembered being pushed off balance and landing awkwardly on his left knee. He knew it was bad when he heard that familiar pop on the inside of the knee. He crumpled to the floor. The ball flew out of bounds and play was stopped as the referee retrieved it.

"You OK son?" the ref asked as Cody sat upright and looked in astonishment at his left leg. He had already rehabbed the knee twice over the past year and thought for sure that his troubles were behind him. This was going to be his year. Playing with the big boys, scoring pretty good for his age, and bringing a new spirit of reckless abandon to the basketball court. Now this.

Not again, not again, not again was all that was registering in his brain.

"Son, are you all right?" the referee repeated.

All Cody could do was shake his head no, as most of his energy and concentration was aimed at trying not to cry. It was bad enough that every single pair of eyes in the Mountain View gymnasium were focused on him. If he broke down bawling…he didn't know if he could take that.

Coach Myers walked up with a look of despair mixed with disgust on his face. Cody couldn't tell which was more evident, but he couldn't look for very long into the coach's eyes. He just stared at the leg.

"What happened?" Coach Myers blurted out, hoping it might just be a cramp or maybe, better yet, an ankle sprain. Ankle sprains heal pretty quickly in young legs. If it was an ankle sprain, Cody could be playing in less than a week.

Cody didn't say a word, he just pointed to the knee.

"Damn!" was all the coach could muster. Now they both just stared at the knee.

"Well, gentlemen, we got a basketball game to play tonight," the ref offered, rather sympathetically, too, as Cody recalled. "Are you going to help this young man back to the bench or do we need to find a doctor?"

As Cody struggled to get up, two of his teammates reached down to grab under each shoulder to help him stand. He certainly didn't want them to carry him off the court, so he gingerly put a little pressure on the leg, but it was too painful to walk. He began wondering if he was going to throw up that pre-game meal right in front of all these loyal Mountain View fans. That, he thought, would be downright tragic. He bent over to let the blood rush back to his head to let his stomach settle.

"How can we help, man?" one of his buddies asked.

"Let's just get the hell out of here," Cody replied.

He spent the next few minutes pretty much alone in the cramped locker room. The Bobcat team manager, a nice if not slight overweight boy named Cooper, helped him down the stairs to the empty locker room. The coaches and players had the second quarter to finish, so they had the room to themselves. He had waved off the assistant coach as they headed down the stairs and now he and Cooper were wondering what they would do next.

What they did was wait for Cody's mom to appear and haul him off to the emergency room, calling Dr. Kalvasian on the way to the hospital.

As Cody lay back on his bed he decided that there was no way he would let his mind wander back to that giant needle episode. He could almost hear the pain train rumbling right here in his room.

His cell phone rang and spared him the recollection.

"Hell-ooo," was his typical greeting, although tonight's version was quite a bit more subdued that his regular. It actually came out more like "low" which is exactly the way he was feeling.

"What happened?!!" Laurel Luckinbill's voice filled the room. "I felt so bad seeing you being carried off the field like that. I just didn't know what to do and all my buds said I should go to you, but I just couldn't, I mean, that would have been so embarrassing with all those people looking at me and then, I wouldn't have known what to say anyway. And, and, and…oh, baby, are you OK?"

"It's not a field, it's a court."

"Say what?"

"In basketball it's called a court, they carried me off the court. Football is played on a field."

"Ooo-kaaay, thank you, thank you very much, I'm so glad we got THAT cleared up. Sorry."

"Yeah, whatever," was all Cody could get out.

"So, what's up with your leg?"

"I screwed it up again…that's about all there is to it."

"Bad timing, huh? Especially since you missed all the festivities after the game. That dance was a killer and you should have seen what Shelley was doing…"

Cody kept listening as Laurel kept talking. Actually, he thought, she could pretty much talk non-stop about anything. They had been going out, whatever that meant at 15, for three months. Cody sure didn't know except that two people hung out together during school whenever possible, which was pretty much just lunch time and had a "date" like going to a movie every once in a while with a bunch of friends. Three months, seems like a long time he thought. She was one of the most popular girls at Mountain View High School and all the boys had a crush on her. There were even a couple of guys that had dared asked her out since she and Cody had become "official." She had said no both times, at least that's what he thought. He really didn't know.

"And then everyone started telling me how sorry they felt for me since you got hurt and weren't going to make the dance…" Laurel continued, but Cody was only catching the gist of the conversation (or was it a monologue, he wasn't quite sure). His mind was wandering to the conversation Dr. K and he had had just a few hours before, the one where the demented doctor had advised him to take up another sport.

Then the call waiting beep brought him back to Laurel.

"Hang on, 'nuther call comin' through," Cody managed to interject. "Hell-ooo?"

"Cody, it's Denny, you OK?"

Denny ("don't you dare call me Denise") Clarke and Cody had grown up in the same neighborhood and were pretty close friends as younger kids. But in high school their relationship had changed. Cody started hanging out with the jocks, some who were actually upperclassman. Denny was resisting the process of turning young girls into young women that high school often accelerates. She wasn't the prettiest girl in town, but her name was rarely mentioned without the word cute attached to it. And Cody had noticed her figure had been developing nicely the past year or so and even though she still wore mostly jeans and t-shirts, she looked a lot better in them than she ever had before. He had to admit, she was easy to hang out with. You could just be yourself with Denny. She was fun to be around.

"Uh…I was on the other line…" Cody mumbled.

"Oh, sorry…hmm, let me guess…Laurel?"

"Yeah."

"Well she's probably still taking and hasn't realized you have put her on hold. We have no more than 15, 20 minutes max before she figures it out."

"Careful," Cody mocked, but he couldn't help but chuckle

under his breath. Denny always had a way of being sarcastic without being nasty and was the quickest wit he knew. He envied that in her.

"Hey, listen, it's getting late and I've gotta finish this up with Laurel and I'm kinda not feeling like talking much anyway so do you mind if we just catch up tomorrow?"

"Oh, no, I understand. I just felt bad when you got hurt and was thinking about you. I'll talk to you tomorrow, OK?"

"Sure, Den, thanks. See ya."

Cody clicked back to Laurel. "Laurel, you still there?"

"That was very rude, don't you think?"

"What?"

"Keeping me on hold for so long, that's what!"

"Like, maybe, 20 seconds?"

"Geez, aren't we in a good mood."

"Well, actually, no I'm in a pretty crappy mood, to tell you the truth."

Silence filled the airways for the next several moments as Cody tried to put his feelings into words. All he could think of was how long a day it had been. Laurel was simply pouting to make him feel bad.

"If you wouldn't mind too much, I think I'd like to try and take a shower and see if I can get some sleep. OK? I mean, we'll see each other tomorrow if I go to school. You wouldn't mind, would you if we just cut this conversation short?" Cody fumbled out a poorly executed exit strategy, but he never did understand how to get out of situations like this. He barely understood what kind of situation this was.

"No, I was just worried about you, baby. I'll catch up with you tomorrow. Sweet dreams. Bye…" Laurel said rather coolly, waiting for more from Cody.

He hung up. He hated when she called him baby.

Cody spent the next few minutes just looking around his room, not the least bit sleepy. His room looked like a disaster. Clothes everywhere, most of them thrown over his desk chair but a decent portion of which had spilled over to the floor. He had managed to pick a pile up when he got home that night and toss them in the corner, but who cares, anyway, his knee was screwed up again. Tennis shoes and sweat socks, still wet and rather pungent, lent a distinctively manly smell to the room. Cody didn't mind, actually he kind of liked it. The smell tended to keep this mom out of his room.

His bookcase and shelving that bordered his room about two feet from the ceiling was crammed with trophies. Soccer trophies, Little League baseball trophies, summer league basketball trophies. Some actually looked rather impressive. Team parents probably chipped in some serious dough to help the coach buy the bigger model trophy after either a winning season to let the players know how proud everyone was, or a losing season to let the players know the parents didn't care if they won or lost. Man, he couldn't figure out parents anymore than he could figure out girls.

He also had a hat rack full of baseball hats, various posters of Michael and Kobe, one of Steve Young, a couple of rock groups and one huge poster of a cowboy riding a bucking bull, the bull being downright hostile trying to get that dude from digging in those spiky spurs into his flanks. Laurel had given him that one. "One stud on top of another," she had said.

Just then he heard a tapping on his window. Lifting the shade he saw Rupert Clarke, Denny's older brother gesturing him to open the window. Cody just sat there wondering what the heck he was doing at this window a few minutes before midnight. He barely knew the guy.

"Hey, Dude, open the window, special delivery and I'm on the clock," Rupert whispered rather loudly.

"Hey, what's up?" was about all Cody could manage after he got the screen out of the window.

"I'm just the delivery boy in this little melodrama, Cody. I have been pledged to secrecy. Actually, my sister paid me ten bucks to personally hand this to you and seeing how's my job here is now officially done, I will retreat back into the shadows from which I came. See you, dude, hope the leg ain't killing you too bad."

He vanished out into the front yard, past the huge magnolia tree, and began to jog up the sidewalk. Cody opened the paper bag and looked inside. He pulled out a white plastic spoon and a large plastic cup filled with peppermint chocolate chip ice cream. His all time favorite.

Denny, he thought. And he smiled for the first time all day.

A THUMP IN THE NIGHT

Thump-thump, thump-thump, thump-thump.

Mitchell Burke stared at the clock, perspiration beading on his forehead even though the room was cool. It read 12:06 am. Exactly ten minutes since the last time he'd looked.

Like Cody Calhoun, sleep would not come easily for Mitchell Burke this night, but for completely different reasons. Sleep never came easily for Burke. At least not for the past few years. His nights were filled with a fear he couldn't escape.

This night was like all the rest. He had gone to bed fairly early, around 9:30 and started to read a sport magazine. Nothing too heavy, nothing too exciting, nothing too engrossing. He was tired from a busy day and a week of restless nights and he just knew tonight would be different. He would fall asleep and stay asleep until the alarm rang in the morning. It wouldn't happen again. Not tonight. Please, God, not tonight.

But it did. Forty minutes or so after he had grown sleepy and turned out the light beside his bed, he awoke in a light sweat. His eyes opened quickly and wide and he took a deep, full breath, one that filled his lungs like he hadn't had a full breath since he'd fallen asleep.

He listened but the room was still. So still he could almost hear the beating of his heart. Which was exactly what he was listening to and what he most desperately wanted to hear right at this very moment.

Thump-thump, thump-thump, thump-thump.

His mind was now wide-awake and he began to re-live all the things that happened that day. It wasn't a special day, wasn't eventful in any way that he could remember, but his mind wandered from one episode of his day to the next.

He'd had a light workout at the gym before work. It hadn't been strenuous, but he'd been especially tired that morning and he was determined not to have any more than one cup of coffee in the morning. He got so wired from the caffeine that he felt like he was racing sixty miles an hour if he had more than one. Of course, he never used to drink coffee. Not until a couple of years ago.

Then he reported to work and saw his usual slate of patients. He loved working with people and helping to mend their injured bodies. He didn't regret for a moment not finishing medical school. He didn't want all the responsibility that doctors endured. So many of them worked with such deadly, dreadful diseases. He liked patients who were curable. At least he could get them back to a reasonable level of living and in the 13 years he'd been a physical therapist, he had never had a patient die on him. Two of his patients had passed away while under his care, but both had died from natural causes, not from the injuries he had been treating.

Why wouldn't his mind just shut up and let him sleep? He'd tried counting sheep and breathing deeply for extended periods of time and he'd even tried the technique of tensing each muscle group in his body, starting with his lower extremities and working his way up to as many facial muscles as he could isolate. Tensing the muscle, relaxing the muscle. Tensing, relaxing, tensing, relaxing.

But nothing. His body was relaxed, his body was tired, his body was exhausted. But his mind was wide-awake.

After work he had a light dinner alone in his home. He'd fixed grilled chicken without the skin, a few raw carrots and two slices of that special sourdough bread he'd found at the boutique grocery store down the block. He had splurged and had a beer. But only one. He never had more than one. At least not in the past several years.

Thump-thump, thump-thump, thump-thump.

He spent the next two and a half hours working on his bike. It was a top of the line road bike that he had got six months ago. Cost him just over three thousand dollars, but worth every penny. He didn't have much else to spend his money on anyway. He had ridden it exactly four times.

He cleaned it from top to bottom. He filled his special cleaning bucket with a mild detergent, spiked with just a little degreasing liquid. Not much, but just enough to cut through the grease that the chain ring had splashed onto the bike. He started by wiping down the handlebars and rewrapping the left handlebar cover. Wrapping the black spongy tape that cushioned his hands as he rode was very similar to wrapping an injured arm or leg, he thought. He had worked meticulously, making sure the wrapping was tight enough to stay secure, but not so tight to stretch it out of shape.

Sleep, go to sleep, you are very sleepy, tomorrow's a big day, you need your sleep. But he couldn't fall asleep.

His mind raced through the rest of the evening. Finished cleaning the bike, reassembled what he had taken apart. Wiped it down one more time to make sure it was dry. Watched a little TV, some mindless sitcom, what was the plot again, he hadn't really been paying attention and couldn't recall exactly if he had watched the whole thing or just turned it off and started on that sports magazine.

The last time he remembered glancing at the green glow of the digital clock it read 1:48. He slipped into a restless, dreamless sleep. But he checked one more time, just to make sure.

Thump-thump, thump-thump, thump-thump.

LIONEL K. FITZHUGH

For the next couple of weeks, life slowed down a lot for Cody Calhoun. Most notably, Cody Calhoun himself slowed down. He was issued a pair of standard, beige-with-the-rubber-armpits crutches and a large, cumbersome brace for his left knee. Dr. Kalvasian gave him a few exercises to build up his strength, but he mostly had to do nothing until the swelling went down. It wasn't easy to take showers either, so he had to resort to baths, but of course, he didn't tell anyone except his mother that he was "bathing." Sleeping was a pain because he could only lie comfortably on his back. All in all, as he looked at life at this particular time… it was a pain.

He returned to school after missing a week, mostly because his mom worked and worried that nobody could look after him if he stayed at home any longer. If it had been up to Cody, he would have been content never to go back to school and face all the questions and stares that kids bombarded him with the day he returned. He could have stayed on the couch at home for the rest of his sophomore year, mostly watching Sports Center and occasionally doing a little homework.

As soon as Cody appeared that first day back at school, Laurel Luckinbill was there to console him. She liked to hang around Cody and tell him how sorry she was that he got hurt. At first, Cody thought it was a pretty nice thing to hear. No problems here feeling a little sorry for yourself. Heck, everybody does it, right? Cody felt a little sympathy was warranted at the moment.

And Laurel could stroke very nicely, thank you. Cody often found himself just getting lost in her looks as she cooed over him. She had long blond hair, natural for the most part, Cody thought, but he didn't care if it was all-natural or parts of it materialized right out of a bottle. Her eyes were mostly brown, big and brown, but they had a sprinkle of orange dotting the brown, like little specs of sunshine, Laurel liked to say. Cody never said that. He never thought that either, come to think about it. Her skin was mostly fair and even in the winter it looked like she had a tan, even if the sun hadn't shined for months. Maybe she goes to a tanning booth, Cody imagined. Her smile was infectious, with perfectly straight teeth, two years worth of the best orthodontist visits money could buy. Her complexion almost perfect, her body…well, Cody tried not to think about that, especially in his weakened condition. She laughed with a little squeak. But she wasn't laughing much with Cody these days, just sort of frowning and feeling sorry for him.

Laurel wasn't the only one to pitch in with a little sympathy. His teachers all asked him either what happened (those who weren't into the sports world) or when he might return to the team (those who were into the sports world) or just how he was feeling. He didn't dare tell them how he was really feeling, mainly because he was still coming to grips with it himself. He knew he was mad, and frustrated, and depressed, and well…mad, frustrated and depressed pretty well summed it up.

His days at school were filled with hobbling to classes, hobbling to lunch and hobbling to practice to watch everyone else but him practice. Inevitably, he was late for most of his classes and his teachers, who were already into their lectures of the day, would nod their heads with sympathy and approval that he was late. His classmates mostly ignored him, but some rolled their eyes, like here comes Calhoun, milking this leg thing so he can be as late as he wants for this lame class.

Denny Clarke also seemed to care about how Cody was handling life. Except she wasn't all drippy sweet with sympathy like Laurel. Once or twice that first week back to school, she would see him in the hall between classes and just give him a smile or a couple of words of encouragement. Like, hang in there, this won't last forever. Or, life sucks, then it gets better, then it sucks, then it gets better. Well, Cody thought, I'm definitely in the life sucks stage, that's for sure.

Only one person seemed to be quite oblivious to Cody Calhoun's left knee, his best buddy, Lionel K. Fitzhugh. Lionel also seemed oblivious to why his parents saddled him with a name like Lionel K. Fitzhugh. He would always say, Fitzhugh is the family name, British, you know old chap, so everyone in the family has that one. And the Lionel is like the train, Lionel Trains, I just keep movin' and groovin'. When anyone asked him what the K stood for, he would always respond. "It's special, my special K," and then he would bust out laughing so everyone within about a square mile could hear him. But nobody ever referred to him as Lionel Fitzhugh. It had to be Lionel K. Fitzhugh. He even made his teachers add in the K if it was left off the class roster list.

On Friday, two weeks after the fateful day Cody tore up the knee, Lionel came up to him after school, as Cody was struggling against the crowd to make his way down the front steps and out the school entrance.

"Say, four legs, what's up this weekend?" Lionel shouted above the din.

"Well, I'm thinking about entering the Boston Marathon, what about you?" Cody replied.

"Oh, yesss, the man has started to recover just a slice of that razor wit, that rapier humor, that fun stuff that had made him a legend around this here high school for oh, these so many months. How long have we been at this school? About 600 months now? Seems like it."

Lionel K. Fitzhugh thought that most of school, except science and music, was a total waste. If he wasn't discovering something new or listening to music, he was bummed out.

"I'll probably just hang out at home and try to beat Laurel off me," Cody offered.

"You wish, dude. Good one, two in a row. You are back."

"Naw, I'm just getting tired of ripping up my armpits with these sticks, you know. I feel like I gotta break out, throw off these chains, get on with life." Cody always seemed to get into the flow of life a whole lot easier when he was around Lionel, who never had any trouble getting into the flow of life. Except that his interpretation of life was different than anyone else Cody had ever met.

In just about everything, Cody and Lionel were complete opposites, which made their friendship pretty unique. Although Cody liked to hang out with the "cool crowd" and not stray too

far from the socially accepted, Lionel K. Fitzhugh was rarely
concerned with what was cool or acceptable. He prided himself
with being different and apart from the cliques that littered
Mountain View High School. When most of the guys had their
hair clipped short, circa 1963, and spiked with lots of gel, Lionel
looked like he stepped out of 1973. His long brown hair flowed
to his shoulders and he was just starting to get enough hair on his
face to start a mean set of muttonchop sideburns, the kind that
were full and bushy and almost reached his mouth.

Someday, I'll grow a full beard and look like Jerry
Garcia, he liked to say. Kids would ask him, who is Jerry Garcia,
you freak. And Lionel would reply, the freak's freak, that's who
Jerry Garcia is, he's grateful he is dead, so he doesn't have to
look at you dweebs all day. Grateful Dead, get it. And then that
laugh again.

To say that Lionel K. Fitzhugh was into music was
probably the understatement of all time. He lived music, he loved
music. About as much as he loved technology. He was a rare
dude indeed. Left brain and right brain, he liked to say. I got the
tunes on the right side, I got the techno on the left side. I'm
double trouble.

Cody dressed pretty conservatively, mostly baggy shorts,
wearing them just about year round. You could do that in
Northern California if in the winters you didn't mind the early
morning chill too much. Sports t-shirts or polo shirts, but rarely
did Cody wear long sleeves or sweaters or jackets. His engine
burned brightly and he was always warm to the touch. Lionel, on
the other hand, always wore bell-bottom jeans and even in the
dead of summer with the temperature reaching 90, he had a
sweatshirt on. While Cody was lean and muscular for his age on
a ramrod straight frame, Lionel was short and a bit soft in the
middle, carrying a few extra pounds. The only similarity in their
appearance was their tennis shoes. Cody always wore the latest
basketball shoe and Lionel loved running shoes. You never know
when you have to escape from something, Lionel would always
say, and better to have a great pair of sneaks on than to try and
run in clod-stompers.

Cody just liked to hang out with Lionel and take it all in.

Lionel was a trip, that's for sure, Cody thought. And right now he could use a trip away from the trouble that was festering in his left knee.

"What say we check out the James Taylor concert? I think I can locate a live webcast of the Cincinnati show." Lionel asked.

"I don't think so, Fitzy. Laurel said she'd call me and maybe we could watch a little TV."

"I keep telling you dude, all that girl wants to do is watch TV and tongue wrestle with you. Now I'm not opposed to tongue wrestling in principle, but when you get past the tongue, what else is inside of that girl? You know what I'm talking about?"

"Only sometimes, Fitzy, that's what makes hanging out with you so special."

"I'm talking like she's a few gigs short of a hard drive, she got the looks and she got the style, but she don't always compute down at the basic human level."

"Huh?"

"She got no soul, dude, she only cares about what she cares about. She doesn't care about what truly matters in life."

"And I suppose you know what truly matters in life, that it?"

"I will tell you, deficient one. What matters in life is what burns in your little chest thumper. What gets you up in the morning, beside java, and what keeps you going all day long. For you, jockstrap, it is the thrill of victory and the agony of defeat. It's your sports. For me, it is the music. Now I love the techno, but my heart listens to the music. For your little chickadee, I seriously doubt that anything in God's green Earth stirs her soul. Except perhaps for the newest shade from Revlon or the newest powder from Cover Girl. Get my drift?"

Cody just stared and shook his head and chuckled. Although he had to admit, he hadn't discovered much stirring in Laurel. "Whatever, that still doesn't decide what we are going to do tonight."

"Well, tonight I will be avoiding all those things that my mom said I was supposed to do this week and surfing for Sweet Baby James. Buzz me and I'll con my mom out of a pizza and split it with you."

"Sounds fine. Hey, by the way, you doing anything tomorrow morning?" Cody asked.

"Just sleeping till noon and dreaming of that Four Tops boxed CD set I just have to have."

"The four who?"

"Four Tops, 1965, sugar pie, honey bun, you know that I love you, can't help myself, I love you and nobody else," Lionel crooned in his not-so-perfect falsetto.

"The reason I asked, if you're not busy with those honey buns, you willing to go with me to the therapist? I can't go it alone with just my mom."

"Therapist as in head doctor? You're loony dude, but not that far gone."

"Physical therapist, for my knee."

"Your knee? What happened to your knee? Hey, you're using crutches. You crippled or something?" Lionel teased.

"You're the one who's crippled, in the head, you Four Tops freak."

"Oh, yesss, zinger! I told you he was back!" Lionel K. Fitzhugh shouted to nobody in particular as they headed for the parking lot behind Mountain View High School.

THE TORTURE CHAMBER

The cold and cloudy December morning matched Cody's mood. Since the latest injury, his mother had been on him almost every day with a bunch of I-told-you-so's. I told you it wasn't completely healed. I told you it was more serious than you were letting on. I told you we should have gone to a physical therapist a long time ago.

The latest I-told-you-so slammed into Cody as he, his mother and Lionel K. pulled into Diablo Valley Physical Therapy, Inc. for his Saturday morning appointment. Cody dreaded the meeting. He feared his knee was worse than he wanted to know and that the cure might be more painful than the injury. He'd heard horror stories of all the agonizing hours athletes had endured coming back from knee injuries.

Lionel K. was drumming on the front seat headrest to an imaginary beat inside his head. He'd been talking about 60's surf music since he'd arrived at the Calhouns for an early morning power shake, Cody figured the Beach Boys were singing about surfing or California blondes in Fitzy's head. The leftover coffee that Lionel K. slipped into the shake when Mrs. Calhoun wasn't looking probably had added to the tempo of the beat.

The office was located in a heavily wooded area of downtown Mountain View, secluded behind a row of doctor offices. As the trio entered the office suite, Cody was struck by the tranquility of it all. The reception area was decorated in warm colors, lots of light browns and beiges. The pictures on the wall were original drawings of San Francisco scenes. The Golden Gate bridge in fog, the new PacBell Park, home of the San Francisco Giants, a wine country scene and several of the ocean surrounding the Bay Area. Overhead, exposed large wooden beams extended to a high ceiling and gave the whole office a kind of a chic warehouse effect.

To his right was the receptionist's office and since she

was on the phone, Cody glanced to his left. Glass doors separated the reception area from a large room full of exercise equipment and people. Cody noticed at least a dozen people each seriously concentrating on a separate machine. Some were drenched in sweat, some were slowing repeating an exercise, staring directly in front of them or at the particular arm or leg they were exercising.

He didn't notice the music. But Lionel K. did.

"I'm in love with this dude, already, man. Can you believe it? An oldies station, playing a little Jan and Dean. Amazing. Makes you want to head to the beach in your woody, doesn't it?"

"Makes me want to change the channel," Cody said.

"Can I help you?" the receptionist interrupted.

"Yes, we're the Calhouns, here to see, uh…Dr.…" Cody's mom was searching in her purse for the appointment slip.

"That would be Mr. Burke and if you'll have a seat, he'll be right with you."

"No need to sit, we can go right back to my office," Mitchell Burke said, extending his right hand to Mrs. Calhoun as he appeared behind the reception desk.

"Mrs. Calhoun, I presume. Oh, sorry, that rhymes just a little too much, doesn't it?" Mitchell said.

"Sarah, please."

"Sarah it is. And which one of you is Cody?" Burke asked.

"Yeah, me," Cody nodded.

"Hey, how's it going? Not the greatest, I guess, or you'd be doing something else on a Saturday morning," Burke said.

"Like sleeping," Lionel K. said under his breath.

"I take it you're here for moral support," Burke said as he shook Lionel's hand.

"I suppose. That and to listen to the music. Just keep me out of that torture chamber." Lionel had approached the glass door and was staring inside.

"No guarantees, man, no guarantees. What was your name again?"

"Lionel K. Fitzhugh."

"Well, I suppose you got enough torture going on just with that name, huh?" Burke smiled and winked at Lionel as he headed through his office door.

His office was immaculate. The only things on his desk besides a manila folder were a computer and a coffee mug filled with pens. In the corner of the office was a 36-inch television and VCR. Shelves behind his desk were filled with what at first glance looked like medical books. In another corner was a full size skeleton of the human body, with all the muscles, organs, arteries and veins in living color running every which way. Cody just stared at it.

"Oh, that's Van the Man. I'll introduce you to him when we devise a plan to rehabilitate this knee of yours," Burke said.

Cody just nodded.

Burke studied Cody for a moment. He checked out his build, his muscle structure, his left leg, which was still wrapped in a knee brace, and his eyes. He didn't notice any fear there.

"You're a basketball player, right, Cody?" Burke asked.

"Uh-huh."

"Yeah, I think I've seen you play a few times. Number 32, right? Started for Mountain View most of the season?"

Cody turned in amazement. "Yeah, right, you know who I am?"

"Sure, I work with a lot of kids from the high school. Word gets around. And I saw you pick that little guard from Crescent City about six times last month."

"Yeah, they benched him after that."

"So, I've been reading the report Dr. Kalvasian sent over. It's pretty complete and I think I have a good idea of what's going on with your knee."

Cody's mom interrupted, "Can you explain exactly what you're going to do, how long it will take, and how much it will cost? I mean, we've never been through this before and we really don't know what to expect."

"Sure, I think I can answer most of those questions this morning, but the how long it will take part will depend on Cody," Burke replied.

He circled in back of his desk and put his arm around the

skeleton. "You see, contrary to popular belief, the human body is not a machine. Men build machines and most machines are built to last only so long. It's called built-in obsolescence. Take your car for instance. Don't you think car manufacturers could build a car that would last more than 100,000 miles? Sure they could, but if they did, they don't make any money, because everyone would only buy a car about every 10 years."

"On the other hand, man did not design or build the human body. God did. And as far as we know, he didn't incorporate built-in obsolescence."

Burke noticed that Cody and his mother had blank stares on their faces and Lionel K., even though he was apparently rocking out to a song in his head, was leaning forward in rapt attention.

"It's like this. Let's go back a hundred years. At the turn of the 20th century, what was the life expectancy of humans?" Burke asked.

"57.3 years for men and 59.9 for women" Lionel quickly answered.

"OK... I'll take your word for it. Really? 57.3 and 59.9?"

"I'm into science and technology and stuff," Lionel replied.

"Great. So my point is today it's closer to 80, right Lionel?"

"Lionel K.. Don't forget the K. Right, 76.8 and 79.6, about, I think." Cody looked at him, rolled his eyes, sure Lionel was making it all up!

"Close enough. So men and women are living an average of 20 years longer at the start of the 21st century. And life expectancy will continue to increase. So in another hundred years, we'll live to be 100, in 200 years, 120, 300 years, 140, et cetera, et cetera. We can at least give that a good chance of happening. But why do some people die at age 50? We don't know. Just that every body is different. Created different, individual. A unique creation."

"Like Lionel K.," Cody mumbled.

"Thank you, thank you very much," Lionel replied, in his best Elvis impression.

"That's why some people are professional athletes. God created their bodies uniquely. Unique muscles, unique bone structure, unique blood supply, everything in a unique package. And he created others, well, not professional athletes."

Cody shifted restlessly in his chair without saying a word, but Burke picked up on his anxiety.

"So how's this apply to you, Cody?" he asked.

"No clue," Cody replied.

"Well, let me put it this way. I can fix your knee, maybe not 100%, depends how much damage there is, but close, real close. But I don't know if God built those two knees you've got there, and especially that left one, to play basketball. He didn't let me in on his plan for you. He didn't give me the blueprint. You are a special athlete, from what I've seen so far, with a lot of heart and soul, and passion for playing sports, am I right?"

"Suppose," Cody answered.

"I know I'm right. But what I don't know is how God built that special body of yours. Me? God gave me great hands, strong legs, a good head on my shoulders. And you'll find out what makes you special. Especially when you enter the torture chamber. But I don't have any spare knees I can give you to replace that left one of yours. You are not a machine."

Cody still looked hesitant.

"No promises is all I'm saying," Burke said. "No promises that after we rehab that knee, it won't happen again. Maybe you've got built-in basketball obsolescence in those knees. Maybe they weren't built to play ball."

Cody just nodded, like he understood.

Suddenly a scream erupted from the rehab room and a loud crashing sound brought Mitchell Burke bounding out of his chair headed to the exercise equipment room. As he arrived, Cody and Lionel K. were right behind them. Sarah stayed in his office, peeking out, looking toward the glass doors.

A large muscular boy was sprawled out on the carpet, grabbing his leg and trying to repress his agony.

"Manny, talk to me, man, what's wrong?!" Burke shouted as he cleared the others away from the stricken boy. A large group of people had surrounded the stricken boy, all with their mouths open wondering what to do.

"It's my hammy…oooowwwwww," the boy managed.

Burke took a deep breath and felt his whole body relax. "Another cramp, I take it."

The boy could only nod as he gripped his leg and tried to straighten it out.

"Just relax. Let me at that bad boy." Burke began to massage the muscle, gripping it at both ends and isolating it so the spasm would subside. In a matter of seconds, the boy's face began to relax and the moaning stopped.

"Rachel," Burke said to one of his rehab assistants, "after you get Manny a very large tumbler of water, will you please review the proper technique for this machine with him, so we don't scare all of the customers away please?"

"Yes, sir, right on it," Rachel replied.

"OK, folks, tragedy averted, emergency over, you may all return to your programs. No loitering to watch the young man squirm. We have work to do. And Rachel, let's change that tape. I think we're all ready to crank it up a notch here this morning. How about a little Journey."

In unison, the group mockingly moaned.

As Burke led Cody and Lionel K. back to his office, he laughed heartily and sung, "Don't stop, be-lieeeeevin," and he burst into a hearty laugh.

Lionel now had a serious interest in this therapist. "Dude," he whispered to Cody, "this guy is wacko, but can you dig it? These are people in major pain…and they're lovin it."

"Whatever. Are you saying you would like to join me in the pain sessions to follow?"

"Uh, no. Moral support, remember."

The rest of the hour they spent in Mitchell Burke's office was an evaluation of the injury and a timetable for rehabilitation. Cody was to report to Mitchell Burke after school on Monday and would spend three or four days a week working on the machines. He was instructed to begin a walking program immediately. Burke then discussed the payment program and gave instructions for filling out the insurance forms.

As they were leaving Burke shook hands with Cody and

Lionel K. and they quickly exited the door into the parking lot. They had seen enough of the torture chamber for one day.

As Burke said goodbye to Sarah Calhoun, he shook her hand and held on just enough so that she couldn't pull it away quickly. He grabbed her right hand with his left and held it with both hands.

"I'll take good care of him, don't worry. He's a strong kid. And don't worry about the money either. We'll work something out, OK?" Burke reassured her.

"OK, you're the doctor," Sarah said.

"Well, not technically, but thanks for the vote of confidence. See ya soon."

As Sarah backed out of the office, she noticed that Mitchell Burke did have great hands and his eyes weren't bad either.

THE LIFE BLOOD OF AMERICA

Cody and Laurel had been sitting on her front porch for almost an hour and he hadn't said more than about ten words the whole time. The winter day had long since disappeared and a chill had entered the Northern California town from the ocean, as it always did. The temperature was quickly dropping toward 50 degrees, a slight wind blew in from the bay and the two were bundled up in winter coats and wrapped together in a bright yellow blanket.

Laurel had been talking about school and what her family was planning for spring vacation and girlfriends and who was dating who. Cody sat motionless, wondering what Monday and a trip to the torture chamber would bring. He occasionally injected one-word answers and offered quick comments, but he was preoccupied. Not bored, you see, because it wasn't often a boy was bundled closely together with a girl like Laurel and got bored. But more than once he found himself wondering exactly what Mitchell Burke had meant when he said some knees may not have been made to shoot hoops.

"Well, would you?" Laurel's question almost startled Cody.

"Would I what?"

"Geez Louise, Cody, aren't you the romantic type?" Laurel moaned as she slid further away from him on the porch bench.

"What are you talking about?"

"When a girl asks that kind of question, she shouldn't have to repeat herself."

"If a girl wants an answer to a question a boy didn't exactly hear, then maybe she will have to repeat it, just this once." The tone of the conversation had taken a turn, for both of them.

"Well...I asked if you wanted to kiss me," Laurel said

softly.

"Well, yeah, I guess," Cody replied, but he made no move to do it.

"You may, if you want."

Cody wondered how his breath smelled and he wondered exactly how many other boys had been offered the same invitation on this same porch.

"Now?" he mumbled.

"Right now."

Cody bent toward her and lightly kissed her on the lips and quickly pulled away to see how she liked it. Laurel grabbed the back of his head and pulled him closer and kissed him hard. She wouldn't let go.

Cody suddenly got claustrophobic and wrenched his face away from Laurel and quickly stood up, knocking the blanket off them and banging his good knee on the porch railing. The Cokes they had been drinking went clanking off the front steps.

Laurel's eyes were opened wide and a look of shock had settled on her face.

"What in the world is wrong?" she blurted. "Didn't you like that?"

"Well, yeah, it's just…" Cody searched for the next word.

"Just what?"

"I don't know, Laurel, it's just that everything is happening so quickly these days. It's like I'm on a roller coaster, it's going way too fast, taking turns I'm not ready for, and there is absolutely no way to get off."

"Are you saying you want to get off of ME?"

"No, it's not that, it's just…"

Laurel nodded her head and held out her arms, moving her fingers and hands, coaxing him to complete the thought.

"I don't know," Cody shook his head.

"Cody, you're a really cool guy and I love being around you. But, lordy, you are frustrating. I'm not used to rejection, you know what I mean. All I wanted to do was kiss you and you pulled away from me like I had AIDS or something."

"Sorry."

"No, sorry doesn't cut it. What the heck is wrong with

you?"

"Wrong with ME? Just because I'm not ready for all this, there is something wrong with me? Maybe, maybe, there's...." He wanted to say there was something wrong with her, but he couldn't bring himself to do it. It felt pretty nice under that blanket.

"Geez, get a speech coach, if you can't get it out." She regretted it almost as quickly as the last word left her mouth. But it was too late, it was out.

Cody looked at her, his eyes narrowed and he felt like running away, quickly. But boys did not run away from girls like Laurel Luckinbill, at least without deep humiliation. He had been hurt by that last remark but didn't want to show it.

"I think I need to go now," he managed to get out, slowly and deliberately.

"Fine...just...fine," Laurel said, just as slowly and deliberately.

Cody nodded and walked off the porch and headed down the street, not looking back. Laurel sat back down, shook her head, and said out loud, "Geez, what did I do?"

Cody headed directly to Lionel K's house, saw his downstairs bedroom light on, and climbed through the bushes to tap on the window. Lionel, as usual, had headphones on and didn't hear him knock. Cody repeated the tapping, this time on the side of the window frame so that it reverberated throughout the room. Lionel looked up and hurried over to the window, mouthing to Cody that he'd meet him at the front door.

"What's up, dude, you look like your dog just died," Lionel said as he greeted Cody.

"You ever kiss a girl?" Cody asked.

"Are you kidding? No telling what kind of diseases you could contract from that species!"

"Terrific, I can see you'll be lots of help in this situation."

"Oh, yeah, you got a situation! Come right in, my boy, and we will get down to the a-nitty, a-gritty in this a-sitty." Cody just shook his head.

As they entered Lionel's room, Cody noticed the room looked pretty much like it always did, littered with cassettes, CDs and even a few record albums.

"Where are the eight tracks, Fitzy?" Cody said, his way of teasing his friend about his obsession with music, a game they often played.

"Stored in the closet right next to the 33s. So you got a girl situation, huh? I got just the music for you."

"Let me guess…" Cody said.

"Don't even bother," Lionel interrupted. "Your knowledge of music dates all the way back to like, Madonna. You know, there was music before 1985, dude."

"Yeah, yeah, who's it gonna be?"

"Jackson Browne. You see, I'm into that era, circa 1971. Lots of guitars, great harmonies, a little country mixed in. Classic Southern California rock and roll."

Lionel swiftly grabbed a CD and slipped it into the tape deck. He searched for the song he wanted as Cody studied the shambles that was once Lionel's desk.

Well I been runnin' down the road tryin' to loosen my
load,
I've got seven women on my mind.
Four that wanna own me, two that wanna stone me,
One said she's a friend of mine.
Take it ee-ee-easy, take it ee-ee-easy.
Don't let the sound of your own wheels drive you crazy.

"Most people don't know that Browne co-wrote that song, everyone figures it was the Eagles, but my man Jackson recorded it on his first album, too. It's just that their version hit it big. I tend to like his better, not so studio-perfect, you know what I mean?" Lionel said.

"Lionel, nobody knows what you mean half the time," Cody teased.

"It's music, Code-man, the life blood of America. I learn about America through the music."

"Yeah, yeah, Rock 'n Roll Hall of Fame. Music historian, we've heard it all before."

Not more than one hundred times had Lionel K. Fitzhugh

told Cody Calhoun his dream of someday working at the Rock 'n Roll Hall of Fame. Lionel had studied the project since it was first opened back in the late 80s and immediately knew it was a life he was meant to pursue. With his knowledge of music, actually quite vast and diversified for a boy of his age, and his technical ability to produce, re-produce, and pirate (on very rare occasions), he knew he was a natural for a life in music. And since he was pretty much tone deaf and couldn't play an instrument to save his soul, he had concluded that a life as a music historian was his destiny.

"Ya see, Jackson Browne is not afraid to voice his opinion about whatever is going on in his world through his music. War, hunger, poverty, but mostly love. You can tell in each one of his songs if he is in love with a woman or if his heart has just been stomped on," Lionel explained.

"Well, I feel like my stomach has been stomped on," Cody offered.

"Laurel?"

"Bingo."

"Hmm. Stomach been stomped, you say?"

They both just sat on Lionel's floor with their heads in their hands listening to Jackson Browne telling them to take it easy.

"Fitzy, I've never seen you with a girl. Ever enter your mind? Girls, I mean," Cody asked.

"Yeah, I figure, I'll wait until I have a good job. Then some decent-looking girl, not great-looking, not a knockout or anything, but you know, decent, real decent, will find me, possess me, love me, and marry me. I'll have precious little input on the whole thing and if I play my cards right, I just may luck out and stay with her my whole life. Nirvana."

"You really think it works that way?" Cody asked, mostly serious.

"Dude, nothing else that women do make any sense in the world to me, so I figure, my dream is as good as anyone's, right?"

"Right," Cody said. "Right."

"Right on," Lionel added.

J-ROD

That same Saturday night, as Lionel and Cody contemplated life and girls, Joe Roddy contemplated algebra.

As far as he could figure, there was no earthly reason any red-blooded American should have to learn algebra. And no possibility that he would ever have any use for it in his entire life. And absolutely no way on God's green earth he was going to pass Monday's midterm test. None, zip, zilch, zero, nada, no way Jose.

He was left with only one possible way out. He would cheat.

Even though football season was over and he was rehabbing a badly dislocated shoulder and would probably miss all of the wrestling season, he could not afford to fail algebra. He knew the school did its best to ignore a lot of misconduct from its athletes, but failing grades were not something they'd overlook. Misconduct maybe, grades, never. He also knew his father would kick his butt halfway to Helena if he was kicked off the wrestling team for grades. Joe Roddy wasn't afraid of many people, but his father scared the crap out of him, especially when he'd had his share of tequila.

Yeah, you could get away with quite a bit at school. Heck, he'd been let off himself with only a two day suspension for that little fiasco in the cafeteria where he'd smashed the food tray into the face of that disrespectful little turd of a freshman. What was his name, Turnbull? Roddy had a pet name for that little turd and he wasn't afraid to use it, again and again and again until the little pecker had tried to start a fight with him.

Imagine, a freshman picking a fight with Joe Roddy, J-Rod, to his friends, the starting middle linebacker on the Mountain View football team and a wrestler who went undefeated his junior year except for the two disqualifications for unsportsmanlike conduct. Roddy had been caught with his thumb buried deep into the eye of his wrestling opponent, his favorite trick, twice last year. He'd have to be a little more careful this season, if he had a this season.

It was so easy to make that little turd (Turdbull or was it Bullturds, Roddy couldn't remember the name, he'd had so many for the little slimeball) get so frustrated that he took a swing at Roddy. It had been so easy to break his little freshman nose with that plate of mystery meat and Roddy silently laughed as Turnbull's buddies had rushed him off to the nurse's office, his newly slanted nose streaming with blood. You could hardly tell the blood all over his face from the meat sauce. It was, in Roddy's opinion, a tasty little incident that helped solidify his ranking as one bad ass.

Cheating wasn't new to Joe Roddy. He'd been caught several times looking at other's work in the classroom and there was even an accusation that hc had forced a classmate to write a term paper for him or face a severely damaged scrotum. The boy had never come forward when Roddy's paper was suspected of not being his own work and each member of the class was interviewed individually by the teacher.

Roddy's time as a middle linebacker wasn't exactly what you call textbook football either. He pushed every rule to the max and had been penalized more than any other football player in the history of Mountain View. Nobody ever kept that kind of record, but nobody doubted his claim, and Roddy's heroics on the gridiron were legendary. What the record books do show is that he'd been tossed out of three games in his two years on the varsity. All for unsportsmanlike conduct.

Roddy almost decapitated a running back with a clothesline tackle last season. Another Mountain View player had the back around the ankles and almost down when Roddy sized him up and deliberately tried to pry his head away from his shoulders. He didn't even wait for the yellow flag to hit the ground as he headed to the locker room, knowing the disqualification was coming. His coach was not very happy that his star linebacker had been thrown out, but they had a sizeable lead at the time so his punishment was only a little extra running at the following Monday's practice.

The other two times Roddy had been tossed were times where he got caught grabbing the scrotum of the opposing player while in the middle of the pile at the end of a tackle. Nut cracking was what he liked to call it. With all those players piled on top of each other, why shouldn't he get all the help he could in making that running back afraid of him by trying to rip his balls off? Roddy considered it a victory that he'd only been caught twice, considering how many running backs in the county must have spent Friday nights icing between their legs after playing Mountain View.

And there was even a rumor floating around the backrooms of pool halls and barrooms of downtown Mountain View that Joe Roddy had persuaded his big brother Buck to enlist half a dozen of his bruising buddies to help him win the starting linebacker job on the football team. The rumor had it that Roddy and his buddies jumped the starting middle linebacker shortly before the first game in J-Rod's sophomore year. They had masks on and beat him so badly he suffered a cracked skull and lacerated kidney and never did play another game for the Lions. Joe Roddy started the next game and every game since. Buck Roddy simply considered it family duty to protect and promote his little brother. All Joe had to do was buy his brother beer for the next three months. A small price to pay for the chance at gridiron glory.

Yes, a little algebra test was no match for Joe Roddy. And if the freaking teacher caught him, well then maybe a little nut pulling or midnight mauling might help discourage him from reporting the minor transgression in ethics.

NO EARTHLY IDEA

After school on Monday, Cody reported to Diablo Valley Physical Therapy for his first session with Mitchell Burke and his staff. He was nervous and anxious. But deep down there was a bit of excitement pinballing in him, too. At last he was going to get some professional help to rehab his knee. He just didn't know the extent of the work needed to get it back to one hundred per cent.

Burke greeted him with a warm smile and an energy bar. Gotta keep your strength up, he said, as he explained in detail what the sessions would include. He gave Cody a small, spiral notebook and asked him to document everything. He wanted Cody to take notes on the treatments and jot down every single thing to do with his knee that seemed even remotely important. When Cody wasn't at Diablo Valley Physical Therapy, he wanted to know what was going on with the knee. Pain levels, strength levels, exercise completed, even feelings and worries, which Cody knew he would have but didn't know if he wanted to share them with Burke.

Cody had been walking without the crutches for a few days and Burke encouraged him to walk as much as possible as part of his therapy. He spent almost an hour reviewing the injury using his skeleton buddy, Van the Man, and detailing how they would combat the injury. Those were the words he used, like it was combat, fighting the enemy. He talked about attacking the muscle groups to build them up, to reinforce them, because they were the best defense against re-injury. He talked about using care, but being aggressive. The best defense is a good offense when dealing with injuries.

Cody also got the lay of the land in the torture chamber, although that's not what Burke called the exercise room. He called it The Coliseum, like in the movie Gladiator, where the battle really takes place. This is where we build you a new knee, he told Cody. But all the time, Cody got the feeling that Burke was only the teacher, that the rehab was totally up to Cody. He was to schedule three appointments a week for the first two weeks, but after that, he could up the ante, so to speak, by coming by up to five times a week. The more you do, the better it gets. And don't forget to log it in the notebook.

Burke introduced Cody to the staff and a few of the regulars. The busiest time at the center was after school during the week and The Coliseum was crowded. Mostly with kids and young adults. Burke had a real talent for encouraging everyone and showing concern for what they were going through. But as he showed Cody the first series of exercises, Cody noticed an intensity he hadn't seen before. Everything was precise and exact. His instruction was specific and as Cody mimicked the exercise, Burke corrected or perfected his technique. All the time getting as much feedback from Cody as he could. Do you understand what I just said? Repeat it back. Got it? Show me. OK, good, show me again. Great. Good job. Always precise, always encouraging.

As Burke and Cody finished up the session, they headed toward the water cooler, which was located next to a row of stationary exercise bikes.

"Your knee won't be ready for those for a week or two, but you'll either learn to love them or hate them. It's great exercise for that knee. Heck, it's just plain great exercise, period."

"You like to bike?" Burke asked.

Cody sort of shrugged his shoulders and said, "A little."

Burke's look grew concerned and he stared at Cody with an intensity Cody hadn't seen before.

"Look, Cody, you and me, we're going to be spending a lot of time together over the next few months and I believe I am the one guy who is going to get you back on the basketball court, if it's meant to be. But you and me have got to start communicating, you know? I've got to know what's inside you if you want me to help. Come with me." He directed them back to his office and closed the door.

Cody slumped into one of the chairs in front of Burke's

desk and Mitchell sat right beside him, turning the chair slightly to face Cody. Before Burke spoke, he took a couple of deep breaths and stared at the floor for more than a few moments.

"What are you afraid of in life, Cody?" Burke finally asked.

"What do you mean?"

"What I mean is, what scares you, what puts fear into you, what keeps you awake at night?"

"I don't know, I never thought about it, I guess."

Burke let the question sit in the air and surround them both. He wanted Cody to start thinking about the one question he'd been thinking a lot about lately.

"I'll tell you what scares me," Burke finally said. "Death"

Cody's eyes opened a little wider and Burke knew he finally had his undivided attention.

"You see, Cody, the little things in life I've learned to handle. I even use them to motivate me. And I've learned to tolerate the unknown. Man, I used to hate the unknown. I wanted to know how things turned out, how they worked, wanted to have all my ducks in a row. Get organized, be organized, stay organized. Anticipate the future, do everything you can to make it happen exactly like you want."

"But as you grow up you find out that that is not the way it works. You cannot have everything figured out. Life throws curveballs when you're expecting the fastball. High heat sometimes when you expect the change up. But, and it's a big but for some people, if you learn to enjoy the spontaneity of life, all the curveballs, then life becomes more of a game to play, rather then a puzzle with no answers."

"And that has exactly what to do with death?" Cody wanted to know.

"Yeah, death, the ultimate bean ball. You're enjoying life, taking it all in, slippin' and a slidin' with it sometimes, but just crankin' with it, rolling downhill with the breeze behind your back, even dealing with all the unknowns…except death. Nobody knows that one. And it can be a beanball heading right toward your cranium and no matter how hard you try, you just can't get out of the way."

"Heavy," Cody offered.

Burke smiled and sat back in the chair. "You afraid of girls?" he finally said.

"No way," Cody said confidently.

"Liar," Burke countered. "You afraid of failure?"

Cody shrugged his shoulders.

"Sorry, shrugging and a slight nod of the head, that did not compute. And your answer was?"

Cody got an exasperated look on his face and said, "Yeah, I guess, sometimes."

"Alright, a breakthrough!" as Burke bounded out of the chair.

"I knew you had it in you. Truth and honesty. Sitting across from a man you hardly know and willing to admit you don't know it all. That's a start, my man, especially from a 15-year-old. Because once you admit you are afraid of something, like failure, you can use that as a great motivator."

"But, Cody, one thing I want you to know. You cannot fail in here. You can only give me your best."

"OK, I can do that."

"One other thing, Cody. I am almost totally certain you have no earthly idea of what your best is. Not many of us do." Burke left the room, silently slipping through the door.

Cody stared off into space and thought about this tall, strange man that talked about failure and death. His mind racing, his thoughts jumping all over the place, he couldn't quite pinpoint his feelings. It wasn't quite fear, at least not the kind of fear he had felt in his life. Like speaking in front of the class and not quite being able to get the words out right, or that first basketball game as a sophomore.

No, this was something different. He had a sense of what Mitchell Burke meant by fear of failure. And a creeping feeling inside of him, way down deep inside, somewhere he hadn't looked before started bubbling to the surface. It was a feeling like he wasn't capable of giving his best. Maybe he didn't have it in him. Maybe...

"Are you going to sit there the rest of the afternoon or are we going to finish the workout?" Burke said lightly, his face looking around the corner of the office door and his big grin breaking the mood that engulfed Cody.

"Oh, is lecture time over?" Cody shot back with a smile.

"I'm working on your mind, too, you know. Not just rehabbing that knee of yours. The knee? It doesn't think, it either works or it doesn't. If it doesn't, we fix it. But the mind, it's always thinking. Sometimes that's good, sometimes it's bad," Burke continued as they made their way back to the Coliseum.

"Bad like how?" Cody asked.

"Bad like thinking too much. You see, sometimes we need introspection, we need to figure out what makes us tick. But other times, we just need to crank. Put your head down and plough forward. You just tap into the source of that motivation, whether it's a fear of failure or a need to succeed, or you just want to impress that pretty little lady in the second row, and you go balls to the wall."

Cody began to understand what he meant and it showed in his face. He was nodding slightly, like he had remembered one or two times in his life when balls to the wall was exactly how he felt.

"OK, Cody Calhoun, let's give me 27 minutes on the treadmill, no elevation, at 3.3 speed. Do not, I repeat do not, under any circumstance try to prove your manhood by breaking into a sprint, or a run, or a jog, or anything other than a walk. In fact, it's almost closer to a stroll, got it?"

"A walk in the park, doc."

"Music, we need music in here!" shouted Burke to nobody in particular. "And none of that rap stuff. Give me some of that old time rock 'n roll! Give me some Sam and Dave!" And he started to shout in a big, bold baritone voice:

You didn't have to love me like you did, but you did, but you did, and I thank you.
You didn't have to squeeze me like you did, but you did, but you did, and I thank you.

Cody programmed the treadmill as he shook his head in amazement at Mitchell Burke. This dude is crazy, Cody thought as he started to walk, staring out the window at the parking lot. He didn't realize it, but he had a big smile on his face.

He carefully upped the speed to 3.3 and settled into the routine. He felt comfortable for the first time today, because he knew for the next 27 minutes, he was on his own. He was rehabbing. His knee was working, and getting better.

Before he slipped into his rhythm, he caught a reflection in the plate glass. It looked like somebody on a stationary bike was pointing to him. He turned slightly to look over his right shoulder and the turn made him lose his balance. He almost toppled over backwards off the back of the treadmill before he righted himself by grabbing the handrails.

"You're in big trouble, Calhoun, if you ever get that thing past crawl speed," Joe Roddy snickered as he shook his head, laughing out loud as he began to crank as hard as he could on the bike.

Cody returned to his rhythm, but it wasn't quite the same. He felt a slight chill run up his back and he shivered.

Mitchell Burke, who had been standing in the outside hallway talking to a new customer, heard every word.

BURKE'S LAW

Over the next six weeks, Cody Calhoun's life was programmed almost to the minute. Up at 6:15 for classes at 7:30. After school basketball practice to watch the team work out. The Lions were mostly losing these days and Cody knew he couldn't do anything about it. Cheering from the sideline during games kept him busy and into the game, but he was dying to play. It drove him crazy to see his teammates throw the ball away or miss a shot he knew he would have made if he had just been in the game.

At practice he was pretty much ignored. The coaches knew he was out for season and they had to work to do. Their work did not include Cody Calhoun, so he practiced foul shots during most of the practice. Cody figured that even without the team trainer rebounding for him, he could still get in 300 to 350 shots during a regular practice. Maybe he'd be the best foul shooter on the team next year.

After practice ended around 5:30 he walked over to Diablo Valley Physical Therapy and to get in his workout. Burke had showed him a few weight training exercises he could do during basketball practice with free weights, but he discouraged much more than that because he wanted to watch Cody's progress and supervise the workouts. He kept telling Cody he'd be on his own soon enough. Just hang in there a while longer.

By his fifth week of rehab Cody was doing all the exercises that Burke had showed him: leg extensions, leg presses, hip extensions, calf raises, hamstring pulls. He had even started to work on his upper body a bit, mainly because he was tired of looking like a toothpick. He graduated from walking on the treadmill to running and eventually to the stationary bike.

Burke showed him how to work the different muscle groups in his legs on the bike and gave him detailed routines of strength, speed and duration. All were properly noted in Cody's spiral notebook, which, except for looking a little ragged from being crammed into his backpack along with everything else, was a precise record of Cody's last five weeks.

Cody was pumped about his time in the Coliseum. He was a quick learner and had pushed himself to do just a little bit more than Burke required. It became a game with them. Burke would give the detail of the exercise, the weight to use, the amount of reps and Cody would put five more pounds on the scale and do five more reps than Burke had asked for. If Burke said to ride the bike for 30 minutes, Cody went 35. If Burke gave him a range of resistance, Cody would push himself to go just a little harder, a little farther.

But he never lied when he recorded the workout in his notebook. Burke looked at it every week and never said anything about Cody pushing it too hard. Mostly he got attaboys or high fives after Burke inspected the notebook. A nod of the head and a big smile from Mitchell Burke was good enough for him.

After his workout, Cody helped clean up the Coliseum, wiping down machines, emptying trash containers, and refilling water coolers. Burke had made a deal with Cody's mother, that if he pitched in and helped in the evening, he would discount Cody's therapy charges. Actually, Sarah Calhoun had only seen one bill for the initial evaluation for $125 and one bill the following month for $25 for a special ice pack for Cody.

After Cody finished his work, he started in on his homework until Burke closed for the day. Burke had gotten into the habit of dropping Cody off at his house on his way home. Every once in a while Burke stayed for dinner. Cody hit the books until he hit the sack. It was a routine without a lot of excitement, but Cody enjoyed it. He knew where he had to be, when he had to be there and what he had to do. He liked routine, he liked that his day was all laid out for him. No surprises.

One evening as Cody was reloading the paper cup dispenser by the water cooler, Burke walked into the now empty Coliseum. "Your mom just called and said she'd be here in five minutes to pick you up."

Cody wondered what was up. "That's all she said?"

"Yep, that's all."

"Something's up. She never comes to get me."

"Cody, you might as well stop trying to figure your mom out. Burke's Law #7: moms are always smarter than their children. Live with it."

"Burke's Law?"

"Yeah, I stole that from a TV show in the 60s. It's on TVLand now. Gene Barry as a private detective, being driven around in a big old Rolls Royce solving crimes."

"The only crime around here is all that 60s music you play. Now I gotta hear about a 60s TV show?"

"It was the golden age, my boy, the golden age," Burke countered.

"Right, right, but you might try living in the present age for once in your life."

"Oh, I live in the present age, I just choose not to listen to the music of the present age."

"You and Fitzy ought to get together and compare cryptic notes about the past. Maybe throw on some 'albums' or listen to some 'eight track tapes' or something."

"Don't be dissing my music."

"You call that music?" Cody said as Van Morrison crooned over the stereo system.

Burke just smiled. It was another routine that Cody enjoyed, bantering with Burke about the music of the 60s and the music of the new millennium. It was playful and good-natured and had become another bond between the two.

As they finished their work and threw uppercuts at each other's music, Sarah Calhoun slipped into the lobby and watched them a moment. Cody had certainly taken a shine to this man, but she wasn't too sure about him. He seemed too good to be true and she had been down that road before.

Sarah's marriage to Frank Calhoun had ended six years earlier, when Cody was nine. As the marriage was falling apart, the Calhouns had sold their home and moved into an apartment. When Sarah returned from work the evening before escrow closed, Frank Calhoun had moved out - lock, stock, barrel and stereo equipment. He'd cleaned out the house of everything of value and left a set of divorce papers.

Sarah spent that evening knee deep in tears and Brillo pads. She cried more for her failed marriage and an unknown future than for losing Frank. And she had to clean the entire house herself that same night because the new owners were showing up two days later to claim their home. Frank didn't shown up the next day at the title company to sign the final papers for the sale of their home. But he did show up late that evening to talk the title company into sending the proceeds check to his personal checking account. It took Sarah five months and a slew of lawyer fees to finally get her half of the money.

Frank Calhoun had been a decent father to his only son, but a terrible husband. He was a drinker and he blamed his unquenchable thirst on his Irish heritage. In fact, he was Scottish and he inherited none of the frugal nature of the Scots. He always spent more than he made as a carpenter either in bars or at the racetrack. When Sarah's marriage was final, she had little furniture, a shabby wardrobe, a nine-year-old boy, a mountain of debts and no job.

Her only saving grace was a degree in accounting that she managed to earn through seven years of night school. When Frank left, she took a bookkeeping job in a high technology firm that made networking equipment for computer systems. The company took off during the Internet boom of the late 1990s and Sarah climbed the ranks within the accounting department, all the way to manager with four wannabes reporting to her. Her salary wasn't great but it paid the bills and she was able to put aside a small amount each month for Cody's college fund. He wouldn't be attending an Ivy League school, unless he happened to earn an academic scholarship, but Northern California had many good schools where he could get a decent education and stay close to home.

As she reminisced where the last six years had taken her, Mitchell Burke noticed her in the lobby and smiled, holding up a finger indicating he would be with her in a moment.

"Cody, let me talk to your mom for a second alone, OK?"

Cody shrugged his shoulders and Burke took that as a signal that he had as long as he wanted. He knew Cody would keep himself busy.

"Hey, Sarah, what brings you here today? Come to see how I've been torturing your boy?" Burke said as he approached her at the reception desk.

Sarah ignored the lure of banter and almost whispered, "Is there somewhere we can talk, alone?"

Burke picked up on her solemn mood and suggested they retreat to his office. Van the Man had been posed in Burke's office chair, his skeletal arms placed around his own neck as if he were choking himself, his legs sprawled across the desk.

"Sorry, over-enthusiastic patients who can't take the pace we put them through here, I suspect," Burke managed as he lifted the skeleton from his chair and placed it on the hat rack it normally called home.

"I'm very, very, very concerned..." Sarah began slowly, "that Cody has been incurring...expenses, let's say, here that...are mounting up, you know, and..." she trailed off and didn't finish the sentence.

Burke's natural character would have let her stumble a bit more and even urged her to get it out so he could understand it, but he quickly grasped that she was talking about money and he jumped to her rescue.

"Sarah, Cody is pretty much on his own here now. He really doesn't take up much of my time. I've got lots of machines just sitting idle and if he wants to use them to strengthen that knee, it's fine with me. And he helps around here with clean up and things, so he's pulling his own weight," Burke said.

"What are you saying? You're not charging us anything for him to be here?"

"You're paid in full as far as I'm concerned."

"Mr. Burke, we appreciate everything you've done for Cody, but we don't want, nor do we expect any charity from you," Sarah said, almost indignantly.

"Mrs. Calhoun... no, I mean Sarah, that's what we agreed on right? You're Sarah, I'm Mitch? Anyway, Cody has got a ...determination in him that I really admire. You see, most kids, heck, most adults for that matter, come here with an injury, they get treatment, they stick with the treatment, for the most part anyway, they get better, they go away. Most want to get better and usually they do. But rarely do I see someone like Cody…"

"Is his knee better? Is it one hundred per cent?" interrupted Sarah, trying to stay on target. She wasn't going to let this man wander off the subject.

Burke wasn't used to being interrupted in the middle of an explanation and he didn't much like it, but he understood Sarah's concern for money. "It's better, it's not perfect, it may never be one hundred per cent," he said. "And I know you don't know me from Adam and you're concerned with the amount of time I'm spending with your son and if I'm going to charge you for each and every visit and the answer is no."

"Do all the other kids that come here get charged for your services?"

Burke took a deep breath, "Most do, some don't."

"And what determines if they do or they don't get charged?"

Burke looked directly into her eyes, bright blue eyes he noticed, but quickly got back to the business at hand, whatever that was, because he had no idea, "I do. It's my business."

"So why isn't Cody getting charged?" she demanded.

"Lordy, would you like me to charge you? I mean I could if you demanded it, but somehow, somewhere, I thought I might be doing you a favor. I can do favors, can't I? It's my business, I do favors all the time. Just the other day, I put the whole football team through a two hour meeting on weight training and I didn't charge the school district a red cent. And guess what? The principal didn't call me up and tell me to charge her, she actually called me up and thanked me. Personally. On the phone. Thank you, Mr. Burke, I appreciate it."

Burke let out an exaggerated exhale, which had the effect on Sarah Calhoun that he wanted. She bit her lip and didn't say a word. Man, he thought, if I have to make her feel guilty about it, at least it's one way to stop where this conversation is going.

"I'm sorry, I didn't mean to…" she began softly.

"No, no I'm sorry. I'm used to being pretty demanding around here and when I couldn't get my point across I resorted to blatant over-exaggeration. Except for the football thing, she really did call."

"It was a very nice thing to do and she should have called."

They both sat there in silence, looking any place other than each other, contemplating where the conversation was headed.

Finally, Sarah broke the silence, tears welling up in her eyes. "I'm worried about Cody, and it seems I'm worried all the time. I want to hold on to him so tight, to know what he's doing, to know his friends, to keep track of him every second of every day. And I know that's not all that good for him, but I just can't help it. I just can't lose him, but I don't know how to hold onto him."

"As far as I can see, you're not losing him," Burke offered.

Sarah looked suspiciously at him. "He spends more time here than at home these days."

Burke knew he was treading on thin ice, that bond between teenage son and mother, one side that is straining to break the ties of motherly love, yet fearful of being independent, the other side desperately hanging on to that love.

"Most of the time, Sarah, he's working really hard on his rehab. Truthfully, I've never seen a kid work harder. And there does seem to be times when he just doesn't want to go home, I'll admit it. But maybe he's just craving a little male bonding. You know, someone he can talk to, an adult, and adult that's, well…not his mother. You know what I mean?"

She nodded, "He just doesn't let me in like he used to."

"He's got two thing working against him. One, he's male. And two, he's a teenager. Put those together and all semblance of a hearty conversation dies. Almost 100% of his answers are either 'yeah', 'uh-huh' or 'fine.'

"You forgot 'whatever'."

Burke smiled and finally Sarah broke out of her frown and smiled warmly at him.

"Listen, about the money," Burke said, "if you're willing to have him put a few hours in here a week, I'll pay him, and he can work off any expenses that way. He'll get his rehab in, I'll get some help with a few projects I have lying around, and you won't have any out-of-pocket expense. Sound OK to you?"

"No charity, right?"

"We'll call it the barter system. Services offered for services rendered."

"How long do you think he'll need to keep up his rehab?" Sarah asked.

"Another month or so before he's ready to really test the knee. I'm one to go a little longer than recommended in rehab. Better safe than sorry, Burke's Law #1."

Sarah looked quizzically at him.

"Old TV show, Burke's Law, starring Gene Barry?" he responded.

"Oh, yeah, right," she said. "The guy with the limousine."

"Well, actually, it was a Rolls Royce."

She looked at him mischievously and said, "Whatever." They both laughed as they headed back out to the Coliseum.

THE FIGHT

Laurel was making little happy faces in the fogged up windows in her brother's 1991 Mustangs as she and Cody sat in the back seat. It was Friday night and the car was parked in front of LaRoma's Pizza Parlor, the local hangout after a Mountain View basketball game.

"It's getting chilly," she said as she snuggled closer to Cody. He had already moved as far from her in the seat as he could. He was quite sure she'd grab him by the seat of his Joe Boxers if he tried to escape out the front door of the two-seater. He braced himself for what was coming next.

"Don't you want to kiss me?" Laurel asked.

Bingo, that's what was coming next, and Cody wasn't all that opposed to kissing her, but he wasn't sure where it was going to lead. He figured he could stall.

"Boy, the Lions sure looked good tonight, didn't they? Man, I wish I was out there. You know, it's killing me just sitting there on the bench not being able to play. It's like the coach doesn't even know I exist, you know what I mean?" Cody fired off. It may have been his longest speech of the past two months.

"Exactly," Laurel deadpanned.

Cody sat there desperately trying to think of something else to say as Laurel moved closer and grabbed his left hand, squeezing softly.

"Cody," she said, "I don't give a rat's little tushy how badly we beat those farmers from Truckville, you know what I mean? I just want you to kiss me like you mean it."

"Sure," Cody said and he leaned in for the kill.

Inside LaRoma's the basketball team was being treated to three large pizzas by Dominic LaRoma, head proprietor of the restaurant and longtime fan of Mountain View teams. His standing offer was that any time the local team won a game, football or basketball ("there aren't any other real sports, are there?" he always said), he would treat the team to free pizza. He wasn't just a generous booster of Mountain View athletics, the old Italian was a pretty shrewd businessman, too. He knew that the jocks brought in the wannabes. Those were the kids that liked to hang out with the jocks. Wherever the jocks went, the wannabes hung out. Deep down they wanted to be jocks, too, but most of them weren't ever going to be part of the athletic upper crust, so they became content just to hang on, listen to the stories of the conquests and offer support and praise whenever they could.

And besides, wherever the jocks went, so did the girls. Wannabes weren't so proud that they wouldn't immediately latch onto any girl discarded by the jocks. Girls rejected by jocks were usually pretty fine women. Even if there weren't any rejects, girls were girls, and wherever girls were, hangers-on wanted to be, too.

Dominic had just finished delivering the third Meat Stacker pizza to the basketball team table in the back part of the restaurant. He surveyed the Friday night crowd and smiled to himself. Another victory, another profitable night. He was a middle-aged man, born in San Francisco, and all Italian. He cherished his heritage and wore it proudly. He had the round face, dark eyes and olive skin of his race and a big, warm smile and a hug to show he was from the country of love, as he liked to put it.

He even dressed the part. He always wore his Mountain View Lions baseball cap and a large white apron, which covered a body that had dipped into the leftover pizzas way too often. He kept his bushy, black mustache full and liked to throw out a 'Hey, Paisano' to his Italian buddies when they entered his restaurant. He even had the Dean Martin song about the moon hitting your eye like a big pizza pie, on the jukebox, mixed in with the latest hits and some golden oldies.

As Santana's "Smile" blared from the jukebox (Dominic always cranked the volume just a little higher on Friday nights), Joe Roddy was holding court, surrounded by his faithful bunch of wannabes.

Even though Roddy wasn't on the Mountain View

basketball team and his wrestling season was over due to the shoulder injury, he still considered himself a top jock, worthy of many hangers-on. He enjoyed crashing these basketball parties for a little free pizza and a chance to pick up one of the leftover ladies. Roddy wasn't unattractive and he usually had a girlfriend, although he didn't stay with any girl very long. He was big and broad and ever since his father got him that acne drug, his face had cleared up, revealing good-looking features. He used his smile to his advantage and was proud to say he never needed any sissy braces to get these big, straight, clean ivories.

That night Roddy was sitting at a table adjacent to the basketball banquet with two of his buds from the wrestling team and their girlfriends. Roddy was giving them a hard time because they couldn't eat anything that night except for Diet Coke. Wrestlers rarely indulged in pizza during the season to make their weight class unless they were the fortunate ones that were trying to wrestle up a weight class and were actually trying to gain a few pounds.

Jim Scales, who wrestled at 165 pounds but weighed closer to 170 was in a desperate attempt to shed the remaining weight before tomorrow's match. He kept one of those tall, 16 ounce plastic glasses nestled in his lap and every minute or so raised it to his mouth and spit into it. He figured he could lose at least three pounds over the next 14 hours to make his weight if he got as much water, in the form of spit, out of him as possible. He'd face dehydration in the match if he got to that point, but no sense worrying about that now.

Roddy kept trying to push the glass over and give him a spit shower, so he kept reaching into Scales' lap to grab the glass. Scales only defense was to knock the hand away and yell "pervert" as loud as he could. The girls thought it was funny and Roddy liked the attention.

Denny Clarke and a few of her friends were in the pizza parlor that night, enjoying a three-cheese pizza, diet drinks and the festive atmosphere. They weren't what you would call hangers-on, but on Friday nights during basketball season, there was no better place to hang out than LaRoma's. Her brother, Rupert, and his buddies were good friends with most of the guys on the team, so they liked to hang also and trade stories about athletic feats. Rupert played lacrosse, an up- and-coming high school sport in Northern California, but since most kids in the school had no idea what lacrosse was, he wasn't considered much of a jock. And what with the kids tacking the nickname basket hockey to his sport, he tended to get more than his share of friendly teasing passed his way.

Joe Roddy and Jim Scales had taken their little spit shower game to the next level. Roddy was both trying to grab the plastic spittoon and kick the leg of Scales' chair out from under him, figuring he'd shower Scales one way or the other. He wasn't going to miss this opportunity. Finally Scales was teetering on the back two legs of the chair. As Roddy made one final attempt to grab the cup, Scales suddenly grabbed the spittoon, pushed the chair back violently and jumped up from the table. It was a disastrous move, setting off a series of unexpected reactions.

The heavy wooden chair slammed into the table where Denny Clarke and her friends were sitting, catching the metal pizza tray that was hanging off the edge of their table. The pizza was catapulted over Scales and headed for one of the unfortunate girls sitting at Roddy's table. She stared transfixed as the pizza, as if in slow motion, flew up a good eight feet in the air, arching toward her. Gravity quickly took over and she got the brunt of four slices of three cheese squarely in the middle of her chest. She screamed.

As the pizza was dancing overhead, Scales' noticed that his table had tipped precariously toward the basketball team. A small plastic pitcher of Orange Crush slowly slipped off the end of the table and landed perfectly upright. Perfectly enough that is to send a shower of soda high into the air, drenching the boys with their backs to the Roddy table. Scales, who later blamed his dehydration, slipped and fell and knocked the whole table down on top of himself. The big metal napkin holder hit him squarely in the crotch.

The only person within spitting distance of the whole mess who was left completely untouched was Joe Roddy. Once he surveyed the scene and noticed he didn't have a spec of pizza or Orange Crush on him, he fell into uncontrollable laughter. He pointed to the girl with the three-cheese pizza decorating her chest and he laughed. He pointed to Jim Scales holding his crotch and moaning and he laughed harder. He pointed to the drenched basketball players and almost fell out of his chair, holding his stomach and bellowing.

Dominic LaRoma knew in an instant that this could be the small spark that ignites a massive food fight or worse yet, a brawl. He'd seen it before so he quickly came running over, assuring everyone that everything was all right. He quickly righted the overturned table, positioning himself between Roddy and the basketball team, and started cleaning up the pitcher and glasses on the floor. In the meantime, Scales had pulled himself up and wiped himself off and began looking around for his spittoon.

Roddy was still giggling and trying to hide his laughter in his hands but doing a poor job of it. Dominic returned to the kitchen to get more towels for the clean up.

"Shut up, Roddy," Rupert Clarke spit over his right shoulder in Roddy's general direction. Rupert had taken the hardest hit and had orange soda dripping down his back inside his shirt.

The demand coming from the usually mild mannered lacrosse player struck Roddy as funny. He covered his mouth with one hand and pointed at Rupert with the other, exploding into another fit of uncontrolled belly laughs.

Denny Clarke couldn't control herself any longer either and half under her breath said "Jerk" so that she was sure Roddy would hear her.

"Listen, squirt," Roddy said as he managed to quickly switch his tone, "you watch your cute little pouty mouth and don't be calling me names, you hear."

When Rupert heard his sister being talked down to, he rose from his chair with his fists clenched and faced Roddy.

The mood in the room quickly turned from Animal House food fight to Old West gunfight. Rupert held his ground and just stared at Roddy. Roddy slowly stood, took off his jacket and placed it on the back of his chair.

"Sit down, Rupert, unless you intend to do something

about it, which would be highly unadvisable." The last word rolled off Joe Roddy's tongue very deliberately as he over-enunciated each syllable.

"Why don't you take your fourth grade humor and your loser friends and get the hell out of here, Roddy." Rupert Clarke wasn't a fighter and it was very much out of character for him to confront one of the school bullies. The demand didn't hold a lot of conviction. Roddy sensed the lack of fight in Rupert and took a step closer.

Just then Denny Clarke, who had a lot more fight in her than her brother, grabbed Roddy's arm and said, "You going buy us a new pizza since your buddy here launched ours half way across the room?"

"I told you to back off, squirt," said Roddy as he pushed Denny away, sending her reeling toward her table.

"Hey…" was about all that Rupert Clarke got out of his mouth as he stepped toward Roddy. Before he could finish his sentence, Roddy, with cat-quick timing, turned toward him and threw a roundhouse right hand punch, which hit Rupert squarely in the jaw and sent him spinning backwards. He slipped on the wet floor, fell over, and hit the back of his head on the edge of an adjoining table. The room froze.

Every eye turned toward Rupert who lay on the black and white tile floor, unconscious. A few of the basketball players cradled Rupert's head and Denny touched his cheek and tried to rouse her brother. Dominic returned to the scene and gently grabbed Roddy from behind by both arms at the elbows. His grip was powerful and his intent was clear.

"Leave and do not come back. Tonight or anytime in the future," said Dominic LaRoma. "You are no longer welcome in my restaurant."

"Get your greasy hands off me. I didn't do a thing. I was just sitting here minding my own business eating your crappy pizza. This jerk," Roddy said pointing to Rupert, "came at me so I defended myself."

"But I will not defend you," said Dominic, "if this basketball team decides to teach you some manners. I advise you to leave and leave quickly." He began to push Roddy not so gently toward the door, keeping himself between Roddy and the rest of the crowd.

When they reached the door, Roddy turned toward the restaurant and shouted "Losers!" He was hailed by every bite of half-eaten pizza in the restaurant.

Rupert was finally regaining his senses but wasn't able to rise above a sitting position. His eyes hadn't cleared and Denny was worried. A couple of boys put fingers in front of his face and asked him how many he saw, but Rupert just sat there, staring, not focusing on the fingers or the fact that he was sitting in Orange Crush and pizza with an entire room full of kids looking at him. Denny kept asking the crowd to give him room and declining Dominic's suggestion that he call an ambulance.

"Maybe we can give him a minute or two and then get him some fresh air," she said. Dominic kept cleaning the floor and straitening tables and chairs as most of the kids resumed their Friday night socializing, leaving Rupert there on the floor, rubbing the back of his head.

"He does not look good. Perhaps you should call your parents and have them pick him up?" suggested Dominic. That seemed to get Rupert's attention and his eyes looked at Denny with a plea for help.

"Let's start with some fresh air," she said as they helped him up and led him to the doorway. Rupert received lots of soft pats on the back and a few compliments that he stood up to Joe Roddy from his teammates. The basketball players seemed to be huddling around one table, plotting revenge.

"Thanks Mr. LaRoma," Denny said as the restaurant owner placed one of the wooden chairs with the red vinyl seat just outside the door so Rupert could sit down. "I'll let you know how he's doing in a minute or two."

But Rupert refused the chair and took a few steps towards the curb before he felt a sudden queasiness in his stomach. He grabbed the fender of the nearest car and immediately heaved every morsel of pizza he had eaten over the past hour and lots of other unidentifiable stomach ingredients. Denny cringed.

"Oh, gross!" Laurel shouted as Rupert Clarke sprayed the fender and hood of the car she and Cody were sitting in. "Gross,

gross, gross."

"Hey, that's Rupert," was Cody's only comment as he started to get out of the car.

"And where are you going?" Laurel said rather coldly.

"Well we can't very well sit here while he's heaving all over the car." Rupert had sent another projectile halfway across the hood of the car as Cody opened the door. "Maybe Denny needs some help."

"Help is not all she needs," Laurel commented under her breath.

Denny seemed surprised to see Cody emerge from the fogged up car until she saw Laurel poke her head out the door. Denny rolled her eyes and shook her head, but Cody didn't notice. He was too busy looking at Rupert.

"Is he OK?" Cody asked Denny.

"I don't know. Roddy punched him and he fell and hit his head pretty bad. I think he may have a concussion or something."

"Maybe he needs some medical attention?"

"No, I'm fine," Rupert mumbled as he wiped his mouth off with his sweatshirt sleeve and spit repeatedly on the sidewalk.

"Rupe, you might be really hurt," Denny said, a concerned look on her face as she grabbed a napkin and began patting Rupert's forehead and cheeks.

"I just wanna go home," Rupert said.

"No way I'm letting you drive home," Denny demanded.

"We can walk home from here, it's not that far, and pick up my car in the morning. I'll tell Mom and Dad it wouldn't start."

"Why don't you just ask one of your friends to take you home?" Cody asked.

"Forget it, just get me home, OK? I don't want all those guys seeing me ralphing all over the place."

Rupert took a few steps away from the car but he wasn't quite steady on his feet. Denny grabbed him under one arm and started to help him. She looked back at Cody with a look that said, are you going to help us here?

Cody looked at Laurel, who was fluffing her hair with one hand and digging in her purse for a stick of gum with the other.

She hadn't even gotten out of the car. He approached the rear door and poked his head inside.

"I gotta help Rupert get home. I'll call you tomorrow."

"You're leaving?! Now?" Laurel asked.

"Well, yeah, Denny needs a hand, so I thought I'd…help…her, er him, I mean Rupert, OK?"

"And how am I supposed to get home?" Laurel knew exactly how she was getting home but it seemed like a spear she just couldn't help herself from tossing right at Cody.

"You said your Mom was coming to get you at eleven thirty, right? And your girlfriends are still inside so they'll keep you company till then. Or your brother can take you home."

Laurel sat pouting in the back seat of the Mustang, not looking at Cody. It was a sure sign he was not supposed to leave her like this, all alone in the back seat of a parked car, a car for parking no less.

"See ya. Sorry," Cody managed as he took off in a trot toward Denny and Rupert, who hadn't made it more than a few yards before they had stopped again.

"Hey, wait up, I'll help." Cody grabbed Rupert under his other arm as the three of them rounded the corner underneath the large yellow and red sign of LaRoma's Pizza Parlor.

After a few minutes of silence, Denny finally looked to her left under Rupert's slumping head toward Cody. "Those windows in that car sure were fogged up," she said.

Cody felt embarrassed and just shrugged his shoulders.

Denny thought for a minute, then a look of mock disgust swept over her face.

"Gross. Gross, gross, gross."

Cody smiled.

THE PIED PIPER

"So tell me again why we are trucking through the early morning chill to get to Mr. Mitch's house," said Lionel K. to Cody as they walked the half-mile from Lionel's house to Mitchell Burke's home the following Saturday morning.

"Mr. Mitch?" Cody asked.

"Well, Mr. Burke sounds so formal and everything and besides, Mr. Mitch kind of has a ring to it, you know. And we just can't start calling him 'Mitch' now can we?"

"Sounds like a gay hairdresser to me," Cody bantered.

"Back to the question: what are we planning to do there?"

"Well, technically speaking, he only invited me, but I figured I may need back up and who better to protect my rear than you, huh, right?"

"Protect it from what?"

Cody shrugged, "Who knows."

"Is breakfast included?" Lionel asked as he rummaged through his ever-present backpack for an early morning snack. He didn't seem to mind the vagueness of Cody's answer.

"Sure, definitely, maybe, I think...I'll ask. He seems like a nice guy and everything."

The two friends walked in silence as the early February sun tried to burn off the Northern California cloud cover. They each exhaled sharply every once in a while to see if they could see their breath. Cody kept thinking about last night's encounter with Denny and Rupert Clarke and wondered about Laurel's reaction to his leaving so abruptly. Lionel continued to dig into his backpack as he whistled an old sixties love song. As they walked, they said little, settling for being on a small adventure with a best friend.

As they rounded the corner and headed down the street where Mitchell Burke lived, Cody lightly punched Lionel in the right arm and kept on walking. It was a ritual with them, a form of communication that said, thanks for being beside me at this particular moment in time. Neither one of them could really articulate the feeling, but the punch seemed to suffice in getting the point across.

In his best Elvis impersonation, Lionel said, "Thank you, thank you very much."

"Whoa, old Mr. Mitch's business must be doing pretty good. This is not a home, it's a mansion," exclaimed Lionel as the two approached the front door of the two story colonial style home.

"Well, maybe in another life he was rich and famous, or his family's rich and famous or he won this house on Wheel of Fortune or something. He sure isn't getting rich as a physical therapist," Cody offered.

They stood on the doorstep and surveyed the house before ringing the doorbell. It was a huge house with a long walkway that led up to a porch surrounded by large, white columns. The roofline jutted up at odd angles in wood shake peaks that concealed a second story. Large windows hidden by wooden shutters surrounded the house, which culminated in the back in the four-car garage at the end of a long, winding driveway. The entire front yard was meticulously landscaped with lots of colorful flowers and blooming shrubs.

"Hello, gentlemen, come on in," Mitchell Burke greeted them as he opened the door to his home. " Glad you're a little bit early. Bagels are on the counter in the garage, help yourself. Just down that hall to your right. I'll be right there."

"Bagels, yummy," Lionel whispered in his best Jim Carey impersonation as they trekked down the hallway to the open door of Mitchell Burke's garage, never anticipating what they would find there.

"Whoa," Lionel said, his mouth staying open with the last syllable as he stepped down into the garage.

"Double whoa," Cody managed.

The garage looked like something in between a large bicycle store and a small bicycle museum. The first sight their eyes were drawn to was a garage wall which had ten bikes stacked in rows of twos, each bike mounted on the wall with a fancy metal bracket. Another wall was shelved from the floor to about three quarters of the way up the wall and filled with neatly stacked bike helmets, spare bike parts, various boxes of different shapes and sizes, bottles and cans of bike lubricants, and tools big and small. And that was only the items easily recognizable.

A third wall looked like a bike maintenance shop, where three bikes were elevated off the floor on different sized stands, each in a different stage of assembly. One was missing both wheels, one was missing the seat and petals and one was only a frame – no wheels, no seat, no handlebars, no nothing. Along the same wall, bicycle tires hung from large pegs.

Scattered on the floor were large brightly colored plastic baskets, some filled with clothes, others with shoes, one with bike tires and tubes and a smaller one with nothing but gloves. Any remaining space on the walls were covered with large bicycling posters, mostly action shots of bikers in competition, the strain and sweat on their faces almost popping off the posters.

Lionel noticed a large card table filled with bagels, cream cheese, jellies, six large containers of juice and three large canisters of what they assumed was coffee since they were surrounded by small packets of cream and sugar. Just as he was about to grab a bagel, the booming sounds of Steppenwolf blasted into the garage, daring you to get your motor running and head out on the highway, looking for adventure.

"Dude," Lionel said to Cody, "we got a rock and roller bicycle maniac living in this house. And who," his voice lowering an octave, "disguised as mild mannered Clark Kent fights a never-ending battle for truth, justice and the American way. He's Superbikeman!"

"Maybe it's just a hobby," Cody offered.

"No, a hobby would be like two bikes, a couple of helmets and a half dozen posters. This is definitely not a hobby. This is more like an obsession, I'd say."

"I'd say that's a perfect word for it, Lionel," Mitchell Burke said as he stepped down into the garage and hit the garage door opener. Both double garage doors moaned into service, slowly cranking open and letting the morning light and cold air in.

"What are you, like a professional bicycle rider?" Lionel asked.

Adeptly avoiding the question, Burke pointed to the bagels and said, "Aren't you guys going to dig in?"

For the first time Cody could remember, Mitchell Burke seemed a little flustered by a question. His eyes darted away from direct contact and he begun to nervously rearrange the bagels that overflowed an oversized platter.

"Me and the Codeman here are usually fairly famished this time of morning, but there is no way I can eat more than like two or three bagels," Lionel said, "but you got enough here to feed the Tour de France." Lionel broke out into a large self-congratulatory smile. "See, I got bike knowledge, oh, yeah."

"Right, name two other bike races, Brainiac," Cody challenged.

"Uh…the Tour de Italy and…uh…the tour…de Germany!"

Cody looked to Burke for confirmation. "He got Italy. One out of two ain't bad," Burke smiled.

"When's company arrive?" Lionel asked.

Burke looked at the large neon clock with the word Campagnolo scripted across the face and said, "Any minute now."

"And who is this company we're expecting?" Cody asked.

"You'll see."

As Cody and Lionel helped themselves to the food and juice, Burke began to take one of the bikes down from the wall rack, grabbed a cleaning cloth from one of the many baskets on the floor and began to wipe the bike clean.

"Mr. Mitch, I sure do like your love of music," Lionel said.

"Thanks."

"But I gotta ask, you got anything from say, oh I don't know, the last 20 years or so? Everything I've ever heard either in your office and now in your home, is like, ancient."

"Well, Lionel, to tell you the truth," Burke began, "I love mostly the music of my youth. It reminds me of what was happening in my life at the time. A song brings back a memory, and the memories are mostly good. And besides, most people my age would say the music of today couldn't hold a candle to the music of their day."

"Sort of like a musical generation gap, huh?" Lionel said.

"I guess you could say that. But you did say you liked the music of my generation, right?"

"Sure, some of it."

"Well anytime you want a lesson in rock 'n roll, soul, country rock or even a little heavy metal, you come knockin to hear a little rockin at my door."

Lionel's eyes widened and he got a huge grin on his face as he begun to gyrate in a dance that resembled a cross between a bad imitation of a football player's end zone celebration and a Texas two step.

"Oh, man, now you've gone and done it. You have released the beast," Cody cracked.

"Anytime, anywhere, any place, I'm a slave to rock 'n roll," Lionel crooned.

Mitchell Burke doubled over in laughter, but recovered in time to start a rather stilted rendition of the Funky Chicken, elbows out like he was trying to fly and legs grinding the clean cement floor of the garage like he was putting out a half dozen cigarettes at once.

Cody merely shook his head in mock disbelief, continuing to munch on a multi-grain bagel, and trying his best not to laugh out loud.

Even the whirl of two dozen bicycles rambling up the driveway didn't halt the impromptu shindig as Burke mouthed the Steppenwolf anthem.

"Like a true nature's child, we were born, born to be wild…"

The riders came to an abrupt stop and stared into the garage in bewilderment. Cody put his hand to his head and turned away in an attempt to hide his embarrassment for his friends, but Burke and Lionel K. just gradually slowed their dance, grinned at each other, shrugged their shoulders and did a double high five.

After a deep breath, Burke addressed the group of riders,

who now had rather disgusted looks on their collective faces, their heads doing a slow shake from side to side in unison, almost like they had practiced it.

"Come on in boys, we're just setting the mood for a great morning ride."

The young riders, whose ages ranged from around 14 to early 20's gradually propped their bikes up inside the garage as Burke made the necessary introductions. Most began to wolf down the bagels, juice and coffee as others started to rummage through the clothing baskets on the garage floor.

Cody watched in amazement as the riders readied themselves for what he learned was a weekly Saturday morning ride. A few riders grabbed tools and began to make minor adjustments to their bikes. Several had their bikes up on a rack and were cleaning chains and gears. Some donned extra clothes or exchanged their clothes for ones in the baskets.

Burke all the while was masterful at directing the mild chaos, pointing out nuances in bike mechanics to several of the riders, reviewing the morning ride route with a young man who looked to be the leader of the group. The two were looking at a large map of Diablo County that Cody figured was at least six feet square and took up most of one wall in the garage. Burke was encouraging to the younger riders. Cody heard short clips of conversation peppered with "do your best" and "ride as hard as you can" and "remember your technique" and "don't worry about the older riders, you ride your ride."

As the riders finished their preparation, Cody noticed that a few had borrowed bikes from Burke and others had borrowed clothing or helmets or gloves. Most of the food was gone and cups lay scattered on the card table and garage floor. Clothes were strewn around the baskets and tools lay scattered. One of the younger riders spent a few minutes before the riders departed to do a quick clean up as the horde began to peddle out into the bright but cold February morning.

Burke motioned for him to join the group, "Go ahead, Jimmy, I'll finish up. Have fun. My money says you'll beat Brownie today."

The boy pumped his fist and bared his teeth and took off

to catch the group.

As Burke began to tidy up the remains of breakfast, Cody roamed around the garage, looking into every basket, examining every bike, fingering the tools. Lionel was first to break the silence.

"You're like a Piped Piper of bikers, aren't you? You play the music to psyche em up, fill em with carbs and caffeine and send them out into the cruel world of monster SUVs."

"Nah, nothing like that," Burke countered. "I like biking. I'm able to help young riders get started, and sometimes, you know, kids just need a little coaxing. Most of these guys were in my rehab center at one time or another, they got on the stationary bike, I encouraged them to try the real thing, they got hooked. Some are very accomplished riders now. End of story."

"So why are we here?" Cody asked.

"Thought you might like to try the real thing. You're physically ready. You, too, Lionel, if you're interested."

"No, thanks, but you two go ahead. I'd rather hang in the cozy garage, have another cup of jolt and see if you got anything I can listen to from, say, the 70s?"

"What do you say, Cody, want to take a little ride? Nothing too strenuous, just to get a feel of things."

"Sure. I'm game."

"Lionel, you'll find my entire collection of CDs, tapes, albums and eight tracks in the first room to your left past the kitchen. You're welcome to rummage around, play anything you like, use the headphones. We'll be back in half an hour or so, OK?"

"Man, I'll be munching bagels for half an hour, take your time."

Burke began to outfit Cody with the bare necessities of the ride, starting with biking shorts, leg warmers and shoes. They tried on various helmets and gloves and Burke fit Cody on one of the remaining bikes from the wall, adjusting the handlebars and seat to fit Cody's height. He spent five minutes reviewing the gear shifting and proper riding technique, trying not to sound too overbearing. Cody took it all in and didn't seem to mind the instruction.

He'd been impressed with the group of riders and noticed a unique friendship tinged with competitiveness that was just underneath the surface. He was anxious to do anything physical again, having spent weeks and weeks in the rehab center working on his knee. As physical as rehab was, it was still work; this looked like fun.

Burke shoved a cell phone into his back pocket and gave Lionel the number, asking him to close the garage door behind them. Lionel waved goodbye as Burke led the way down the driveway and Cody cautiously followed, all the time looking down at the bike. It almost looked to Lionel like Burke was towing Cody with an invisible line, Burke riding smoothly, Cody wobbling ever so slightly.

Lionel grabbed his third bagel of the morning, a fresh cup of coffee and headed to the music room, his body already moving to the sound in his head.

THE TRIPLE BEES

Over the next several months, Cody and Burke rode as much as the weekend weather would allow. Burke always the teacher, Cody the absorbing student. They traveled mostly short, easy routes around the neighborhoods, each ride going a little further than the one before.

Burke showed Cody all the riding techniques: when to ride out of the saddle, how to pump the pedals for even, steady strokes, how the gear shifts worked. They rode side by side, speaking often, although Burke did most of the talking.

When the Northern California weather turned to rain, they spent Saturday mornings in Burke's garage, along with several of the riders that made up Burke's Biker Brigade. Lionel had given the group the name out of respect to Mitchell Burke and his willingness to teach Lionel as much about the history of rock 'n roll as he did Cody about biking.

Mitchell Burke didn't much like his name in the group's moniker, especially when they considered having the name screen printed on their biking jerseys. The group tried different variations and eventually settled on The Triple B's, that evolved into The Triple Bees, because it sounded close to the Killer Bees. And it had a nice ring, yet there was just a hint of secrecy behind it, like a special club where you had to know the password to get in the clubhouse door. Except that Mitchell Burke's door was always open. To everyone. Everyone including Joe Roddy.

Burke had challenged Roddy to start to ride with the group not just because it would be good rehab for Roddy's and his damaged shoulder, but because Mitchell Burke thought he could rehab Joe Roddy. The temperamental teen didn't much like bicycle riding, but he never backed down from a challenge. And he knew that hanging around the squeaky clean Mitchell Burke couldn't hurt his already tarnished image. Burke figured that the rigorous routine of the rides might just keep Roddy off the streets (or on the streets as the case may be) and keep him close so Burke he could keep an eye on him. Burke seemed to be able to influence Roddy when he was at the rehab center; maybe it would work in other parts of his life.

Burke would often start out each Saturday morning ride explaining a riding or maintenance technique. One morning he showed how to patch a flat tire without taking the whole tire and inner tube off the rim, a great timesaver to a road rider. Another time he explained a training technique to get a more consistent pedal stroke by imitating wiping something off the bottom of the shoe on the upstroke. He always stressed teamwork, often using the techniques of professional riders. He emphasized the boys work on the method of drafting, one cyclist just in front of the other, breaking the wind resistance for the second rider, each rider taking his turn in the front so that all riders conserved energy.

Although Lionel K. never rode with The Triple Bees, he loved hanging around the group, and not just for the bagels and Beach Boys. Lionel had an inquisitive mind and he loved mechanics and electronics. He had already taken apart his MP3 music player, rewired his mother's car stereo system (now it really rocks, he said), and helped fix Burke's 1970s style turntable (to listen to "those big, black Frisbees" as he called vinyl albums).

As Burke began to work with the more serious riders, cyclo-computers and heart rate monitors became an important part of the training. Lionel was always the first to program the devices, even learning how to customize several models to offer more than the original designer had intended. He also developed a tracking system on Burke's iMac computer to record each rider's progress, in riding speed, mileage, endurance, heart rate, and blood pressure. He argued that if he could just take a very small blood sample of each rider before and after a strenuous ride, he'd have his proof. No one volunteered.

Once Cody's time came to start rides with The Triple Bees, Mitchell Burke stopped riding with him. Now the group was the teacher and the there was no better place to learn how to ride than on the road with a group of dedicated riders.

Cody's rehab was officially over, although he still came to the center to work his knee on the machines. Basketball season was long gone and the Mustangs hadn't yet organized their summer program yet, so Cody didn't have any b-ball commitments. Burke kept punching home the fact that a long, hard bike ride was one of the best ways to get in shape. But deep down he knew it was only a matter of time until Cody started playing hoops again. So he encouraged Cody to keep coming to the center to get the knee back to 100%. He even added a few killer jumping exercises to work his basketball muscles back to top form.

Cody had been on the courts a few times since the injury, but not in any contact games. He spent a couple of Sunday afternoons just shooting around at the local park by himself, trying to get the feel for how his knee was going to hold up. He was tentative and slow on the knee, very conscious of his every twist and turn; hesitant to do much, but wanting so bad to try to do it all.

After frustrating weekend days of homework and a little shooting around, he'd come home and spend evenings tinkering with the bike Burke had loaned him. His mother would come out to the patio of their rented townhouse and try to get Cody to talk about his frustrations, but Cody wasn't too sure he knew exactly what they were or how she could help.

Sometimes he'd talk about his knee and how it felt, but more often he talk about his cycling. His mother could see the gleam in his eye as he talked about learning how to ride and competing with the older boys in The Triple Bees. She liked the group and was reassured that Mitchell Burke had a firm hand on the pulse of the riders. And she liked that Cody would spend time on his new hobby rather than sitting in front of the TV and watching obscure teams she'd never heard of compete in college basketball.

Sarah Calhoun felt life was getting back to normal. Cody was feeling much better physically, Mitchell Burke was a good influence on him, her job was going along without conflict, and Lionel was well, Lionel. A little crazy at times, but a good friend to Cody, almost like a brother.

Then Mitchell Burke turned up the heat.

PREPARATION

"It's not even called a race, it's called a ride, and it's for charity, so there will be a lot of just everyday riders, nobody special," Mitchell Burke explained to a few of The Triple Bees one Saturday morning before their ride.

"When is it?" Cody asked.

"It's the last Saturday in April. They start early in the morning, like you guys are used to, and they have several courses to choose from. I'm thinking you guys could do the 50 miler. Stick together as a group, see how fast you could do it. I mean, some of the other Bees have been riding races for years. It's about time you guys got the feel of some very minor competition. And 50 miles, with the hills and everything, would be a good test for you."

Burke had picked the newest members to talk to that morning, asking them to stick around after the main group of riders had started out.

"What do you mean it's a charity ride?" somebody asked.

"Well, many charities organize large bike rides to raise money. They get lots of volunteers, put together well-stocked rest stops, map out a route, and it becomes, well, how would you say it, an event. This one is organized by the American Heart Association, and if you guys were interested you could get people to pledge money to you for every mile you ride or just a lump sum for the day."

"You mean we gotta raise money to do this thing?" Joe Roddy interjected.

"You don't have to, you just have to pay an entrance fee. But you could raise money; it's a worthy cause, let me tell you. Heart disease is the number one killer of men and women in the U.S. And I'd be happy to pay your entrance fees as my donation."

"Are you riding too," Cody asked.

"Nope, I'm leaving the hard work to you. I'll be manning one of the rest stops."

"Chicken," Roddy whispered almost under his breath.

"Like I said, it's not a race, there is no competition, just use it as a training ride," Burke said, ignoring Roddy's remark.

There were four new riders that Burke had singled out that morning to ride in the charity event and as they prepped their bikes, Burke continued to describe the event. Three of the four, including Cody Calhoun, began to get excited about testing themselves on a course with lots of other riders. Joe Roddy kept throwing darts at the idea.

The 50-mile course would be a nice stretch for all four of them, since that was about the distance each was riding during an entire week. To do it all in a day would be a push, but Burke had no doubt they could all finish. Besides, the days were staying lighter longer as springtime blossomed and they still had three weeks to prep for the ride.

Many members of The Triple Bees, who had been with the group for more than a season, were entering competitive rides and these charity rides were a good entrance for the new riders to see if they liked the whole scene. Some kids liked to ride alone or with a group of friends, but if any were going to do more than just Saturday morning rides, they had to test themselves. Some of the kids Burke had introduced to cycling as a way to rehab injuries had jumped into the sport in a big way, even competing in national age-group races.

Over the next two and a half weeks, the four riders, Cody Calhoun, Joe Roddy, Freddie Greensmith and Patrick Canaby trained up to five days a week on their bikes. Three of the four, Roddy excluded, even began to raise funds by asking friends, neighbors, parents and grandparents to contribute if they finished the ride. Burke had instilled in them that not finishing was not an option, so they asked for contributions for completing all 50 miles.

The day before the ride the four gathered at Burke's house after school. They arrived in a combined state of tension, excitement, fear and apprehension. Most all feelings were mixed in some combination in each boy. Burke worked with each one as they prepared their bikes for the ride and gave general instructions on how he thought the ride should go.

"This particular ride will have a few accomplished weekend riders," Burke began, "young studs who are just using it as a training ride. They'll ride balls out for as long as they can. Most of the other riders will be a mix of over-age riders trying to relive a little glory to families out for a joy ride. Please, please be careful of inexperienced riders. In no way should you jeopardize anybody's safety so you can go fast. Take it easy, enjoy the ride, be careful."

Burke had explained that there was no official starting time or a start gun that sounded to begin the race. Riders arrived according to how many miles they were riding, registered, and started on the course, map in hand, when they were ready. The four Bees had decided that they wanted to be the first on the course, so they had agreed to arrive at 6:30 and be ready to pump when the course officially opened at 7:00.

"Work on your drafting, switching leads about every half mile or so. Stop at the rest stops and refuel, but ride hard when you're on the course," Burke continued. "And in a race… sorry, ride like this, the motto of the day is 'let nobody pass you.'"

"What do you mean by that," Roddy asked.

"I mean that the four of you should be able to outride anybody on that course, so don't let anybody pass you. Easy enough, right?"

"Sounds like a loaded question," Cody quipped as he smiled at Burke.

"No. No hidden agendas. If somebody flies by your group, just catch them. At the end of the day, you just want to be able to say, you were the best riders out there and nobody outclassed you. That's all I'm saying."

"Sounds like you're throwing down a challenge," Cody said.

"No, who, me? Never."

Burke left them alone in the garage to work on their bikes. The boys were quiet with their own thoughts. For all of them this would be a new experience. For Cody, Freddie and Patrick, they looked forward to the ride almost like a first kiss. Exciting, oh yeah! For Joe Roddy, he was just looking for a way to beat the other three to the finish line.

Burke put an old Beatles cassette on the stereo and as the four boys continued their routine bike maintenance, Paul McCartney crooned about the long and winding road.

CATCH US IF YOU CAN

Saturday morning broke cool and crisp with heavy cloud cover. Each boy had eaten a big breakfast and pumped themselves full of liquids. When Cody's mother dropped him off near the registration booth, he spotted Freddie and Patrick already waiting in line. Cody jumped out of the car, grabbed his gear and bike and joined them. He didn't even wave to his mom as she drove off.

The large parking lot was just beginning to come to life. Registration tables were the first order of business and the lines were beginning to fill. There was a long table with coffee urns and bagels off to the right and a short distance away volunteers were setting up tables in preparation for the post ride lunch. Volunteers at two large tables, adjacent to the registration table, were handing out free ride t-shirts. At another table, more volunteers were passing out route maps. Riders in all colors and shapes and sizes were milling around, talking, eating, and looking at the ride maps. The long line of green portable toilets was almost as busy as the registration table.

"Hey," was all Cody said as he got in line behind Patrick Canaby to get his bib number. The other two just nodded to him and continued checking their clothes, shoes and bikes. The registration table was divided into groups, last names beginning with A through D to the left, E through I next, and so on down the table. Freddie was beside them in the adjoining line, munching on an energy bar.

"I got a feeling I'm gonna need as much energy as I can get today, dudes," he chuckled as he broke into a big smile, his teeth all full of energy bar. The other two cracked up, almost giggling. They didn't realize it, but it was one way to relieve a little of the nervous tension surrounding the three.

As Patrick reached the head of the line and begun filling out the short form disclaiming any liability for the American

Heart Association, Roddy rode slowly by, his number 1318 fluttering on his back. He had a big grin on his face, but it had no resemblance to the ones quickly fading on his giggling buddies.

"See you losers at the finish line," he blurted as he jumped out of his saddle and pumped quickly out the parking lot and onto the course. He was out of sight in a blink of an eye.

The three Bees just stood dumfounded in line until Cody said, "What the heck is he doing?"

"Leaving us in the dust, I'd say, offhand," Patrick deadpanned.

"Nice teamwork," Freddie spat.

"Forget him, the three of us will work as a team. Just forget him," Cody said, trying to refocus the group. But in the back of his mind, he was thinking, let's catch the son of a bee.

After they all registered, the three riders quickly helped each other pin their numbers to the back of their jerseys, made a last minute pit stop and accelerated out of the parking lot. They were young, energetic, pumped up from tension and excitement, and just a little ticked off at Joe Roddy. It made for a fast first few miles.

As they hit the five-mile mark, they settled into a steady pace, each rider taking his turn in the lead, the other two riding less than a foot behind the rider in front of him. They weren't quite what you would have called a well-oiled bicycling team, but their work over the past few weeks had paid off. Their pace was quick and the early start time left the course almost empty.

The first rest stop was at 11 miles into the race, a perfect place to stop if you were doing the 15 or 25 mile loop, but The Triple Bees felt like they were just getting warmed up. They slowed a bit off their pace to see if Joe Roddy or Mitchell Burke was anywhere to be found but when they noticed only a few volunteers milling around waiting for the crowds certain to come, they all three stood in their saddles in unison and pumped back onto the course.

As they pulled out of the rest stop, Cody noticed a pink fluorescent sign with large black letters taped to a stop sign. It read "Go, Codeman." Nice touch, Cody wondered. Nobody else in the pack of Triple Bees seemed to notice. Cody wondered who put the sign up, probably his Mom, but when would she have time to do that? Did she even know the course? Lionel? But he wouldn't use pink, would he? Cody didn't have much more time to think about it as the pace quickened.

Cody Calhoun was the undeclared leader of this pack. His stamina was better than the other two riders, even though at almost 16, he was a full year younger. His bike held the only cyclo-computer and he kept a close eye on two monitors, distance traveled and miles per hour. Burke had given them a target range of 15 miles per hour and they were well above that at 19.5. But Burke had reviewed the route map the day before and noted that most of the elevation in the course was between the 15 mile mark and the 25 mile mark. Cody knew they couldn't keep this pace through the hills, but all three riders seemed fresh so he continued to set a brisk pace.

As the climb through the hills began, Cody noticed that he was often in the lead. The other two riders started to labor after a few miles and their pace slowed dramatically. Cody tried to stay on his saddle to conserve energy as Burke had taught them. But Freddie and Patrick were often standing and pumping, a sure sign to Cody that they were going to tire quickly. He stayed in front for the next five miles, keeping a pace that allowed both riders to stay close but kept them challenged, too. His mind slowly shifted from Joe Roddy to his buddies as he did his best to pull them through the hills.

The course continued to wind through the Northern California foothills and as the three solitary riders hung their heads and pedaled, the sun began to break through the overcast sky. Since large redwood trees surrounded them, they took no notice, but one by one they started to shed clothing. First they unzipped jackets; then they peeled them off and stuffed the light windbreakers into their jersey back pockets.

By the time they hit the 28-mile marker, most of the hills were behind them. After a lengthy descent they hit a short incline and saw the rest stop. Cody was still in the lead and indicated they would stop by pointing his right hand out to the right and slowing his pace. All three riders were relieved for the short break and needed more nourishment.

As they were eating bananas and filling their water bottles, Mitchell Burke approached. "How are you guys feeling?" he asked.

"I'll be feeling much better on the way down that hill, that's for sure," said Patrick through a mouthful of banana.

"Where's Joe?" Burke asked.

"We were about to ask you the same question. He decided to fly solo and the last time we saw him was at registration," Cody said.

"Well I've been here since before seven and he hasn't stopped here. There's only been a handful of riders before you guys."

"We'll catch him," a steely eyed Cody remarked as he finished filling his jersey pockets with two energy bars. "You guys ready to go?"

Patrick and Freddie shot each other looks that indicated they were by no means ready, but shrugged their shoulders as if to say why not.

"Let's roll," Cody commanded as he snapped into his pedals.

"If I don't see you at the finish line, let's meet back at my house first thing tomorrow morning, I want to know how it went," Burke yelled at the riders as they pulled out.

For the next 20 miles Cody was almost always leading the three Bees. Occasionally, Patrick would take the lead downhill because he loved the speed, but when the pulling was hard like on slight inclines or into head winds, Cody was the one leading the way.

With a little over two miles to go, all three riders were fatigued. Freddie and Patrick hadn't spoken in miles and both were suffering from saddle sores and cramping calf muscles. Cody had never ridden this far in his life and his body was reminding him of that fact every chance it had. His neck and shoulders were sore and he kept swiveling his head to relieve the tension. His legs felt like he was pushing a wheelbarrow under water. His hands were so tired they were numb on the handlebars.

As the boys exited a stretch of curves on a lonely two-lane suburban street, they came upon a long straightaway. When

Cody looked up and retook the lead from Freddie, one of the few times he'd been in front in over an hour, he noticed a single rider about four or five hundreds yards away. It was Joe Roddy. They were too far away to get a feel for how fast he was riding but Cody was sure Roddy had to be feeling as bad as the rest of the Bees, because he didn't look like he wasn't cranking all that fast.

Cody managed to say, "There's Roddy, let's get him." He immediately rose from his saddle and his bike responded like a pony heading back to the barn.

"You get him, I got nothin'," Freddie croaked.

"Me either, I'm done," Patrick responded. "How far to the finish?"

"Less than two miles," Cody said after looking at his computer.

"Go ahead, man, we'll be fine. Waste him."

As he was about to take off in pursuit of Roddy, Cody remembered Mitchell Burke's pre-ride talk about sticking together and riding as a team. He had pulled the other two riders throughout much of the race, but he realized they all had worked hard over the past four hours. His loyalty to the other two riders overtook his need to catch Roddy, and he sat back down in his saddle. He didn't have much left himself.

"Let him go, let's finish this thing together," he said.

The two riders could barely manage a smile. They rode the final two miles in suffering silence.

As they crossed the finish line to the cheers of a dozen or so volunteers, they immediately headed to the food tables. Roddy was sitting in a chair slumped over sipping lemonade.

"Hills get the best of you, J-Rod," Cody said sarcastically.

"Good afternoon, ladies, glad to see you finally made it," Roddy said as he straightened up and smiled in a weak attempt to look less terrible than he felt.

"Get lost," Freddie mumbled as he and his two friends headed for the hamburgers.

BUTCH AND SUNDANCE

Lionel K. arrived early the next morning to get all the information about the ride. He was taking this tracking thing seriously. He showed up in his Mapei cloth biking hat, turned backwards, bright yellow fleece sweatshirt and extra baggy shorts and sandals. (Lionel always claimed his upper torso got cold but never his legs or feet, so don't make a big deal out of it, OK?). His laptop computer was already booted when he rung the doorbell.

Cody had slept much of yesterday after the 50-mile ride, but this morning he felt great. He'd eaten three bowls of cereal for breakfast and two bananas and was making a protein milkshake in the blender as the doorbell rang.

"OK, give me the stats first, then coffee second," Lionel K. said as Cody opened the door. "On second thought reverse that order."

"Good morning to you, too, Fitzy," Cody smiled.

"Hey, I'm working here. Please excuse me if I neglect the obligatory salutations and want to get right down to business."

"You're working?"

"Well, I've just declared myself your official statistician hyphen bike mechanic. Hey, how did that baby hum, yesterday? I bet you never even heard that chain the entire race, did ya?"

Cody just shook his head and motioned Lionel back to the kitchen. Lionel busied himself finding an outlet near the kitchen table and plugging in the laptop as Cody poured him a mug of coffee. Cody retrieved the cyclo-computer from the garage and handed it to Lionel.

"You haven't touched this since the race, have you?" Lionel asked, almost accusingly.

"Ride, not race, ride."

"Well from the looks of this baby, you dudes were racing. Flat out, pedal to the metal, cranking," Lionel commented as he clicked through the readings on the small, wristwatch-sized device. "I wonder if I can sync this puppy to the laptop, like a hand-held, you know, with some kind of wireless technology?"

"Why? There's like 5 things you track."

Now it was Lionel's turn to shake his head. "You just keep riding, Butch," Lionel drawled in his best Western accent, "because that's what you're good at." It was a reference to one of their favorite videos, Butch Cassidy and the Sundance Kid, and a knock at Cody's lack of sophistication when it came to computers.

As Cody was heading back to the blender, the phone rang. "Grab that will you, Fitzy?"

Lionel picked up the cordless and in his best Scottish butler voice said, "Calhoun residence, how may we be helping you today?"

"Is…Cody…there?" a familiar voice asked.

Lionel cupped his hand over the phone and mouthed the words, "It's Laurel" to Cody.

Cody shook his head and mouthed back, "Tell her I'm not here."

Lionel dipped his head, raised his eyebrows and shrugged his shoulders as if to say if you weren't here, what would I be doing here? Cody got the message and quickly followed with a mouthed version of "Tell her I'm in the shower."

"The master Calhoun is indisposed at the present time, missy. He's in the water closet," Lionel said to Laurel.

"The what?!? Is that you Lionel?"

"Tis, missy, tis, and the water closet is what you would call the bathroom, mum" Lionel said in his Scottish brogue.

"Tell him to call me," she asked and before Lionel could continue, she hung up.

"Brrr. That woman is cold, she just hung up on me. Is that an ugly way to treat the help or what?"

Cody had an uncomfortable look on his face, shook his head and let Lionel ramble on in his Scottish accent a while longer. Ever since the night at the pizza parlor when Cody had left with Denny Clarke, Laurel had been acting differently. He wasn't sure if it was because he left with Denny or because he wasn't too anxious to participate in Laurel's sexual games in the back seat of her brother's car.

Cody was confused about his feelings for Laurel. She was drop dead gorgeous, as popular as any girl in school and everyone wanted to date her, but something wasn't quite right between them. He never really felt comfortable around her. She wanted him to do things that he didn't want to do and he wasn't just talking about making out in back seats of Mustangs. She wanted to sneak a couple of beers from her folk's refrigerator and drink it in the woods with him. She wanted to skip class and play video games. She wanted to kiss him way more than he wanted to kiss her. And that drove Cody a little crazy.

Was he OK that he didn't want to kiss the prettiest girl in school? Was he weird because of that? Maybe she was just cooler than he was, Cody thought. Maybe she's just more mature. Maybe she's just more developed, sexually, than he was. Maybe they just weren't right together.

"Earth to the Codeman, Earth to the Codeman, come in please, we have lost frequency," Lionel mimicked in a scratchy, low voice trying to bring Cody back to the conversation.

"Sorry."

"Well you were either thinking how much you liked her or thinking how much you don't like her and I can't quite tell which it is. But from the fact that you have me lying now for you, I'm thinking you're thinking it's the don't like. Am I right?"

"I'm not really sure what you even said," Cody joked.

"Don't try to change the subject. What's going on with you and the chill queen?"

"Come on, we're do over at Mr. Mitch's soon. We can talk about it on the way." The two friends packed up their gear, locked the front door and headed down the street in the general direction of Mitchell Burke's house. Cody walked the bike Burke had loaned him for the ride and Lionel lumbered along beside him. Lionel was ready for all the dirt, but he knew Cody well enough not to press him. He'd talk when he was ready. They walked on in silence, Lionel almost too anxious for the conversation to begin and Cody almost too confused to know where to start.

THE WHITE BOX

As they approached the door to Mitchell Burke's home, they had been walking for almost a half an hour. Although they had talked on and off during the trip, they made absolutely no progress in understanding the situation and now Lionel was as confused as Cody was. But then again, he never claimed to know much about the opposite sex, one of the few boys in Cody's class who actually admitted that they were clueless when it came to girls. When they rang the doorbell, they were both lost in their thoughts, Cody as confused as ever and Lionel wondering if music and technology were enough to sustain him in life. Were girls actually necessary at all?

"Hey, how did it go, how do you feel, what was it like?" Mitchell Burke machine-gunned Cody with questions as he opened the door.

"Pretty cool… really cool," Cody smiled.

The three of them drifted into Burke's den and he continued to ask questions. Cody's mood changed immediately as he retold the story of the ride, almost mile by mile. Burke was patient with him as he expressed his feelings, his techniques, his anger over Joe Roddy, his exhilaration. Meanwhile, Lionel downloaded the stats into the laptop, hooked it up to Burke's color printer and was printing out a summary of the week's training and a detailed summary of the ride.

"There's been one question I've been avoiding asking, but it's probably the most critical question of the day," Burke continued, "how's the knee feel after 50 miles?"

When Cody hesitated, Lionel chimed in, "Actually, it was 52.7 miles, for the record."

Burke just nodded and kept his eyes on Cody, waiting for his answer. "It's OK," was all that Cody offered.

"No pass, try again. More detail, please."

Cody just shrugged his shoulders and kept quiet.

"Son, haven't we been through this before," Burke started in a lecturing tone, "about how you have to communicate…" Then he caught himself, lowered his head and raised a hand as if to apologize. Now it was Burke's turn to stay quiet as Cody collected his thoughts.

"Well about halfway through, it started to hurt a little."

"Show me where."

Cody pointed to the inside and outside of the kneecap.

"Describe the hurt. What did it feel like?"

"Not really painful or anything. More like weak or tired."

Burke let out a silent sigh and felt a sense of relief come over him. "Good, tired is good. Pain can even be good, but it sounds more like fatigue than anything."

Burke had moved closer to Cody and was now sitting on the footstool in front of Cody's chair with the left knee in question firmly in his muscular hands. He manipulated Cody's knee ever so gently, moving the knee slightly side to side, bending it slowly and pressing his thumbs into suspected tender spots. He did the same to his right knee, too, so Cody could compare the two.

After Burke was thoroughly convinced that Cody had done no damage to his knee, he commented, "It's fine, nothing to worry about, it's just a little tired. Probably like the rest of your body."

Cody nodded, relief in his eyes. Lionel pumped his fist, triumph in his gesture.

"Tell me how you felt around the 40 mile mark," Burke asked, changing the subject.

"The one thing I most remember is how bad my butt felt."

"You'll get used to it, what else?"

"No, I mean it really hurt."

"Pretty soon, after more rides, it just goes numb."

Lionel's face contorted into a grimace and he very quietly uttered, "Awwwe!" as his eyes went to his crotch.

Burke tried to hide his smile as he pressed on, "How did your legs and your lungs feel?"

"I felt good, I felt I had lots left. And then when I saw Roddy, I got pumped."

"But…" Burke left the sentence open so Cody could complete it.

"But I thought I should stay with the guys and finish the race together."

Burke sat back and pondered the scenario. He had prepped the riders as much as he could prior to the ride, going over lots of different situations they may face. But he didn't anticipate the stunt Roddy pulled. And he had forgotten that Cody had been ingrained as a team player. He was impressed with the time the three riders clocked and correctly concluded Cody had led the pace most of the race. Even though it wasn't really a race, Roddy made it one and Cody had reacted like a hound dog on the scent of a fox.

Burke was also onto the scent of something, but he really wasn't quite sure what. He probed Cody for more.

"Could you have caught him?"

"I could have blown him away. He was gassed and I had a lot left."

"What do you mean a lot left?"

"Anytime I jumped out of the saddle and cranked, I just flew. My legs were tired, but I've always been able to call up the reserves. I hardly ever get tired."

"Could you have maintained a quicker pace?"

"How much quicker?"

"Lionel, what did they do?"

"52.7 in three hours, six minutes and 12 seconds, so they averaged almost exactly 17.0 miles per hour," Lionel proudly said after checking his charts.

"Could you have averaged, let's say, 19 miles an hour?" Burke asked.

Cody thought for a moment, like he was reviewing the course in his mind, "Maybe. There were a lot of hills. Probably. But it wasn't a race, right, it was a charity ride?"

"Two things I forgot to tell you. One, it's always a race. And two, when it comes down to the last mile or so, the last push, if you can win it, win it."

Cody was confused, "So the heck with my teammates?"

"No, absolutely the contrary," Burke explained. "Your

teammates brought you to a point where you, or any one of them, had a chance to win the race. Or in this case, to catch Roddy. That's how a team works in a bicycle race. Sort of like the Three Musketeers, all for one and one for all. If you win, the team wins. If anybody else on the team wins, you win."

"Codeman, it's like a b-ball game, dude. If you score 30 points and the team wins, you're the hero. If you score zip and the team wins, everyone's a hero," Lionel offered.

"Precisely," Burke chimed in.

"Exactimundo," Lionel said with gusto.

At exactly the same time, both Lionel and Cody said, "Cool" and gave each other a high five.

"So, Cody, are you ready for the next level?" Burke asked.

Cody had never even thought of this level until a few weeks ago, but answered, "Maybe, what is it?"

"Training."

"I thought that's what I've been doing."

"No, you've been rehabilitating your knee, mostly."

"Feels like training."

"Does it? It hasn't felt like fun?'

"Well, yeah, mostly it's been a lot of fun."

"Good, but sometimes training isn't always fun. Basketball practice isn't always fun, is it?"

"Yeah, it is."

"Running sprints, conditioning, that's fun?"

"Ah, right, no fun."

Lionel had drifted over to Burke's music collection and was sifting through a stack of CDs. Most titles he didn't recognize, but one caught his eye.

"I do believe," Lionel said in a low voice meant to interrupt the conversation, but in mostly a polite way, "that what we have here is a CD from the current decade. Alanis Morrisette? Somehow it just not you, Mr. Mitch."

"She's got a bit of an edge, I like her. Besides, it was lent to me by a friend of mine."

Lionel thought to himself that he'd never seen Mitchell Burke hang with anybody who wasn't a patient of his or a bicycle freak. "Let's crank it up and groove," he said, slipping the CD into Burke's elaborate sound machine.

"This training would include you, too, Lionel, if you're up to it," Burke said as he coyly brought Lionel into the fray.

Lionel crunched his eyebrows together and furrowed his brow, slightly closing one eye as he turned to Burke. "As long as I don't have to sweat."

"Nope, Cody's gonna be doing all of the sweating, and then some."

That last statement, said with emphasis, got Cody's attention. "What's the 'and then some' part?"

"We'll get to that. Lionel, your part is fairly simple, but extremely important. I want to be able to track Cody's progress in much more detail than what you've been doing so far. And there will be times when I'll want to talk to him in the middle of a ride. And we'll want to make that bike seem like it's part of him, like a third leg almost. Think you're up for that?"

Lionel rose, walked over to Cody and put his arm around him and said in a mock serious tone. "We are a team, like Matt Damon and Ben Affleck, like Luke Skywalker and Han Solo, like Jackie Chan and Chris Tucker, like Butch and Sundance, like… Regis and Kathy Lee, like Homer and Marge, like…"

"Quick, get back to the two guys theme," Cody interjected.

"…like Simon and Garfunkel, like, like, like, Bugs Bunny and Daffy Duck…"

"Nobody knows whether Daffy is a girl or a guy."

'I'm pretty sure he's a guy."

"With a name like Daffy and that terrible lisp?"

"Good point, he could be somewhere in between, let's discuss that further since I'm all out of gas on this buddy, buddy thing."

Burke smiled, shaking his head. "I get the point. Lionel, look inside the garage, in that small storage room, right beside where the bikes are hanging up." Burke reached inside the kitchen cabinet door, found the key he was looking for among a row of keys neatly running the width of the door. "This should open it," he said, tossing the key to Lionel. "I'm looking for a box marked HRM, for heart rate monitors."

As Cody Calhoun and Mitchell Burke began to discuss the details of "the training" as it would become known, Lionel K. Fitzhugh headed toward the garage. He unlocked the door to the closet and as his eyes adjusted to the dark, he pulled on a chain dangling in front of him. A single light bulb overhead illuminated the small, musty smelling room.

The room measured about eight feet square and three sides were shelved from floor to ceiling with deep, wooden shelves. Two walls were stacked high and deep with boxes. One entire wall was stacked with white cardboard boxes, the kind with lids on top that people use to store important papers and files, each box displaying a year in large, black handwritten numbers.

Lionel traced the boxes back to the year 1975 and then his eyes moved across and down the shelves, stopping with a box in the bottom row marked 1991. Most years were represented by at least two boxes. As he quickly looked around, he saw no box dated later than 1991. Funny, he thought. He wondered what happened to the last ten years or so.

As Lionel looked for the box marked HRM, he noticed most of the boxes including the ones marked with years, were tightly taped shut with gray duct tape. Not the way a box would be sealed if intermittent access were a possibility. A few boxes on the middle wall were brown cardboard and had its tops folded into the box so that inquisitive eyes, like Lionel's, could peer into the top. Several looked like they held old bicycle parts and a couple contained nothing but old bike pedals. The third wall contained four bike frames. No wheels, no handlebars, no gears, just frames.

Just as he saw the HRM box, he noticed a single white box, slightly askew on the bottom shelf with "photo albums" neatly printed on one side. The duct tape at one end of the box looked like it had been pulled away slightly, leaving just a small opening. For a few seconds he just stared at the box, thinking the temptation to look inside would pass. When it didn't, he kneeled down, slid the box slightly toward him, peeled the duct tape off and peeked inside.

The box was filled with old photo albums. Lionel reached in and grabbed the album lying on top. He sat down on the cold, cement floor and held the album on his lap. He knew in some way he was trespassing into a time in Mitchell Burke's past life. These photo albums weren't displayed in the house where anybody and everybody could pick them up and look inside. They were in a locked room off the garage, in old boxes sealed with heavy-duty, don't look inside, duct tape. Lionel noticed for the first time he had broken out in a slight sweat and his mouth was dry.

The album he had in this hand was labeled PARIS, 1986. He flipped open the cover and sat there stunned at the picture he saw staring back at him. Mr. Mitch, he thought, you've been holding out on us, big time.

Lionel straightened up the little room exactly as he had found it and returned to the house. Cody and Burke had begun to write down a sequence of training rides to build his strength and endurance. Lionel's job was to figure out how the heart rate monitor and the cyclecomputer worked and to design a means to communicate with Cody while he was riding.

But his mind kept drifting back to the white box and the photo of Mitchell Burke in Paris.

COMING OUT OF THE CLOSET

Lionel K. Fitzhugh avoided Cody Calhoun as much as he could over the next week. On the one hand he was dying to tell Cody the secret he had uncovered in Mitchell Burke's garage. On the other hand, he knew he had somehow crossed the line, he had dug too deep into the secrets held in the garage. If Burke had wanted anyone else to know what Lionel knew, why had he hidden them so deep? It was like buried treasure that no one was to supposed to find. And even if they found it, they were not supposed to open it. Lionel knew that it couldn't have been more clear not to open the boxes if Burke had posted a sign saying, NO TREPASSING, DO NOT OPEN.

Now Lionel was in a predicament. He didn't want to be around his best friend for fear he couldn't hold the secret in. But they were having so much fun with this biking thing. Cody was really getting into the racing and Lionel was really getting into everything else about it.

Lionel didn't want to be around Burke because he felt ashamed. Ashamed he had broken the trust Burke had shown him. Burke had sent him into that closet looking for the heart rate monitors, knowing those secrets were close enough to touch. But he had trusted Lionel not to look and Lionel had failed him.

Throughout the week Lionel wasn't his usual self. The secret was like an infection, just festering below the surface, and it affected everything Lionel did. When he was in school, his concentration was lost. When he was listening to his music, every song seemed to be about betrayal or guilt. Innocent questions people asked him made him paranoid. Even his food didn't taste as good. He often got a far away look in his eyes during meals and fantasized that he had been tried in a court of law, found guilty of trespassing, theft, felony possession of a secret too big to know, or some other heinous crime and was now eating his last meal.

Only one thing could possibly be good about his ordeal: at least he felt guilty about what he had done. As the week wore on, Lionel began to feel better about his guilt. OK, so he had done something terrible, but at least he felt guilty about it. It could be worse; he could feel nothing at all. He thought, I bet there are lots of kids who would have absolutely no remorse whatsoever about what I did. They wouldn't even think it was bad. I, on the other hand, am feeling miserable about this. I am crushed, I'm devastated, I'm lost, I'm…I'm…OK, I'm a martyr. Yes, I can live with being a martyr, actually it's kind of cool. No, that's wrong, too, isn't it? Martyrs are only people who have done something wrong and then talk themselves into feeling good about being guilty. At least he was right about one thing, he was lost all right.

Although Lionel had been avoiding Cody all week, he couldn't avoid the Saturday morning trip to Burke's that had become their ritual. They would meet at Lionel's house around eight and walk the half mile to Burke's home where Cody picked up his ride schedule for the day or met up with a few other Triple Bees for a nice little 40 miler. He still borrowed one of the six bikes Burke had in his garage. Baseball season had hit Northern California as it always did in early March and some of the Bees had early morning games so every once in a while, Cody was on his own.

This Saturday morning turned out to be quite a bit different for both of them. Burke answered the door, welcoming them in, his hand covering a slight smile, one that he was having a hard time suppressing. As Lionel and Cody headed for the kitchen, ready for a bagel and some java, they both stopped dead in their tracks. There at the blender, surrounded by what looked like half the produce aisle at the local supermarket, was Denny Clarke.

She had her long, dark hair pulled back in a ponytail and wore a red, oversized Stanford sweatshirt, black running pants and new Nikes. Her back was turned as they entered the kitchen and with the whir of the blender, she didn't notice them at first. She had what looked like a recipe book out and was peering down into it as she groped for a banana just out of her reach.

Surrounding her were several small plastic bags filled with different colored powders, a variety of white plastic bottles, and a couple of small dishes filled with orange, brown and clear pills. Cody thought that if she had a white lab coat on, she'd look just like a crazed pharmacist.

Cody grabbed the banana and held it like a gun, saying, "Stop what you're doing, move away from the blender or I'll have to plug ya."

"Very funny," Denny said, noticing the trio behind her. "Now make yourself useful and start peeling."

"Besides the fact that I'm drastically opposed to kitchen work of any kind, my mind keeps racing with the question, what are you doing here?"

"Well, basically, I'm experimenting with a new high carb, high protein shake."

"I can see that, I meant what are you doing in this particular kitchen experimenting with a new high carb, high protein shake?"

"I was talking to Mr. Burke about a project I'm working on in school, sort of like a science project, where I'm learning about nutrition and we got to thinking about the Triple Bees. And he was telling me his theories about carbs vs. proteins and the right mixture for long endurance sports and I was telling him mine, so he invited me to try a couple of my ideas on you guys," Denny blurted out. It seemed a little too rehearsed to Cody.

Cody looked skeptically toward Burke, who nodded quite unconvincingly and gave a slight shrug of the shoulders. This meant to Cody that he was covering for Denny, but he couldn't quite figure out exactly what he was covering up. Cody also didn't seem to mind much at all that Denny Clarke had invaded the male sanctuary of Mitchell Burke's home. He also noticed that for the first time he could remember, Denny was wearing a little makeup. She normally had a very natural, well-scrubbed look, but never tried to look overly pretty. Today she had just a hint of eye shadow to highlight her bright blue eyes. He liked what he saw.

"OK, only one question, how come it's green?" Cody asked, pointing to the large stainless steel industrial strength blender sitting on the counter.

"A secret ingredient. Try it, you'll like it."

Cody looked at the concoction with a contorted grimace as Denny poured it into a glass. "Looks delicious," he managed as she handed him the drink.

"Lionel?" she asked, holding up the half filled blender tumbler.

"Uh, no thanks, I'm not doing any long distance endurance things today, so I think I'll just stick with the organically grown and packaged high octane, no carb, no protein, brown, I repeat, brown coffee."

"I'll try a little," Burke chimed in. Denny gave him a thank you with her eyes.

Cody took a small swallow with a grimace on his face and quickly found out he liked it. The shake had a decidedly sweet taste and Cody could detect hints of banana and strawberry and lots of other tastes he couldn't identify.

"Well?" Denny asked.

"Not bad," Cody replied.

"Good, very good," Burke said, "What's in it?"

"Lots of good stuff, most of which, if I told you, our bike rider here would turn up his nose and give me a hard time about," she said pointing toward Cody.

"It's just my job to give you a hard time, which by the way, you deserve," Cody said as he gave her a mock jab with his fist to her upper arm.

Lionel rolled his eyes, which only Burke noticed, as the give and take between Denny and Cody amped up.

Cody grabbed a bagel and was beginning to add some cream cheese, when Denny stopped him. "Hey, Cody, would you do me a huge favor and not eat that bagel before your ride? I really do want to find out if that shake has enough of everything in it to help you through the ride today."

"This is gonna last through 40 miles?"

"Probably not the whole 40, no. But I want to see how far you can get on it, so take a few bagels with you and let me know when you start to run our of fuel. OK?

"OK, but if I bonk at like five miles, I'll come looking for you."

Denny Clarke didn't say it, but that didn't sound like such a bad idea to her. Lionel saw the look in her eye and rolled his eyes again.

After what appeared like an awkward silence, Burke clapped his hands together and said, "OK, what are we up to today? Cody, it looks like you're on your own. You got a plan for your ride?"

"Not really."

"Well, I do, come on out here and look at the map." They headed to the garage to look at the wall as Denny started to clean up the mess she had made. Lionel drifted over to the stereo system and was rifling through Burke's collection of CDs.

"So you said you wanted to do about 40 today, right?" Burke asked.

"Sure, whatever."

"Good, why don't you follow Ryan Road out to the reservoir, take it completely around, then head back on Stoops Highway, until you hit up with Ryan again, then come back the way you came. That'll give you a few hills, one big climb on Stoops and probably very little traffic most of the way."

"Denny, what about you, you up for a little ride?" Burke asked as she came through the door from the house.

Cody's eyes grew huge as he didn't quite believe what he was hearing. Denny? Ride? With me?

"Oh, my mom's got a whole list of things for me to do today, so as soon as I clean up everything here, I'm heading back home."

Cody felt a gigantic sense of relief wash over his entire body.

"But, Cody, since you're heading out toward Ryan Road, mind if I tag along on my way home?" she asked.

"Tag along like running beside me or something?"

"No, ride along. I rode over on Rupert's ten-speed. It's a little old but Mr. Burke helped me clean it up a bit."

"Oh, Mr. Burke did, did he?"

"Hey," Burke replied, "I'm a gift to the entire community. I do not discriminate against the female gender."

"You're a gift all right. Yeah sure, I'll ride along with you over to Main Street," Cody relented.

Lionel had returned to the music room. He grabbed a pair of headphones and began to settle into a CD he'd been wanting to listen to for a long time, The Allman Brothers Greatest Hits. A true hippie group from the 60s, he thought. But at least you got to hear their greatest hits and not some bad collection of stoned-out songs filled with lots of guitar and drum solos. Besides, if Cody and Denny were leaving that would give Lionel a chance to rid himself of this guilt he was feeling, especially if he could bring himself to ask Burke about the contents of the white box. But he didn't know if he had the nerve.

After Cody and Denny left, Burke tapped Lionel on the shoulder. He removed the headphones and said, "Whassup?"

"Just wanted to talk with you for a minute," Burke answered.

"Well, hey, if you're busy or something today, I'll just head back home or work on that Trek in the garage. I'll just quit bothering you, you know, don't mean to be a nuisance or anything." The guilt was creeping up on Lionel and he was feeling like he needed to escape.

"Relax, Lionel, you can chill here as long as you want. I just wanted to know how you're enjoying your role as second banana. I mean you seem to want to tackle all the behind the scenes kind of stuff, like keeping times for Cody, working on the bikes, programming the heart rate monitors. You OK with that?"

"Yeah, sure. It's me. I'm no jock, but I got a mind like Einstein when it comes to mechanical stuff. I dig figuring out how things work and how to make 'em work better. Besides, Cody's my best friend and someday he's gonna be a star. I don't know in what, maybe a cycling star, but in something. You know, he's just got something about him. Makes you want to hang with him."

"He is a good kid, real determined, I'll say that for him."

"Oh, no, Mr. Mitch, he's way more than that. He's a stud. He puts so much pressure on himself to perform no matter what he's doing. And he loves the pressure, he thrives on it. Me, I don't much like pressure, kinda chokes me, leaves me short of breath. I freak. But Cody, man, he eats that stuff up. I admire that in him and I suppose that's why I like being around him. Sort of like a groupie you might say. I want to be there right by his side when he hits it big cause it's gonna be so cool to see that."

"You're a good friend, Lionel," Burke said.

"I try…" Lionel responded, then looked at Burke and reluctantly accepted the compliment with "…thanks."

Lionel flipped the switch on the stereo so that the Allman Brothers could be heard throughout the house. Burke's home was wired with speakers in almost every room and with a single flip of the switch, the song *Whippin' Post* had filled the home.

"You know, for what looks like burned out hippie freaks, these almond guys rock and roll."

"Allman, no d," Burke corrected him.

"Oh, yeah, right," Lionel said, checking the CD cover. "Were they really brothers?"

"Some of them were, imagine they still are if they're still alive. As I remember, they had a tendency to…well, die."

"Bikers, huh? I mean the motorcycle kind."

Burke nodded his head, "Like I was always told, two-wheeled motor vehicles and drugs do not mix."

As Burke headed back to the coffee maker for his second cup, Lionel flipped through the upright CD holder. "Man, you got quite a collection."

"Come with me, you ain't see nothin' yet," Burke replied as he headed toward the garage. "Oh, I gotta find that album, Bachman Turner Overdrive," as he broke into song.

B-b-b-b-baby, you just ain't see nothin' yet

Lionel looked up nervously as Burke mentioned the garage and all the feelings of guilt swept over him again. The camaraderie the two were building over rock 'n roll and bicycles was nice, but Lionel couldn't escape the feeling that he had betrayed Burke's friendship. And he wasn't quite ready to admit his failure.

As Burke was rummaging through a bunch of boxes in the

garage, Lionel reluctantly entered. He quickly glanced toward the locked door that hid the white boxes and glanced away. Had Burke seen him look in that direction? He noticed his mouth was dry and his heartbeat was increasing. What would he say if Burke asked him if he'd been looking in the white boxes? Would he lie and say no? Would he break down and confess everything and throw himself on the mercy of the court? Was he going crazy here or what?

Maybe he should just blurt it out. OK, it was me, I did it. I was the one. Don't blame any Killer Bee or the cleaning lady or the guy who mows the yard or the unknown gunman on the grassy knoll. Me, Lionel K. Fitzhugh, I'm the guilty party here. Guilty as charged. I can take my punishment like a man. String me up, or lock me away, or make me eat 17 of those horrible green protein shakes. Anything but this torture of guilt!

"Hey, Lionel, I said give me a hand, will you?" Burke repeated.

"Oh, sure," Lionel replied as he grabbed the end of a somewhat small, but extremely heavy cardboard box. "Man, what's in here, the original stone tablets from the Ten Commandments?"

"Nope. Just a lot of rocks. Rock 'n roll, that is," Burke laughed.

Thankfully they were bypassing the dreaded locked door and heading directly into the living room. Burke opened the box of vinyl record albums, which had just an old, dirty beige strip of masking tape holding it together. In Lionel's mind this just verified the fact that the white boxes, secured with heavy duty gray duct tape, were much more important than a treasure like old rock albums. He knew now he was in serious trouble. The guilt just kept growing.

Burke grabbed a Rolling Stones album and slipped it onto the turntable. He meticulously wiped the vinyl disk off with a soft cloth and blew gently at the needle on the arm before using the remote lever to connect needle to groove. The raunchy sounds of Mick Jagger quickly filled the room.

"Most people were into the Beatles right about this time, but for some of us, it just wasn't cool to like them," said Burke.

"We wanted to associate with a group that was a little more rebellious, and the Stones fit the bill perfectly."

"Rebels, were they?" asked Lionel.

"Compared to the Beatles, yeah."

"So was it like they were mean and nasty, like you couldn't quite trust them, like they'd steal you blind if you let them?"

"More like you wouldn't trust them with your girlfriend, I suppose."

"But not like they were liars and cheats, just not squeaky clean, right?"

"Very few of us are squeaky clean, Lionel, and for those that pretend to be, there's usually a skeleton hidden in the closet somewhere," Burke said.

Lionel thought, don't say it, no, don't say it, please, dear God, don't let me say it.

"Or a white box?" Damn, I said it, why did I say it? It just came out, I had no control, but now, I'm dead for sure.

"Huh?" was Burke's only reply, but he was looking at Lionel intently.

Lionel just shook his head, but no words came out.

Finally Burke said, "Lionel, you look like you got something you just have to get out of your system, but you don't know how to let it out."

"OK, OK, I can't stand it anymore. The guilt is killing me. I confess, it was me. I did it, I was the one. I uncovered your big secret!"

"What big secret is that, that I'm a closet rock 'n roller?"

"No, worse, a closet bicycling champion." There, it's out, I can't take it back. Finally, a big weight off my shoulders, I can breathe again. Whew, thought Lionel. Now comes the hard part.

Burke just stared at Lionel, not saying a word, his eyes narrowing and his brow furrowing. Lionel couldn't ever remember seeing him like this. Usually he was calm and cool or intense and vocal. But rarely just squinting and frowning.

After a long silence, maybe a full two minutes but what seemed like a full twenty minutes to Lionel, Burke finally said in an even, controlled voice, "How'd you find out?"

Lionel detected there was very little anger in the question, more curiosity. "I was checking for those heart rate monitors in the closet and I saw the box, with the dates, and…well, I guess…I opened one. Sorry."

"That was a long, long time ago," Burke said, and then, smiling, added "in a galaxy far, far away."

"You're not royally ticked?" Lionel was amazed, it was like a last minute death row call from the governor. Hold the cyanide pellets, this man may not be as guilty as originally charged.

"Maybe a little disappointed, but I'm not mad. It happened, not much I can do about that."

"But *what* happened?!" Lionel could hardly restrain himself, he had so many questions.

Cody and Denny rode in silence for the first mile or two. He was anxious to get on with his training ride, but he had to admit, Denny wasn't all that bad to be around. She sure didn't make him feel crazy like Laurel always did.

Denny was in heaven. Secretly she had been riding the rejuvenated bike almost every day. Nothing real strenuous, but now she was in good enough shape that at least she wasn't wobbling all around and heaving like an old lady with a smoker's hack. She was peddling effortlessly, and even though she knew Cody was taking it easy on her, she wasn't embarrassing herself. And every once in a while she would speed up, startling him, so that he'd have to pump a little harder to catch her. It became a little game.

They rode on without saying a word.

Mitchell Burke was silent, too. Lionel was giving him plenty of space, not pushing to ask all the questions that were swirling around in his head. Burke pensively flipped through the box of record albums, seemingly looking for one in particular.

He finally found the one he was looking for, slipped it out of the cardboard cover and then the white paper sleeve. He handled the record by holding it in the creases of his hands between the palms and his fingers, but neither the palms nor the fingers actually touched the album. Then he placed his middle finger of his left hand in the small hole in the center of the record and his thumb on the outside perimeter. Still nothing was touching the grooves. Burke then meticulously cleaned the disk with a small white special cloth.

When the ritual was completed and the album in place, he slid the needle to the song he was looking for, and dropped the lever. A very distinctive guitar lick filled the room as Burke cranked up the volume.

"You can't listen to this softly," he commented without looking at Lionel.

Lionel didn't say a word but nodded knowingly.

You get up every morning to the alarm clock's warning,
Take the eight fifteen into the city.
There's a whistle up above
People push and people shove,
And all the girls are trying to look pretty.

As Randy Bachman continued to belt out *Takin' Care of Business*, Burke leaned over and turned the volume down just a bit.

"This used to be our ride song. We'd crank this baby up before a big ride and it would just fill your brain for hours and hours. You couldn't get it out of your head. We'd even sing a line or two out on the road. I guess it became something like our anthem."

"Who is 'we'?"

"Team Volvo. It was a professional racing team, sponsored for about three years by the car company. We rode mostly the international circuit, heck, that was about all there was back then in the early 80s. But that was a long time ago. A lifetime ago."

"So how come you hide it in the closet? I mean, you were an international racing star, I saw the clippings in the box. Why cram that part of your life away?"

"I have other things in my life to sustain me now," Burke answered. "Some people like to live in the glory days of their past and they never seem to live in the present. My present is my practice now, my victories come every day working with people to make them better."

"Yeah, but it's one thing to brag about everything you did in the past," Lionel pressed, "but another thing to hide that past in a box in the garage. Especially since you still are really into bikes and everything. Just seems weird to me. I mean, if Cody knew you were a racing stud, he's be so smacked out."

"Exactly my point. I don't want people to be smacked out because of what I did in the past. I want them to be smacked out over me for what I can offer to them today."

"I suppose, but…you're not ashamed of what you did, are you? I mean you didn't get busted for steroids or any performance enhancing drugs, did you?"

Burked smiled for the first time in about an hour. "No, I was clean. And no, I'm not ashamed of anything."

"But you hardly even ride anymore. Just those little training rides around the block with the Codeman when he started ridin'. How come?"

Sweat broke out on Mitchell Burke's forehead. *Thump-thump, thump-thump, thump-thump.* It was never far away, that feeling. But too close to share with this young boy.

"I have my reasons. Like I said, another lifetime ago," Burke replied, trying to hide his uneasiness.

Cody and Denny rode on, finally starting to talk, and mostly about bikes. Cody began to open up a bit and once he got started talking about the feeling he got when he finished a hard training ride, Denny began to understand why he was so committed to the sport. She would ask him a question about training or bikes or bike clothing and he'd just talk. It was nice to hear him talk, she thought.

She wanted to ask him about basketball, because she knew he wasn't playing that much anymore, but she couldn't get up the nerve. She wanted to ask him about a lot of things, but she didn't have the nerve for that either.

After a couple of minutes of silence, she asked, "How's the shake doing?"

"Too soon to tell. At least it didn't give me gas," Cody said as he smiled slightly.

"Well, I suppose that's a plus."

"Yep."

She looked over at him and smiled back, swerving her bike precariously close to his and then quickly away again, barely avoiding a crash. Cody swerved out into the traffic lane and quickly got his bike under control.

"Jeez, I'm sorry," Denny cringed.

"No problem, just keep that bad boy under control. Hey, Denny, now it's my turn to ask you a question."

"Fire away."

"How come you're so into biking these days?"

"It's just a great way to test out all my nutritional theories, for one thing. You know I'm into all that stuff."

"Yeah, I know."

"And I'm really considering going into some health field. Maybe like Mr. Burke or occupational therapy or a sports trainer or something. I don't know yet. I gotta go to college and everything, but I like that kind of stuff."

"That's cool. Sometimes I wish I knew what I wanted to be when I grow up," Cody said.

"Well, for me, it just seems like I get pulled in that direction a lot. It just seems right or natural or like I was meant to do it. You know the feeling?"

Cody thought about the way he felt on a bike and he replied, "Yeah, I do."

After another minute of riding, Cody spoke up again, smiling. "Say, Denny, any other reason you're into biking these days?"

She smiled back, "I've got my reasons."

"So you don't want me to say anything to Cody about all of this, do you?" Lionel asked Burke as they were putting the albums back into a storage compartment in the wall.

"Cody needs to find his own passion about riding, Lionel. He's got to learn for himself if this is something he's doing to get in shape for next basketball season, or…if it's something else to him. I don't want my past to influence his future. If he wants to get serious about riding, he knows I'm here to help."

"But, it's so cool, and I mean, he really respects you and all. I would think he'd want to know."

"Lionel, being a pro racer isn't all that glamorous. Mostly, it's just lots of long, hot hours training. And very few people make any money and gather any fame. Most just give it up after a couple of years and go on with the next phase of their life. That's what I'm trying to do."

"But you were a champion…"

"I won one stage of the Tour de France. Big deal. Guess where I finished that year: sixty second out of a field of 90. All told in my entire racing career I barely made enough money to pay my bills. Nobody even heard of me before. Name me one other American that's even won the tour besides Lance Armstrong."

"Greg Lemond."

"OK, good, now we've named all the famous American bicycle riders. Exactly two."

Lionel got up the courage for his next argument. He swallowed hard and took a deep breath. No sense stopping now, he thought. "But you didn't do it for the fame or money, did you?"

Burke was caught off guard by the question, which happened to be right on target. Pretty perceptive of this young man, he thought. No, he hadn't done it for fame or money. But he wasn't ready to tell Lionel the real reason he rode bikes. Or the real reason he stopped. So he threw Lionel off the scent.

"No, I did it for the girls."

Lionel's eyes grew wide and he got this sheepish grin on his face. "Oof," was all he could say as he tried to keep from cracking up.

"Bike stud!" Lionel finally shouted.

"Mum's the word. Nothing about this to Cody, right Lionel?" Burke said.

"Oh, mommy!"

"Lionel."

"Hey, hey don't worry. My lips are zipped."

SHERBURNE HILL

Even though the nights were still chilly in Northern California into May, the days began to warm up and the daylight hours lasted longer. Perfect for bicycle riding. Burke had devised a weekly training schedule for Cody that included six days of riding, four days of weight lifting and one off day without any training, a complete rest day. Cody chose that day to be Friday since it gave him time to hang with his friends or catch a movie.

Cody had decided to skip the spring basketball league that all varsity players were "strongly encouraged" to attend. He told Coach Myers that he was still rehabilitating his knee with heavy physical therapy, weight lifting and conditioning, which was all true. When Myers had consulted with Mitchell Burke, he felt satisfied, at least for the time being, that Cody was doing all the right things to make it back to the team in time for summer leagues. Cody missed his buddies on the team and the fun of playing in the spring league because it was just playing games and no practicing. But he didn't miss the fear that he could hurt his knee at any time. He didn't like playing with that fear and he was content to pass up the next month or two of basketball to get the knee back to 100%.

What Cody hadn't figured on was how much fun he was having on the bike, especially during training, which in his mind was just another word for practicing. Even the word training had a much better ring to it. Why did other sports call it practice, he wondered? Sounds too much like work.

He also had a bike that almost flew it was so fast. Cody had transitioned from working off his physical therapy to working for Mitchell Burke. He continued to tidy up the office and therapy rooms a few evenings a week and assumed the filing chores from Burke's secretary. It didn't pay a lot of money, but he was able to save enough to start looking for a new bike. Burke had been loaning Cody a bike and as nice as it was, it was just a little too big for Cody's body type. Burke was almost six foot two and weighed close to 220 pounds. Cody was built more slender at just over six feet and weighing 160 dripping wet. Burke suggested that a smaller frame built to Cody's body would give him more efficiency on the bike and help him from getting fatigued so quickly.

Cody's mom didn't have much money to kick in to help, but Burke had quite a few friends in the bike business. So before he knew it, Cody was shopping for a new bike. With $200 his mom gave him, his savings from work, and birthday money, Cody had close to $1000 to spend on the bike. He was all ready to spring for a lower end composite bike with off the rack components, like gears and wheels, when Burke stunned him by offering to sponsor him in the purchase of the bike. Cody didn't know what that meant, so Burke explained the deal. Burke would help purchase a quality, upper end bike and in exchange Cody would agree to ride it. Sounded like a sweet deal to him, but Cody's mom had balked until Mitchell explained the details.

It was something that was quite common in the bicycling world, Burke explained to Sarah Calhoun. A sponsor would help a young rider with gear and other expenses as a way to promote the sport. In turn, since it was typically a business expense, sponsors were able to write off the expense just like it was advertising. Sometimes the rider was expected to print the name of the sponsor on the bike or his jersey, but mostly, the only thing the sponsor really wanted was the rider to ride – and race. Especially at the amateur level where big name sponsors weren't involved, local bike shops and sugar daddies to the bicycling world often helped out younger riders. Cody was right, it was a sweet deal.

The brand new Cannondale CAD 7 all aluminum bike with upgraded Campagnolo components and wheels fit Cody perfectly. He had spent almost an hour in the bike shop getting measured for the bike before it was purchased and another hour after it had arrived and been assembled in the final fitting. He'd even had his new bike situated on the stationary bike trainer so he could pedal and get his seat and pedals adjusted. It almost blew him away when the bike shop owner had taken a plum bob and hung it from his knee to make sure his pedal stroke was completely straight up and down while in motion. Cody had never known that the science of bike riding was so intricate. He had basically gotten on any old bike and pedaled like crazy until he was too tired to pedal anymore. Burke was now showing him that pedaling was important, but so were a whole lot of other things.

Of course, Lionel K. Fitzhugh was present during every phase of the purchase of the new bike. He became such a sponge for information about how the bike was constructed and assembled that the bike shop owner finally offered him a job in the store. Lionel turned it down, although he was flattered, because he had a job of his own. Number two man to Cody Calhoun, the newest sponsored bike racer in Northern California.

For Cody's six days on the bike each week, Burke had a schedule planned at least four weeks out. Lionel's job was to research the training ride and produce a map for Cody to follow, at least until Cody knew the routes by heart. He used Mapquest or Yahoo on Burke's computer system to find the exact route and a color map for Cody to stuff into his jersey in case he got lost. Lionel was also in charge of the cyclo-computer that was attached to Cody's handlebars. It tracked distance, speed, average speed and heart rate. Lionel's job was to keep these statistics and to devise a way to graph them in Microsoft Excel and Draw so he could get an even better picture of how good a shape Cody was in.

Cody's job was to ride. Burke had him working on technique, speed, and endurance. Some days he simply rode as hard as he could for the length of the ride, which could be anywhere from 40 miles to 60 miles. Other days he worked on speed training, or as Burke called it, intervals. He'd pedal at top speed in a big hard gear, mimicking an all-out sprint, for up to two minutes. Then slow down to regular speed for eight minutes. Then to all-out again and back to regular, repeating this pattern for a majority of the ride.

Some Saturday mornings before Cody left on his training ride, Burke would work with him on the stationary bike in Burke's garage, concentrating on his technique. Pedal stroke was a big deal to Mitchell Burke and he was always tweaking with the way Cody pumped his legs. Burke taught him how to not only push down hard during the stroke but also pull up on the pedal as it completed its circle. It's like wiping gum off the bottom of your shoe on a doormat, Burke would explain. And consistency was a big deal, too. Keep pedaling hard all the way through the stroke, don't let up, don't rest at the bottom of the stroke, keep pumping, keep pulling, don't forget your left leg, and so on. It was like a mantra to Burke. Cody often wondered how he knew so much about pedal stroke.

And Mitchell Burke was always concerned with Cody's left knee. It was the one damaged in basketball and the initial reason that Cody had come to therapy. Burke examined the knee almost daily, looking for indications of swelling or pain and using his strength test by asking Cody to hold the knee out straight and then having Burke try to move it one way or the other. Burke was always satisfied with the progress in the knee, at least as far as Cody could tell. He would say something like, OK, good, looking good today, great, no problems here, as he was putting Cody through the paces of a knee examination.

But most of Cody's training came on the bike, on the road. Burke changed the routes and the routines daily. The rides were challenging and Burke always found a way to make them a contest. On flat rides, speed was often the name of the game. Could Cody cover the ride maintaining an average speed of 20 miles an hour? If the route contained some hills, elevation Burke called it, then the speed challenge might be 16 or 17 miles per hour for the duration of the ride.

When the rides were mostly elevation, mountains as Cody called them but in Northern California, hills were about as big a name for them as you could give, heart rate became the game. Cody was to maintain a certain heart rate over the course of the ride. Burke always seemed to know exactly how high the heart rate should be without actually having Cody fall out of the saddle from exhaustion or lack of oxygen. Cody was amazed at how precise Burke's knowledge of heart rate was, since there were times when he knew he could in no way make it up the next hill keeping the heart rate that Lionel had given him earlier in the day. But he could, and he did, at least most of the time.

Some days Cody worked on his breathing technique. (Who knew there was a technique to breathing, Cody wondered? Wasn't that just the way God make human beings? Air goes in, air comes out. What's the technique about that?) In through the nose, out through the mouth was the basic instruction, but Burke would vary it by making Cody concentrate on really blowing out hard on the exhaling part. He said that forced air out of the lungs and the natural reaction was to suck it in just as hard as you could. Cody only had to think about the first part, the out, and the in part just followed naturally.

Cody also worked on acceleration. Burke would make him accelerate over the smaller hills, trying his best not to slow down. You beat guys going up the hills, not coming down them, Burke always said. Most people get bogged down when they see obstacles in their way, but if you develop the techniques of pushing over obstacles, then you'll look at them as a challenge, and you'll eat them up. So Burke would lay out a course full of small, rolling hills and the technique of the day was to "accelerate to the top."

Often Cody would find himself pushing past what he thought was possible in his conditioning. In basketball games, there was a rest stop about every 30 seconds. The ball goes out of bounds, a foul shot is taken, something stops the game and gives the body a chance to take a breath. Burke's idea of training on the bike included very few rests. But he built Cody's conditioning gradually so that only through Lionel's graphs did they all see the progress. From day to day on the bike, it was just training to both Cody and Lionel, but when you looked at the statistics on paper, they all could see how Cody was getting in shape. The miles he rode increased, the speed in which he rode them increased, and his heart rate just kept getting stronger.

Then one Saturday morning, Burke threw a wrench into the works. Cody and Lionel had arrived at Burke's home right on schedule at 7:00 am. Burke's garage was equipped with a keypad entry system and both the boys had been given the combination. They would help themselves to whatever supplies or riding clothes they needed from the garage, get the bike ready to ride, fill the water bottles, discuss the day's ride, have a few snacks. Burke would often not even be awake before Cody was gone and Lionel was puttering, either in the garage with one of the bikes or in the den with one of the CDs. This Saturday morning was different. When they arrived, Burke was already dressed and ready for the day.

"Change of plans today, gents. It's Sherburne Hill day."

Lionel's eyes narrowed and he looked at Cody like he'd just been given a single clue to a diabolical plot to overthrow the world. He arched his right eyebrow and narrowed his left eye. "Sounds dangerous," he said.

Cody's confidence was high on the bike, since the last week or two he'd been hitting his targets for speed and heart rate, so he saw no mystery in the statement. "Bring it on," was all he had to say.

Burke had a slightly smug look on his face as he commented, "Lionel and I will be joining you today, at least for the evaluation part of the ride."

"Whew, dude, you had me going there for a minute. When you put together the hill part and the joining part in one sentence and added my name in there, I thought for sure, unless I was motorized in some way, it would be certain death. You know what I mean?"

"It may very well feel like death to Cody. But I assure you, Lionel, you and I will be warm and comfortable in the GMC," Burke replied.

Cody's smile quickly vanished.

"I see you're just about ready, Cody, so Lionel and I will meet you at the foot of Sherburne Hill, at the intersection of North Main. Do you know where that is?"

"Yeah."

"It's about five miles, a nice warm up for you. See you in about 20 minutes?"

"Sure." One-word answers were about all Cody could come up with. That death word kept rattling around in his head like a pinball gone berserk.

Burke and Lionel jumped in the SUV and drove down the driveway. Mitchell Burke motioned to Cody to be sure to shut the garage door after he left, and they were gone. Cody finished his mental checklist in preparation for the ride, but he wasn't concentrating. Rattle, rattle was all he heard.

"So mysterious one, what's up with Sherburne Hill?" Lionel asked as they headed to the rendezvous site.

"We are about to see what your friend is made of today, Lionel."

"I'd say mostly protoplasm and water. And a ton of heart, if you get my drift."

"He's gonna need at least a ton."

Cody arrived at the juncture of Sherburne Hill and North Main a few minutes after Burke and Lionel and most of his fear had left him. He rode fast and hard, lopping at least five minutes off the time he was expected to arrive. The morning was cool and crisp, the air clean and the traffic light. He was ready for the challenge.

Sherburne Hill was located off the main drag and only merited a small street sign tacked to the telephone pole, unlike most of the neighborhood where illuminated green and white street signs proudly hung over the streets, proclaiming their splendor. Sherburne Hill's sign looked like it had been there way before the fancier lighted signs arrived in town. The road narrowed quite a bit from the broad streets in the neighborhood and the quality of the road didn't seem quite as good. The nice smooth blacktop stopped about 50 yards up the hill.

"You ever been up this road?" Burke asked as the three of them assembled in front of the SUV.

"Rode by it a few times, but never up it," Cody said matter-of-factly.

"It's 4.2 miles to the summit, where the road forks off two ways. The right fork heads out toward the freeway, the left to a private cattle ranch. The computer all set, Lionel?"

He nodded, "Heart rate monitor, too."

"OK, Cody, let's see if you can make it up averaging nine miles an hour. Take a mental note of what the computer says at the summit and take it easy coming down. This is a climbing test, so I don't want you killing yourself on the descent, got it?"

"Got it," Cody shouted as he sped away up the hill.

"I mean it. Real easy coming down, those switchbacks are killers!" Burke shouted. Cody waved his acknowledgement as he accelerated and switched to a lower gear.

The first mile was a gradual ascent and Cody didn't have a problem beating his target. He was even able to enjoy the scenery. Sherburne Hill was not much more than a roughly paved mountain road. It was barely two cars wide, Cody thought, but he doubted he would see any vehicles. There were no houses on the road and it looked completely deserted. The hills surrounding him jutted up quickly from the road. A small stream paralleled the road on Cody's right side. He wondered from studying geology in science class if the stream had etched the pathway from mountaintop to the valley bottom over the course of several thousand years. Or was it million years? He couldn't remember. Large eucalyptus trees hugged the path and hid it from the sun.

Abruptly at the second mile marker, the hill got nasty. And steep. Cody first switched down a gear, then another, and finally found his biggest granny gear as he settled into a comfortable pace. He tried staying in the saddle to conserve energy as Burke had taught him, but several times had to rise up from the seat to keep his momentum.

He looked at the cyclo-computer and was shocked to see the large digital mile per hour number hovering at 7.5. Even with his quick pace on mile number one, he knew it wouldn't take long for his average speed to drop. Lionel had programmed the computer to display the current miles per hour in the large dial and average miles per hour to appear in the smaller readout in the upper right hand corner of the gauge. Every time Cody looked at the smaller, average number, it was falling. He picked up the pace.

Quickly the scenery faded from view and he only concentrated on the road and the dial. Every once in a while, he looked up to see Sherburne Hill continuing to climb in front of him, but the road was so narrow and curvy that his vision was limited to no more than ten or twenty yards. After a while he knew better than to look. It just kept going up and up.

Cody looked at his gears to make sure he was in the

easiest one. Man, there's gotta be another one on the chain ring, he thought. He was now out of the saddle and pumping down hard on the pedals. He tried to remember the techniques for climbing, Burke had reviewed them enough, but he was finding it hard to concentrate. He remembered to pull up on the pedals and push down on the pedals and he remembered to blow out hard for more air in his lungs. He pushed on.

After about a mile of this steep ascent, the hill relented and gave him a break. The road narrowed even further, now no wider than a pickup truck, and gradually leveled out. Cody fell into the saddle and caught his breath but at the next corner was again forced to jump up out of the saddle and exert maximum effort. This was no ordinary hill, he thought. He also thought about cursing at Mitchell Burke. But he knew this was a test and he knew, somewhere down deep inside that he was prepared for it.

His only saving grace was that the dense tree coverage kept the road cool. Even so, Cody was dripping wet. He'd unzipped his jersey and his body kept telling him to drink water to stay cool and hydrated, but every time he took a sip from his water bottle, it threw his breathing off. He was trying to suck as much of the dry, cool morning air as he could. Oxygen, give me more O, more O, please. Sweat dripped onto his sunglasses so he took them off and quickly shoved them into a back jersey pocket.

His lungs ached. Every breath forced air in, but he couldn't seem to get it deep enough. Cody tried to expand his diaphragm and breathe deeply, but the air never seemed to get below his throat. He couldn't force it down enough before he needed another breath. He knew he was breathing too quickly but he couldn't slow it down without slowing his pace and it was dangerously teetering around nine MPH as it was. Any backing off now, especially not knowing what lay ahead in the final two miles, could be tough to make up.

His legs were burning, especially his thighs. He wasn't used to spending this much time out of the saddle and he desperately wanted to sit down. But, in fact, he knew that if he sat, the bike might just stop altogether. Technique, where's the technique? Down hard, up hard on the pedals. Breathe in through the nose, out the mouth. That doesn't work, Cody thought, not enough air coming in through the old nose portal. Let's go, air in the mouth, air out the mouth. More air, more air.

A strange thought then came to Cody. It was a scene from an old Star Trek episode where Captain Kirk was demanding more power from Scotty, the guy in the engine room.

"She can't take much more, Captain, she's gonna blow," Cody heard in a distinctively Scottish accent. He felt Scotty's pain. Oh, boy, did he feel it.

He looked at the mileage. 2.7 miles down, 1.5 to go. He actually thought right then and there that he wasn't going to make it. He wanted to stop, just get off the bike now and breathe again. Every fiber in his body was in full protest. His lungs screamed at him. Get off! His lungs howled! No more, give it up! His head pounded from lack of oxygen. I'll turn the hammer off if you quit! Is that my vision blurring? Am I going to pass out, fall off the bike and land in the stream?

Then the hill relented again, leveling out. Cody thought, maybe a few more strokes. I can make a few more strokes. Don't quit just yet. Maybe I can hang on. Breathe, dammit, breathe. The bike was now wobbling a bit and Cody had unconsciously started to traverse the road as much as the narrow pavement would allow. He was trying to cut down on the steepness of the hill by riding not directly up but from side to side. All he could think about was reaching the top now. It had to be soon.

Then he saw one more steep ascent and he almost quit. I can't make it, no way. But he kept pedaling, one foot, then the other. Right, left, right, left. His head slumped down, he looked at the pedals, trying to will them out of sheer effort, to keep going. He didn't care about the target rate, he only cared about making it to the top. He switched, almost pedal stroke to pedal stroke, from sheer despair and defeat to pure determination. Keep going. No, quit. No, keep going. No, really, quit. No. Yes. No. Now his mind was the battleground, his body had already lost the fight.

Meanwhile, at the foot of Sherburne Hill, Lionel and Burke passed the time.

"I really would like to be able to talk to Cody right about now Lionel," Burke commented. "Do you think you could figure out a way to put two-way communication on that bike?"

Lionel frowned, thinking immediately of how to do exactly that. Burke knew before he asked the question how to do it, but he wanted Lionel to figure it out himself.

"I'm sure there's a way. Gotta be one," Lionel muttered.

"Good, work on it. I'd like to be able to talk to Cody and have him talk to me. I'd be real interested in his heart rate and his oxygen level at a moment like this."

Meanwhile, Cody saw the next crest in the unrelenting hill and let the faint hope enter his mind that it was the last one. Mercifully, it was. He saw the fork in the road a mere fifty yards ahead and that gave him the boost to finish the climb. As he came to the top of the hill, he clicked out of his pedals and slumped over the handlebars, grasping for air.

After a few minutes in recovery, he remembered to look at the mph dial. It read 8.6; he'd missed the target, but at this particular moment he just felt glad that he hadn't quit. At least he'd made it to the top.

Cody enjoyed the cool breeze in his face on the ride down Sherburne Hill. He followed Burke's advice and took it easy, keeping his fingers close to the brakes and applying them generously. Cody noticed more of the scenery on the way down; somehow he'd missed a lot of it going up. How did I miss all this? Where was I on the trip up the hill? He coasted back to the starting point and found Lionel and Burke talking in the SUV. When they noticed his arrival, they popped out of the car.

"And the final reading is…?" Lionel asked as Cody pulled his Cannondale up to the pair.

"Eight point six," a sullen Cody answered.

"Not bad, not bad at all. I never thought you'd even get close to a nine on that hill. Killer wasn't it?" Burke said.

"Damn straight. Thanks for the warning."

"Sorry, you're right. In most cases you'd have upfront knowledge what the course is like before you tackle it. I apologize," Burke countered.

"Whatever."

"OK, so this time, since you know the course, let's see if you can beat the 8.6," Burke suggested.

"This time? You mean next time, right?" Cody asked.

"No, I mean this time. Now."

"No way. I can't do that again, man."

"Ah," Burke countered, "that's your mind talking. Probably your biggest battle going up that hill was your head. I'll never do this, when does it end, I gotta stop. I hate that Burke. No way can I make it. Stuff like that, right?"

Cody didn't answer.

"So this time," Burke continued, "you know you can do it. So go do it again. Simple as that."

"Simple for you, you're not doing the pedaling," Cody said in not much more than a whisper.

'Yeah, but he could," Lionel blurted out, getting a grimace on his face the moment he said it. It was like the words just escaped and before he could stop them they were out. Burke gave him a stern look, but looked away quickly.

"Yeah, right!" Cody said with an attitude.

"Cody," Burke started, "you said you were ready to take it to the next level. You've done some good training over the past few months, really worked hard, progressed a lot. You're a well-trained athlete now. But I don't understand this attitude. You asked me to coach you…"

"I never asked for a coach," Cody interrupted. "You're a…, not like a coach…"

"No, I'm a coach," Burke continued calmly. "Like it or not, you need a coach. Having a good friend like Lionel is nice, it's great, nothing better in the world than that. He helps you, takes care of you, looks after you, hangs out with you. He even has started to learn about the bike and what makes it click. But he doesn't push you. He's too close to you. And he doesn't know that's what you need. That's my job. To figure out what you need and right now you need hills. Lots of hills."

"You're pushing too hard," Cody shot back.

"What? One time up that hill is suddenly too hard?" Burke said, his voice rising noticeably. "Heck, I've had kids go up that hill three, four times in a row without stopping. I mean just sprint to the point you're standing, turn around and bust butt back up. Some of the premier riders around here do it time and time again all day long. One time and you're done? Give me a giant, freakin' break."

Cody looked at him with a meanness Lionel had never seen in Cody before. Hate was closer to it. Cody's eyes had narrowed, his lips were clenched together, he suddenly spat on the ground, took a long drink of water and spit it out.

"Screw you," he mumbled to Burke as he suddenly pulled his bike up and pointed it back toward Sherburne Hill. He punched his cyclo-computer back to zero and clicked into his pedals. Then he took off with a vengeance back up the hill.

As he disappeared around the bend, Burke looked at Lionel, who had a wide-eyed look on his face and was wondering what just happened there. Burke said with a smile, "Nothing like a little motivation to help you get the legs churning, eh?"

A look of realization came over Lionel and he said, "You planned that, didn't you?"

Burke shrugged, "I just went with the flow. It's all part of the program."

Lionel nodded.

Cody returned to the rendezvous spot shortly with a big 'I told you so' grin on his face.

"9.2!" he shouted from thirty yards away. He pulled up next to the SUV as Burke and Lionel emerged. His chest was puffed out like a wrestler defying the screaming crowd in a World Wrestling Federation match.

As Lionel was congratulating him and checking the computer, Cody kept staring at Burke, who was busy jotting something down in a notebook and pretending to ignore Cody.

"Well?" Cody finally said, a bit of cockiness in his voice.

Burke quickly glanced up from the notebook and said, "Well done. Now try for 9.5."

"Now?" Cody said, almost shouting.

"Right now," Burke said calmly. "And I want you to concentrate on your left leg, the one you injured. Pedal extra hard with that leg, pull up hard, push down hard. Up hard, down hard. Hard left, hard left, hard left. Got it?"

"Yes sir, you bet, no problem." Cody began to swing the Cannondale back around.

"That's yes sir, coach, to you," Burke said with a big grin on his face.

Cody pulled away, heading up Sherburne Hill a third time, "Yes sir, coach," he said, now almost inaudible to Burke. Almost. Another thirty yards up the hill, he smiled and muttered to himself, "Screw you, coach."

Twenty-five minutes later he returned. His jersey was soaked and his water bottle empty, but he was grinning through gritted teeth.

Lionel waited in anticipation for the results. Cody was deliberately holding out on the two. Finally both his hands shot into the air, and he bellowed, "9.7!"

High fives all around and a few back slaps from Lionel. As Cody was filling up his water bottle from the big jug in the SUV, Burke gave him a one-arm hug. "Nice job" was all he said, but Cody felt the pride grow inside him. It didn't take much of a compliment from Mitchell Burke to swell his chest.

After a snack and a bit of explanation on the hill to Lionel, Cody got instructions from Burke for the rest of the morning's training ride.

"Now, while your legs are heavy, get in some distance work. Spend another hour on the bike and we'll meet you back at my place. Lunch is on me," Burke said. Lionel smiled broadly at the thought of lunch on Mitchell Burke. He could almost smell the home made chicken enchiladas now.

The two got into the SUV, swung it around and headed back toward home as Cody was searching in his seat bag for something.

"Just gonna make a seat adjustment before I head out," he explained. Lionel gave a thumbs up and the SUV pulled away.

When it was out of sight, Cody waited another minute and turned the bike back toward Sherburne Hill. As he stomped on the pedals, he mumbled to himself, a steely determination in his voice, "Now for 10.0."

SO HAPPY TOGETHER

"If you think I'm pushing that boy too hard, Sarah, you have to let me know," Mitchell Burke said to Sarah Calhoun as he poked at the pasta primavera on his plate. "You know him better than me and you know his history, I mean his, eh, his emotional history. Not his physical history, I'm okay there. Well, you know what I mean," he finished and started piling pasta into his mouth.

"You mean his psyche? How emotionally strong he is?" Sarah asked.

"Yeah, kinda."

"Yeah, kinda what? What kind of answer is that? You sound just like Cody. Two-word answers. Men." She was about to add can't live with them, can't live without them, but she was also trying to be serious, so cut herself off quickly.

Burke kept eating, finally noticing that the pasta dish Sarah had prepared for them was delicious. The pasta was firm, yet done and the vegetables were crisp not mushy, just the way he liked them. The sauce was a light olive oil with various spices he couldn't name and didn't care because it was all topped with fresh ground Parmesan cheese. Burke would eat just about anything if it was topped with fresh ground Parmesan cheese.

"This is really delicious," he said to Sarah, his mouth still half full, one angel hair dangling from his lips.

"Don't change the subject," she answered, trying to stay on subject but she was betrayed by the smile that crept across her face. Try as she might, she couldn't help smiling whenever she was around Mitchell Burke, who slurped a dangling noodle into his mouth with an over-exaggerated smack and a wide-eyed look. She almost lost it. He reminded her of those dogs in the movie *Lady and the Tramp* when they both got hold of the same piece of pasta and started sucking on it until their mouths met. She got lost on the mouths meeting part as she smiled and ate and stared off into space.

"Earth to Sarah, report in please."

Upon reentry, she just smiled at Mitchell Burke. "You did change the subject, you know," she said very quietly.

"Not really on purpose. I just wanted you to know how much I was enjoying the meal. And the ambiance."

Sarah looked around her modest apartment, littered with ten-year-old furniture and five-year-old carpet. The walls were standard issue light beige and the drapes looked like they'd shrunk at least eight inches off the floor from repeated laundering. The furniture was old, out of fashion, and a bit worn looking. Decorations weren't exactly skimpy, but by no means would they be called elaborate. Sarah had a nice homey touch with the way she decorated her house and everyone felt welcome in it, but she didn't have the money to do all the things she wanted to.

At least she had been able to set a lovely table, even if she did say so herself. She had purchased a nice tablecloth and a set of place mats and real, cloth napkins. No paper napkins for tonight. But her silverware was still ragtag, a mish mash of too many trips to bargain basement sales. And the wineglasses were not real crystal, but at least they were fairly new and hadn't been ravished by a film of dishwasher soap. She scrubbed them extra hard earlier in the day just to be sure.

"Ambiance? Here? Right."

"Well, what I meant was, beautiful day, beautiful meal, and beautiful lady, that's ambiance to me."

"OK, now it's my turn to change the subject," Sarah said a little too quickly. "What did you mean by Cody's emotional history?"

"What I meant was he might be a little fragile, what with all you and his dad went through."

"You have no earthly clue what his dad and I went through. Have you ever been divorced?" Sarah asked, although she knew the answer was no.

"No, but I can imagine what you went through and what Cody went through. My folks were divorced, too, you know. And that was back in the 50's when it was a pretty rare event. People in small towns just didn't do that kind of thing back then and there weren't all those studies done on the effects on the children. But people figured out pretty quickly that the adults were hurting and the kids were hurting even more." Burke went back to swirling his pasta around on his plate like an artist looking for the right mixture of color but not finding it.

Sarah felt ashamed that she'd jumped on Burke so harshly and she didn't exactly know why she'd done it. She was so over Cody's father, she thought. But sometimes the mere mention of his name made her do and say things that weren't really her; at least not the person she'd become since the breakup.

"I'm sorry, I had no idea," was all she could muster.

Burke smiled warmly at her and said, "You don't need to apologize. You didn't know. And you're probably right, I don't know what you went through."

They ate in silence for a few minutes but it wasn't awkward silence. Burke was contemplating how quickly Sarah was willing to apologize and admit she'd been wrong (even though he didn't think she was). Sarah was thinking how amazing it was that Mitchell Burke didn't get defensive or angry or want to argue, even a little bit. He had simply accepted her apology. Done deal, no more to say, don't worry about it. She wasn't used to a man who didn't have to win ever single argument (was that even considered an argument?) or be right about everything. Most men she knew had a very hard time admitting they were wrong.

After a minute or so, he asked, "Do you thing Cody is fragile, emotionally?"

Sarah only had to think about it for a second. "I personally think he is the strongest 16-year-old young man I've ever known. He's my rock. When I'm fragile, he's there. He doesn't always say the right thing, but he knows how to be there for me. It's hard to put into words, but he knows when I'm down, like he senses it or something, and he'll do what he can to lift me up. He talks basketball or bikes or girls or something that he can get excited about, and then he gets me excited about it too."

Sarah hadn't practiced this speech, and in a way, she was discovering what Cody brought to the family for the first time herself. But the more she talked the more she got excited and the more her admiration for her son grew.

"Or he'll talk about you, Mitchell."

"Me?" Burked asked somewhat startled.

"He admires you very much. He thinks you did a great job getting his knee back in shape, but I also know he respects how you've coached him on the bike. You've pushed him but he's not complaining. At least not to me. And Lionel tells me almost anything in the world I want to know and he hasn't mentioned it."

"I admire him a lot, too. Not many kids his age would go through all that hard rehab to get back to playing shape so quickly. And he's ten times stronger now than before he was hurt. He's so focused sometimes, he reminds me..." his thought trailed off and he began to swirl the pasta again.

"Of you?"

Burke nodded.

"I would think that would be a good thing, Mitchell," Sarah said as she reached across the table and softly squeezed his hand.

HOW COULD I DANCE WITH ANOTHER?

Just about the same time Sarah Calhoun was looking dreamily into the eyes of Mitchell Burke, Cody was pulling into the parking lot of Denny's restaurant. He'd borrowed his mom's car and even though it was a 1993 Volkswagen Jetta (such a chick car, like almost every Volkswagen ever made he thought), at least he had his driver's license now and a whole lot more independence. Denny Clarke called earlier in the day and when Cody mentioned that his mom and Burke were laying claim to the apartment for the evening, she suggested they grab a burger if that sounded OK to him.

It sounded more than OK to Cody. When pressed where he wanted to meet her (he wasn't really allowed to date much, his mom was so over-protective, so he really couldn't pick her up at her house), Denny's popped into his mind. You know, date with Denny at Denny's. It sounded pretty cool at the time. Now it sounded down right juvenile. How in the world did he ever come up with that? She's gonna think I'm a total dork. He kept worrying about the restaurant and the old chick car and quickly spiraled into a downright ugly self-inflicted Cody bashing, tattooing himself with everything from bad skin to bad haircut (damn you, Supercuts), stopping just short of declaring himself the devil child.

But when he turned into the parking lot and saw her standing there…(like the old Beatles song Fitzy is always playing, well she looked at me, and I, I could see that before too long I'd fall in love with her)…he forgot about his skin and his hair. Denny Clarke had that effect on him. He just liked being around her. She never pressured him into being something he wasn't and she always accepted him just the way he was, warts and all. (Man, he was glad he didn't have warts; I guess it could be worse). They'd been hanging out together more and more lately. Denny hadn't really gotten into the biking scene much, but still liked to experiment with her killer protein shakes. She often would consult with Lionel on the impact of a certain shake concoction she'd brewed up and how it affected Cody's performance on the bike.

In one of their talks at Burke's house after Cody had hit the training trail, she's confided in Lionel that she had been the one to tack up the "Go, Cody" signs on the first race he'd ridden back in April. Being the good friend and confidant that he was to Cody, Lionel quickly broke the confidence that same day and told him every word. Denny didn't really get mad at Lionel, although she faked it pretty good for a day or two. She actually knew Lionel would tell Cody and deep down, hoped that he would. Sometimes boys are so predictable, she thought. Good thing they are!

As Cody checked his look in the rear view mirror one more time, he smiled. Denny usually made him smile, sometimes just thinking about her did it. But she also had a really good sense of humor. She didn't tell jokes or anything, she just seemed to laugh a lot. Mostly she'd laugh at herself, cutting herself down ever so slightly, so the other person would look better. She wasn't judgmental about other kids too much, always saying something like, "well, they probably have it tough at home," or "being a teenager is never easy, is it?" Then she roll her eyes, get a little smirk on her face like she just pulled a joke on you by making you feel sorry for the other kid, then start to giggle. Cody liked her giggle.

"How's the big romantic rendezvous going at home?" she asked Cody as he strolled up to the entrance of the restaurant.

"No clue," he replied and then he quickly remembered his mom's advice about not answering her questions with two word comebacks. "And I guess I really don't want to know, you know?"

"Bull, you want to know every gory detail, just like me. I'd like to be invisible right now, standing in that apartment, taking notes, are you kidding me?"

"Yeah, you're probably right," Cody conceded. But he really wasn't too sure he wanted to know any details, but he might as well make Denny think he agreed with her. His mom had told him that, too. Don't be disagreeable.

The restaurant wasn't very crowded and the middle-aged hostess, who wore the standard brown Denny's uniform, seated them in a booth by the front window. Denny noticed that the hostess looked older than she probably was, and had a weird thought that the color of the uniform had actually seeped into her being. Her eyes were brown, her dye job was mostly brown and even her skin was fading into a yellowish brown. From the smell of her breath, the cigarettes she chain-smoked probably had a lot to do with her skin color. Denny was always fascinated with what people put into their bodies and how often it came seeping back through their pores. The hostess made her cringe a bit and Cody noticed.

"Something I said?" he asked.

"What? Oh, no. I was just wondering how long that hostess had been working here. She probably has a whole lot going on in her life. And her feet probably hurt. Mine would if I had her job all day."

Cody smiled at the sympathy Denny displayed. Just then he thought of Laurel and how she never, ever had a sympathetic word to say about anyone. Man, he thought to himself, I haven't thought of Laurel in a long, long time. Good.

"What?" Denny asked.

"Huh? Oh, nothing." Great, Cody thought, at least it was a three-word answer if you count huh as a word.

Two older gentlemen seated at the counter traded today's newspaper sections back and forth, speaking little. Only the rustling of their papers broke the silence. A family of five was seated across the restaurant, the three kids looking like they were between the ages of one and four. The mother looked a bit disheveled, her hair falling in her face, her blouse stained with what might be blood, but probably was spaghetti sauce. The father was holding the youngest child in his lap trying to make him stop squirming by spoon feeding his something green from a little jar. Another couple sat in a booth three booths away from Cody and Denny and munched their dinner without saying a single word. Other than that, the restaurant was quiet.

When the waitress came to take their order, the same

brow-drenched hostess that had seated them, Cody was tempted to go for the Grand Slam breakfast, served anytime here at the great American greasy spoon, but he changed his mind. Denny would probably have frowned at all the fat, so he ordered the club sandwich after she waved him to go ahead and order first. Good variety of meats, grains and vegetables, he thought, in a good old club sandwich.

"Good choice," Denny commented as she continued to scan the menu. "I think I'll have the Grand Slam with double sausage, no bacon, and an English muffin. And juice, orange juice. You can never get enough vitamin C," she said to Cody.

"Good choice," he mimicked back to her, with just a bit of sarcasm tinged with humor in his voice.

"What?" she asked.

Cody just shook his head and smiled. Do you think she did that for me, he wondered? That would be just like her to order something she didn't like so I wouldn't feel bad ordering the same thing, or worse.

"Did you want to change your order?" Denny asked.

She did do that for me, didn't she? "Nah, I'll stick to the good variety of meats, grains and vegetables. But throw in the fries, please. And a coke." The waitress finished scribbling the order on the grease stained pad and loped lackadaisically back toward the kitchen.

"How's your mom doing?" Denny asked after an awkward moment of silence.

"Fine, why?" Shoot, two words.

"Well, I don't know, it's just whenever we talk, she seems a little troubled."

"When do you two talk anyway?"

"When you're not around, I guess," Denny smiled.

"I don't know what's bothering her. I try not to give her much grief."

"I just thought that maybe she was a little emotionally fragile, what with everything that's happened."

"What everything?" Cody asked, a little more irritated.

"Well, not everything lately, I mean, things are OK, right? I just meant that with Mr. Mitch in the picture now, maybe she a little…I don't know…gun shy."

"What do mean by that?" Cody asked, too ashamed to admit he didn't know the meaning of the phrase.

"Just that sometimes when a woman's been hurt before, it's a little scary jumping back into the mix again, that's all. I didn't mean anything, it's probably none of my business," Denny gracefully tried to exit this particular line of conversation.

"Hurt before like by my dad? Is that what you mean?"

"Yeah, I guess," Denny said, looking like she was practicing origami with her napkin, anything to not look into his eyes.

"Look, you don't know squat about my mom being hurt."

"I know, I'm sorry, let's change the subject."

Cody looked down at his silverware and noticed that at least half of yesterday's breakfast was still caked on his fork. The thought crossed his mind as quickly as water over a dam. He took a deep breath.

"Look, no offense taken. But my mom is a rock. She's always there for me, whatever I've needed, whatever it's taken, she's done it for me. When my dad bailed, she cried for a while, mostly at nights when she thought I couldn't hear. But she never gave up. I think she had a job in about a week. A year later, she got a really good job. And for being my mom and all, she mostly knows exactly what I need. Not always. Sometimes she throws up a bunch of airballs, but I know she's trying. So I'm not too hard on her. She always seems to say the right thing to keep me up. And she's always been at every game I've ever played. That means a lot, you know."

Denny nodded slowly, keeping her eyes glued to the large glass sugar dispenser that she was twisting in her hands.

Cody continued, "And she never gives me grief about my friends. Actually, most of my friends like being around her, you know?"

"I like being around her," Denny offered with hope that he would forgive her for something she wasn't quite sure she'd done to offend him.

"Yeah, she likes you, too."

"She does, how do you know?" Denny asked, her eyes

finally meeting his.

"She told me. We talk you know," Cody replied, his tone softening.

"Oh…well…I admire her and everything she does. I'm always amazed at how much she accomplishes in life. Sometimes it seems I can barely get myself up and out of bed without a major catastrophe. And she seems to handle almost everything in stride. Nothing seems to rattle her. She's very together, like some kind of superwoman or something."

They sat in silence for awhile. When the meal was served, the waitress absentmindedly switched the plates, Cody ending up with the Grand Slam. For a minute he stared at it, forgetting that he hadn't ordered it. Denny politely cleared her throat and stole a look at the gigantic breakfast.

"Right," Cody said finally, switching the plates.

"You remind me of her," he finally said.

"Your mom? Me?"

"Yeah. It's like you always have it together."

"Thanks," she said, her eyes searching for his. For a second she wanted to reach across the table and grab his hand, but they were both wrapped around the sandwich.

"Thanks a lot." She settled for that and smiled deep inside.

THE CHOICE

The next morning Mitchell Burke was awakened by the sound of a bouncing basketball. He slowly shook himself awake and noticed he had a headache. Never should have had that second glass of red wine, he thought. He threw the covers off, swung his legs over the side of the bed and sat up, turning his neck from side to side to try to ease the paid in his head. The bouncing ball wasn't helping the process. It must be Cody. He and Lionel were the only ones with access to the garage and the sound was definitely coming from that direction of the house.

He shuffled over to the phone system on his bedroom desk and punched the button on the elaborate console that read Garage. A small beep proceeded his question, "Cody, is that you?"

He waited as Cody ran over to a matching console mounted on a wall of the garage. Cody sheepishly answered, "Yeah, sorry. You up?"

Am now, Burke thought, but he answered, "Be right down." He slipped on a pair of sweat pants, his flip-flops and a San Jose State long sleeve tee shirt. He liked rooting for the underdog and he couldn't remember the last time the Spartans were favored in anything.

When Burke entered the garage, Cody was sitting on a small step stool, dribbling the basketball from one hand to the other. He didn't hear Burke open the door but seemed lost in his own world. A Creed song played lowly in the background and Burke hesitated a few moments before announcing his presence. Cody's back was turned slightly, his head slumped, his chin on his chest. But he wasn't watching the basketball as he deftly switched it between hands and through legs, he was looking past the ball to a place only he could see. Burke saw worry and what might be confusion in his eyes. Burke let the moment linger.

Finally, the song ended and that seemed to jostle Cody

from his trance. He turned and noticed Burke standing in the doorway.

"Hope it's nothing too serious," Burke quickly commented before Cody had a chance to ask him how long he'd been standing there.

"What?"

"Whatever seems to be bothering you."

"Ah, nothin," Cody slowly replied.

"Wanna talk about it?"

Cody shrugged his shoulders and went back to dribbling the ball. Burke took that as a yes, but proceed slowly and carefully.

"You like Creed? They're a little too heavy for me," Burke asked.

"Heavy as in heavy metal or heavy serious?"

"The metal part. I can't really say I've listened to the words closely enough to figure out what they're trying to say."

Cody stood up, went over to the stereo console and fingered the play button to find a song on the CD.

"Listen to this one," he said.

The melodic guitar of *My Sacrifice* filled the room.

"What was that first line?" Burke asked.

"'When you're with me, I'm free,'" Cody replied.

"You know, when Frank Sinatra sang, you could understand the words."

"When Frank Sinatra sang, there were probably a lot less words in the English language."

Burke didn't reply, but playfully mimicked a knife stabbing him in the heart, then added a slight twisting motion to the imaginary blade.

"Is he talking about a woman?"

"Don't know, maybe," Cody said, then added, "maybe something else."

The two continued to listen, and after Cody had cranked up the volume, he returned to his perch on the stool and picked up the basketball. Burke busied himself with sweeping off the indoor outdoor carpet, but kept stealing looks at the teenager.

When the song ended, Cody turned the volume back

down, but didn't seem eager to jump back into the conversation.
He slowly walked over to the Cannondale, picked a dust rag and
began to wipe the bike down with his right hand. But he kept the
ball in the left one.

The "sacrifice" in the song suddenly hit Burke like the
proverbial ton of bricks.

"When does the summer hoop season get underway?" he
asked Cody.

"They're already playing pickup in the gym four days a
week after school. It's called Open Gym, but it's really spring
practice. I think summer league games start the week after
school's out."

"How's the knee feeling? Ready for basketball?"

"Yeah, it's fine," Cody replied, but slow enough to
convey hesitancy.

"But…" Burke waited for Cody to complete the thought.

"But what?"

"The knee is fine, but…"

Cody just shrugged and returned to wiping down the bike,
which was already cleaner than newly hand-scrubbed linoleum.

Burke decided to take another tact. "Did you ever notice
there aren't a lot of six foot white guys in the NBA?"

"Duh," Cody stated.

"Or playing college ball for that matter."

"What about John Stockton? He's the NBA's all-time
leader in assists."

"Yep, that's one." Burke countered.

"What's your point?"

"Well I guess my point is, sometimes people come to
crossroads in their life. They can either go left or right, but they
can't keep going straight. You know, like a T in the road?"

Cody nodded but didn't reply.

Burke continued, "And most of the times, most but not
all, most of the times, that's not an easy decision to make.
Especially if you've always envisioned going in the one
direction. You see, life always presents choices. There's rarely a
time where there isn't a choice. The trick to life is often just
making the choice, one way or the other, right or wrong. Tons of

people are dead in the water cause they can't make the decision. Freezes them up, stops their progress."

"Can't have your cake and eat it, too," Cody nodded an understanding.

"Not quite. It's more like you can't decide between the pumpkin pie and the pecan pie at Thanksgiving, so you don't have either."

"Couldn't you just have a little of both?"

"Sure that's an easy decision to make when you're talking about pie, but it sometimes doesn't work when you're talking about life."

"Actually, I believe we were talking about cake, not pie."

"Right, I stand corrected." Burke smiled and slightly shook his head but continued, "So if I may be so bold, you're standing there dribbling a basketball with one hand and cleaning your bike with the other. Is this like a T in the road? Can you have your b-ball and your bike or do you have to make a choice?"

Cody shrugged again, "I dunno."

"That's why I brought up the whole thing about six foot white guys in the NBA. You're a very talented basketball player. If you work really hard and dedicate yourself you could probably play ball in college. You'd enjoy it, have a great time, maybe even be BMOC."

Cody scrunched his face like Burke was speaking a foreign language.

"Oh, sorry, Big Man on Campus, BMOC."

"That's like a Frank Sinatra reference, I take it."

"Right, ancient history," Burke conceded.

"And your point is…" Cody asked again.

Burke took a deep breath, hesitated, and decided to plunge ahead. "You have a chance at being really, really good in basketball," he said slowly for emphasis. He took another deep breath, go ahead, Mitchell, let the kid in on it, don't hold back, right between the eyes, it's the time.

Cody raised his eyebrows in anticipation of the rest of the thought.

"And you have a chance of being…great…on the bike,"

Burke exhaled like he had let go a secret he'd been holding in forever.

"Huh? What do you mean?"

"You're the best I've seen in a long, long time on the bike, Cody. Really."

"How would you know, you're a physical therapist,"

"I know, I've got a little experience in this field."

"Yeah, like what? What experience do you have in this field?" Cody shot back, a little too emphatically, a little too offended. Burke suspected something was about to hit the fan.

"A little," Burke said meekly.

"Oh? From what Lionel K. Fitzhugh tells me you've got a hell of a lot more than a little experience in this field, don't you?" Cody turned his back and slammed the basketball against the garage wall. It caromed off the wall, struck a plastic bin full of helmets and sent them flying in different directions. Burke didn't speak until the last one stopped spinning.

"I see Mr. Fitzhugh has let the cat out of the bag. Just as well, I suppose."

"More like a tiger than a cat," Cody spat.

"I probably should have told you," Burke conceded again.

"What else haven't you told me? Or my mom?"

"What do you mean by that?" Burke said in a quiet, calm tone.

"You just seem to be all of a sudden a man of many secrets. And…I don't know!" Cody couldn't find the words.

"And you think I'm keeping secrets from your mom?"

"Are you?"

Burke thought about it for almost 15 seconds and finally said, "A few, I guess."

"She deserves better than that."

"You're right, she does," Burke conceded for the third time.

The two were lost in their thoughts for several minutes. Cody felt almost betrayed. He'd trusted Mitchell Burke with a big part of his life. Not just his knee rehabilitation, but with his friendship and his feelings. He'd let Burke get close to him like no other man since his father. And look what good it had done him.

Burke was considering his options. He wasn't a man to tell his secrets easily, even to a young man like Cody, who had become more than a friend or a protégé. Should he tell him about his past? And if he did, should he tell him everything? It had been a very long time since he'd shared his innermost feelings and fears. Was this teenage boy willing to be his confessional? Should he burden Cody with it all?

Burke started slowly, "You know that T in the road we were talking about? Sometimes when a man my age keeps traveling down one straight and narrow road for a long time, he never sees the T's in the road. It seems like he doesn't even notice the options, he's just set in his ways, nose to the grindstone, eyes focused in front."

"I don't have a clue what you're talking about. Speak English, will ya."

Burke was fidgety and kept scratching imaginary itches. His heart was beating faster and his stomach felt queasy and sour. He took another deep breath. "OK, I was a champion bicycle racer. Came close to winning it all, top of the world type thing. Tour de France. But I didn't and it almost crushed me. I spun into a deep, deep depression after I couldn't ride anymore." Don't go there, Mitchell, keep something back, the kid can't take it.

"It's painful to talk about. And sometimes a man has to let go of his past and make a new future for himself. I didn't want to stand on my past successes, heck, I hurt to think about them. I made a new life as a physical therapist. The past is past." There, that's enough, you've gone quite far enough, Mitchell, almost to the T in the road.

Cody wasn't sure what to say. His mom was the only adult in his whole life who had ever divulged feelings like that to him before and he didn't know how to react. He felt better inside that Burke had told him the truth, but somehow he wasn't totally satisfied.

"Is that it?" Cody finally asked.

"In a nutshell."

"English, please."

"I mean that's the short version, the condensed version."

"Anything else I should know about?"

What, is this kid clairvoyant? Burke thought to himself. "That's pretty much it."

"In a nutshell?"

"A nutshell, right."

"So you just didn't tell us cause it's too painful to talk about?"

"When you get close to the mountaintop, but you don't quite make it all the way up, it's not just painful, it's almost, I can't find the word. It's…"

"Crushing," Cody said.

"Yeah, maybe that's it."

Cody thought about the times his father had broken promises to him and knew the feeling. "I think I know what you're talking about, almost the exact feeling." Cody stared off into space, lost in his thoughts.

Burke shook himself from his fog, sensing an opportunity to turn the conversation from the abyss he didn't want to go over and get back to his original point.

"But I never regretted heading up the mountaintop. It's better than staying on the flats and coming to all those T's in the road. There aren't a lot of T's on a mountain, you pretty much have your choices eliminated for you. You just head up."

Cody's attention now turned away from the wall back toward Burke. He seemed engaged again in the way his friend wanted to steer the talk. So Burke pressed on.

"You're different from me, Cody. Better than me, really. You've already faced heartbreak in your young life and fought right through it. It's made you tougher. I never had to face defeat until I was much older in life. I was born with a silver spoon in my mouth, which means I had it all handed to me, never had to work too hard for success. When I hit the wall, it hurt. Nearly crushed me. Took me a long time to even confront it. But you're different. You've already hit walls and bounced off them. It's made you resilient. Do you know what I mean?"

"You mean my knee?" Cody said.

"I mean your father…and your knee. But mostly your father."

Cody looked down at the indoor outdoor carpet and nodded knowingly. He couldn't look into Burke's eyes.

"I don't see you as a sad boy, mad at the world because he doesn't have a father around. I see you as a young man who has hit that wall and bounced back. It may have hurt, I suppose maybe it may have even crushed you at the time. But you bounced back. Not everyone does."

"You bounced back, didn't you? I mean, you started over and made a success of yourself again, didn't you?" Cody asked.

"In a way, I did, sure. But it took me a long time. I never saw the T in the road for, what seemed like, well, a very long time."

"Until you met my mom?" Cody snuck in a smile.

"This conversation is heavy enough without going there, isn't it?" Burke smiled back.

Cody nodded, "I guess."

"And like that Creed song said, sacrifice is making a hard choice. It is a sacrifice, you do have to give up something. But most of the time, when you come to the T in the road and you make the decision to go right or left, the road suddenly, miraculously, smoothes out. You leave the agony of the decision behind, you concentrate on only one road, not two. You get your focus back, you can see what direction you're heading."

"We're talking bikes or basketball here, aren't we?"

"We could be."

"Are you saying I have to choose between the two?"

"Absolutely not," Burke quickly answered. "A young man your age can leave his options open, but at some point lots of open options just begins to look like indecision and lack of focus. That's why in college they make you declare a major."

"But this particular decision would be really hard. I can see the T, but I can't see the best road to take."

"Then maybe the T is far enough in the distance that you don't have to veer one way or the other just yet."

Burke let that sink in for a minute, then he continued, "But don't get so close to the T that the decision has to be made in a split second. If you wait until the T is right in front of you and have to make a hard left or a hard right at the last possible second, sometimes you don't make the turn and you go crashing right into the T."

Cody finished wiping down his bike, then cleaned the chain in silence. Burke retreated to the kitchen to make coffee and look for something to eat. After twenty minutes, Cody loped into the kitchen and announced that he was going for a ride. Maybe a long one. See ya, if you're not here when I get back, I'll use the code to get into the garage or maybe just go straight home. Thanks for the talk, appreciate your honesty, just don't treat my mom bad cause even though we didn't talk about that, we should have. I'm not quite sure I understand all the reasons you didn't tell me your past, but I guess you have your reasons, so what's it to me, it's really none of my business, it's just that I felt hurt, almost betrayed, in a way.

But he didn't say all that. Actually, he said none of that. He simply finished working on his bike, put his cycling gear on and took off. No thanks for the talk, no goodbye. Just gone.

It was another cool, crisp May morning in Northern California. Cody knew it would be warmer the longer he rode, so he was almost underdressed for the morning chill. He had put on his wind vest over his cycling jersey, but his arms and legs were bare. At first the wind brought goosebumps all over his body, but he relished the shock of the cold. It made him concentrate on his pedaling and quickly elevated his heart rate. He wanted more blood pumping through his system because he knew it would warm him. And he wanted to concentrate on the cycling because he didn't want to concentrate on T's in the road or hard lefts and hard rights.

He quickly cycled out of the city limits and headed toward one of his favorite routes. He pedaled past the ritzy neighborhoods with guard shacks and iron gates. Past the strip mall with Starbucks and Jamba Juice and toward the open country roads. In this neck of the city, housing was popping up quicker than microwave popcorn but if you pedaled long enough and far enough you hit what would be called the closest thing to a country road. They were actually long stretches of pavement connecting the back of one township to the front of another with ten miles in between.

The people who moved here liked the solitude of the country with the conveniences of the city. Ten miles wasn't too far for a gallon of milk or a video but far enough to see the stars at night and listen to an occasional cricket. Those were sights and sounds you almost forgot about when you lived spitting distance from your neighbor. The not-so-wide open spaces at least gave people the chance to have a garden to grow pumpkins or tomatoes or almost whatever their heart's desire, because anything would grow in California. Some city slickers even had a horse or two. In Northern California there was still room for a ride, even if most of the time it was only around the white fenced circle corral.

Cody passed a veterinarian clinic that looked like it specialized in more than just dogs and cats. It had a large acre or two of corral attached to the side and several horses grazing on bales of hay. He looked to his left and saw the new middle school, a West Coast cross between an elementary and junior high school and it was the last building in sight. Another mile or so and he made the turn on Montgomery Road and he busted through the last bond of the city.

Cody loved these country rides. You rarely saw a car and if you were adventuresome enough and didn't mind getting lost every once in a while, you could meander through these roads for hours on end. Even though each county maintained their portion of the road differently, they were still in pretty good shape. Easy winters with ten or fifteen inches of rain and not-too hot summers meant the road crews could concentrate on re-striping the city streets and ignoring the country ones.

The roads were mostly at right angles to each other, probably just paved divisions between the old farms that used to litter the landscape. The farms were mostly still there, but few looked like they were still working. Cody rode by lots of old farm machinery that had grass growing up through the rusting metal. He could recognize the old tractors but the other equipment could have been moon rovers for all he knew.

In sharp contrast to the old farm machinery, Cody was well-oiled and raring to go. Months of riding six or seven days a week had conditioned his body and his mind. He now found the slight uphill grades easy targets and relished knocking them off at the same speed he maintained on the flats. When he encountered the longer hills he jumped out of the saddle and used his upper body to help pull him up and over. Each hill and each long stretch of level road became a challenge to ride faster. His body responded when his mind pushed him to ride harder. On this particular day he noticed he was almost never out of breath. It seemed the harder he pushed, the faster he went and he couldn't push himself fast enough to get winded. He remembered days like this on the basketball court. Every shot went in, you never got tired, your coordination seemed to be perfect. In the zone, some people called it.

Was it just that on this day in May his body was performing better than usual? Was the adrenaline pumping more today than on other days? Was he more in sync? Was it just that he felt better or thought he felt better?

The rolling hills were still bright green, the greenest they would be all year, after an unusually rainy April. In a month or two, without rain, the grasses that covered the hills would turn golden brown. But now, just after the rainy season, with sunny afternoons, green dominated the landscape. Cody noticed a few cows grazing lazily on the gentle sloping pastures. As he rode by he tried to startle them by yelling moo at the top of his voice, sort of a rebel yell with a Midwest farmer flare to it. One brown cow slowly looked up but never lost the rhythm of his chew. The black ones and the two-tones never even noticed his presence.

Light, puffy clouds dotted the blue sky like gigantic cotton balls. Except for the occasional rebel moo and the constant whirl of the Cannondale's chain, Cody rode in silence. He liked it that way. As much as he didn't want to think of T's in the road, his mind kept coming back to them. Cody always felt in a heightened state of awareness when he was on the bike. Maybe it was a reflection of his concentration. Maybe he was relaxed enough and his body was so occupied that his mind had a chance to open up. Maybe it was just the endorphins kicking in. Whatever it was, most of the time things just seemed to clear up. Troubles seemed smaller, good ideas more in abundance, the future brighter.

Cody let his mind drift towards basketball. He loved that sport and the competition but it didn't give him the thrill of a solo bike ride through the hills at top speed. He loved being together with his teammates--joking, slamming, talking, just hanging. But on a bike he was in total control and depended on nobody else. He was not only the leader of the pack, he was the pack, too. He was the general in charge of strategy and the troops in charge of artillery. The brains and the muscle.

He loved performing in front of a crowd, even though high school basketball crowds were dwindling these days. But he sometimes hated the incompetence of his teammates. He had been reprimanded more than once by Coach Myers for yelling at a teammate when his passes hit them in the hands and caromed out of bounds. But on the bike, he only had himself to blame if something went wrong.

Cody kept powering through the late morning sunshine. He unzipped his vest, then eventually pulled to the side of the road under a large oak tree, took it off and stuffed it into his jersey back pocket. He nibbled on an energy bar and drank from his water bottle. His mind swirled around T's in the road, basketball, bicycles, Mitchell Burke, even Denny Clarke.

He didn't consciously notice at the time, but he was at the intersection of Logan Territory Road and Irvington Highway. The two came together at right angles just north of the Alameda County line. From a thousand feet in the air or maybe even from the top of the hundred year oak tree, you could plainly see they formed a perfect T.

THE CRASH

Buck Roddy had been framing a sidewalk and pouring cement all day at his job with Robert Evers Construction and he thanked God that it was Friday. The job with the small construction company, which did mostly residential work, paid pretty well for a 19-year-old, but at times the work was much harder than he liked. He was a big, strong guy and he liked to kid himself that he kept in pretty good shape, but his belly was already bulging and he tended to put on weight, even when he was hauling sacks of dry cement in the hot sun.

He would have much rather been the owner of the company, Bob Evers, who seemed to do a lot of supervising and not much work. Roddy thought Evers spent way too much time on his precious cell phone and he figured half the time he was placing bets on sporting events instead of anything related to construction work.

This particular Friday, Roddy and two other workers were building a new sidewalk and driveway in a ritzy neighborhood on the north side of Ruby Ridge, California. The new lot where the house stood was fairly steep in the front yard and the three young men had spent a good part of the day hauling wheelbarrows up and down the gently sloping terrain. The unseasonably hot May morning didn't help.

Even with a struggling national economy, money always seemed to flourish in Northern California so construction work with the Evers company was plentiful. Actually, Buck could only remember two days in the last three months when he'd given them a day off. He would have much preferred a day off about once a week. Five days a week for up to 10 hours a day was too much for Buck Roddy, no matter what the pay. His mind often wandered during the tedious, backbreaking work to what a nice, comfy security job with a clean uniform in an air-conditioned building might pay. Even if the pay was way lower, he might jump at the chance. Plus, it would be a nice stepping stone to the police force, which was Roddy's dream job. Wearing a gun, driving a fast car, telling people what to do and being able to hide out for hours at a time without supervision seemed like heaven on earth to Buck Roddy.

The two other workers had become friends with Roddy in the three months that they'd been working together. Felix, who was a short, lean Mexican with a neatly groomed, pencil thin mustache, was the hardest worker and never said much, although every once in a while he would surprise the others with a detailed interpretation of a building technique in almost flawless English. Buck never bothered to learn his last name, Martinez or Rodriquez or something like that, and although he like Felix because he could take a joke and laughed easily, deep down he knew the Mexican in the straw cowboy hat set a bad example in front of Bob Evers. He worked too hard and took his job way too seriously and if Evers had to fire someone because of lack of work, it sure wouldn't be Felix.

The other member of the trio was John Zecharius, or Johnny Z as Buck liked to call him. They had been high school buddies on the football team and since meeting in the ninth grade had been almost inseparable. They like all the same things: sports, girls, and beer – and not much else. They could always find a pick-up basketball game at the outdoor courts where their size and muscle came in handy and beer was plentiful, even if you weren't twenty-one. Girls were much harder to come by, but every once in a while they found two girls attracted to the big, dumb, jock type, although Buck couldn't remember the last time it happened.

Johnny Z was built almost identically to Buck, well over six feet tall and tipping the scales in excess of two-fifty. They both favored the same look: tight blue jeans, t-shirts, big, brown construction boots and baseball hats, but never worn backwards like those younger wussy kids did. Today Johnny had a black Arizona Diamondbacks hat on with the rattlesnake logo. He thought it made him look mean and he liked to look mean.

The day was winding down and Felix was finishing the detail work on the driveway. Buck and Johnny gathered the sawhorses to place at the street level and were looping the yellow caution tape across them and over to the sidewalk. After the area was secured, Buck headed back to his car to grab what was left of his lunch. He'd saved a little meat from the Subway sandwich and was eager to place it on both sides of the driveway. Maybe a nice little doggy or kitty cat would stroll across the newly poured cement, leaving little footmarks that were sure to send the pompous owner of the home up the proverbial wall. That's how Buck Roddy's mind worked; he enjoyed injecting just a little torture in other people's lives. It gave him a rush.

"OK boys, once you get the street sweeped up a little more, I think that'll wrap it up for today," Bob Evers said as he tugged on the caution tape to make sure it would hold. "Then we can start the Friday safety meeting."

All three grinned and picked up their pace knowing that safety meeting was the code word for ice cold Budweisers in Evers truck. It had become a Friday afternoon ritual that Buck had suggested and encouraged. Evers didn't much like the idea of supplying beer to minors, but he wasn't opposed to pouring down a few cold ones on a hot day so he wasn't hard to influence. Besides, he read somewhere where employees needed a little motivation to keep working hard and since he wasn't big on speeches or compliments, he figured beer might do.

When the three finished their cleanup, they joined Evers in the short drive to the end of the cul-de-sac. Even though only a few families had moved into the new neighborhood, Evers didn't want to risk being seen drinking beer in front of one of his construction sites. And the home site at the end of the cul-de-sac hadn't even had the foundation poured yet, so you could still see the hills. After looking at brown dirt most of the week, it was a pleasant diversion to gaze up at Mount Diablo.

Buck Roddy and Johnny Zecharius both took off their shirts and boots, pulled old lawn chairs from the back of the truck and stretched out with their first beer. Roddy checked the cooler as Evers distributed the fruits of the week's labor and noticed that if he drank fast, he might get more than his usual allotment of two. The first one went down fast, quenching a dry throat.

Bob Evers made small talk, mostly about sports and upcoming jobs for the trio, but Buck and Johnny weren't paying much attention. Evers thought this Friday afternoon ritual was a great time to do a little male bonding with his employees, but he mostly liked to talk about himself and his successes. A 50 year old man spouting off about all his conquests couldn't keep the attention of young men whose minds wandered quickly to women. Even Evers' stories about sports seemed a little outdated to Buck. Who the heck ever heard of some of these old farts he keeps harping about? Man, at least try to talk about somebody from this century!

Buck Roddy purposely hadn't consumed much water during the hot afternoon, knowing he'd get a quicker buzz that way. Halfway through his second beer he got that familiar feeling he craved so much; his head got a little fuzzy, his troubles seemed a little farther away and his crude jokes got a little funnier – at least to him. Felix and Johnny Z laughed loudly when he told a joke about Arab terrorists, but Evers wasn't much amused. He liked the three young men who did his dirty work for him, but that didn't mean he had to laugh at what was mostly junior high humor. When Buck grabbed a third beer from the cooler, shook it up and sprayed Felix with it, Evers knew it was time to close shop for the week and head to his favorite watering hole.

As he drove off, the three men walked the short half block to the construction site to pick up Roddy's car. Both Felix and Johnny Z had ridden with Buck that morning because neither of them owned a car. It beat walking and Buck only charged a dollar a day for gas money.

Before he unlocked the door to the 1982 Buick LeSabre, Buck slapped himself in the head, feigning stupidity. "Man, I almost forgot, I got a present for you peasants!"

The two looked at him like he was going to pull another one of his practical jokes on them. They each took a step backward away from the car.

"No, I mean it's a good thing. Boy, you two just need to find a little trust in your heart. When have I ever let you down? Well, I mean lately, you know?"

Johnny Z said, "Yeah, yeah, yeah, what's the surprise already?"

"Just a little contribution to the Friday party, compliments of my old man," Buck said as he popped the trunk to the LeSabre, reached in and pulled out a small Igloo cooler he had hidden underneath a dirty blanket.

"Man, from the looks of what's in that trunk, I'm ain't trustin' nothin' that comes out of there," commented Johnny Z. Roddy's trunk was littered with an assortment of old shoes, fast food wrappers, soda cans, dirty t-shirts, various sports equipment, a gym bag, and miscellaneous items that could only be classified as garbage.

"You'll be singing a different tune, big boy, when you find out what old Buck has in his little Igloo icer." Roddy held the cooler up to his chest as if showing it off and slowly opened the lid to reveal four more beers.

"What did you do, rob a leeker store?" Felix giggled in his high pitched Mexican accent.

"Nope, just my old man's stash in the garage. Nice of him to keep it stocked for just such an occasion, isn't it?"

Actually Buck Roddy's father, Joe Roddy, Sr., did keep his garage refrigerator stocked and he really didn't mind if Buck took a few beers every once in a while. After all, he thought, that's what young men do and what's a few beers gonna hurt anyway. He and his wife Shirley had gotten into many a heated argument over the contents of the refrigerator and the easy access by the two boys, but Joe Roddy, Sr. never lost an argument with his wife, especially when it concerned beer. So every Thursday night on his way home from work, he stopped at Beverages 'n More and bought two cases of beer. The manager of the liquor chain on most Thursdays had it ready and waiting for him behind the counter.

Buck Roddy had packed the mini cooler that morning with four Budweisers and plenty of ice, and when he opened the cooler, he let out a nice big "Ahhhhh! Nectar of the Gods." The two men each grabbed one and settled into the LeSabre.

The interior of the car wasn't much better than the trunk. Scattered about were old candy wrappers, cigarette butts, six months worth of mud on the floor mats and enough dust on the dashboard to wonder what the original color was. Roddy turned up the radio, Johnny Z grabbed a half-filled bag of two-week-old Cheese Puffs and Felix just kept giggling as the afternoon wore on.

As Buck Roddy cracked open his fourth beer, Cody Calhoun pulled out of his garage on his bike to try and get in at least a 30 mile training ride before sunset. It was going to be tight, but if he kept a decent pace and the clouds didn't roll in off the coast too quickly, he just may have enough light. Since he'd been delayed at school, he was running late. He didn't bother to hook up the transmitter that Lionel had rigged up for him; he knew Lionel was deep into that history project due tomorrow and wouldn't have time to talk to Cody anyway.

Cody mentally mapped out his course as he headed to the canyon road. He reset his computer to track his mileage. As he was flipping through the settings, he noticed he'd been riding a lot since installing the device. His accumulated mileage was 1600. That was 1600 miles in the past two months since Lionel had put the new computer on this bike. Not bad, he thought.

He figured if he rode out against a small headwind for at least 15 miles into Walnut Grove, circled the mall and headed back through Ruby Ridge, he'd notch the 30 with time to spare, even though traffic might be heavy on a Friday afternoon. Since he knew many people avoided the freeways around rush hour and opted for city streets to avoid the mind-numbing crunch of bumper to bumper traffic, he'd have to be creative and find side routes on the ride that would take him into the hills and new housing developments.

How in the world people spent hours every day in their car driving to and from work was beyond Cody. He wondered how people kept their minds busy as they slowly poked along. Radio these days was filled with either mindless talk show hosts mouthing off about almost anything they knew little about or commercials. And radio commercials, Cody had already figured out at an early age, were mostly written to get your attention, so most of them were totally stupid. I guess they write them to jolt people out of their stupors, he thought.

Cody was lost in his thoughts as he jumped on the pedals, maneuvered through the late afternoon traffic and searched for roads that would take him away from all the disgusting car exhaust fumes. He could almost tell the age of the car he was trailing by how bad it smelled. And diesels were the worst. He headed toward Walnut Grove.

Buck and the boys were nursing their last few beers, knowing that the prospects for getting more were slim. They told stories about girls, mostly lies. Felix just sat in the back of the LeSabre and giggled a lot. He was a happy drunk. At age 20 he was making almost as much money as his father, who owned a small landscaping business, and he had a whole lot less in expenses than his dad. He loved the outdoors, the physical labor and the artistry of construction work.

As he sat in Roddy's car, barely listening to the banter in the front seat, he admired his work across the street on the new driveway and sidewalk. He'd made a few suggestions to Bob Evers on how to add a little more curve to the sidewalk and helped him estimate how to make it level, taking into account the slope of the yard. Although Evers hadn't said so outright, he smiled at Felix's ideas and used every single one of them.

Buck Roddy grew silent as Johnny Z was describing the attributes of one Cheryl Snodgrass, a senior at Mountain View High School.

"Man, if it wasn't for her last name, she'd be almost perfect. I wonder if she puts out?"

"Huh, what're you babbling about?" Roddy said.

"You musta been dreaming about her, too, from that far away look in your eye."

"Nah, I'm just making a plan."

"For what?"

"More beer."

"Then keep planning, don't let me stop you, that what you're good at."

All three sat and listened to a Metallica CD that Buck had managed to steal from his brother, lost in their thoughts. Felix thinking about money, Johnny about Cheryl and Buck about beer.

Cody was in a groove. His legs felt strong since he had ridden the day before and the temperature was ideal. Even though the day had turned out warm, his speed and a slight breeze kept him cool. Traffic was tolerable and he found several side routes to take him away from the heavy congestion. Since the T in the road conversation with Mitchell Burke, he seemed much more focused. His training rides were faster, his endurance better, his attitude always high. He didn't dwell on the subtle yet powerful change, but he knew something was different.

It was almost like the time he finally gave up on his dad. His father had left the family for good when Cody was just a young boy, but for the first few years he'd show up unexpected at the door and ask to see Cody. His mom would see the glimmer in the innocent, hopeful eyes of the youngster and let his dad stay for a day or two. Although she never let Cody out of her sight when her ex-husband was around, she didn't interfere much with the play between the young boy and his father. The three of them would spend hours at the park and his dad would follow Cody all through the playground structures, climbing, crawling, sliding, swinging and jumping.

Around his dad, Cody was fearless. He always pushed the envelope a little more each time they were together. He wouldn't climb the big slide with his mother, but when his father was in town, they couldn't get him off it. On the swings, his mother would only push him so high, but his father made him feel like he was almost going to do a full 360-degree circle. His mother tried to hold him back just a little, trying to protect him. But his father pushed him to be daring and attempt something he didn't think he could do.

But even when the days were filled with long trips to the park and hot dogs on the way home, Cody knew it wasn't going to last. Every time his dad came to visit, Cody would fight going to bed because he didn't want to wake up and find his dad gone. In bed, fighting to stay awake each night, Cody could hear his mother and father fighting. He didn't know why but they never seemed to get along. His mother rarely said bad things about his dad, but he could see the hurt in her eyes every time his name was mentioned. Cody had always loved his dad and he supposed he always would, but he didn't like to see his mother so sad. And when his dad wasn't around, his mother wasn't sad.

As he grew older his dad was around less and less. When Cody was 10 his dad got a job in Colorado and he could only remember seeing his dad once since then, at his grandfather's funeral. Maybe it was because Cody was older or his dad had changed or that he was grief-stricken over the death of his father, but it just wasn't the same between the two of them. Or maybe Cody was just mad because his dad hadn't been to see him in over three years.

Since the funeral his dad had called every once in a while, usually on Cody's birthday. But the calls became less frequent and finally stopped. His mother had explained that his dad had remarried, pity the poor girl, and was thinking about starting a new family. Cody was crushed. If his dad were giving up on Cody and his mom as family, then Cody would give up on his dad as his father.

His mother had always preached to Cody to depend on himself – and not his father – for the really important things in life, and now Cody was going to finally take her advice. No more tearful good-byes when his dad left after a visit. No more hoping he'd show up soon again. No more waiting for birthday calls or unexpected visits. No more wishing that his mother and father would reunite and they'd be a real family again. No more dad.

When Cody finally made the decision to give up on his dad, he spent a long time just being sad. Once the sadness subsided and the wound scabbed over enough that the hurt didn't hurt so bad, Cody began to heal. And once the healing started, Cody's life took a turn for the better. He got into basketball and poured all his emotion and effort into it. He got focused, he found a purpose.

At some point, and Cody didn't remember when this actually happened, he figured out that once he cut the cord to his dad, he became his own man. Maybe earlier than most kids and maybe with more scars, but with a new sense of power and a new determination to be fearless on his own. He'd have to push himself now - he knew that - and he liked the idea.

Buck Roddy pulled the brown LeSabre up to the curb in front of his next-door neighbor's house. It was part of his plan. If he could sneak into the house, steal a few more beers, and sneak out again without his mother hearing him, he would be a real hero to Johnny Z and Felix. Of course, with all their freaking giggling in the car, he couldn't sneak up on a cemetery at this rate.

"Shut up, you buttheads!" he loudly whispered as he slowly closed the car door until it barely clicked shut. "I'll be back in two minutes, just keep it down."

Buck approached the single story ranch style house from the neighbor's yard, heading toward the side gate, using the large pine tree that separated the two properties as cover. The gate was never locked and only held shut by a deadbolt on the inside. Buck quietly reached over the gate, slid the bolt open and entered.

His mother was usually in the kitchen by this time of day preparing dinner or in the master bathroom preparing to go out if his dad was feeling generous. Either way, Friday night was steak night for Joe Roddy, Sr. and if he couldn't get a decent one at home, he begrudgingly took his wife out to dinner. The kitchen was directly adjacent to the garage, but the bedroom was at the far end of the house from where Buck now stood motionless, listening for sounds of his mother.

Buck knew his plan would fail if the garage door were locked. But that morning he unlocked it in anticipation of just this moment. In fact, Buck was always unlocking the door and his mother was always loudly complaining that someone was leaving the garage door unlocked and what would happen if a burglar found it that way. Today, Buck was the burglar.

He tried the door handle and slowly turned the knob. It didn't make a sound because once a week for the past six months, Buck had put a little WD40 on it to keep it squeak free. It opened and he slipped into the darkened garage. For a moment he let his eyesight adjust, but in his condition, he wasn't sure if it would adjust quite right to the darkness. The only light in the garage came from the base of the near wall where the tiny ventilation screen projected the fading afternoon sun.

Buck reached the fridge, which stood right next to the door that lead into the house, and slowly pulled on the handle, trying his best to make no sound. It opened and he deftly, for his condition at least, shoved three beers into his jeans jacket. Just as he closed the refrigerator door, the light in the garage went on and the door to the house opened.

Buck thought quickly. As his mother took the first step into the garage, Buck yelled, "Boo!" and his mother screamed, clutching both hands to her chest. She kept screaming (for what seemed to Buck forever but in reality was about five seconds) until she noticed it was her son. Buck at first started to laugh loudly, but then noticing how terrified his mother was, thought better of it.

When she finally settled down, she immediately said, "Oh my God, Buck, what are you trying to do, scare me right into my grave, you moron?" Buck didn't like her tone. Then she slapped him upside his head, knocking is baseball cap to the floor.

"Jeez, you didn't have to hit me, I was only playing around."

His mother was still trying to get her breath and control her pounding heartbeat. "You scared me half to death," she said to him in a mood none too playful.

"Sorry," Buck managed to mumble.

"I suppose your brother's in on this, too," she said as she cautiously looked around the garage for her youngest, Joe Jr.

At that moment, Buck remembered he was supposed to pick his brother up from after school detention, but he'd forgotten. He couldn't hide the look of stupidity on his face.

"Don't tell me, you forgot. Oh, Buck, you're beyond help."

Buck immediately saw his chance for escape. "We had to work late. Don't worry, I'll get him right now. They probably found a few more reasons for him to do more detention anyway, the little criminal." He punched the garage door opener and headed for the door.

"Don't talk about your brother that way. He hangs around you too much."

"Yeah, yeah, later," he said as he headed toward the LeSabre.

Buck loved it when a plan came together.

Cody had reached Walnut Grove in good time, made the circle around the mall and headed for the rolling hills that led over to the high school. The road would be a lot less congested than other routes, especially since school had been out for over two hours. Because he was making such good time, he decided to add another thirty minutes to the ride. If he could get over to the reservoir and make the loop around it in under thirty minutes, he could shoot by the high school and still get home in plenty of time before dark. So he pushed it. When he hit the deserted Carnaby Reservoir Loop road, he turned onto it and cranked even harder. Nothing to do but pump hard for the next few minutes and see how fast he could make it around. With no traffic to contend with, nothing could stop him now.

Buck Roddy took his time driving over to the high school. After all he had a beer to drink and a couple of buddies in the car that were at this precise moment, admiring him. Why rush? After they got out of his immediate neighborhood, Buck pulled over into a cul-de-sac and they popped the beers.

Cody made the reservoir loop in 26 minutes according to his cyclo-computer. He slowed ever so slightly at the end of the road, checked the time and the distance he had to go to get home and glanced at the fading spring sunlight. He slipped on his cycling vest because it was getting a little chilly and the vest had glow-in-the-dark stripes across the back of it, just in case he became hard to see on the unlit country road. No sense taking any chances now.

Buck Roddy started the LeSabre and noticed as he pulled out onto the main drag that his timing was a bit off. He accelerated a bit too quickly as he pulled out of the cul-de-sac into traffic and jerked everyone's head back, then realized he had miscalculated how close he was to the oncoming dark green truck. The truck slowed dramatically and blasted him with the horn. Buck's only response was the single finger salute. Felix and Johnny Z roared their approval as the truck passed them and returned the insult with fervor.

Buck turned the LeSabre toward the high school and gunned it. His little brother was probably good and steamed now; he'd been waiting for over an hour. It was a few minutes after five o'clock, the sun was setting and Buck Roddy was feeling no pain.

Buck pulled up in front of Mountain View High School and saw Joe Roddy sitting on the bus bench, throwing rocks into the empty parking lot below. As he noticed the battered Buick, he fired a rock at it, just missing the front headlight but putting a noticeable dent in the right front fender.

As Joe opened the door and got in his brother smacked him playfully but painfully up side his head. "I suppose in some perverse way, the old Buick deserved that. After all, it was real late pickin' your sorry butt up today. But don't ever let it happen again."

"Wish I'd hit the headlight, butthead."

"Don't be mad little brother. I got a surprise for you that should take the edge off that attitude you're showing." Buck Roddy tossed J-Rod the final Budweiser.

"Thanks, Dork, but you still owe me one," Joe shot back.

"I don't owe you jack and either you show a little appreciation for that refreshment or you can walk your sorry ass home."

Joe popped the top and kept his mouth shut as his brother turned off onto Wayland Road. It was the long way home, but there would be less traffic and it would give Joe time to finish his beer. He figured it was Buck's way of doing him a favor. He rolled down his window to let the cool afternoon breeze clear the stagnant air in the car.

Cody was feeling no pain either. The ride had been smooth, his legs strong and his newfound conviction had taken him beyond the typical fatigue that can creep into training rides. He decided to push himself even further and when the turn-off for Wayland came up suddenly, he veered to the right and stood to crank on the peddles. There was no bike lane on this road and it would take a little longer to get home, but the traffic would be lighter than the main drag. Cody felt confident he'd be home by five thirty.

Buck tipped the can back and drained the last sip from the beer he'd been nursing since he left his house. Joe was still sulking in the back seat, sitting next to Felix, not saying a word. An hour of detention and an hour waiting on a bus bench on Friday night had done a number on his mood.

Buck turned toward the backseat and with his left hand on the wheel, crushed the can against his head and fired it toward Joe. A direct hit, the can bounced off his head and struck Felix in the mouth, numbing his lip.

Buck cracked up, "Score, double score!" Joe grabbed the empty can and was about to slam it into the back of Buck's head, when Buck turned around to the back seat, saw what was coming down and ducked his head, hitting his forehead on the steering wheel. An expletive deleted shot from his mouth. And everyone, including Joe Roddy, burst into uncontrollable laughter.

With tears of laughter blurring his eyesight, his right hand rubbing his swollen forehead, and five beers streaming through his bloodstream, Buck had little left to drive the lumbering LeSabre. He didn't even notice the back right tire slip onto the soft shoulder of Wayland Road.

Cody heard it first. The sickening sound of a car too close behind you, churning dirt on the shoulder.

"Look out!" Johnny Z managed to say as Buck squinted in the fading daylight toward Cody. He slammed on the brakes, but that only compounded the problem. The LeSabre was only about ten yards in back of Cody, traveling almost on its own at 37 miles per hour. The back right tire had no traction when Buck banged the brakes and that caused the rear end to slide to the right. Buck was slow to react and had no idea in his corrupted state how to get the car under control.

Cody felt a tingling sensation of danger sweep through his body, every hair stood on end. The road offered no place to go. As he glanced back over his left shoulder, he saw the brown LeSabre barreling toward him sideways.

He looked directly into the eyes of Joe Roddy as the rear passenger door hit his rear tire. To J-Rod it seemed to happen in slow motion. He saw Buck panicking in the front seat, trying furiously to turn the wheel. He saw Johnny Z cover his eyes with his hands and turn his head away from the crash. He looked into the terrified eyes of Cody Calhoun just before impact.

J-Rod screamed at the top of his lungs, "Buck!!!"

To Cody, it happened in a split second. He saw the car, then he saw sky as his world was turned upside down, literally. Cody's bike did a head-over-heels somersault, landed briefly on its front tire, careened 180 degrees to the right and quickly slid down a muddy embankment toward a drainage ditch. The LeSabre came to a stop in the middle of Wayland Road and the four young men in the car finally breathed again.

"Did we hit something? Was that a bike?" Buck managed to say through clenched teeth and trembling lips.

Cody didn't feel a thing. The complete disorientation of the crash sent him into a state of total confusion. He survived the initial somersault in relatively good shape. But his helmet had struck the road pavement before the bike slid down the hill. He lost consciousness but that may have been to his advantage. He wasn't able to feel his right collarbone suddenly snap in two or the rocks on the side of the fifteen-foot slope gash deeply into his right leg. And he wasn't able to feel the barbed wire suddenly and painfully stop his descent down the hill as it slashed into his back and lodged deep within his muscles from mid-back to mid-thigh. He came to rest against the four-by-four wooden post that held the barbed wire firmly in place surrounding the property of Jim and Edna Finch, who were at that precise time vacationing in Maui.

Buck Roddy quickly gained enough sense to know that he was drunk, he'd just hit a bicycle and that he'd better get the hell out of there. He gunned the Buick and never looked back.

The sun set in the hills overlooking Wayland Road and all was quiet. It was 5:28.

THE SEARCH

"Jesus, Buck, you gotta go back!" Joe Roddy screamed from the back seat. He was sure it was Cody Calhoun and no matter how much he disliked Cody, he knew he had to be hurt.

"Like hell. We been drinking beer for two hours and we all smell like a brewery, you included you little twerp, so what do you think the nice policemen are going to say when they arrive, sirens blaring, onto the scene of the crime? 'Oh, no problem, stupid little law anyway, that no drinking and driving DUI thing, you boy's just be on your way now, we'll clean up this mess.'"

"He could be hurt," Joe managed to argue.

"We could be hurt a lot more if we get caught here. Now shut up and let me think." Johnny Z and Felix had quickly sobered up and both were silent.

"At least call the police on your cell phone and leave an anonymous tip that there was an accident," Joe offered.

Buck thought for a moment. "Nope, they can trace cell phone calls. We do not want to be implicated in this," Buck said nodding his head like he was trying to convince himself. The others picked up on his conviction and slowly nodded, too.

"Implicated? Hell, you probably killed him!" Joe shouted.

Buck turned off Wayland Road and quickly pulled over to the curb. Joe thought that he had regained what little sense he had and was going to turn around and go back. Buck leaned over the back seat, grabbed Joe by the shirt and looked directly in his eye with his most menacing glare. "Never…I repeat, never, say a thing about this to anybody or you are dead meat. Got it? Not a word. Never. Dead. Comprende, little brother?"

Joe pulled his shirt away from his brother's grip and said, "Got it." But all he could see was the bike somersaulting down the road and he wondered if Cody was really dead.

Cody knew he wasn't dead, but he didn't know where he was or what had happened. He gradually regained consciousness and realized he was looking at the side of a hill and it was now dark. He was still disoriented and for a moment he shook uncontrollably; his overheated body had cooled quickly in the evening chill. Luckily, his helmet had absorbed most of the shock of his collision with the pavement. As he tried to gain control over his trembling, he concentrated on taking a few deep breaths.

He hadn't yet surveyed his injuries and when he first began to feel his body, he didn't think he was hurt too bad. He was lying on his left side and as he tried to move, pain shot through his right shoulder and arm. He decided that OK, a little arm pain might not be too bad. So he lay there for a minute or two and kept his right arm pinned to his side.

He felt sick to his stomach and wondered if he would heave. At least there wouldn't be much in his stomach except that banana he had about an hour ago. That wouldn't be too bad, heaving that up. Then he noticed his headache. As a matter of fact, he noticed his head was killing him. But he could move his head and his arm, so a headache probably meant he had only banged it on something on the way down.

His sunglasses had flown off his head and his helmet was askew, covering most of his vision, what little of it he had considering the darkness, his condition and how he was wedged into the ditch. Cody managed to reach up with his left hand to find the buckle to the helmet and unsnap it. The helmet fell away in two pieces. Weird, Cody thought. Why was his helmet split in two? And how come I can't remember what day it is?

Cody sat there. He was confused, disoriented. He was wet...and cold. And after about fifteen minutes of lying there, he figured if he could crawl back up to the road...what was the name of the road he was on? He couldn't think of it...weird again. But if he could make it to the road, he could find help.

As he tried to move, he noticed sharp pains all along his back, butt and legs. He couldn't move. He noticed the barbed wire. And he noticed he was skewered to it.

When Cody hadn't come home by six o'clock, Sarah Calhoun called Mitchell Burke to see if Cody was at Burke's office working out after the ride. Burke said he hadn't seen Cody all day, that he had probably just tacked on a few more miles onto his training ride. If he wasn't back by six thirty, call back and they would figure something out.

When Burke hung up, he immediately called Lionel.

"Lionel, are you in direct contact with Cody through the transmitter?" Burke asked before he even said hello. Lionel picked up on the urgency in his voice.

"No, man, I was at the coffee shop after school working on my science project with a couple of guys, so we decided not to hook it up today. Why?"

"Maybe nothing, but Cody hasn't come back from his training ride and he's overdue, that's all."

"And it's pretty dark," Lionel added.

"Yeah, but he's used to riding in the dark."

They both were lost in their thoughts and neither said a word for almost a minute.

Burke finally broke the silence, "Can you track him? Can you find out where he is?"

"I don't think so, if he doesn't have the receiver with him, I can't talk to him and there's no way to hone in on the signal."

After weighing his options, Burke said, "I'm going to look for him. What's the log say he was riding today?"

Lionel opened up the software program that tracked Cody's workouts and scrolled down to today's date, "It says 30 miles from home to the mall and back, but he almost always adds to the prescribed route. Pick me up on your way and we can figure out where he might have added on another five miles."

"I'll be there in three minutes. Be waiting outside your house, bring your laptop and ...Lionel, bring some flashlights."

Burke phoned Sarah back and told her he would pick her up in five minutes. The hunt was on.

Mitchell Burke's SUV was loaded. Leather, Bose sound system, OnStar satellite, automatic climate control. As he jumped into the backseat, Lionel noticed that the truck (you really

couldn't call this thing a car) had almost every imaginable option
built in. But probably the most important add-on was the Global
Positioning Satellite connection that Burke was now fiddling
with. The full color screen showed what looked like a street map,
complete with street names, freeways and distances between
major intersections.

"OK, Sarah, see this function here? It'll widen the area
that we can view on the screen," Burke motioned to the dial on
the system as Cody's mom turned the interior light on to better
see the unit.

"Lionel, tell me again the prescribed route we think Cody
was riding tonight."

Once Lionel described the circle of travel that Cody was
riding, Burke widened the four-color map on the GPS screen to
include the coordinates. After about three minutes of work, he
had the map of the route Cody was traveling on the screen.

Sarah Calhoun looked worried. "That's a lot of territory to
cover."

"Yes, it is, but we have help. On my way to pick you up I
phoned as many Triple B's as I could get a hold of. I've got
Collins, Baranski, Steinberg and Clarke ready for our
instructions. I want the B's to take the two northern grids,
northwest and northeast. Lionel, you take the cell phone and start
banging numbers. Do you know how to get to the directory on
this thing?" he asked as he handed Lionel his phone.

"Got it. Is that Rupert Clarke or Denny?"

"Denny."

"Bang, it's ringing now."

Burke flipped on his high beams and flashed them to an
oncoming police car and the two cars stopped in the middle of the
street. Burke rolled down his window and had a short
conversation with the policeman.

"OK, the Mountain View police have the middle two
grids, west and east. We'll take southwest and southeast."

Sarah looked at Mitchell Burke with a bit of amazement
and asked, "How did you get the police involved so soon. We
don't even know if he's missing."

"Well, it's not the whole force, but a couple of buddies of mine are cyclists and they were more than happy to help."

Lionel meanwhile was giving directions and coordinates to the last of the B's and asking them to check back on the cell phone every five minutes. Burke pointed the SUV south on Madera Street and punched it. He wanted to get to his section of the grid to start the search as soon as possible. The clock on the dash read 6:35 and the temperature had fallen to 52 degrees.

A light rain started to fall.

Mitchell Burke got many headlights flashed at him from oncoming cars as he had kept his high beams on. A few cars behind him honked as he crept along at about 15 miles per hour, slowly covering his grid, looking for any telltale signs of a downed bicyclist. Lionel was in the back barking instructions over the cell phone to the other searchers; what to look for, where to look, keep your headlights on, the radio off so you can hear, roll down your windows, I don't care if it is raining, you can see better and hear better, and so on.

Sarah Calhoun sat in the front seat, mostly worrying, but always with the large searchlight flashlight pointed to the right side of the road, moving from bush to tree to sidewalk to ditch to fence to anything that might have entrapped Cody.

Burke was using his hands-free cell phone in the car checking answering machines at his office, his home, Cody's home and Lionel's bedroom.

Cody lay on his left side, one half of his helmet under his head for a pillow. He had managed to salvage two items with his right arm, even though the pain was excruciating, his water bottle and his glasses. He joked to himself that he certainly wouldn't go thirsty and if the sun happened to come back out anytime soon, he'd be well protected.

He had noticed that he would have been in almost total darkness, but a halogen street light not more than thirty yards from him was beginning to glow. Thank goodness that this part of the city at least had streetlights and even though many were on timers, this one seemed to be waking up at just the right time for

Cody. Not that it was going to help much, but at least it wouldn't be totally dark.

Every time he moved the barbed wire dug more deeply into his flesh. Great, I'll look like all those football players with the barbed wired tattoos on their arms, except mine will be the real thing, it will run all the way down my backside and you'll only be able to see it if I'm stark raving naked!

Cody was still mostly entangled in his bike, one foot still clipped into his pedal. As he gingerly moved the bike out from underneath him, he noticed a half of a red reflector light still strapped to the seat post. Suddenly he had an idea. It was a long shot but what else did he have. He began to search for the other half of his potential guiding light.

Burke's SUV slowly passed the high school and came to the intersection of Wayland Road and Monte Sereno. He pulled over to the side of the road.

"OK, troops, what would Cody do here? Take Monte Sereno back toward home or loop around Wayland?"

Sarah said, "Well, Monte Sereno is the quickest way home from here, it was getting dark by then, we think, so…I say…uh…Monte Sereno. Turn right."

Burke did nothing. Then he looked at her, smiled gently and leaned over to give her a kiss on the cheek. Sarah was startled but she smiled back.

"Good girl, great mother, perfect mother thinking. OK, boys think just about totally opposite of mothers, so we go left." He swung the SUV to the left and headed down Wayland Avenue.

After searching in vain for the other half of the reflector light, Cody reached out and yanked the remaining half away from its cradle on the seat post. He flicked it with his left hand toward the road above him but it sailed wide right and landed about two feet short. He then reached behind him and unzipped the small bike bag from underneath his saddle that carried a few small tools and two small nitrogen canisters that he used to inflate flat tires.

He began throwing everything he could up to the road. Hey, maybe somebody will notice and investigate, what could it hurt?

Lionel had a break from the cell phone action and was looking up through the sunroof of the SUV, trying to think of anyplace in the world Cody might be except on Wayland Road. He was worried about his best friend, but he didn't want to find out in about three hours that Cody was studying late at Laurel's house. No way, he thought, that girl hasn't been in the picture for some time now. Good, for Cody, that is.

His attention almost didn't come back to the road in time. Almost.

"Stop the car," he said quietly, but loud enough that Burke heard him and stopped.

"What?"

"Back up a few yards, slowly."

"What, what, did you see something?" Sarah said as she saw Lionel peering out the window.

Lionel held his hand up to quiet her. "Shush. Quiet."

There, he noticed it again as Burke slowly backed down Wayland Road, his car's emergency flashers making the only sound, clink, clink, clink, clink, clink, clink. A light reflecting off of what looked like a small, brass canister, just like the nitrogen canisters a few of the Bees used for quick tire inflation.

"Stop here, I'm getting out," Lionel said.

He quietly climbed out of the car, all the times his eyes trying to find that reflection again. What we have here is a signal, he thought.

All at once without warning at the top of his lungs Lionel K. Fitzhugh yelled, "CODY CALHOUN. ALI, ALI IN FREE!"

Both Burke and Sarah jumped. So did Cody.

"Yo, down here, Fitzy," Cody managed to say barely audible at street level.

"Contact! We have contact, the Eagle has landed! Let's get some light over here!" Lionel yelled back to the SUV as he bolted over to the ditch where Cody had been lying for over an hour and a half.

As he ran to the side of the wet road, Lionel lost his footing, slipped in the loose, wet mud just off the pavement and headed down the ditch butt first. He quickly smashed into Cody's injured right arm, driving Cody's backside deeper into the unrelenting fence.

"I found him! I found him!" Lionel yelled back up the slope.

"Oww," was about all Cody could muster. But at least Lionel was right, he was found.

SOME SERIOUS SCARRING

The paramedics worked for a good twenty minutes freeing Cody from the barbed wire. Actually, they didn't quite free him from all of it. They basically used wire cutters to extract Cody, leaving a large hole in the Finch fence and a good deal of barbed wire still in Cody's backside. They said they had to leave something for the surgeon to do once Cody got to the hospital. Funny guys, those paramedics, especially when it wasn't a life-threatening situation or their own backsides that were punctured.

Cody was loaded onto the stretcher face down with his right arm tightly wrapped close to his body. His mother rode in the paramedic van to the hospital, gently crying, but not hard enough for Cody to see. Burke and Lionel followed in the SUV.

It had been a slow night at the emergency room of Mercyhurst General Hospital when they got the call that a bicyclist was arriving soon with multiple injuries and a large chunk of barbed wire puncturing half of his body.

The three nurses who heard the dispatch call hovered around the admittance desk, wondering what might show up and what the cyclist might look like with barbed wire tattooed on him.

Dr. Mathew Hiney broke up the bunch, saying, "Ladies, you'll be the first to know once we get a look at this young gentlemen. Now could you please prepare a place for him? Set up an IV and heat up some tea, he may be suffering from a little hypothermia. It's getting cold out there and from the preliminary report, he might be suffering a little exposure."

Mathew Hiney was tall and thin and slightly balding, and just a little too gangly to be called handsome, but he had the calm demeanor that all emergency room doctors needed. He always wore green hospital scrubs just a little too loose for his frame but he displayed a well-scrubbed, almost antiseptic look about him, like he showered with Lava soap at least twice a day. But his big

brown eyes and warm smile instantly made the frightened friends
and relatives that rushed into his domain feel more at ease. As a
doctor, he knew that the loved ones of the victims needed care
and attention, too. Fear and anticipation could really run a
number on mom or dad's body or mind. More than he liked to
remember he had to work on the mental state of mind of the
loved ones who brought the emergency victims into the hospital.
He knew if somebody you loved was in serious medical trouble,
there wasn't much else that could be more painful.

Cody, however, was in very little pain as the ambulance
pulled up to Mercyhurst Hospital. The medication he'd received
had taken full effect and he felt almost tranquil as they rolled the
gurney into the emergency room. Dr. Hiney immediately took
charge of the staff that scurried around Cody, giving directions to
the two nurses who eagerly nodded their understanding and
started to work.

He then approached Mitchell Burke and Sarah Calhoun,
who were hovering around the admittance desk looking very
concerned, "Are you two the parents of this young man?"

Sarah looked sheepishly toward Burke and said, "I'm the
mother." She let go of Burke's hand, not even realizing that she'd
been holding it.

"And I'm the coach," chimed in Burke, as he grabbed the
hand back.

"OK, good, nice to meet you both. I have the preliminary
report from the medical technicians that brought the boy in.
Nothing life threatening, but I imagine you're both quite
concerned. Here's a quick scenario of what will happen over the
next few minutes."

Hiney looked at the chart in his hand that had already
been started for Cody. "First, we'll check him out here in the ER.
We'll continue the IV of fluids, he may be a little dehydrated and
get him some antibiotics. Is he allergic to any that you know of?"

"No, nothing," replied Sarah.

Nodding and noting, Hiney continued, "Then we'll take
some x-rays. He said his arm was very painful and the tech said
he thought that maybe the collarbone was fractured. I'll also want
to take a picture of his left leg, just a precaution, he's scraped up

pretty badly there, and of his lower back. Then he'll be prepped for surgery. That will consist mainly of closing up that wound on his backside and taking care of anything else we may find in the meantime. Any questions?"

Sarah looked flustered and began to stammer, "Well, will he…is he…I mean, will he be alright?"

"The short answer is, he'll be fine, but let me get to work and I'll update you as I go. Probably fifteen or twenty minutes, OK?" He turned and headed into the emergency room.

Sarah let out an audible sigh and squeezed Mitchell Burke's hand tightly. Lionel and a few of the Triple Bees had begun to gather in the cramped waiting room. After Burke answered questions and thanked everyone for all the quick work in assembling the help team, everyone began to handle the emergency in their own way.

Burke took care of Sarah, getting her a cup of coffee and helping with the paperwork. Lionel held court in one corner, recapping the rescue and describing in detail the extent of the injuries Cody had sustained. A few of the Bees came over and wished Mrs. Calhoun their best and headed back home. The waiting game began.

Denny Clarke watched the scene unfold from just outside the emergency room door. She was too afraid to go inside. She couldn't bear to hear any bad news about Cody. When the first of the Triple Bees left and noticed her, she felt like a chicken and mustered up the nerve to walk through the door. She stood in the doorway as tears welled up in her eyes. Sarah noticed her and instinctively walked over and gave her a hug.

"He's a little banged up, they think he may have broken his collarbone, but the doctor assures me he'll be just fine," she whispered into Denny's ear.

All Denny could do was cry and nod her head. Finally she managed to say, "I feel like such a fool."

"Why, for crying? Hey, I just stopped crying about five minutes ago myself. It seems like I've been crying for hours, so join the club. And besides," Sarah pulled away from the hug and looked Denny in the eye, "that's nothing to be ashamed of.

Crying's a good way to let the emotion out. I personally don't know how all these men can be so stoic."

"It ain't easy," Burke said softly as he handed her a box of tissues, winked at Denny and headed back to his chair.

Dr. Hiney emerged from behind the swinging door to the ER with what Sarah thought was a slight smile on his face; nothing huge or anything, but he certainly didn't look grim.

"If you want to follow me," and he motioned to one of the private offices adjacent to the waiting room, "I'd be happy to discuss what we've found out about your son so far."

Sarah began to follow him, but noticed that everyone that knew Cody who was still in the waiting room had risen to their feet and were craning their necks to hear a word about their friend. She saw the anticipation in their eyes.

"Would you mind, Doctor, giving us all a quick review of how he's doing? Then maybe you and I can talk a little more in detail if you need to," Sarah asked.

"Not at all, please gather around folks." He waited until the fifteen people still in the waiting room surrounded him.

"Cody has a few minor injuries and two fairly serious ones. He has a second-degree concussion, which we'll watch closely for the next couple of days. It could have been much worse. I dare say that helmet he was wearing may indeed have saved his life." Here he paused and looked at everyone in the small crowd, trying to make his point that they all had better wear their helmets without saying as much.

"He has a very nice, clean break in his right collarbone. After we get it set, it should heal nicely in four to six weeks. No other fractures that we can detect right now. Those are the two serious injuries. We've cleaned out the wound on his backside and that will require quite a few sutures I'm afraid, but it wasn't too deep, there doesn't seem to be any muscle damage, so except for standing up to eat his dinner for a week or so, no major problems."

"He also has a few minor lacerations and assorted bumps and bruises, but I anticipate he won't feel most of those in a matter of days. He's generally in good spirits and resting comfortably, for the most part, right now. Any questions, folks?"

Lionel's hand shot up, "Will he have any major scarring going on after all is said and done?"

Most of the group smiled and the tension was immediately relieved. One of the Triple Bees punched Lionel in the arm. And the group started to talk quietly among themselves

"Well, as a matter of fact, there will be some scarring," and the group immediately sobered up and quieted down. "But unless he takes his pants off while he's standing up eating that dinner, you probably won't be able to see them," Dr Hincy smiled and nodded knowingly.

The small crowd started to disperse. Lionel, Denny and a few others started to question the admitting nurse as to the whereabouts of vending machines, saying good news always made them hungry. Burke and Sarah pulled Dr. Hiney aside.

"Got another second, Doctor?" Burke asked. "I've been working with Cody rehabilitating a serious knee injury and I just had a few questions."

"Sure, and as his coach," as he looked from Burke to Sarah Calhoun, "and mother, there is something I'm sure you'd be interested in seeing on his x-rays."

As they headed inside the swinging doors to look at the x-rays, Dr. Hiney explained the few cuts and bruises on Cody and the treatments. He detailed what they'd be looking for as symptoms of Cody's concussion. When they reached the monitor to view the film of Cody's collarbone, Hiney pointed out the fracture, but Sarah could barely see it.

Mitchell Burke saw her confusion and took charge. He asked all the right questions. How severe was it, how long to heal, what restrictions would the boy have, what exercises would he have to do to help the healing process. Burke knew all the answers, but he wanted to make sure Sarah heard them, too. They also reviewed the other x-rays the Hiney had ordered.

After reassuring Burke that both of Cody's legs appeared to be fine except for a couple of patches of nasty road burn, Dr. Hiney was drawn back to the x-ray of Cody's chest, the one where the collarbone break appeared. He seemed to be mesmerized by something, because he didn't even hear Sarah's question about bacteria.

"Jeez, I never noticed this the first time I looked at this," Dr. Hiney mumbled softly, almost to himself. His look was nowhere near troubled, Burke noticed, it almost appeared bewildered.

Sarah quickly rose from her chair and furrowed her brow, but Burke grabbed her hand and squeezed reassuringly.

"What is it, Doc?" he asked, almost nonchalantly Sarah felt.

"Well, wow, this is pretty unusual. See this here," he was pointing to the middle of Cody's chest, "that's your son's heart and it is, by far, the largest heart I think I've ever seen, maybe a third bigger than a normal, like a fully-grown man's heart."

"That's terrible," Sarah said, barely audible.

"No, that's fantastic. From every indication, it's a perfectly normal, red-blooded American beating heart, if you'll pardon the pun," Hiney said.

"He is an athlete, Doctor, a damn good one, probably the best cyclist we have in this county, maybe the state," Burke interjected.

"And will you look at those lungs," Hiney interrupted. "They're huge! I mean monsters. We need to do a few tests on this boy, I mean don't get me wrong, they all look perfectly normal, but we should check them out just to be sure. You know, eliminate any potential problems, but they look healthy as all get out to me."

"What are you saying, Doc?" Burke asked, but he thought he already knew.

"What I'm saying is, that young boy of yours," he said looking at both of them now, "well, it's no wonder he's great on that bicycle. He has the inner machinery, the heart and lungs, of a fully-grown, mature adult male…even bigger. Biggest heart and lungs I've every seen, no doubt about it," he said to the x-ray of Cody Calhoun, shaking his head in bewilderment. "Awesome."

VISITATIONS

Cody spent the next couple of days in Room 421 of Mercyhurst General Hospital and he was generally miserable the entire time. The first day he shared the semi-private room with a chatty man with a compound fracture of the left leg. Even if Cody could find a comfortable position to lie in, which was impossible, the man never stopped talking, and Cody couldn't have gotten any rest if he'd tried. It didn't matter if the man knew about a subject or not, off he went. Looks like it might rain, usual for May isn't it? Then he was onto a complete dissertation on the annual rainfall in various spots around the globe. Did one side of Maui actually get 10 times the rainfall as the other side? Do I care one way or the other? Man, I better not mention anything that is remotely related to math. A complete soliloquy centered on mathematics might actually bore me completely to death! Luckily for Cody, he was spared that cruel demise; the man was released the following morning.

That second day was filled with short walks around the nurse's station and back to his room sandwiched around visits from his mom, Burke, Lionel, a couple of the Bees and Denny. The nurses wanted him up and moving as much as possible and even though the strolls were painful, it actually beat lying in bed. At least he could stretch his muscles a bit and start to work on getting the soreness out of his body. Cody had been reassured that the broken collarbone would heal quickly, in a matter of weeks. There was little if any muscle damage along his backside, since the puncture wounds weren't too deep. But 47 stitches had been needed to close the wounds. They would probably remain for a week or 10 days and leave some permanent scarring, but really, all in all, it could have been much worse.

His head still hurt and he couldn't remember much of the crash, but the doctor said the concussion was mild and in a few weeks he'd probably be completely over any lingering side effects like confusion or lack of memory. Cody thought he'd just as soon forget what happened anyway and as long as he was on a quick road to recovery, what the heck, all cyclists crash sometime, don't they?

Near the end of the second full day in the hospital, just after Cody had finished a scrumptious meal of mystery meat on a bun, tapioca pudding and green beans, a knock on the door interrupted a momentary pain-free siesta.

"You awake? Can I come in?" asked Coach Myers.

"Yeah, sure, Coach, no problem," Cody mumbled as he rubbed the sleep from his eyes. "How ya doin'?"

"I guess the better question is how are you doin'?"

"Getting better all the time, every day. Doc says I should be outta here tomorrow probably."

Cody spent the next five minutes describing the injuries and the likely timetable for healing. All the time Coach Myers was shaking his head, frowning and pacing slowly around the cramped hospital room. He looked very serious and didn't say much, only interrupting Cody with short, quick questions about any permanent damage or loss of range of motion. He didn't seem concerned at all about the concussion. He'd seen enough of those over his 30 odd years of coaching to know boys got lots of concussions. Some weren't even diagnosed as concussions in the early years of his coaching days. Probably just a headache, son, take the rest of the day off but be ready to bust butt tomorrow at practice.

After Cody finished, Coach Myers finally spoke, "Son, it's probably none of my business, but I just gotta ask, when in the sam hill are you gonna give up that infernal bicycle?"

"What?" Cody replied, almost in shock.

"Well, son, the way I see it, that thing almost got you killed. And here it is supposed to be a way for you to get that bum knee of yours back in shape. You're lucky you didn't tear both of them knees up and then where would you be. Back at square one, not even at square one, you'd be way behind square one."

Cody wasn't sure exactly where square one was, but it sure sounded like no place he wanted to be.

Myers continued, "Now you got a bum shoulder, and it's your shootin' arm, too. Those things don't heal overnight. I know plenty of kids that once a shoulder goes, it stays gone for a long time, sometimes good, but sometimes bad, too, you know. Man, you're just lucky you didn't break a leg or your back or something even worse."

Cody wasn't sure exactly what would be worse than breaking your back but he was sure he never wanted to find out.

"Did I ever tell you about that Logan kid? What was his name, Kyle, yeah, that was it. He was racing cars one night, not legally or anything, just him and a buddy. Wrapped it around a tree and smashed his left kneecap. Never could get that boy to jump more than about a millimeter off the ground after that. And before that, he had a pretty decent jump shot. Not after. Took him almost two full years to get back on the court in any competitive situation and senior year he barely played at all. Shame, real shame."

Cody just sat and listened to all the gory details of one injury after another. He supposed Coach Myers would get back to him in good time, but he was beginning to feel like he was being preached to, and Cody didn't much like it.

Myers was dressed as he usually was in a red polo shirt, khakis and tennis shoes. Cody couldn't remember when he wore anything else. Even during basketball games, he wore the same outfit, sometimes substituting penny loafers for his Nikes. The khakis always looked a little worn and the polo shirt a little small, probably due to the fact that the coach had let middle age go directly to his ever-growing stomach.

"People tell me you been racing that bike all over three counties the last few months. I've seen ya once or twice myself. But I haven't seen you at all at spring ball. You plan on comin' back soon? That knee should be prett'near healed by now, don't ya think?"

Cody felt instinctively that he'd come to the T in the road. The question was: go left, go right or stay right where you are?

"It's feeling OK," Cody answered. Maybe if he idled a while just where he was...

"Well, school will be out in another few weeks, and then we hit it hard for summer ball and camps. Even if you're not 100% by then, I expect you be at the camps helpin' out, gettin' some shootin' in. We gotta get you back on the court. You been away too long."

Cody didn't reply. Of course, there was no opening for a reply, not really a question anywhere in there, was there?

As the silence got a little uncomfortable, with Cody not knowing what he was supposed to say and Coach Myers not exactly saying everything he wanted, the door to the hospital room slowly opened and Denny Clarke stuck her head through.

"Oh, sorry, I didn't know you had company. I'll come back later," she said as she slid back out the door.

"That's OK, Miss Clarke," Coach Myers said, "I was just on my way out."

Denny demurely nodded her head and entered the room quietly, her arms behind her back. She sidestepped to the left and waited for the coach to leave.

"Well son, hope you're outta here real quick. Hospitals can be a dangerous place." Coach Myers came near the bed and stuck out his right hand. Cody had never seen the Coach shake hands before, he'd always said he didn't like getting too close to the boys, whatever that meant. Cody reluctantly offered his left hand, Coach Myers pumping his hand slowly up and down, holding the grip a little longer than normal and squeezing a little tighter than comfortable.

He leaned closer to the bed and in a quiet voice, almost a whisper, said, "And you might consider putting that friggin' bike in mothballs, permanently." He turned and walked toward the door, nodding in Denny's direction a goodbye and never looking back at Cody as he exited the room.

Denny looked at Cody and gave a mock look of fright, her eyes getting bigger and her mouth curling down. Cody smiled at her and although she instantly had lifted his mood, he was still a little stunned from what just happened. He had seen coaches get tough, even mean, with players before, but Coach Myers' performance just now was pure, backroom intimidation. Subtle maybe, but heavy-handed nonetheless. Cody instinctively knew he didn't like it, but he really didn't know what to do with it. He just let it sit for a while.

"Whatcha got behind your back?" he finally said to Denny.

"A little healing, energy surprise," she answered, revealing one of her now famous shakes. (You really couldn't call them milkshakes, because she never used milk, ice cream or sugar. All natural, all good for you.)

"I used some special herbs for quick healing, like echinacea, and lots of Vitamin C and B. Plus some stuff that if I told you what it was, you probably wouldn't drink it. So it'll just be my little secret." She handed him the large, white Styrofoam cup with a lid and straw.

Cody slowly sipped, smiled as he sucked and nodded that it was tasty. Since he left most of his dinner on his plate and this tasted cool and a little sweet, it was a nice retreat from the sour conversation that had just taken place.

After a few more hearty sips he asked Denny, "Remember that talk we had about you being drawn to the health field some day?"

"Yeah, sure."

Cody took another few swallows, put the drink down on the metal tray that was attached to the bed and squirmed to get comfortable.

"What if you're drawn in two different directions?" he finally asked.

Denny immediately thought he was talking about her and Laurel Luckinbill. She quickly became nervous and uneasy. Her normally perky smile vanished and she started to unconsciously fidget, pulling at her ponytail and twisting her head back and forth, trying to loosen suddenly tight neck muscles.

Lost in his own thoughts, Cody didn't notice her uneasiness. He wished he were out on his bike. It always seemed easier to think on the bike.

"What do you mean, two different directions?" Denny finally got up the nerve to ask.

"This is hard for me to talk about, you know," he quietly answered.

"Well, I'm a pretty good listener. You could try me."

"It's just that I've always loved basketball and now I love the bike and it seems like everyone is trying to make me decide among the two, that's all."

"Do you have to make a choice now?" Denny asked as she took a long, deep breath. Her anxiety dropped away.

"I'm thinkin' I do, yeah."

"Why?"

"I'm losing my focus. Like I'm being pulled in two opposite directions. Like my body is being stretched like a rubber band. I can feel it in my body somehow. It's like pressure. I'm tense. Sometimes I just wanna scream, to let off the steam. Is that right? For a kid my age to feel that way?"

Denny shrugged, "I feel that way sometimes."

"Well at least since I'm gonna be out of action for a while, I can try and figure it out. Maybe I'll just lie here, ask for another shot of that Demerol and relax. Maybe if I'm relaxed, I can figure it out. I got to."

Denny so much wanted to tell Cody that he didn't have to struggle to figure it out. That it would come to him. That he would feel it, down deep somewhere. But she herself couldn't put it into words. She didn't know why she wanted to pursue helping people, making them feel better or perform better. She just knew she felt better when they did. But she didn't consciously make up her mind. She just did what felt right to her.

She leaned down to him and kissed him gently on the cheek. Cody got a whiff of her; she smelled fresh and clean, not heavy on the perfume like some of the girls he knew. She stayed close to him, looked into his eyes and said, "Whatever you decide, you'll be the best at it. I just know it."

He nodded, looking away, almost embarrassed at her sincerity. Then she hugged him, gently at first, and when he hugged back, she squeezed him a little harder. He winced as his shoulder twinged a bit and said, "Oww," as he glanced at his injured arm.

He could see sympathy in her eyes as she gently backed away. He wanted to smell her again and he liked the sympathy, but she quickly retreated to the foot of the bed. He stared at her for long enough to make her look away and start tidying up his bed sheets. She was wearing faded jeans and a hooded sweatshirt, but she wore them well, he thought. The jeans were tight, but not especially low cut like most of the girls were wearing these days. And the sweatshirt was zipped down an inch or two more than usual from the nape of her neck. He stared at the curve of her neck and the cross necklace she wore. His eyes drifted toward her face. She wore little make up, just a little eye shadow. Her dark hair was pulled back from her forehead in a ponytail, and when she looked up, her emerald green eyes caught his stare. He looked away.

"You better drink more of that shake. It'll make you feel better."

You make me feel better, he wanted to say, but didn't. After some small talk about school and proms and biology class, Denny smiled at him tenderly, with that look of sympathy again and moved toward the door. Don't go, come closer, hug me again, I don't care if it hurts or not, he wanted to say, but didn't.

"See ya, get better," she said as she waved goodbye.

"Thanks for the shake."

"My pleasure. Bye." She moved through the door and was gone.

No, my pleasure Cody thought. Suddenly he felt better, his shoulder didn't hurt as much and his body wasn't tense anymore. He hadn't figured anything out just yet, but he was a lot closer.

THE SET-UP

After three days, numerous needle punctures and way too many body pokes and blood tests for his liking, Cody was released from the hospital. Except for a sore shoulder, a slight headache and a backside that felt like it was stapled together, he felt pretty good.

Saturday morning he made plans to walk over to Mr. Mitch's house and since Lionel was already there working on the damaged Cannondale, his mother insisted she walk with him. He wasn't too keen on being seen walking with his mother, but she'd been great with him over the past few days, waiting on him hand and foot, shoulder and rump, so he figured he owed her at least this. Sometimes you just have to give your mother the satisfaction of doing motherly things, even when you don't want to be mothered.

Even though his mom wanted to drive him over, Cody insisted on walking. Actually, it was more comfortable walking than riding, but that wasn't the main reason he wanted to hoof it. The doctor said he needed to get some exercise, that it would help the healing process, and Cody wanted to do everything he could to heal. He didn't much care about being careful about the stitches in his back and rump, another thing his doctor had emphasized, so even though walking might pull them apart a bit and leave a little more scarring, Cody figured it would be a badge of courage if nothing else.

It was almost 9:30 when they finally shuffled up to Mitchell Burke's home. From the outside, it looked pretty quiet, but things were jumping inside. As they approached the front door, Cody heard the music, although he didn't recognize the tune. Somehow it didn't sound like a Lionel K. Fitzhugh selection.

Burke answered the doorbell in gray sweatpants and a red Stanford tee shirt. "Oh, yes, the wounded warrior up and about ready to conquer new worlds I see. Come in, come in. The coffee is hot, the music is rockin', all is right with the world again on a Saturday morning."

Cody couldn't help but smile at Burke's exuberance. Shaking his head, he asked, "What is that you are listening to?"

"REO Speedwagon, my boy. They rocked the 70's."

"Oookay."

"Actually, I promised Lionel I'd introduce him to a few of the rock 'n rollers that never made it out of the 70s. Morning, Sarah."

"Morning, Mitchell."

"Lionel's in the garage working on the bike and Denny's in the kitchen working on Lord knows what, so take your pick."

"I'll take you up on that offer for coffee," Sarah said.

That sounded good to Cody, too, especially since he knew the coffee was in the kitchen, but he didn't want to be too obvious so he headed without comment to the garage.

"I'll tell Denny you're here. She's got something new she wants to try on you," Burke said as Cody headed out the laundry room door.

"Great," he mumbled under his breath. Another concoction from the blender, probably filled with all kinds of healing roots and berries. But he couldn't mask the smile that stayed glued to his face.

"Dude, good to see you in the land of the living again. I was worried, man," Lionel said as they knocked fists as a greeting.

"Thanks bro, how's the 'dale?" Cody asked referring to the black bike now perched atop the work stand and missing at least one wheel.

"In the healing process, just like you. Actually, not bad considering. We replaced the back wheel, it was bent beyond help. Now I'm replacing a few spokes on the front one, but I think she'll live."

"Those hoods look pretty gruesome," Cody noted, referring to the handlebars and brake hoods, which housed the braking mechanism.

"Yeah, they'll probably need new cables, too. But it

doesn't look like you're ready to ride quite yet, so I have a little time to put her all back together again."

"Sooner than you think, so don't dawdle."

"Working it here, boss, working it here," Lionel shouted as he picked up the truing tool and began to work on the front wheel.

"How'd you get coerced into listening to…something, something, something Speedwagon?"

"REO Speedwagon, and actually, they kinda rock, in a heavy metal kinda 70's way, you know."

Cody winced, "I'll take your word for it."

"Take your word for what?" Denny asked.

"Oh, hey," Cody smiled. "That REO Meatwagon is a band just waiting for a reunion tour."

"Speedwagon, Speedwagon. Don't be dissin' rock 'n roll, no matter how old the rockers," Lionel poked back.

"Well the volume is a little less intense in here and I wanted to try a new technique on you Cody. Care to join me in the parlor?" Denny asked.

"Do not, I repeat, do not go into the parlor with that woman, whatever a parlor is, said the spider to the fly," Lionel deadpanned.

"Very funny. This way please," Denny countered.

As the two exited the garage and REO Speedwagon cranked into *Ridin' the Storm Out*, Lionel shouted above the music, "Like a Christian to the lions, dude."

Denny led Cody into what Mitchell Burke called the rec room although most homes would have designated it the family room. Burke had a big screen TV as the center of attraction and a multitude of devices hooked into it, including TiVo, Nintendo, and a DVD. The room adjoined the kitchen and was decorated in mostly browns, reds and oranges in a manly, Western motif. A big brown leather couch, a reclining chair, lots of throw pillows, even a handmade Indian rug in beige surrounded a brick fireplace.

Cody was instructed to sit down in the recliner and Denny sat on the leather ottoman in front of his feet, which were now propped up as he was almost vertical to the floor.

"I just finished this reflexology class at the community college and we've been learning how every part of the body has a corresponding touch point in the feet," she said as she began to unlace his K-Swiss tennis shoes.

"What's a touch point and what are you doing?" Cody asked, looking skeptical.

"A touch point is kinda like a direct link to certain places in the body. For instance, there are places on the tips of the toes that are directly linked to the sinus regions in the head. So if you had a cold, massaging those points should help clear your sinuses."

"Except I don't have a cold."

"I know. I just used that as an example. Besides you've got so many sore spots on your body after a fall like that, I figured I could work on the whole foot," Denny said as she began to take off his socks.

Cody instinctively drew his knees up, pulling his feet away from her. He wasn't too sure about any of this. A foot massage? What's next, she going to lie me on a table with only a towel covering my scarred backside?

"What's wrong?" Denny asked, taken aback that he wouldn't let her touch his feet.

"I don't know, it just seems kinda weird, you know?" Cody mumbled.

"Well the protein shakes were kinda weird until you got used to them, weren't they?" Denny quickly shot back, a little indignantly. "Now, come on, it's not going to hurt and it might help, too. Put those big dogs up here and lean back and relax." She patted the foot of the recliner and Cody slowly gave his feet back to her.

Both Sara and Mitchell had overheard the exchange from the nearby kitchen and were stifling laughter, inching closer to the counter that separated the two rooms.

Denny started with Cody's right foot, putting one hand on his ankle and the other on his toes and rotated the foot in a circle. She began to knead the arch with her right thumb, still gripping the ankle with her left hand. She hit a tender spot and Cody flinched and let out a small yelp. She was patient with him and he got used to the technique. Whenever she found a tender spot she would concentrate on the surrounding area instead of directly squeezing and pressing on the tender area. Eventually Cody began to relax and they talked about school and classes. Every once in a while Denny would inform Cody what location on his body a tender spot on his foot was connected to.

Sarah and Mitchell drifted into the room and sat on the leather sofa. "Cody, do you remember anything about what happened that day of the crash?" Burke asked, sipping on his second cup of coffee.

"Not really," he answered, shaking his head. "I remember turning onto Wayland Avenue and then waking up in the ditch."

"How about the sound of a car or a truck?"

Cody looked up toward heaven as if the answer was hidden behind the ceiling fan. "Nope, nothin'." He wanted to find out what had happened to him, but his head was still clouded, still fuzzy. There were big lapses in what he could remember; the doctor told him that he might feel that way for a month or more. He didn't like it, now knowing what had happened to him.

From the hallway leading back to the garage, Lionel could be heard calling out for more caffeine and bemoaning bicycle wheels. As he entered the rec room, he saw Denny working on Cody's left foot and immediately stopped in his tracks. His face looked like he'd just swallowed something that he neither liked nor recognized. His left eyebrow arched high and his right eyebrow dipped low.

"I hoped you washed those puppies before you actually touched them," he said to Denny.

For a moment she stopped the massage and slowly swiveled her head toward Lionel, "Why?"

"The boy is an athlete. Need I say more?"

"Forget him," Cody drawled. "Please proceed. And I think my esophagus is a little sore. Could you see if you could find the corresponding esophagus spot and work on that a bit?"

Denny squeezed hard on the fleshy part of his little toe, causing him to call out, "Ouch!"

"And this little piggy cried wee, wee, wee all the way home," she said, smiling smugly.

"The doctor said your memory might come back a bit over time. Let's see if we can jog it a little," Burke stated.

"Shoot," Cody replied.

"The highway patrol found tire marks in the loose dirt on the same side of the road as you were, about thirty yards from the spot we found you. They're speculating that a moving vehicle might have struck you. But we've got no identifying marks on the bike, like paint from the vehicle, and no eyewitnesses. So unless we come up with something, well, we've got nothing. Take us through as much of the afternoon as you can remember in as much detail as possible."

Cody began to tell the story of the bike ride that ended up at the hospital. Denny stopped the massage and sat cross-legged on the floor in front of him. Lionel filled his coffee cup and joined the group, grabbing a banana on the way. Sarah put both hands near her ears like she was ready to clamp them down quickly to block out the gory details. Burke grabbed a pencil and pad to take notes.

Cody detailed the afternoon ride, noting how heavy the traffic was, how fast he was going, how hard he was working. He threw in small details that most of the group ignored but that Mitchell Burke found fascinating; like when he downshifted a gear or two and what his heart rate was at certain times. After five minutes of weaving his way through the ride, bringing him right up to the point of turning onto Wayland Avenue, Cody suddenly stopped. He looked like he was searching for something.

"What?" Burke asked.

Cody shook his head like he couldn't quite put his finger on it. He sat in the recliner, his eyes shifting from right to left like he was looking for something but couldn't remember what.

"OK, let's shift gears for a moment," Burke said, breaking the silence after a few seconds. "At that time of day on Wayland Avenue, what kind of traffic would be driving by there?"

"Well, not many commuters, there aren't a lot of homes out that way," Sarah said as she began to pace the room. "And it was too late for school traffic, it was probably after five o'clock when the accident happened."

"Maybe, but maybe not," Denny chimed in. "What about detention? How late does that go?"

"Exactly four thirty," Lionel offered. "Been there, done that."

"What about spring sports? Baseball players or track guys?" Cody asked.

"Possible, but not necessarily probable since Sarah said there aren't many homes out that way."

"Hey, I got it," Lionel said. "Friday afternoon, a little out of the way, almost Bay Area back roads. Dopers or drinkers looking for a little privacy maybe?"

"You might be on to something. That would explain why the vehicle slipped off the side of the road," Burke mused. "And why they left the scene of the accident."

"Well, I hate to say this," Sarah said. "It sounds like kids then, doesn't it? Not that kids are necessarily the only ones it could be."

"But the most likely I suppose," Burke said.

"Sad, but true," Lionel concurred, nodding his head up and down. Cody and Denny offered no rebuttal.

"If it was kids, chances are it was kids from Mountain View High, right? So let's set a trap and see what we catch," Burke smiled at the group.

"What do you mean a trap?" Cody said.

Burke held up a finger indicating for the group to wait for his answer as he headed into the garage. He emerged in less than a minute with a few electrical devices in his hand. He laid them out on the cast iron coffee table.

"Most of the Bees know we've been experimenting with audio transmission with Cody, right?" he said to Lionel.

"Exactimundo. We've been using a wireless device on him for about a month now. So?"

"But we weren't in contact that day, were we?"

Lionel said, "No, we didn't have it hooked up, you know that."

"Yes, but does anybody else know?" Burke said.

"What do you mean?" Cody asked.

"What if we spread the word that we did have you hooked

up that day?" Burke replied. "And that we've been experimenting with recording the transmission, as a way to gauge your training."

"Huh, you're losin' me here," Lionel said.

"Well, suppose we let on that the day of the accident, we recorded Cody's ride. Every single second of it."

"Are you saying, Mitchell," Sarah interjected, "that we claim we have audio of the accident and maybe we find a clue on the tape, like a voice or something?"

"This is beginning to sound like a Columbo episode," Lionel said.

"Who?" Cody asked.

"Peter Falk, nasty old raincoat, lazy eye, always gets the bad guy to fry himself by asking all these questions. Detective series," Lionel said.

"Got it. The vast wasteland."

"Misspent childhood."

Both Cody and Denny nodded their heads.

"Are you, Mitchell?" Sarah asked, getting the kids back on topic.

"Exactimundo," he answered, trying to sound like Lionel.

"But if we don't have anything like that, wouldn't that be…lying?" Denny asked in a soft voice.

"What's your point there, little lady?" Lionel said. "Oh, yeah, the lying part, not a good thing, right?"

She nodded.

"Anybody got any better ideas?" Burke asked. "I don't much like the lying part either. But I don't much like the part where Cody was munched up and spit out and left to…well…hang on the barbed wire fence."

"So what do you have in mind, Mr. Mitch?" Cody asked.

"Lionel, you start working on the audio recording part. Go to Radio Shack, start figuring out if it's even possible. Get one of those small recorders and begin experimenting with recording off the transmitter that Cody uses. If you need someone to be out on the road, use Denny. She can hook up Cody's transmitter and ride out a few miles while you're recording. But do it quickly, today or tomorrow if possible. We want to get the word out at school that we may have something here."

"I'll talk to the guys down at the station and let them in on the plan. They may have some good ideas on how it can play out. Or some things to watch out for."

"What about me? What can I do to help?" Cody asked.

"Number one, young man, get healed, feel better. Then we'll talk about how you just may start to suddenly regain some of your memory."

Cody smiled. He looked forward to being healed, that was for sure. But he looked forward even more to being part of the trap.

SCHOOL BUZZ

Within a few days the buzz around Mountain View High School was that Lionel K. Fitzhugh was a technological genius. He had figured out not only how to be in constant voice contact with his numero uno bike racing pal Cody Calhoun but also how to record Cody's voice directly onto the hard drive of his laptop computer. Rumors floated around the school that Mitchell Burke must have big plans for Calhoun if he invested in the technology to record voice contact for training rides.

Lionel purchased voice recognition software and quickly learned how to use it to recognize Cody's voice. Once the software was installed and he had instructed Cody on the patterns and terminology to use, he left Cody alone in the garage to practice recording his voice.

Cody quickly got the hang of it. He and Burke had devised a short list of terms to use, like heart rate, speed, topography and others that described both Cody's physical and mental condition and a verbal portrait of the bike route. Within a few hours he and the laptop were communicating. The software for the most part could recognize Cody's voice and record it onto a hard drive. Since they had the basic technology down, they didn't worry too much about the details. By the end of the weekend, they knew enough to begin the ruse.

The Triple Bees often met during lunch at school, mostly just to hang together. Sometimes they talked biking, but a few of the boys weren't quite as hardcore about the sport as others in the group, so the talk drifted, mostly toward girls.

But on Monday morning, Lionel made sure the lunchtime conversation stayed on track, the technology track. He outlined the hardware and software he used to record Cody's rides, being just vague enough to draw little scrutiny. He described the quality of the recordings with vivid detail and precise recollection, a feat indeed considering Cody had only walked about a block away to mimic actually riding and recording. Lionel had recorded just enough, an hour or so, to make a file full of Cody's voice. He proudly displayed how the system worked from his laptop.

Lionel also speculated how much detail the recording could capture, including not only Cody's voice, but peripheral sounds, too, like cars speeding, horns honking, dogs barking, and maybe even voices yelling. He described one voice on the recording that wasn't Cody's, but sounded like someone saying, "get the freaking bike out of my way" or something close to that. Nobody actually mentioned Cody's accident. Lionel was determined not to be too obvious with the trap, so he just kept planting seeds. He figured the more he planted, the better the chance that one would actually take root.

Joe Roddy had never officially been part of The Triple Bees. After he finished his rehabilitation at Burke's office, he'd continued to ride by himself a little on the weekends for a few weeks, but eventually quit. He claimed it was bad for his football training because he was losing too much weight with all the biking. He was much more concerned with adding a little bulk to his frame; the coaches all said strength and power came from weight and muscle, so Roddy figured that if he was losing weight he was losing power. And that was something he definitely didn't want to lose.

There was a buzz around campus as Lionel held impromptu demonstrations before school, at lunch and in science class. Somehow, Lionel had talked Mr. Schoenfeld, his science teacher, into letting him demonstrate the software package, even though they were studying electrical current and there was only a small connection between the two. Electrical current was the lifeblood of a computer, Lionel argued, and since he displayed so much passion about the subject, the teacher relented and gave him five minutes to show off his project.

Joe Roddy got wind of the buzz by mid-day and was all over it like white on rice. He had absolutely no interest in the technology of it all, except the small reference Lionel was sure to mention at every opportunity – that the recording device was so sensitive, it could pick up peripheral sounds. Although Roddy would never be described as intellectually bright, he was cunning, so he tread carefully on the information. If it was true that Fitzhugh had rigged up some device to record Calhoun on his rides and if by some far flung chance it was working on the day of the accident, then Roddy realized there could be a trail that led somebody back to the Buick. He kept his eyes and ears open the entire day but said nothing to indicate his interest.

Late that night, after the Roddy family dinner of pork chops and gravy, Joe traipsed up to Buck's room and knocked on the door. Loud heavy metal music almost drowned out the "enter at your own risk" reply. Joe closed the door behind him.

"Turn that junk off, we got to talk," Joe instructed.

"Since when are you the one givin' directions around here, puke face?" was Buck's reply.

"Since I discovered we got trouble, trouble with a certain hit and run accident the cops have been investigating for the past week or so, that's since when."

Buck hit the remote control on his Aiwa sound system, making the room dead quiet. Joe indicated silently with hand signals that he should turn it up a notch or two. Buck rolled his eyes and turned the system back on and dialed down the volume. A constant guitar drone filled the background.

"OK, Sherlock, what's the big mystery?" Buck said impatiently. "I got places to go and people to see."

Joe pulled a chair over close to where Buck Roddy was lying on his unmade bed. He had to clear a small mountain of magazines out of the way to get the chair close enough to communicate in a whisper. "Fitzhugh has been braggin' all day that he's been recording Calhoun on training rides. Claims he's figured out how to be in contact with him and actually recorded his voice onto a computer."

"No kidding," Buck replied in mock wonder, "let's call the newspaper. That's front page stuff for sure, for sure, Sherlock." He burst out laughing in a low guffaw, only half-heartedly trying to stifle how stupid he thought his younger brother was.

"There's more," Joe replied, quite confident that he would put Buck in his place in due time. Besides, he was used to his brother laughing at him, but more often than not, Joe got the last laugh. It wasn't hard to outmaneuver Buck.

"There'd better be, asshole, cause so far, you're wastin' my valuable time."

"The twerp claims that the recording device he's rigged up can capture all kinds of sounds when Calhoun is riding. Sounds like dogs…and cars…even other humans."

That got Buck's attention. He rose to a sitting position and faced Joe head on. "What else does the little shitface claim? Did he mention the accident?"

"No, nothing. But he said he's been recording Calhoun for weeks now."

The two sat in the disheveled bedroom, littered like a homeless shelter, alone to their own thoughts for a minute or two before either spoke. Buck's room mirrored his slovenly lifestyle. It was layered with clothes, sports magazines, empty soda cans, shoes, hats and other assorted debris. His mother had long ago given up the ordeal of having Buck clean it himself. She refused to even step foot in the room and if the cleaning lady didn't do her best to tidy it up once every two weeks, no telling how deep the strata would have piled.

"What are we going to do about this, Buck?" Joe asked. "What if they can somehow connect us to the accident?"

"No way on Earth they can do that. What we're gonna do is nothin'. Except for one thing, keep our mouths shut. And for damnsakes don't open your trapdoor about this to Johnny Z or Felix. Those buttholes will soil their pants and start to go all spineless if they get wind of this. And besides, that little techno twerp has probably got nuthin'. He's just blowin' smoke for all we know, just bragging about some new computer crap."

"Well we know the cops are involved cause of that article in the paper. It seems they're hell-bent on finding out what happened," Joe added.

"Exceptin' they don't have squat. We checked out the Buick and there was absolutely no damage that we could tell."

"That whole car is damaged."

"My point exactly. How could they tie any mark on that car to that little tricycle Calhoun was ridin'? No way."

"What about tire tracks? Suppose they got a way to match

the tire marks in the mud to our tracks, like fingerprints or something?"

"What are they gonna do, go around checkin' out every single car in Northern California and compare it to those tracks?"

"Yeah, maybe."

"No maybe. They got better things to do. They got real crimes to solve, like robberies and murders."

Joe thought to himself, hit and run is a real crime, a felony he supposed. You just can't almost kill someone on the road and run away from it. And if they could prove that alcohol was involved, then you'd really be up the creek without a paddle in a leaking boat.

"And Joey-boy, don't go taxin' your little brain too much about this. You're pretty good in the muscle categories, but your brain ain't a muscle you need to be exercisin' right now. You let me do the thinkin' and we'll get through this just fine. OK?"

Joe wasn't too sure his brother could think himself out of anything. The Roddy boys weren't known in the community as thinkers, they were known as doers, and it sure seemed like something needed to be done right about now.

"Here's the plan, Joey-boy," Buck said, rubbing his hands together with anticipation like he was ready to sit down to a Thanksgiving dinner feast. "First, you hang around the techno twerp a little more than usual. But don't do nothin' suspicious. Don't be asking a lot of questions, just hang out and listen. Find out what they know and report back to me."

"And what, fearless leader, are you going to be doing when I'm doing all the work?"

Buck smiled, slowly crossed his fingers together like he was going to pray and cracked all the knuckles on both hands. He then clasped his hands behind his head and lay back on his bed. "I'll be planning the strategy on how to destroy the evidence."

KARL SPINKS OF THE CHP

Mitchell Burke met Officer Spinks of the California Highway Patrol at the scene of the accident on Wayland Avenue Tuesday afternoon about a half-hour after Mountain View High School had adjourned for the day. Cody sat in Burke's SUV listening to 95.7 The Rock. It played a lot of heavy metal and he was in a heavy metal mood. It had been almost six days since the accident and he was getting restless. The weather was warming up nicely, perfect for training rides. Daylight savings time had kicked in and summer was bumping up against him like a dog in heat. Perfect for bike riding.

His shoulder was still stiff and sore but he had been moving it gingerly for a couple of days now. The doctor said he wanted to immobilize the collarbone, but Cody had secretly been moving the elbow away from his side, like he was doing the chicken dance and flapping his wings. His stitches were healing nicely and probably would be removed in a week or so. They still looked nasty, but a few of the young ladies at school seemed very interested in their exact location and he liked the extra attention they gave him. And Burke kept telling him all young men have a few scars on their bodies. All it meant was that they were in the battle, not sitting on the sidelines. The rest of his body was still banged up, but the soreness was better every day.

He still couldn't remember what happened that evening, but his memory was getting better. He now recalled the ambulance ride to the hospital in short snippets, almost like snapshots in a photo album. His mom's worried face with her hands covering her ears from the shrill of the siren, the uniformed emergency technician hovering over him, the scenery speeding by the back window of the ambulance. Someday the doctor assured him it would be more like a motion picture with each frame leading to the next. Right now the frames were sometimes all mixed up, a frame out of sequence popping up at the oddest times.

"Mitch, you know I'm willing to do all I can to help solve this one, but tell me again why I'm here?" Officer Karl Spinks questioned as he took out his notepad.

"I owe you one, buddy, and I really appreciate you coming back here again. I'm just trying to get Cody here," he motioned to the boy to come over to the conversation, "back to the scene so it might jog his memory a bit. Plus I got that photographer from the Valley Herald to come and take a couple of shots. Maybe we'll get them into the paper and maybe our villain will get a little scared. You told me yourself in these hit and run cases, it's often the conscience that solves the crime for you when the evidence doesn't pan out."

"I said it's a long shot at best. If we don't have any evidence, we rarely nab the perp. These hit and runs happen all the time with bicycles. If the rider doesn't get a glimpse of the car or driver and there's no physical evidence, then we don't have much to go on. Hey, Cody, moving better I see. How ya feeling?"

"Better, thanks for asking," Cody said as he approached them.

As Burke and the officer talked, Cody checked out the highway patrolman. He was dressed in the standard uniform of the California Highway Patrol. His raven-colored hair was cropped in a fashionable and practical buzz cut. Aviator mirror sunglasses protected his eyes, giving him a hint of secrecy and anonymity. He was dressed all in tan from the short sleeve uniform top and tee shirt underneath to the motorcycle pants with the baggy thighs. His knee-high black leather boots looked like he had shined them that morning. Cody noticed the extra bulk of his upper body and concluded it was a combination of weight lifting and a bulletproof vest. Too many whackos on the highways and byways of the Golden State to not get all the protection you can.

His equipment was impressive, too. He carried a pistol on his waist belt along with a slew of other devices Cody couldn't identify. A microphone headset wrapped around his right ear and protruded down to his mouth. But most impressive was the brand new Harley Davidson motorcycle propped up just off the street.

The bike glistened in the morning sunlight, its black and white color pattern highlighting its bulk and power. Officer Spinks kept the bike immaculate and Cody thought it looked like it was delivered direct from the factory that morning. Even the white front and rear fenders shined. The saddlebags surrounding the rear wheel, really more like small suitcases, were polished to perfection, their chrome latches reflecting sunlight like stars twinkling in the night.

"She roars, too," Spinks said to Cody as he noticed the youngster eyeing the bike.

"I can only imagine," Cody replied.

"Well, I guess I can hang around and get my picture taken," Spinks said to Burke. "The chief says it's never a bad thing for the public to see their law enforcement officers in the line of duty. But you realize I can't get involved in your little scheme to trap the perpetrator. No way I can let our friendship leap the bounds of hard evidence."

"I totally understand and I would never ask you to jeopardize your integrity, Karl. Just you being here, letting me bounce ideas off you, getting your picture taken, it's a big help. We all really appreciate it," Burke answered.

"OK, OK, you don't have to suck up or anything. Glad to help." Spinks and Burke were old friends and poked fun at each other easily.

"How did you get the Herald to send a photographer out here? Most of the time we can't get them to show up when we think it's necessary. Or they show up at all the wrong times. Never when you want them to."

"It's not what you know, it's who you know," Burke smirked.

"It must be nice to wield such power over the third estate," Spinks said directly to Cody.

"Again, I can only imagine," Cody weakly answered.

A small silver Honda pulled up and parked behind the motorcycle. Cody saw two men emerged, one carrying a large camera, the other poking his head into the backseat, searching in a large cardboard box located in the backseat. He pulled a small spiral flip-top notebook from the box and sauntered up to the group as the camera man looked at the scene in front of him and gauged the sunlight from every angle by walking in circles and looking alternately up at the sky and through his camera lens. Both men were dressed in jeans and looked no older than 25.

"Hi, we're with the Valley Herald. I'm Tom Blackledge, features editor and that's Matt Coverdale, photo-journalist," said the young man with the notebook but making no attempt to shake hands.

Burke immediately offered his hand and warmly shook both men's' hands and introduced himself, Cody and Officer Spinks. As the conversation meandered around the weather and recent crime waves, Cody drifted over to the bike to get a closer look but stayed within earshot of the dialogue. He felt uncomfortable around someone who seemed to be taking notes and talking at the same time. Blackledge was in constant motion, either talking in short, clipped sentences or scribbling madly in his little notebook as he paced around the scene.

"So how's the investigation going Officer?" he asked Spinks.

Karl Spinks didn't immediately answer. As a stall tactic he scratched his chin and furrowed his brow like he was deep in thought. He had been around long enough to know you didn't say the first thing that came to mind when talking to reporters. He also didn't want to destroy Mitchell Burke's plan to fudge the actual hard evidence in the case in hopes of getting the offender to confess, however long that shot may be.

"We've got some solid leads but nothing we're ready to reveal quite yet," the officer said, shifting almost imperceptibly from foot to foot but keeping his outward composure.

The photographer Coverdale was taking shots of the ditch where Cody had crashed, even placing Cody in one of the shots. He told Cody to look down into the ditch and look forlorn, that it might make a good picture. Cody had no idea what forlorn might look like so he just plain looked into the ditch. Maybe he'd get lucky and the photo guy might think he was trying to look forlorn. No such luck.

Next the photographer drifted over to the conversation between the reporter, the Highway patrolman and Mitchell

Burke. He motioned Cody to join the group, then he backed away and started taking pictures. Blackledge slowly backed away from the scene because he knew he wasn't the story and his editor wouldn't want to see him in the shot. Cops and victims were OK, but reporters in the shot never flew.

As the photographer took pictures, Blackledge walked over to the Harley and pulled his cell phone from his pocket. Burke thought that the reporter was losing interest and he knew if they didn't give him more to report, there would be no story in tomorrow's Valley Herald. Burke also knew that when you talked to a reporter nothing was off the record, so he would have to choose his words wisely. He ambled over to the reporter and patiently waited for him to complete his call.

Blackledge flipped the phone closed and nodded nonchalantly to Mitchell Burke that he was ready to talk if he had anything, but that he was important so let's get on with it, I don't have all day, I've got a job to do here.

"I don't know if this is vital to the case and it might not be anything at all, but we've been experimenting with some technology for some of our riders," Burke said.

"Some of whose riders?" Blackledge asked as he drew his notebook from his back pocket. He deftly flipped open the pad and had his pen ready to go before Burke could answer the question. Karl Spinks noticed the two in conversation and walked over to them but pretended to get something out of the motorcycle's rear compartment. He didn't necessarily want to be involved in the give and take but he sure wanted to know what was being given and what was being taken away.

"My company helps sponsor some of the local bike riders around here. Young Mr. Calhoun is one of them. They're called The Triple Bees, but don't ask me where they came up with that name. It's been so long and the legend has grown so much about the name I can't even remember." Of course he remembered how the group got his name, but he wanted to meander through this conversation, he didn't want to sound like he had this story down pat or anything. Play it cool, Burke, don't give him too much.

"And we're developing this technology to record our riders when they're in training, you know, so we can work on their technique, their riding style, their times, things like that," Burke continued. "It's similar to how the Highway Patrol communicates from dispatch to their patrolmen. Isn't that right Officer Spinks?"

"Oh, sorry, I didn't catch all of that," Spinks lied. Now he wasn't real glad he'd been close enough to the conversation to be drawn in. What the heck was Burke doing and why the heck am I involved in it? Well, I've come this far, might as well give a little more rope.

"I was just telling Mr. Blackledge here…"

"Oh, man, call me Tom, please."

"Sure," Burke smiled to himself, "I was just telling Tom here how the technology we're working on is similar to what the CHP uses to record their officers."

"I don't exactly know what you're doing," and here Spinks gave Burke a very direct look, hoping Blackledge would miss it, "…with your technology, but it sounds pretty similar. You see, son," turning to the reporter, "in this day and age, law enforcement has to record almost everything to prove that we're doing our job. Used to be in this fine country of ours, people respected law enforcement, now everyone's trying to find fault with what we do. You know, I've been involved with minor traffic accidents on the freeway, doing my investigation, and had one of the victims of the accident jam a video camera into my face, recording my every move. Everyone's hoping to catch us making mistakes, maybe sell the tape to one of those sleaze TV shows and make a buck. It's pretty discouraging to tell you the truth," the officer continued, shaking his head.

Burke noticed that Blackledge had stopped writing. He'd probably heard this story before. But he was going to let the reporter pick up the scent of the story without leading him directly to the stink of it all.

"So, what exactly does this recording technology have to do with this hit and run case?" the reporter finally asked.

Good boy, you've got the scent back, Burke thought. Now pick your words carefully, Mitchell. Slowly, slowly.

"Well, we think there's a possibility…that this…technology will lead us to the perpetrator, as Officer Spinks would call them," Burke said.

Leave me out of this, Mitchell, don't go anywhere near me, Spinks thought.

"How?" the reporter asked, now writing again in the notebook.

"Well if we have the recording of what happened that day to Mr. Calhoun, and we can find something in the tape, like a voice, somebody shouting or maybe somebody getting out of the car and talking, deciding to stop or to run, then we might have a clue, don't you think?" Burke said, throwing the idea back to the reporter.

"Do you have something like that?" the reporter inquired.

"It's quite possible, a little too early to tell I'm afraid, but it's…very…possible," Burke said slowly.

The reported finished writing a note, then looked up at Burke. "We mostly like to report facts in our newspaper," he said, not confrontationally, just matter of factly.

"And I wouldn't ask you to do anything else," Burke replied. Well, maybe I would, but I can't figure out how to get you to do it.

"Tom, let me have a word with you, please," Karl Spinks said, motioning to the reporter to join him on the other side of the motorcycle.

The two talked for over five minutes. They had turned their backs to the group, purposely Burke thought, so the photographer had nothing good to shoot. At one point, Spinks put his hand over the notebook so the reporter could not write in it. Another time, he put his arm around his shoulder, a gesture that didn't look altogether fatherly to Burke, but closer to arm-twisting. By the end of the talk, the reporter was nodding his head almost constantly and Karl Spinks was smiling, winking his eye and nodding agreement. Burke wondered how the officer had maneuvered the young reporter to his viewpoint, but he figured he'd find out soon enough.

When the conversation ended, the reporter shook everyone's hand and said his good-byes. The photographer had long since put his camera away and lost interest in the whole story. The two got back into their Honda, waved amicably and sped away. Burke looked to Spinks.

"What happened? What did you tell him?"

"I told him I couldn't tell him everything I knew, which was true, right? I told him we needed his help in catching the sleazeball who did this, which is true also, right? I told him if he could file the story with what he had, indicating he could fill in a few of the blanks himself, it would help the investigation immeasurably, which is also nothing but the truth, am I right? Now I did make it sound like we were this close to nabbing the guy," Spinks said, holding his index finger and thumb a half inch apart, "which I suppose is not…quite…the truth, but I didn't actually say anything of the sort, just kind of implied it."

"Then I told him how much the good citizens of this fine city wanted to find the person or persons who committed this crime against this fine, outstanding young man and how a photo in the paper and a story just might help us do that. Which, if the Lord is my witness, is the truth, the whole truth and nothing but the truth. Now, it's up to him."

"And as I recall from this whole dissertation, from the time you dismounted that hog of yours over there, you never once, to my recollection," Burke added, "ever mentioned anything that wasn't the gospel truth."

"That's the way I see it," Spinks agreed.

SOUND BITES

The next morning on page three of the Valley Herald, which was the beginning of the local section of the paper, there was a nice, big picture of Officer Karl Spinks of the California Highway Patrol and Cody Calhoun of The Triple Bees overlooking the scene of the crime. Unfortunately, the story accompanying it was rather short, having been edited down to give more space to the story of the local middle school that had been vandalized by what was thought to be a gang of bitter, outraged thirteen-year-olds.

The hit and run story mainly highlighted Cody's recovery and a rehash of the work that the patrolman had already accomplished: a tire track mold, conversations with neighbors and the victim, (who was still a little hazy on the whole thing), a search for physical evidence. And a very small reference to a certain technology, similar to what the Highway Patrol uses to record their officers, that just might lead to the first real break in the case. Thank you very much, reporter Tom Blackledge, now let the fun begin.

Cody was the talk of Mountain View High School that morning, even more than he had been for the past week. A few of the students, mostly girls, had copies of the paper and were passing them around for all to see. Except for a few sports photos and an annual shot of the local drug enforcement officer who was permanently stationed on campus, the high school didn't get a whole lot of recognition in the news. Even though they had added a second gymnasium and a swimming pool along with a new wing of classrooms over the past two years, high school education wasn't something most readers wanted to see in their local newspaper.

Better to put the local sports scores, including the Catholic basketball league scores of every grade all the way down to third (where the final score could actually be in single digits), than to cover the trials and tribulations of education in California. Most citizens just didn't want to be reminded that their state was usually last in almost every national testing standard with no end in sight for anything different. The editors of the local paper knew what their readers wanted to see every morning and it wasn't coverage of Mountain View High School. So Cody's picture was actually big news on the campus.

Lionel K. Fitzhugh was also doing his part to fan the flame. He had his mom drive him by the newspaper rack in front of the supermarket before school and had purchased every paper available. Lionel dropped quarter after quarter into the hooded paper stand and extracted a single paper for each coin. He knew he could have slipped one quarter in, lifted the lid and lifted the whole stack of papers, but he figured he was dangerously close to a streak of something less than complete honesty and he didn't want to press his luck.

Once at school, Lionel had cut out the picture and article and asked the school office secretary if he could tape it to the inside of the office window, where most tardy kids came to report in the morning and problem kids came to report almost constantly -- a hub of activity at the school all day long. He left other copies in the cafeteria, the library, the weight room and in the outdoor amphitheater that served as a meeting place for most students on their way to class and during breaks. He kept two copies stuffed in his backpack along with his tape recorder.

Lionel had spent the day before at home, playing hooky from school, claiming a sore throat and a terrible sinus condition to his mother. Since he rarely missed a day, his mom figured he needed the day away and had no qualms leaving him alone while she went to work. As soon as she had driven out the driveway, Lionel got busy. He began collecting sounds on the recorder, mostly car sounds. He had hidden in the bushes in front of his house to record the traffic on his neighborhood street, started his dad's old 1957 half-refurbished Ford Fairlane, and even found an old *Dukes of Hazzard* TV show on cable. He suffered through a whole episode of Boss Hogg trying to catch the Hazzard boys just to get a few sound clips of the suped-up Dodge they drove.

He also recorded his own voice in disguise. One time he

placed the microphone in his pillow case and shouted "look out" into a baseball hat from across the room. He found his voice was indistinguishable but that was close to what he was looking for. He then tried placing the microphone into a cardboard box, a wastebasket, an empty fish tank and in his dresser drawer. He finally popped the screen out on his bedroom window, hung the microphone out the window and down the side of the second story of the house, closed the window halfway and shouted toward the window, in various voices including his rendition of the friend in the movie *Ferris Buehler's Day Off* on the phone with Principal Ed Rooney.

By the time he arrived at school that morning with all the copies of the Valley Herald, he had over twenty good, muffled sounds on his tape recorder that meant absolutely nothing but sounded like valuable clues in an ever-developing mystery. During mid-morning break, the twenty minutes between second and third period when most kids ate their lunch, Lionel was playing the sounds to a gathering group of students and explaining what each one could or could not mean. He didn't claim that these particular sounds were gathered on the fateful day when Cody Calhoun was bounced from the highway or that they were even recorded at all from a moving bicycle. But he sure inferred all that – and more.

Cody kept a low profile most of the day. He didn't much like being the center of this charade and didn't know what to say when kids asked him questions. Unlike Lionel who seemed to have an answer for anything, Cody often just shrugged his shoulders and mumbled something unrecognizable. During the mid-morning break he sat munching on a salami sandwich in the back of the crowd that had gathered around Lionel. Sitting a few feet away and all alone, most conspicuously alone because he almost always had hangers-on following him likes flies on a plow horse, sat Joe Roddy.

J-Rod was intently interested in the crowd gathering around Lionel K. Fitzhugh. He wasn't concerned with the usual things that captured his attention – lunch and girls. He kept focused on the tape recorder but didn't get close enough to actually hear what everybody was listening to.

Since he couldn't actually hear anything, his mind started to imagine what the techno twerp had on the recorder. And Joe Roddy wasn't a real imaginative soul. If you couldn't see it, feel it, smell it or touch it, to Joe Roddy it probably didn't exist. So his mind reverted back to what it could see: the day of the accident in living color.

Roddy could see the interior of the old Buick and his brother and friends in all their drunken stupor. Come to think of it, his brother was pretty much of an idiot to be driving around with that many beers flowing through his veins. And those brain-dead lackeys he hung around with had absolutely no contribution to society that he could detect. No redeeming value, no purpose, no use. And why the heck did he have to be in the car that day? What had he done to deserve that?

As he leaned forward, straining to hear a snippet of sound, his mind raced back to the day of the accident. He went over every detail of the ride up Wayland Avenue. He remembered the joking and teasing going on in the car. He saw Johnny Z giggling and bouncing in the seat to the music. He noticed the Mexican – what was his name? Who cares at this point? He noticed him quietly grooving to the beat, his head bobbing, his eyes closed, a quiet drunk no doubt.

He vividly saw his brother at the wheel, slurping his beer, concealing it as best he could but in his condition doing a piss-poor job of it. He remembered Buck smashing the last beer on his forehead and firing the can into the back seat, where it hit J-Rod in the forehead before ricocheting and hitting the Mexican.

Lionel was shushing the group to be quiet and listen to the upcoming sound bite, but Joe Roddy was miles away, in another time zone, another day, milliseconds before the old LeSabre had smashed into Calhoun. He remembered the car fishtailing to the right as slight concern crossed his brother's face when he realized he was no longer in control of the Buick. Nothing too serious, nothing like panic, just concern. He saw his brother spin around and grip the wheel with both hands in an effort to get back on course at the same time the car jerked to the right.

Roddy was staring at the group surrounding Lionel but not seeing, his eyes glassed over, staring off into space. But his mind was projecting the accident back across his eyes like a video he'd seen a hundred times before. Each time it reran, he picked up more details. This time as the car was veering to the right, he noticed a bicycle and its rider directly in front. The rider seemed almost imperceptibly to peddle faster. Maybe it was J-Rod's imagination. Hey, I might have an imagination after all! As the car uncontrollably slid sideways over the asphalt, the rider looked back over his left shoulder.

A new scene in the movie crossed in front of his eyes, a scene he hadn't recalled before. As the bike rider looked back, Joe Roddy saw himself in the back seat of the LeSabre, like he was looking over his own shoulder, screaming at the top of his lungs…

"Buck, look out!!"

First, the frightened look on Calhoun's face. Then, contact. The bike flying off to the right. The car desperately trying to right itself on the highway, with no help from Buck Roddy. Joe spinning quickly to look out the passenger side rear window to see what had happened to Calhoun. The Mexican stupidly mumbling something like aye, carumba. Johnny Z sobering up in a nanosecond. Buck spinning the wheel like he was driving a bumper car at the county fair.

Joe Roddy shivered at the thoughts spinning through his mind, shook himself out of his trance and looked to his right – directly into the face of Cody Calhoun. He freaked. His eyes opened wide, his mouth dropped open and he grimaced, like he'd seen a ghost from his past.

He took a deep breath and concentrated on looking straight ahead. After a few seconds of getting himself under control, he slowly turned back toward Calhoun and saw Cody staring at him.

"What are you looking at, asshole?" Joe sneered.

"Nothing," Cody shot back. But rather than look away, which would have been his typical tactic, he kept staring at Roddy. Something strange was on the face of Joe Roddy, something that Cody had never seen before. Was it fear? Was Joe Roddy scared? Of what?

Roddy desperately tried to keep his hands from trembling.

What the heck was going on here? He never once in his life could ever remember his hands shaking. Maybe he was getting that shaking disease, what was it, like Michael J. Fox had? Maybe it would creep up his body eventually and soon he wouldn't even be able to control when he took a dump. Hey, was that my imagination working there? Or am I losing it?

That damn Buck, he got me into this. I wouldn't be sitting here, shaking in my boots, afraid to stand up for fear I won't be able to put one foot in front of the other without looking like a spasmodic if it wasn't for him. He's always pulling my chain and getting me into trouble. I'm not half bad on my own, but his influence and his legacy for that matter, just the fact that I'm his brother, that's already two strikes against me. Well, if we get in trouble for this, I'm not going down. I wasn't driving the car. I didn't drink myself stupid and almost kill Calhoun. I was just sitting in the back seat minding my own business, wasn't I?

Joe Roddy took a couple of deep breaths, slowly so nobody would notice, and stood up. He stared straight ahead as he tested his legs by shaking them out a bit. They seemed to be working fine now. He turned to his left, away from Cody Calhoun and slowly, almost strolling, walked away. He had to find Buck right now. He had to talk with him.

Roddy walked past the amphitheater lawn toward the school parking lot. He scanned the lot and the road leading to it for a victim. He needed a ride and he needed it now. Finally, he saw a red, '65 Mustang slowing to pull into the school. He knew the car and the driver. Perfect, he thought. He picked up his pace and caught the car before the driver found a spot to park in the crowded lot.

Roddy pulled open the passenger door and got in. Frankie Potts was startled to see him.

"Hey, dude, whassup?" he managed to say as Roddy settled in.

"We're outta here, let's go," Roddy said.

"Man, I can't leave, I'm gonna be late for English and if I'm late again, I'm fried," Potts complained.

"Either you drive or get out and let me drive. Your choice. I got a very important meeting I need to get to and I need to get there in this car and fast."

"Man, I can't let you drive my car. My mom will kill me."

"Your choice."

Frankie Potts contemplated the situation as he heard the bell ring to end the break period. This didn't seem like any choice at all he thought. Finally, he opened the door and got out.

"Just be careful, Joe," he said as he walked toward the school.

"No problem. I'll park it right here and leave the keys under the mat."

Frankie Potts shook his head as he walked away. What a jerk.

Joe Roddy cranked the ignition and pulled out of the parking space. What a loser.

FLASHBACK

Joe knew that Buck and the boys were working a small construction job just off the freeway north of the school in Walnut Grove. Buck had mentioned this morning that they were putting in a patio around a new swimming pool in the backyard of some high tech big shot. Joe punched in Buck's number on his cell phone and after three rings, Buck answered and gave him the street name and number. Joe said he'd be there in five minutes and Buck said he'd count the seconds.

Joe didn't know what he was going to say to Buck and he pretty much knew Buck wasn't going to say much back that was any too brilliant, but he had to get this new information off his chest. It was bugging the crap out of him. What if that Fitzhugh stiff really did have something on that recorder? What if they could tie the Roddys to the crime? What would happen to me? I'd probably get kicked off the football team at the very least, maybe even get probation or something. They wouldn't put me in jail or anything, would they? I'm only 17, aren't there laws against putting minors in jail?

Joe Roddy hadn't noticed that he did indeed have an imagination and at this particular moment, it was totally out of control.

Joe found Buck's car parked in front of a large, Tudor style home in a ritzy neighborhood. Joe could always tell how upscale the community was by how many different species of palm trees the homes had in their front lawns. It must be some type of status symbol or something to dot your property with trees like the ones he saw as he got out of the Mustang. Short ones, fat ones, tall ones, skinny ones.

The six-foot tall wooden fence that cordoned off the backyard of the big shot's home had a section removed to allow the construction crew access to the rear patio. Buck noticed the Mustang pull up and was glad for the break, even though Bob

Evers had been a slave driver lately and hated for Buck to take even a cigarette break. He must be losing big money on college basketball these days, Buck thought.

"Adding grand theft auto to your rap sheet, little brother?" Buck said to Joe as he climbed the steps to the fence.

"Eat me. We gotta talk."

"Some of us have to work for a living," Buck said as he reached into his jeans for a Marlboro, deftly ejecting one from the flip-top box and lighting it with a cheap BIC lighter that was decorated to look exactly like a can of Budweiser beer.

Bob Evers, who was in the backyard supervising the laying of concrete, glanced at the brothers and motioned to Buck to make it snappy by moving his right hand in a circular motion. His left hand held his cell phone close to his ear.

"That guy is beginning to bug me," Buck said, smiling and mouthing OK back to Evers. "What's on your mind, little brother?"

"Did you see this?" Joe said, handing Buck the morning edition of the Valley Herald.

Buck grabbed the newspaper and quickly scanned the picture staring back at him. He read the headline and the first few sentences.

"So?" he finally said to Joe.

"So…so Fitzhugh has been strutting around school with a ton of those, plastering them up everywhere. And he's got some recording of something that sounds like cars hitting bikes, if you know what I mean."

"I have no earthly clue what you mean?"

"Well, I didn't actually hear what was on the recording, but lots of guys have been saying that he's got a recording of the accident. They say Calhoun was wired, like the article says, and that Fitzhugh is close to nabbing the crooks who did it."

"Sounds like a fairy tale to me," Buck mumbled almost under his breath.

"Buck, wise up, what if they can tie us to that crash? We're dead meat, man."

"What, you think they got some data base somewhere with all the sounds of car engines, dating back to the Model T, like those fingerprint files they have for criminals and they're gonna match the sound of my Buick to that recording and then come slap the cuffs on us and haul our sorry asses away?"

"Well they got something, that's all I know."

"They got squat, which is exactly what you know, squat."

"What are we gonna do, Buck? If I'm involved in this and they find out, they'll kick me off the football team or put me on probation or something."

"You are involved, little brother, and don't you forget it. You were in that car just like all the rest of us, so there ain't no ifs, ands, or buts about it. And they sure as hell will do more than kick your lazy butt off football. Think jail time, dude."

"Jesus, Buck, what are we going to do!?"

"We aren't going to do anything, especially you. I, on the other hand, am going to think of a way out of this mess. You know, if I didn't have to pick you up from school that day, you little criminal, none of this would have happened," Buck said, jabbing Joe in his chest with his finger.

"Just cool your jets and let me figure something out," Buck continued. "Whatever you do, don't go ballistic on me. Keep your trap shut, stay away from Fitzhugh and Calhoun, and try not to lose control of your bowels, OK? I'll figure something out. Now get back to freshman biology or whatever class you happen to be failing this period and let me get back to work."

As Joe Roddy climbed back into the borrowed Mustang, Buck pulled another Marlboro from the pack. He took a deep drag and never heard Bob Evers yelling at him to start doing his share of the work.

Later that day at the home of Mitchell Burke, Cody, Lionel and Denny gathered to download the day. Burke had left the office early to join them. As they sat around the kitchen reviewing the Herald article, Lionel talked almost non-stop about the different demonstrations he'd done with the tape recorder throughout the day. He summarized the reactions to his news of possible clues to the hit and run, detailing almost each student and teacher's response to hearing the tape. Everybody was interested, but nobody fell on their hands and knees and asked forgiveness for the sins they'd committed.

While Lionel pontificated, Cody sat back and reviewed his day. He'd kept pretty much to himself, concentrating on looking at other people's faces to see if he could detect any deviance from normal. He kept coming back to the encounter with Joe Roddy.

During a lull in Lionel's speech, Burke directed the conversation to Cody, "Did you notice anything different today Cody?"

"Just once, when Lionel was showing everybody the tape recorder at morning break. I was sitting not too far away from Joe Roddy. He looked over at me and caught me staring at him. And he almost freaked. Like he thought I was going to slug him all of a sudden out of the blue. His face freaked out and his hands came up suddenly, like to block a punch or something. Really weird."

The description caught Burke's attention, "What do you mean freaked?"

"Like he was watching a horror flick and the bad guy jumps out from behind the door with a knife or something. Freaked…like scared…like jumpy, startled I guess."

Denny said, "I've never in my life seen Joe Roddy scared of anything."

Lionel jumped into the conversation after a brief rest. In his best Rod Serling voice he mimicked the beginning of a *Twilight Zone* episode.

"Imagine this…you've just witnessed an event never seen before by our hero. A typically surly boy, always in control, always cool, sees what by most who observed it, a rather normal event. A rather good-looking boy is demonstrating his newest invention before a small crowd. When all of a sudden, surly boy freaks out, like he's seen a ghost, an apparition maybe. That starts a downward spiral, all the way into…The Twilight Zone."

Then Lionel started to hum the theme song to the 60s TV show, doo-doo, doo-doo, doo-doo, doo-doo. As he finished the song, he raised his hands and screamed like he was in a horror flick himself. Everyone jumped, Mitchell Burke almost falling off his barstool and Denny knocking over a jar of her famous green, mystery powder. They both frowned at Lionel, who grinned sheepishly and sat back down.

Cody was startled, too, by Lionel's antics, but in a much different way. As Lionel screamed and raised his hands to his face, it wasn't Lionel's face that Cody saw. It was Joe Roddy's. In a still photograph, framed in glass. The glass of a car window.

All eyes drifted to Cody as he stared off in space, a worried look on his face, like he lost something very important and was afraid he couldn't find it again. Finally, Lionel broke the silence, "Sorry, man, I didn't mean to freak you out. You OK?"

"I just saw something…like a flashback or something," Cody said, his voice barely audible. Denny noticed that he had lost the color in his face and that his hands were trembling.

"Describe it," Burke said softly.

Cody swallowed hard and took a breath. He tried to focus on a fuzzy image that had come to him in an instant and then was gone. Slowly it came to him again and he described what he saw.

"Me…on the bike…riding…suddenly looking back over my shoulder…at Joe Roddy…screaming."

"Who's screaming?" Burke asked.

"Roddy."

"Where is he?" Burke again.

"In a car," Cody answered.

"Is he driving?"

"No, in the backseat."

"What else?"

"His hands are up, in front of his face, he's screaming."

Then Cody flinched spasmodically like he was trying to duck an invisible punch. His breath came in gulps, tears filled his eyes. He stared off into space, but only he could see the motion picture flickering in front of his eyes.

"Then what?"

"I'm down…I'm hurt," he said, a tear trickling down his right cheek.

Denny reached over the counter and took his hand, but Cody never felt it. She felt tears welling up in her eyes, too.

"Anything else?"

"Blackness…nothing." He shivered.

Cody tried to compose himself as the image faded from his view. He shivered again and tried to wipe the tears away from his eyes without anybody seeing. Denny came around the corner and with her index fingers wiped his cheeks, then gave him a hug, whispering in his ear that everything would be OK.

After a moment Lionel asked, "What just…happened here?"

"Cody's getting his memory back," Burke answered.

"I'm not so sure I want that memory back," Cody replied, still hugging Denny tightly.

A light went off for Lionel, "It was Roddy! That dirty son of a…!" he spat.

Burke nodded, "It was Roddy all right, but he wasn't driving the car. We still don't know who was at the wheel. Cody, anything else?"

Cody shook his head, his normal breath slowly returning, the trembling leaving his hands, the tears drying up. But he wasn't quite ready just yet to let go of Denny, who was gently stroking his hair.

"Now what?" Lionel asked.

"Now we figure out who was driving the car," Burke answered, already grabbing for his cell phone.

THE ACCUSATION

"How bout we just beat Fitzhugh to an unrecognizable pulp?" suggested Johnny Zecharius as he and the Roddy brothers hovered around a small Hibachi in the Roddy family garage.

"Brilliant," Joe said. "That'll really throw them off the scent."

"You got any better ideas, retard?" Johnny Z shot back, trying to muster a menacing glare.

"Pipe down, you imbeciles, I'm tryin' to think," Buck shouted as he delicately turned the polish sausages over on the charcoal grill using a large, flathead screwdriver as his cooking utensil.

After a moment or two of silence, Joe asked, "Where's the Mexican? He's just as much of part of this as we are. He should be here helping us."

"Helpin' you what? Think up more idiotic ideas?" Buck asked.

"Doing something. He should be here," Joe said, sulking in his plastic lawn chair.

"He's probably got his nose plastered close to Evers butt somewhere, that faggot. I think all of a sudden he's forgotten every single word in the English language. I told him to be here tonight but he played dumb, like he didn't understand what I was talking about," Johnny Z explained.

"Just as well, he'd be no help to us," Buck said matter-of-factly.

"You know, we wouldn't have to pulverize Fitzhugh. We could get those guys that helped us out when Junior here needed to make the football team," Johnny Z offered, gesturing toward Joe.

"Naw," Buck countered. "Besides, I think at least two of 'em are doin' time now anyway."

The three sat in their cheap lawn chairs, passing around a

bag of potato chips, sipping on Mountain Dews and looking like master criminals planning the next big heist. They spoke in hushed voices as Buck had instructed.

"We could conveniently make Fitzhugh's backpack disappear. Set up a diversion plan, he'll never see it coming. Then, poof, all the evidence is gone, just like that," Joe said, snapping his fingers like the idea had just come to him out of the blue. Poof, with one snap, all his problems vanished. He leaned back in the chair, proud of himself.

"That might work," Buck acknowledged. "But they probably got the real live evidence stashed away somewheres. Fitzhugh probably just made a copy that he's prancin' around now."

"Well, it's a start," Joe said. Johnny Z nodded that it was at the very least a start. "And we sure as shinola gotta do something. We just can't sit here waiting for them to show up and throw us in jail, can we?"

"You been watchin' too much TV, little brother. We don't know what they got. Probably nothing," Buck said.

"Probably ain't good enough for me, we gotta do something!"

Buck carefully placed the screwdriver on the grill and stood up. He then turned quickly toward his brother and placed his size 12 in the middle of his chest, sending Joe sprawling over backward, the lawn chair collapsing.

Buck kept his foot down tight, adding pressure to Joe's ribcage. "You…got…to cool your jets, man. You're getting' way too excited over this," Buck said with a controlled anger just below the surface. "You weren't drivin' that car, now were you? And you didn't have a bunch of beers in your belly, now did you? And you don't stand to be charged with hit-and-run now do you?"

Joe found he was having trouble breathing and he knew if he tried to escape, his brother would only find another way to hurt him, so he merely shook his head no.

"So cool it. We'll figure something out here and you getting' all panicky ain't helpin," Buck said as he lifted his boot off his brother and went back to cooking his sausages.

Just as quickly as his anger came, it disappeared. "Where do you suppose Fitzhugh is getting all his technology? He's not smart enough to be doing this all on his own is he?" Buck wondered.

"Probably from that physical therapist," Joe offered, rubbing his ribcage and straightening his chair.

"Who?"

"Burke. Those guys are always hanging out at his house."

"Who guys?"

"Fitzhugh and Calhoun. And most of the local bikers. But mostly just Fitzhugh and Calhoun."

"Why are they hangin' out there? What are they, faggots or something?" Johnny Z giggled.

"Tell me more," Buck demanded, ignoring Johnny.

"What's to tell? A bunch of guys meet there before they do their training rides. He provides them with gear and stuff, you know, helmets, jerseys, heart rate monitors, stuff like that."

"What's a heart rate monitor?"

"A little computer. Keeps track of how hard your heart is working."

"Too bad they don't have one of those for the brain," Johnny Z offered, trying lamely to get into the conversation.

Buck gave him a concerned look, like why did you interrupt me, again, with your idiotic banter? Johnny's smile left and he looked away.

"So they're into computers, huh?" Buck asked.

"Big time."

Buck continued to turn the sausage with his screwdriver. He constantly turned them over and over again, almost absentmindedly. Johnny Z's mouth started to water and he went to grab one to toss into a waiting hot dog bun. Buck cracked his knuckles with the screwdriver but never looked up from the grill. Johnny backed off into his chair, staring all the time at the sausage.

"Maybe it's this Burke guy we need to worry about then, instead of Fitzhugh," Buck said finally.

"What do you mean?" Joe asked.

"Well if Burke is supplyin' all the gear and stuff, chances

are he's supplyin' the technology that this recording comes from."

"Probably."

"And as we all know, to solve any problem, you have to get to the root of the problem. It sounds like our root problem is this Burke guy. And if he is, then all the evidence will be at his place. So instead of beatin' up Fitzhugh or stealing his little bitty backpack, I say we concentrate on Burke."

While Buck thought about what that actually meant, Joe and Johnny sat and nodded their agreement. Buck continued to turn the sausages.

Mitchell Burke met Karl Spinks at the Mother Lode coffee shop just off Interstate 680. It was a breakfast and lunch only place that mostly serviced the truckers who made the daily runs between Sacramento and San Jose and the rest of the Bay Area. Even though it was Saturday morning, it was the middle of Spinks' workweek and he was in full uniform.

The 60s style coffee shop had a counter with swivel seats covered in red plastic and a dozen booths, each with the old flip-a-page mini jukeboxes. Burke and Spinks sat in the booth closest to the kitchen. Burke slipped a quarter into the music machine and selected a Temptations song. The distinctive beat of *Papa was a Rolling Stone* started softly. Burke searched for a volume control knob to turn it up but found none.

"What's up? Sounded important over the phone," Spinks asked as he looked over the menu.

"Cody's memory is coming back. He can ID one of the passengers in the car that hit him."

Spinks laid the menu down slowly and looked directly into Mitchell Burke's eyes. "He's positive?"

"Absolutely."

"No question about it?"

"None whatsoever."

"Who is it?"

"Joe Roddy, a kid in his class at school."

"You said one of the passengers, he wasn't the driver?"

"Nope, don't think so."

"Tell me how Cody came to this revelation," Spinks asked, taking his notebook from his front shirt pocket.

Burke retold the entire story leaving out no details. He had recounted it in his mind several times since earlier that morning when he first heard it. He finished just as he was draining his second cup of decaf. Spinks hadn't looked up the entire time, but kept scribbling in the notebook. He didn't look enthusiastic to Burke.

"Well, at least it's a positive ID. But I have to tell you, Mitch, it sounds a little shaky. All of a sudden out of nowhere, the victim has a flashback of the crime scene, placing a perpetrator in the car that hits him. The DA will listen to Cody I'm sure, but he's going to want more to press charges. This is just a my-word-against-yours type of case. Hard to prove in a court of law. And with all the hard core cases flooding the courts these days, prosecutors don't like to take on something that isn't pretty clear cut, open and shut. All Roddy has to do is present a credible alibi and we don't have much to stand on."

Burke was deflated. He had thought the case was just about solved, just a few of the tiny details to wrap up and then all would be right with the world again.

"So what do we do now?" he asked Spinks.

"I suggest we go talk to this Joe Roddy and see if we can scare a confession out of him," the officer answered, putting his notebook away and motioning to the waitress for the check.

As Mitchell Burke and Karl Spinks were tracking down the address of Joe Roddy through the CHP database, Buck and his cronies were polishing off the polish dogs in the garage and plotting their next move.

"We gotta destroy the evidence and all things point to the evidence being in this Burke house, right?" Buck asked no one in particular. Both Johnny Z and Joe nodded uncertain agreement.

"If we act quick and destroy the original evidence, then all these sounds that Fitzhugh has on his little tape recorder are just that, sounds. Nothing that ties anything to us, right?" Buck asked again. The two nodded again.

"So we either break in and steal it…which could prove

difficult…" Buck said, thinking out loud, "…cause we really don't know what we're looking for…do we? Well, do we?"

The two diverted their eyes from Buck and shook their heads no.

"So that doesn't leave us many options," Buck concluded.

The three sat in their lawn chairs and stared down at the grease spotted garage floor. Neither said anything for almost five minutes.

Finally, Buck punched the arm of his chair in triumph and smiled broadly, "So I guess we have to torch the whole place!" Both Johnny Z and Joe dropped their jaws and widened their eyes at the same time, thinking the same thoughts but saying nothing out loud. Buck is one crazy fool, that's for sure.

Within fifteen minutes of finishing their coffee at the Mother Lode café, Karl Spinks had the Roddy address and was back on Interstate 680 heading north. Mitchell Burke wasn't invited on this excursion and was told to get back to his office and keep his cell phone on, but otherwise, stay clear of the investigation for a while. Spinks was in contact with his dispatch officer who was reading directions to Spinks via his radio. He quickly found the address in a cul-de-sac of homes nestled close to the freeway.

The neighborhood was typical middle class California. The track homes were probably built 35 or 40 years ago, and the original owners had departed long ago. The new crop of owners were just trying to buy into the real estate craze that had swept through the Golden State over the past generation or two. Most were first time homeowners that overspent for small, poorly constructed homes in hopes that the prices would continue to escalate. But huge mortgage payments left little for maintenance or upkeep on the houses, so by now, the lush landscaping was way overgrown, the houses desperately needed painting and repair, and the whole neighborhood looked worse for the wear and tear.

As Spinks pulled up in front of the Roddy household, he noticed an old beige Buick LeSabre leaving the cul-de-sac, noting the distinct color of the car, but thinking no more about it.

Buck also noticed Spinks and through the rear view mirror saw the motorcycle stop in front of his home. He quickly grabbed his cell phone and punched in the number eight, which immediately dialed Joe's cell phone.

Joe picked up on the second ring, "Yeah?"

"Listen and listen good," Buck talked quickly, his adrenaline flowing. "There's a CHP cop in front of our house, just getting off his bike. Go get mom and get right in her face and tell her she has to agree with everything you say, no matter what, got it?"

"What! I can't do that…"

"Shut up! You can do it and you will do it or we're all dead! Now get her and tell her. Tell her to play dumb and just go along with everything you say. You don't know anything about the accident except what you read in the paper. Got it?!"

"What?" Joe's mind was swirling as he ran from room to room looking for his mother. "Yeah, yeah, I got it!"

"Listen, listen. And mom picked you up that day from detention at school and brought you right home. Mom picked you up, not me. Got it?!"

"Yeah! Got it, got it!"

"Now go!" Buck screamed into the phone, then thought of one more instruction. "And relax, take a couple of deep breaths, just relax. You don't have to open the door right away. Make him wait a minute until you're under control. Do good, man, we're counting on you. Call me when he leaves." He clicked off the phone.

Joe found his mother, Shirley, sweeping off the back patio near the swimming pool. She was dressed in workout clothes and a baggy sweatshirt.

Joe Roddy approached her almost in a panic. "OK, mom, the doorbell is going to ring any second now and it's gonna be a cop. He's gonna ask questions and you need me to answer them. Just let me do the talking, OK?"

"What in the world are you babbling about?" Shirley Roddy demanded.

"Listen, I could be in trouble and you can help me out of it," Joe said, grabbing his mother's arms with both hands. He felt like shaking her and telling her to shut up and just be quiet and let me do all the talking, but he knew his mother well so he took a different approach. "You gotta help me out her, mom. I really need you now." She dropped the broom.

"What kind of trouble are you in?"

"I'll explain everything to you after he leaves..." The doorbell rang. "I promise, every detail, in all honesty, but I can't do it right now. Just play along with me, OK?"

She softened slightly, "I suppose..."

"Just one thing, you remember that day last week when I had detention and Buck picked me up? Just say that you picked me up that day, OK?"

"Buck's involved with this?! I should have known. What did he do...?"

"Mom, mom, I promise, I'll tell you everything, but not right now. I have to get the door. Remember you picked me up that day. Just be cool and play along and after he leaves, then we can sit and talk, OK?" Joe got that pleading look in his eye that his mother couldn't resist, never could, so she reluctantly nodded and instinctively started to straighten her hair.

Joe approached the door and took several deep breaths, trying to calm himself. His hands were shaking a little so he made a mental note to shove them into his pockets as quickly as he could. He opened the door a foot or so and Officer Spinks turned his head around and looked him directly in the eye. This is not good, he thought, we're all dead.

"Hello, son, my name is Officer Spinks of the California Highway Patrol. Are you Joe Roddy?"

"Uh, yeah, what's this about?"

"Just a few questions, son, mind if I come in?"

"Well, I'm not sure..."

"Of course, officer, please come right in," Shirley Roddy said, all what-can-we-do-for-you smiles and sincerity.

"Thanks, ma'am, you must be..."

She stuck out her hand and shook his vigorously, a little too vigorously Joe thought. "I'm Shirley Roddy, Joseph's mother."

As she shook, she almost pulled him into the hallway.

Man, settle down there, mom, you're going to pull his arm right out of the socket. And Joseph, you haven't called me Joseph, well, ever.

After exchanging pleasantries and offering the officer a cool drink, Shirley settled them all down in the living room.

"I'll come right to the point," Spinks began. "Son, you've been implicated in a very serious traffic accident."

"What do you mean implicated?" Joe asked, fumbling for words. He could feel the sweat starting to form on his forehead and under his arms.

Shirley Roddy looked at her youngest son and saw him start to crumble. He had always tried to put on such a hard exterior, trying to live up to the examples – good or bad – of his father and older brother. But he rarely succeeded. He wasn't as tough as they were and that's what she really loved about him. She knew he was a good boy deep down inside, that he just needed a chance to prove himself, to prove that he could succeed in this hard world. And she was determined to help him as much as she could. It was the least she could do as his mother.

"Perhaps, Officer…Spinks, is it?…you could start from the beginning. What's this all about?" Shirley Roddy inquired in a most controlled manner.

"I'd like to ask the boy here a few questions about a hit-and-run accident I'm investigating, if you don't mind, ma'am."

"Not at all, go right ahead. Should I be writing anything down here? Hold on second, let me get a pad and pen," she countered as she quickly scurried into the kitchen. At least she was within earshot of the conversation and as she rumbled around in the junk drawer it gave her a little extra time to think. She immediately decided that she wasn't going to let anything bad happen to her baby boy. She would defend him, even if it meant lying for him. At least until the highway patrolman left and she could get Joe alone. All right, Shirley, collect yourself. Your number one priority here is to protect your boy.

She returned to the living room and motioned for the officer to continue.

"Like I said," Spinks said, eyeing the youngster very carefully, "you've been identified as a participant in a recent hit-

and-run. Could you tell me where you were on the afternoon of May 3?"

Joe looked confused like he didn't know May 3 from November 3. "Huh, when?" he managed.

"Last Tuesday, May 3, approximately five o'clock in the evening."

Shirley Roddy was careful not to speak for her son, she didn't want to seem like she was answering the questions for him, but she was ready to jump in if he needed her. She leaned forward in anticipation of his answer.

"Uh, Tuesday…that was the day I had detention at school I think, so by five o'clock I would have been home by then I guess."

Well, it was at least an answer, not much of one, Shirley thought, but at least he got it out.

"You don't seem to sure about that son. You want to try again?"

Time for a little help. "Officer," Shirley interrupted, "sometimes my son can't remember what he had for breakfast, he's so busy and everything. Think, Joseph, last Tuesday."

"Yeah, I know, that was the day, like I said, when I had to stay after school for detention."

"And then I picked you up about four o'clock, wasn't it?" she said to both of them. Then to the officer, "I remember cause he's got his driving permit and I let him drive home. He needs all the practice he can get," she said with a smile, like she was sharing an inside joke with the officer.

Something about her manner bothered Spinks. And every time he looked at the boy, he looked like he was going to blow breakfast back up for inspection so they all could find out exactly what he'd had.

"How long were you driving after she picked you up, son?"

"We came right home, so probably fifteen minutes or so. However long it takes to get from here to there."

Spinks looked to Mrs. Roddy for confirmation and she smiled and nodded but said nothing.

"What were you in detention for, son?"

"Uh…" Joe stammered, looking at his mother.

Help time again, "Is that really pertinent to the case, officer?" Shirley asked in a sweet little voice.

Spinks had the feeling he was being double-teamed so he backed away. "No, probably not, ma'am." He fingered through his notebook looking for another question, but he seemed to be at dead end.

"Is it possible that this is a case of mistaken identify, officer?" Shirley Roddy asked in a voice not quite as sweet as before.

"Anything's possible, ma'am. Mind if I look inside your garage at your vehicles?"

"I suppose so," Shirley responded, thrown off a bit by the question. "What exactly are you looking for?"

Two can play this game, Spinks thought. "Clues," he said.

Buck Roddy sat in the beige LeSabre with Johnny Z two blocks away in a neighboring cul-de-sac. His mind raced. What if the CHP has something to tie him to the hit-and-run? Was it possible that all those recordings that Fitzhugh was prancing around with really could produce a link to his car? To him? And if so, how was he going to get rid of the evidence?

All he knew was that he couldn't just sit around and do nothing. No telling how long that cop would be inside the house. He could be asking junior what he had for breakfast for all I know. Then Buck put his limited knowledge of construction to work for him.

"Say, Z-man, suppose we can put our hands on a little of that dynamite Evers keeps bragging about that he keeps stored in his garage?"

"What for?" Johnny Z looked at Buck skeptically.

"Might need it. Let's go." He punched the gas and headed in the direction of Bob Evers' home.

Karl Spinks walked around the only car he found in the Roddy garage, a 1998 black Jeep Grand Cherokee with the gold trim package. He didn't know what he was looking for, he was certainly no detective, but he'd always heard them say, just keep looking, you never can tell when you might find something. He bent down and looked at the tires, looking for mud, but found the car sparkling clean, like it had been to the car wash recently. He knew this was Shirley Roddy's vehicle and that she kept it immaculate from the looks of things.

He inquired if there were other cars in the family and Shirley Roddy described her husband's Honda and her son's Buick. He asked when the two gentlemen might be home so he could take a look – it was just a tactic, he really didn't think he needed to look at the other cars, that really was out of his jurisdiction, but what the heck, it didn't hurt to ask. And he wanted to see the look on the kid's face when he asked. Joe was keeping a pretty low profile, hovering in the doorway that led back into the house, his hands stuffed deep into his jeans. He looked away when Spinks asked the question.

Spinks asked a few more questions – where the husband worked, where the son worked – and took down all of Shirley Roddy's phone numbers including her cell phone. As he was writing down the information, it occurred to him that neither one of them had asked him exactly who had been the victim in this hit-and-run. That seemed very odd to him, it was usually the first question people asked.

As he walked back through the house to the front door, he thanked them for their time in a very professional manner. Not too friendly because he didn't want the boy thinking he had a friend in the officer. In fact, he wanted Joe Roddy to think exactly the opposite.

"I'll probably have one of our detectives question the boy again, ma'am. We usually turn over the case to the detectives after we've done our initial investigation. You should be expecting a call in a day or so," he said as he handed her his business card. He handed one to the boy, too, on his way out the door and noticed the boy's hand shook slightly as he accepted it.

DYNAMITE

Buck knew that Bob Evers always played golf on Saturday afternoons at his country club. He also knew that if Ever's wife wasn't out shopping she was sitting at the nineteenth hole at the club getting a head start on her husband who would soon join her. Saturday night's all right for drinking.

Since the Evers Construction Company was a small outfit and Bob Evers liked to impress his little group of laborers with the better things in life, he often had them out to his home. Mostly, he liked to invite them over for an impromptu barbecue in the summer months. Give them a few beers, show them around the house, let them drool over his trophy wife, just generally show them a good time. It made them feel part of the family and built a little loyalty, which just might help keep the boys going if and when times got tough. Besides, he always wrote it off as an employee expense.

So Buck had been through the entire home – and garage – of Bob Evers and he knew exactly where the dynamite was hiding. Evers had even given him the six-digit code to get into the garage, because Buck often had to pick up tools or supplies to take back to a job site.

Buck and Johnny Z pulled up in the lumbering Buick and parked in the Evers driveway. If by some chance, Evers was actually home, Buck had an excuse all ready. He just needed a small bag of cement to do a little work around his house; he'd pay Evers back next week.

Buck punched in the code, which was not too hard to remember since Evers said it was his wife's measurements, 38-24-38. Somehow Buck doubted it. He'd seen her in a bathing suit and the 24 part was washed away a long time ago by too many nineteenth hole martinis.

Buck wasn't necessarily dressed for undercover work, so he strolled into the garage just like he normally did, but his mind was racing. He slipped on his jean jacket so he had a place to stash the loot. All he could think about was destroying this Burke guy's house. His adrenaline was pumping. He had broken out of his menial routine and was planning something big. This is where I belong, he was thinking. He never thought about the illegal side of things, his mind didn't work that way. He just wanted to put together a plan of destruction.

Buck didn't have the capacity to think rationally in this case. He wasn't thinking, well if I do this thing I'm planning, here are the consequences, big boy. His mind was one track wide and it didn't matter which track he was on. The windows on the train were closed, no looking out at other tracks, just full steam ahead.

Once he located the dynamite in the corner of the garage, Buck estimated just how much he needed. He knew Evers would miss it immediately and Buck would be suspect numero uno, but he'd cross that bridge when he came to it. Evers had stolen the gelatized explosive himself from a demolition job in Oakland last year. So what if the federal guys up there screwed up and let some of their precious cargo escape unnoticed. That wasn't Evers problem, he'd always said and Buck knew he wouldn't be able to put up much of a stink since he'd stolen it in the first place.

Buck wasn't planning to blow up the whole house, that would be too suspicious. He just wanted to use the explosives to create a diversion. He stashed a small package of the explosives and a few blasting caps in the inside pocket of his jeans jacket and quickly left the garage, his mind racing back again to Mrs. Evers as he punched in her measurements to close the door. Stay on track, Buck, stay on track.

Buck looked at Johnny Z and saw the ultimate accomplice – willing, energetic and fairly capable. Well, at least minimally capable. Throughout the day, Buck had been putting the idea in Johnny's head that this was some kind of an adventure and that he just had to come along for the ride. Buck was painting the picture of what the future would look like if they didn't do something and it wasn't pretty. He said it was just like insurance, they couldn't afford to live without it.

It hadn't taken much to get him to go along with the plan,

especially since Buck wasn't exactly telling him the whole plan. Johnny's job was to create a diversion. Buck wanted the house empty when he set his plan in motion. He was quite sure he could burn down the house and all of the evidence, but he wasn't exactly sure he wanted to kill anybody in the process.

The two wasted the rest of the afternoon planning the details, waiting for the cover of darkness. Buck knew they had to act fast, that the highway patrolman was hot to trot and getting hotter all the time. He also knew his little brother wasn't up to the job of snowballing and although he was proud of his mother for jumping in and bailing the little guy out, he wasn't sure she could keep it from his father. And once his father found out…well, the old man was a loose cannon and there was no way to predict how he might go off. Better to act now – and decisively – before things got out of hand.

Buck had made a short trip to the supermarket to pick up what looked like a large hypodermic needle. Instead, it was used to inject turkeys and chickens with a basting sauce and made of thick plastic rather than thin metal. But for Buck's purposes, it was perfect. He also purchased a number of different sized light bulbs.

Buck and Johnny sat cramped in Johnny's bedroom listening to music, talking quietly and getting psyched up.

Cody was getting antsy to get on the bike, so he and Lionel trekked over to Mitchell Burke's house that afternoon to work on the Cannondale. Denny met them there, figuring she might get another opportunity to try a new technique out on Cody or at the very least, learn a little more about this sport that enthralled them both. Burke was at the office catching up on paperwork.

Lionel had worked on the bike almost constantly since the accident. With Burke's direction and a sizable cash infusion, he'd purchased the parts that needed to be replaced and inspected everything else. Like any vehicle, the frame was the foundation of the Cannondale and luckily it hadn't been damaged in the crash. The back rim and derailleur were damaged beyond repair and had to be replaced. Putting a new rim on was a piece of cake for Lionel, but he'd spent the better part of a morning learning to attach the derailleur system and realigning the chain. He had also straightened out the handlebars, replaced one of the brake hoods and the saddle.

During the overhaul, Lionel cleaned every part meticulously. Burke taught him the value of a clean machine, how it made the efficiency of the bike so much better and the rider's job so much easier. Lionel took it to extremes, hand cleaning the bike from top to bottom. He even purchased a little bottle of touch up paint from an auto parts store and had every small nick and one big scrape in the frame coated like brand new. The paint was almost a perfect match. He rode the bike up and down the street in front of Burke's house as he adjusted the gearing, but was anxious for Cody to try it out under real conditions.

Cody had another bike loaded onto the stationary trainer in Burke's garage and was trying to find a comfortable position to get a little peddling in. His backside was still tattooed with stitches but except for a little discomfort on the seat of the bike, it wasn't as bad as he thought. His right knee, the one with six stitches directly over the kneecap was his big problem. Every time he pedaled, he was afraid to bend the knee completely because the stitches pulled. They were due to come out in a day or two, but Cody couldn't wait. He'd read Lance Armstrong's book about recovering from everything from bike crashes to brain cancer and thought, hey, am I going to let a few stitches in my knee keep me from my bike?

As Lionel was busy attaching the chain to the Cannondale and Denny was fixing a power shake for everyone, Cody found a pair of sharp scissors, like the kind used to cut hair in a barber shop, in Burke's upstairs bathroom. He looked at the black stitches in his knee and poked at them with his finger. Almost no pain, just a little soreness, that's a good sign. And it looked healed. He studied how the stitches were tied. Sticking the point of scissors under one stitch, he cut it, first on one side of the knot, then the other. Then taking a deep breath, he yanked it out.

To his relief the skin didn't split open. He was right, it was healed, at least enough for government work. He proceeded to take out the other five stitches, experiencing only a little sharp pain with each tug. Then he gingerly bent his knee, almost expecting the skin to split open again. But it held.

Now he wondered what to do about the ones in his butt.

He returned to the garage and jumped back on the trainer. The knee definitely moved better now, without restriction. But he still had to stand to pedal since all the black little ropes holding his butt together pulled against each other and made sitting uncomfortable. Lionel noticed his return and loped over to the trainer to take a look.

He poked at the knee, "Healed up nicely," he said, like he had a medical degree.

Then, "Did you take them out?"

Cody nodded with as much bravado as he could muster, like it was no big deal.

"Cool."

"Now if I could only get the ones out of my butt, I might be able to get a little training in," Cody said, looking expectantly at Lionel.

Lionel looked at Cody, then at his own hands, nice and greasy with the recent chain maneuvers, then finally got the drift of the request.

"No way!" shaking his head violently. "Not even a slim chance."

Just then Denny entered the garage carrying two plastic cups. "No way what?" she said.

Both Cody and Lionel looked at her, then each other. Their thoughts connected. They both smiled, saying simultaneously, "Way!"

Buck and Johnny stared out of the bedroom window, looking at the fading sunlight and feeling the adrenaline gush through their veins. Buck had filled the hypodermic with gasoline from the lawn mower in the garage. He patiently injected about two ounces into six light bulbs by penetrating the soft black epoxy surrounding the metal end of the bulb. Maybe six was too many but then again, maybe not. He thought of himself as a surgeon as he performed the intricate work. The music pumped louder and louder, acting like a drug on their consciousness, stimulating them.

Johnny's part of the plan was relatively easy: create a diversion. He took a small square of the dynamite and stared at it intently. It looked like one of those small packages of cream cheese that came in a foil wrapping once you took it out of the box. He knew Kraft didn't make this particular variety though.

Buck had assured him that dynamite was safer these days than ever before. And it really wasn't used like Hollywood portrayed. They both had seen many a Western cowboy movie where the hero had lit a stick of dynamite with a match and thrown it, only to have it explode when it landed. Pure fiction, Buck said. Never happens that way in real life. Buck had read about dynamite in a book recently. The old stick kind was a combination of sawdust and nitroglycerin, but sometimes the nitro actually bled out of the casing. Big problem if you happened to touch it and get it on your hands. Good way to lose one.

But the new stuff was called gelatized dynamite and it came wrapped in foil so the nitro couldn't leak out. Much better, Buck assured him, much safer.

Buck did the electrical work. Evers had taught him everything he knew about this sort of thing and Buck had become the main guy on the small crew when it came to anything electrical. Buck inserted one end of the blasting cap into the dynamite. Once he'd removed the cover to his cell phone, he rigged the other end of the cap to the ringer on the phone, attaching the wires to the speaker circuit. Johnny watched him and wondered where he'd learned this skill. Buck offered no explanation and Johnny figured he just as soon not know. Johnny checked again that he had plenty of pocket change to make a phone call. As the sun set, they slipped on dark sweatshirts and dark hats and headed for the LeSabre. Showtime. Buck pointed the Buick toward the city park close to Mitchell Burke's home.

Buck dropped Johnny off at the park after reviewing the instructions for what Johnny thought must be the hundredth time. He wasn't a dumbass. He could do this, no problem. All he had to do was find a quiet spot in the park – easy enough this time of day – bury the dynamite under some large object, like the tall slide, and make a phone call. Piece of cake. He checked his watch again and patted the change in his pocket.

BOMBS BURSTING IN AIR

"And me without my digital camera," Lionel joked looking at Cody bent over the bathroom sink. His pants and underwear were slipped down below his waist and Denny was adjusting his hips to get view of his stitches. Only the little baby butt crack appeared above his shorts and Denny was careful to only expose as much as she needed for each and every stitch.

Cody was thinking how easy it had been to talk her into helping him. Actually, once she got over the fact that he was going to take them out anyway, and see, the knee held up just fine, and no, I'm not going to wait to go back to the doctor, she jumped at the chance to help. She got a slight smile on her face and a faraway look for just a second.

"Hand me the scissors and bend over," she said.

The barbed wire that Cody had been impaled on didn't cut his skin as much as it had punctured it. Most of the stitches were small and not too deep and in many of the places where the wire had ruptured the skin, the doctor decided to let nature do its job without the help of stitches. So Denny carefully extracted each suture and in her mind figured that since she'd had a little training with all of her health related classes, she was almost as qualified as a nurse. She was at the very least going to use that thinking if Cody's mom asked why in the world hadn't they waited for the doctor.

Lionel did not stay to watch. He retreated to the garage, finished the chain, washed up and headed to the music room.

After she completed the work, with each stitch Cody's pants slipped down a millimeter more, she made sure he stood still as she swabbed him with an antiseptic she found under Burke's bathroom sink. Except for stinging a bit, Cody felt great and was glad to be free of the binding.

"Thanks, you do good work," Cody smiled at her as he pulled up his pants.

"Any time, big boy," she answered, leaning into him and kissing him lightly on the lips.

At that exact second, a huge explosion rattled the windows in the bathroom. They both looked out the second story window toward the north and saw parts of what looked like the slide at the nearby park being emancipated from its earthly moors, blasting right into space.

Lionel didn't hear a thing. A timeless version of *We Won't Get Fooled Again* by The Who was rattling his brain through a choice set of Bose earphones.

When Johnny Z punched in the last digit of the phone number of Buck's cell phone, the connection was made and enough electricity surged through the blasting cap for ignition. Immediately the small, inconspicuous gelatized dynamite exploded with a powerful force. Johnny had positioned the charge near the base of the large, twelve-foot high slide, which was located in the southern section of the park. The explosion provided enough force to strip the bolts holding the slide to the foundation and splinter both the aluminum slide section and each one of the steps leading to the top of the slide into different projectile missiles. Neighborhoods up to a mile away heard the sound, but nobody witnessed the actual explosion or saw who was responsible for it.

Johnny Zecharius watched his handiwork from a nearby 7 Eleven store, where he had made the phone call to the cell phone that detonated the slide. He was giddy with his success. He was almost skipping as he headed back to the rendezvous spot that Buck had designated. I did my part without a hitch, he thought. Now it's up to you, Buck.

Cody and Denny, overcome with curiosity, rushed down the stairs and headed out the front door. Lionel was still lying on the couch in the music room and except for a slight pause in his concentration to wonder what that vibration was he sensed (probably a little earthquake, no big deal), he never moved.

Buck waited, hidden in a cluster of birch trees, across the street from Burke's house and saw the Calhoun boy and some unknown girl rush out the front door heading in the direction of the park. I love it when a plan comes together, he thought. He waited another sixty seconds to make sure nobody else was in the house before slipping in the front door and heading for the garage.

He immediately found the water heater and severed the natural gas line that led to it with his pocketknife. He inhaled the aroma of gas and got a gleam in his eye. Then he unscrewed the light bulb over the doorway between the garage interior and the house and replaced it with one of his gasoline filled bulbs. He waited to admire his work, knowing that when the light bulb was turned on, the small spark to the filament would ignite the gasoline, burst the thin glass bulb and send a torrent of little gasoline fire bombs in all directions. When those bombs mingled with the natural gas filling the garage, ba-boom, skyward!

He then froze as he heard sounds coming from the house. Who was there? Who could that be? Everyone was out of the house, what's going on? Buck switched off his flashlight and was emerged in a sea of darkness. His mind raced. He could try to make a break for it out the side door but the chance of getting caught was too great. He could hit the electric garage door opener, but that would be too slow for him to make it out before someone heard and came running. He could hide in the garage and hope that nobody came to investigate, but then he ran the risk of getting blown halfway to Nevada.

He moved toward the side door but tripped over a bicycle trainer and dropped his flashlight. It rolled under the small pallet that supported Burke's garage refrigerator. Buck frantically got down on his hands and knees, sweeping the floor in front of him with both hands looking for the beacon. He found nothing and decided to head in the direction of the side door. He rose to his feet, looking like Frankenstein's monster, arms outstretched trying to feel any obstructions in front of him. He lumbered stiff-legged toward the door.

He found the wall of the garage, but no door. He traversed first to the right and ran into an assortment of garden tools hanging on the wall of the garage. A shovel clanged to the cement floor and bounced once, clanging again. The sound make Buck stop for a split second. His hesitation would prove to be costly.

He headed left and finally felt the door. He grabbed the doorknob but it was locked from the inside. Where was the deadbolt?! He could now definitely smell the gas with every breath. His head hurt and his stomach felt nauseated, but he couldn't tell if it was from the gas or from a mixture of too much adrenaline and too much fear.

Just as Buck found the deadbolt and began to relax a little with freedom only a doorway away, Lionel flipped the switch to the garage light from the laundry room. He had heard the shovel crashing to the floor and thinking Cody and Denny were now in the lighted garage, he wanted to plunge them into darkness so he leaned against the door in case they tried to come back into the house.

The spark in the filament ignited, the bulb burst, the gasoline flew in every direction, and the natural gas embraced it like a long lost lover. Buck turned to see the gas explode just as he opened the door to freedom. Too late. Close but no cigar.

The explosion was nowhere near the one Johnny Z had conducted at the park, but it was enough to propel Buck out the side door and slam him headfirst into the wooden fence like a bug on a windshield. He collapsed in a heap, unconscious but alive. It also blew the front garage door off its hinges, puncturing the door in several places. It looked like somebody had thrown bowling balls at it from the inside. The door where Lionel waited was blown inward toward the house and Lionel went with it. He was hurled against the wall of the laundry room and the door hit him in the head, breaking his nose and knocking the wind out of him. He slumped to the floor, stunned and in pain, grasping for breath.

Since seven fire trucks and a bevy of police cruisers had convened on the park like locusts to honey, it didn't take long for several of each to respond to the second explosion to rock the neighborhood in the last half hour.

Not enough time had elapsed between when Buck had severed the gas line from the water heater and the light bulb explosion. Another fifteen minutes or so and half the house could have been blown to smithereens. As it was, there was enough gas in the garage to do some real damage to the garage structure, but the house was pretty much undamaged.

Lionel managed to crawl out the laundry room and head toward the front door just as a fireman was approaching.

"Anyone else in there?" he shouted, helping Lionel to his feet.

"I think two friends are in the garage," Lionel managed, blood dripping down his mouth and covering his tee shirt.

After instruction, three firemen pried open the front garage door enough to shed light on the interior of the garage. Several small fires were flickering, one centered around the big baskets of clothing and one where rolls of paper towels were stored on an interior shelf. After opening the door enough to get a hose on the fires, they quickly doused the flames. They also smelled the leaking gas and one brave veteran of the squad entered the garage to cap the hose.

Just then Cody and Denny came running up the sidewalk, thinking maybe the whole neighborhood was being attacked. They spotted Lionel being attended to by a paramedic. The three friends huddled together, Lionel bleeding, Denny crying softly and Cody trying to be strong and comfort them both.

A thorough search of the premises turned up Buck Roddy, still unconscious on the side of the house. After an initial diagnosis, he was eventually placed on a stretcher and taken to the front of the house, which had became a staging area for the injured. Buck would be sore for a long time and had suffered numerous facial lacerations and a concussion from the face plant on the wooden fence, but nothing life threatening.

Cody identified Buck as he lay on the stretcher and quickly pointed out that he was no friend of theirs and more than likely the culprit responsible for the explosion. As the attending officer heard that statement, he began to treat the house as a crime scene. In the ensuing twenty-four hours, the police found the extra gasoline filled light bulbs in Buck's car and his fingerprints in several places in the Burke garage. They read him his rights in his hospital bed and booked him on several counts of felony property endangerment.

Johnny Zecharius' name was never mentioned in the interrogations of Buck Roddy. Even in Buck's weakened condition, he kept his criminal wits about him and his mouth shut. He confessed to attempting to blow up Mitchell Burke's garage but gave no motive or reason for his temporary bout with the dark side. He did admit to stealing the dynamite from Robert Evers's garage and managed to convince the police that no accomplice was necessary when he blew the city park slide skyward. He told the truth when he confessed to rigging the bomb to explode by calling the cell phone attached to the blasting cap.

The police, including California Highway Patrolman Karl Spinks, did not believe all of the details in Buck's story. Everything fit nicely together except that there was no motive. Officer Spinks mentally tied the hit-and-run accident involving Cody Calhoun to the bombing of Burke's garage, but had little hard evidence except an image of Joe Roddy in Cody's shaky memory. He quietly let the concocted story about the recording devised by Burke and carried out by Lionel K. Fitzhugh slip beneath the surface. Since they had Buck on much more serious crimes and repeated interrogations of Joe Roddy proved fruitless, especially with a good lawyer and his mother present at every session, Spinks decided to put the investigation on the back burner. Burke, Cody and Sarah Calhoun reluctantly agreed.

Joe Roddy kept a low profile throughout the investigation and never quite recovered his tarnished bravado. Friends noticed that he continually seemed much more paranoid than circumstances in a typical teenager's life would dictate. He gradually lost his posse, those buddies who hung around J-Rod because he was so sure of himself and so full of himself. His lack of self-confidence and the inability to get the close-up image of Cody Calhoun's face just before impact out of his mind, preoccupied J-Rod much of the time. His mother continued to shelter him from the police and eventually got the whole story out of him. His father never heard it all, especially when he mentioned that it might be good for Joseph to attend Culver Academy, a military school in Indiana. His mother would hear none of that, she wasn't going to lose her youngest.

Johnny Zecharius reported every day without complaint to his construction job and coaxed Robert Evers into teaching him every thing he knew about electrical. When he turned twenty-one, he became a regular fixture at a local bar, where everybody knew his name.

With his stitches removed and his well-conditioned 16 year-old body healing rapidly, Cody Calhoun quickly returned to bicycle riding. He started riding even before his broken collarbone was completely healed. He had lost more than a month of training and his recovery was slow, but there were no lingering side effects of the crash. His memory returned to full capacity over time, so gradually that Cody didn't seem to notice. He never remembered of all the minute details of the crash day, but in many respects, he didn't mind at all that every second was not present and accounted for. Cody had enough scars on his body to keep most of the incident all too fresh in his here and now. And besides, his mother told him, the past is the past.

He started to date Denny Clarke openly and affectionately, and she even let him call her Denise on occasion. She learned how to massage his tired legs after long training rides and became a true confidant of his fears and dreams, his almost closest friend.

That privilege remained with Lionel K. Fitzhugh, who learned how to be a first rate bike mechanic and a top notch connoisseur of all music from Elvis to Nelly and everything in between. Mitchell Burke made sure Lionel learned the music of the 60's and 70's, except for disco, which he never mentioned. The three friends became almost inseparable and would have except for the fact that no matter how hard she tried, Denny couldn't set up Lionel with any of her girl friends when she wanted a little time alone with Cody.

Sarah Calhoun and Mitchell Burke became close over the next several months but never quite fell in love. At least not the head-over-heels, gooey-eyed kind that makes you ache inside. Sarah was guarded with her heart, having suffered the ultimate wound from Cody's father. She cherished her time alone where she relished in her independence, and she spent long hours at her job, where she practiced a newfound self-confidence. Mitchell was at times distant, seeming not to want to commit too much more than being close friends. His practice was flourishing and at times he could be seen early in the morning or late at night working with a special patient, paving the road to recovery one exercise at a time. Sarah and Mitchell spent a lot of time together, held hands any chance they got and talked long into the night over late suppers, often staying up later than Cody. But Burke always went home to his remodeled house, declining any invitation to take their relationship to the next big, vulnerable step.

Buck Roddy pleaded guilty to the bombing of Mitchell Burke's garage, but from the advice of his lawyer, threw himself on the mercy of the court. He claimed he had been under a lot of pressure in his life and had been drinking too much. In fact, he didn't remember why on earth he was in Burke's garage in the first place, that he had meant to be in Robert Evers' garage, picking up extra supplies. He must have had an alcohol blackout. The presiding judge believed little of what Buck had confessed to, but his heart and soul had been formed in the 1960s while attending a rather liberal West Coast law school. The judge looked at Buck's record, which wasn't spotless, but none too tarnished compared to the others he saw on a regular basis. He let Buck off easy, six months in an aging white-collar facility just north of Sacramento and an additional 12 months of probation.

CODY RIDES AGAIN

As the summer approached, Cody was glad to put his sophomore year of high school behind him. The basketball injury, the rehab, the bike accident, the bombing. That was a lot of life to pack into one year, even for a resilient boy like Cody Calhoun. He rarely looked back at it and never wondered why it had all happened to him. As soon as school shut down in early June, he slept until noon for eight straight days, getting in his riding later in the day. He figured after such a long year, he deserved a bit of a rest.

When Coach Myers approached him the last day of school and handed him a summer basketball schedule, Cody didn't take it. Just never put out his hand, never offered to accept the coach's invitation to rejoin the team. Cody had missed almost the entire season and all of spring ball, but Coach Myers knew his ability and had always assumed he was part of the Mustangs. But Cody's direction had changed.

He couldn't really pinpoint an exact time when he knew he'd given up basketball. Maybe it was the moment Coach Myers left his room that day in the hospital. Maybe it came upon him more gradually during long training rides in the country when he felt free and most like he figured he should feel about himself. Maybe it was a whole combination of things a 16-year-old can't quite put together, parts of a puzzle that may only be visible in the rear view mirror years later. Cody didn't spend much time worrying about where or when it happened.

The coach didn't put up much of an argument that day, but the hurt and disappointment were apparent in his face. He didn't try to hide his feelings like most coaches do, he wanted Cody to know how much he liked him and respected his ability to play ball. He said if you changed your mind, come and see me and we'll see what we can do about getting you back on the team. No guarantees, mind you, but I realize it's been a tough year on you and maybe you just need time to think about it some more. Call me, keep in touch, OK? I'll be keeping my eye out for you this summer.

But Cody's thinking was done. Time to move on. Time to ride.

The first couple of weeks back in the saddle, Burke stayed away from influencing Cody's training schedule. And it had progressed from bicycle riding to bicycle training. Cody wasn't in it just for the endorphin rush at the end of a long ride or the frequent massages he could coax out of Denny if his legs were hurting. He wanted to compete.

Lionel had picked up on Cody's need for speed - and competition – and encouraged him to talk to Burke. Lionel knew what Mitchell Burke was capable of and he correctly assumed that Burke could teach it to his best bud.

At Cody's request, Burke put him on a vigorous, sometimes grueling training schedule after he determined that Cody's injuries had healed. Each week Burke prepared a list of seven training rides for Cody and emailed it to him and Lionel. Each day Cody rode, rarely taking a day off. Each evening Lionel checked the Cannondale over, washing it at least twice a week from saddle to spoke.

As June turned to July, the weather heated up and the training rides did, too. Cody's drive and determination fueled his desire to improve. Lionel kept immaculate records, downloaded from Cody's cyclecomputer with the wireless connection he'd rigged up, and recorded everything in the laptop. He not only recorded the length and duration of each day's ride, but also things like cadence, average and maximum speed and actual workouts performed. Lionel also devised a way to chart progress in heart rate, body fat, weight, anaerobic threshold and VO2 max.

Denny's role in Cody's training changed, too. She quickly went from a casual observer and an interested party to a constant companion, from tinkering with his food intake to full-time nutritionist. Most riders have an ideal riding weight and work diligently to maintain it, watching their diet microscopically. Cody was, at 16, still growing and putting on weight, but Burke didn't want him to go overboard in watching calories. So Denny watched his diet as best she could. He gradually gave up the junk he liked, including soft drinks and fast food, and incorporated lots of carbohydrates and as much protein as he needed.

Denny also got Cody on to a vigorous stretching program to keep his muscles toned and supple. His thighs, calves, hamstrings and gluts were bulking up under the riding schedule and his other leg and back muscles had to be stretched and strengthened to keep an overall balance. Cody still worked out at Burke's therapy office for upper body strength and conditioning and because he just liked hanging out there.

As the summer progressed Burke encouraged Cody to ride at the outside velodrome in San Jose, one of the few outside tracks still operating in the United States. Cody entered the amateur races to build his balance, sprint speed, endurance and competitiveness. Burke also knew he'd meet other young men his age and older who had a burning passion for two-wheelers. It didn't take Cody long to figure out how to ride the special track bikes that didn't have gears or brakes and once he did, he start winning races on the banked course. He also found fellow compatriots to ride with during training who pushed him to ride harder and faster.

These seasoned riders were different from the boys in The Triple Bees. They were serious about their sport and many had dreams of turning professional. Some, like Cody, had sponsors who helped them with everything from equipment to race entry fees to traveling expenses. As they rode with Cody they taught him the techniques of drafting, cornering, sprinting and climbing. And they taught him how to be tough, tougher than he ever imagined he could be. They didn't take many days off and they rarely rode anyway other than hard and fast. On the rare occasion that Cody didn't ride with who he began to refer to as simply "The Boys," he wondered what ride they were doing that day.

The Boys always tackled the tougher climbs surrounding the Bay Area. In a three-week span in August they conquered Mount Hamilton, Mount Diablo, Mount Tamalpais and all the smaller hills from Santa Cruz to San Francisco. A typical day's ride was anywhere from 45 to 85 miles at a pace that would drive lesser riders out of the group. But Cody hung tough and on days that he couldn't keep up, The Boys waited for him at designated stops.

Cody began to build a bond with this group of freewheelers, but it was different than The Triple Bees or Lionel or other friends he'd had over the years. These young men were single-minded and focused. They rarely spoke about anything but bikes and rides. They were friendly, but they didn't make lasting friendships with other riders in the group. Someday they knew they'd be competing against one another and they didn't want to let a friendship get in the way of kicking somebody's butt up and down the highway.

Although local bike races had been dwindling in California over the past decade or so, probably because of the dwindling economy, Cody did manage to find several to compete in during the summer. He worked his way up from the beginning Category 5 designation, quickly moving to Cat 4, Cat 3 and Cat 2. By the time he reached Cat 2 status, most of the races were between 25 or 50-mile competitions over a designated one-mile loop through downtowns. Some were associated with craft shows or bike extravaganzas or other attractions to get people out enjoying themselves and spending money. During each race there were always prize laps that offered rewards more than the typical medals and trophies, anything from wristwatches to cycling gear. Cody always managed to come away from these races with something: cash prizes, gift certificates, clothes and always respect from the other riders. He always rode hard and fair; he built up a reputation in the state as a rider to be reckoned with. He just didn't know when his reckoning would come.

Mitchell Burke, however, did.

It came with a professional bike race called the San Francisco Grand Prix, an annual event that snaked its way through what the chamber of commerce called "the most beautiful city in the world." Between 75 and 100 pro riders came to San Francisco each fall after the European riding season to battle the 125-mile course, which was laced with killer climbs and enthusiastic fans. The cyclists rode a ten-mile loop ten times, then a different five-mile loop five times. The longer loop traversed up Filbert Street, one of the steepest hills in the city, and Broadway Street, another long climb. The smaller loop was nestled close to the bay and the financial district and was flatter and faster.

Burke knew the promoters of the race, old cronies from his days on the circuit. They had planned a preliminary race before the main Grand Prix with up and coming cyclists as a showcase for the Junior USA cycling team. Most of the riders have proven themselves over the past year and were slated to join the Junior Men's team, made up of 17- and 18-year-olds, the following spring in Colorado. A few slots in the riding field were open to invitation and Burke had pulled a few strings and twisted a few arms to secure one for Cody. The preliminary race would take place early in the morning before the professional riders hit the streets of San Francisco and cover only 25 miles.

Burke, Cody and the entourage of Denny and Lionel met in the city the week before the race to look at the course. They drove each of the loops a half dozen times early one morning, looking at all the obstacles and learning the course. Burke had seen the race the past two years and took the lead on strategy.

"It's gonna be a sprint, no doubt about it. Only 25 miles, twice on the big loop and once on the little loop," he said as they parked his SUV and stared up Filbert Street.

Cody gaped up at the long climb in front of him. The hill consisted of three separate climbs, each separated by a small plateau, just wide enough to let a cross street intersect.

Burke saw the look in his eye. "Yeah, it's steep. About an 18% grade, which means if you stop pedaling, you fall over backwards."

"Dude, keep pedaling," Lionel offered.

"Great strategy, thanks," Cody said back.

"Suck air into all those little aureoles in your lungs," Lionel offered.

"In the pro race, you'll see the riders take this hill strong the first two or three laps, then start to back off and traverse it," Burke said, zigzagging his arm back and forth to mimic how a snake moves to explain the technique of riding across the hill during the climb to reduce the steepness.

"But for two climbs, I suggest you go straight up," he

continued. "Go as fast as you can, try and stay with the leaders and don't let up once you hit the crest. These guys are in shape and they're going to try and drop you by powering up the hills and keeping the pace up on the downhills and flats."

Cody nodded in acknowledgement but just kept staring up the monster hill. Denny grabbed his hand and squeezed her encouragement, almost like trying to will her strength into him by passing it through their hands. He didn't let go.

"We'll be in radio contact with you through the ear piece, but they're not going to allow support vehicles to follow the riders," Burke explained, "so if you get a flat, you're out of the race."

Lionel made a note to remember to put some sealant into Cody's tires to add a little more protection against flat tires.

"So the strategy is…," Cody asked.

"Do your best, that's the strategy. These guys are veterans for their age, but you are, too. You don't have all the races like they do behind you, but I'll put you up against anybody," Burke said.

"Stay with the leaders and never back off. You can rest after the race," he continued. "Try and stay close to the front, but don't try to drop anybody until the final lap. If you've got it in you the last two to three miles, jump on it and drive to the finish line. Last year's pro race was decided by less than twenty yards and that was after 125 miles. So this could come down to a sprint over the last 100 yards."

"Old buddy, let me summarize," Lionel expounded. "Balls to the wall, take no prisoners. It's time to pump…you up," he said in his best imitation of Dana Carvey on Saturday Night Live.

"Let's do it," was all Cody said. But the stare had turned to steel.

FILBERT

Race day broke cloudy and cool, normal for just about any day in San Francisco. Burke had sprung for a room at the Hyatt for himself, Cody and Lionel, to prevent them from getting up in the middle of the night and making the long drive into the city in the morning. Race time was 7:00 am with warm ups beforehand.

Denny and Sarah knocked on the hotel door at 5:30 with breakfast, but Cody wasn't asleep. He hadn't slept much at all during the night. Adrenaline, nerves, excitement all mixed together.

Lionel had insisted that the Cannondale spend the night in the Hyatt, too, and it did, tucked nicely in the corner of the room, not too far from where Lionel slept. He resisted cleaning it again, you'll rub the paint off it for goodness sakes the other two said, but he was up early wiping it down with a towel.

As the group walked to the starting area, the sun was just peeking over the bay waters and the streets were already bustling. A helicopter circled above, no doubt getting some early morning footage for one of the local TV stations, who were setting up their broadcast booths and going through their feed checks and sound checks. Other booths serving food and drink were coming alive – booths for energy bars, sports drinks, bike shops and even local charities. Saturn, the carmaker and official sponsor of the event, was putting the finishing touches on their display adjacent to the grandstands. Foot traffic was light but Burke assured everyone that by the time this preliminary race was over, people would be jamming the start line and several key spots along the route. Motorcycles seemed to be everywhere, those that were clearing the streets in anticipation of the race, and also including policemen patrolling and spectators getting a feel for the route the easy way. Bicyclists seemed to multiply right before his eyes. Mostly they were just riding around taking in the sites, showing off their speed and style, enjoying the festivities.

Cody noticed a huge TV screen just in front of the starting line, no doubt ready to broadcast the main race. An announcer stood on a podium, stuttering a single word repeatedly, check, check, check, check. Metal waist high barricades were already in place, cordoning off the start area, the grandstands and leading off down the street, taking a sharp left-hand turn, standing quietly like silent sentries ready for the battle to commence.

As he warmed up on the city streets close to the start/finish line, Cody did his best to avoid the cable car tracks while at the same time checking out the competition. Most riders were faceless warriors, with their helmets and reflective sunglasses covering any emotion. Their bikes were mostly expensive models that looked brand new and their clothing was colorful and plastered with sponsorships. The pink outfits of the Saturn sponsored riders stood out like flamingos on steroids.

Burke had given Cody a new outfit the day before fashioned after the Scottish flag. The white jersey had a large rectangle in the front and back in dark sky blue with a large white X centered in it. Matching blue shorts and socks completed the look. Gotta dig down deep into your Scottish heritage today, my boy, he had said with a slight Scottish brogue. Even though the weather was chilly, around 55 degrees, Cody wore only the short sleeve jersey during warm-ups. A cup of coffee, a pre-race caffeine ritual with many riders, had both warmed him up and added to his jitters.

As Cody warmed up, Burke, Lionel and Denny tested the audio system they would use to keep in touch with him. Burke had decided long ago that he'd limit his instructions to mostly encouragement, so after their sound checks were complete, Lionel took the liberty of pumping a little music to Cody to psyche him up. He chose the Bachman Turner Overdrive song that Burke had used during his Tour days.

You get up every morning to the alarm clock's warning,
Take the eight fifteen into the city,
There's a whistle up above
People push and people shove,

And all the girls are trying to look pretty.

Cody didn't seem to mind; he'd heard the song a couple of times before and it sure did have a driving beat that got him going. He was ready.

An announcement was made for the riders to gather at the start line. Instructions were broadcast and everyone acknowledged the motorcycle with the large American flag blowing proudly from the rear seat that would be the pace car, leading the riders through the course. A second pace vehicle, a Saturn VUE would follow the motorcycle, giving Saturn its money's worth for sponsorship. It was also filled with four pre-selected teenagers whose sole job was waving their arms out the windows and using a loudspeaker to get the gathering crowd enthusiastic for the riders. Cody noticed that the gathering crowd hadn't quite gathered for the preliminary race and wondered if their arms would be tired after the 125-mile circuit. Realizing that actually helped him relax, knowing he didn't have to do the whole 125. Only 25 big ones, baby, let's do it!

Twenty five riders plus Cody lined up single file across Embarcadero Street, one shoe latched into a pedal, one on the street, heads all down in concentration. Riders ready! Then, bang, the starting gun. Burke had warned Cody about the start, to stay back, to start slow, to stay out of trouble. It wouldn't be the first time during the race that Cody would ignore his advice. He bolted toward the front, jostled by several riders, almost going down, but managed to keep his balance by pushing off the rider to his right with his hand. The rider shouted at him but a "steady, steady" coming from Burke into his right ear drowned out most everything else.

He rounded the first hairpin turn mixed in the lead pack, but all the riders were tightly bunched behind him.

The city was just beginning to wake. Saturday morning walkers and coffee hunters glanced at the pack of riders with curiosity. Several spectators, who had already secured their spots along the route with lawn chairs and coolers, looked up from the morning papers to watch. Several people hung out second or third story windows to gawk. Small cafe and restaurant owners were starting to place tables and chairs on the sidewalks. Business would be brisk today.

Most wondered who these riders were, knowing that the main event didn't start until nine o'clock. The Saturn pace car had a small sign on each door announcing the race, Under 18 Junior Men's Invitational, but it was hard to see and most people weren't looking at the car, they were looking at the riders.

The pack stayed bunched as they snaked their way through the first several miles, looking like a school of fish or a flock of birds, all moving in unison, communicating by some unknown force. Cody stayed near the front, still operating mostly on adrenaline, amazed at the speed and power of the riders. He never wondered if the adrenaline would run out, he was too thrilled to be in the hunt.

Burke communicated with him, asking him for readings off the cyclo-computer, like miles per hour and revolutions per minute to get a sense of the pace of the ride. Cody also conveyed heart rate from the monitor strapped to his body, but he was having a hard time relating to the information. That was Burke's job. Cody's was to ride and listen to the instructions.

In such a small group there weren't many riders on the same team so the pack worked together, changing leadership every couple of hundred yards or so, to cut the wind for the other riders. But the pace was relentless. The strong riders would stay near the front, as Burke had predicted. Near the end of the race, in the last lap or so, the pack mentality would disintegrate and it would be every man for himself, hell bent for the finish line. Cody aimed to be in that lead group.

As Cody relayed the information back to Burke, Lionel entered it into the laptop to compare against their preset goals. They noticed Cody's heart rate was elevated, but decided to give him time to settle into the pace. Maybe it would come down. At this rate, would he have the stamina to compete for 25 miles?

Cody didn't notice. He was too busy trying to stay with the group and stay out of trouble. The streets of San Francisco were well maintained, but a series of tracks from cable cars and electric transit buses crisscrossed the avenues like waffle patterns gone berserk. If you weren't careful your tire could get caught in a groove. It would be a quick and painful fall and an early exit from the race.

In the back of his mind and a mile up ahead, the Filbert hill loomed.

Two blocks from Filbert, Cody bolted in front with another rider, both to take his turn in the lead and to be in a prime position for the ascent. As they rounded Kearny Street, Cody could almost feel the power in the group as the riders all jumped out of their saddle as if commanded. He heard the shift of gears and grunts and grimaces as they drove up the first section of the monster hill.

By the third section, the pace had dramatically slowed, steely determination had taken over and the only sounds were hard breathing and pedals cranking. A few solo shouts of encouragement came from the small crowd of onlookers. Cody felt like his lungs would burst. He sucked down hard into his chest to find air, but each time he tried to dig deep, his next breath would come too quickly. His thighs burned with a fire from knee to hip. He didn't dare lean back to put more weight over the pedals for fear he'd fall over backwards, so he shifted his torso lower and moved his butt back over the saddle to search for more power in his hamstrings.

He'd fallen behind six or seven riders as they crested the hill, but somewhere deep inside his mind, which desperately was crying for relief, he remembered Burke's instruction. Push over the hill, stay close.

He pushed and said a small blessing for all the treks up Sherburne Hill.

The lead riders were accelerating down the hill and Cody followed, taking huge, deep breaths and blowing out hard in an attempt to regain his breathing. As he closed the gap between his position and the lead, he experienced a huge surge in confidence, like a second wind sweeping him up from behind and catapulting him along. He flew down the hill with the knowledge he belonged. He could keep up. He could *win* this race!

For the next several miles, Cody stayed aggressive, taking the downhills with increasing speed and staying tight in the corners. The riders began to bunch up again until they hit

Broadway. It was steep and long but not as bad as Filbert and Cody hung with the lead pack. A sharp left at the top of Broadway took them through a perilous journey of hairpin turns all at speeds close to thirty miles per hour.

Cody relayed vital statistics back to Burke and the others but there weren't too many corrections they could make or suggestions they could offer. His heart rate was too high, but if he backed off now, nearly a third of the way through the race, he may not be able to catch up. His RPMs were high, too, but the same held true there. Burke decided to let Cody run his own race for the most part. The riders crossed the start/finish line and the small group of supporters for all the riders cheered.

Cody was feeling strong and confident, so he pushed out in front again to try and put some distance between himself and a small group of riders who surged to the front. He opened up a twenty five-yard lead heading back to Filbert Street, where the crowd was a little bigger than before. He rose from his saddle and powered up the first hill, sitting down for only seconds on the plateau, then stood up again for the second hill, down again and up again. The last hill almost depleted his breath but he pushed over the top and headed downhill in the lead.

He tried to keep the lead through the winding streets heading toward Broadway, but the more experienced riders caught him and bunched again at the foot of the hill. Cody powered up, trying to drop them and surged over the crest in the lead again, but again within a mile, the twelve riders forming the lead group clustered together again.

Burke was right, this was going to come down to a sprint.

Of the twenty-five riders that began the race, as mile eighteen approached, only three had dropped out (both on the second lap at Filbert), twelve were bunched in the front and the remainder strung out over several hundred yards behind them.

As Cody crossed the start/finish line again, he looked directly at Burke and nodded, like a silent communication, some unknown signal. Burke nodded back and gave two thumbs up, which was the most encouragement he had to give. It was all up to Cody now. Burke knew he could no longer help the boy.

The last five-mile loop was mostly flat, virtually a circle

with lots of left turns. Cody's legs were burning but he figured everybody else had burning legs, too. The friendly chatter through the first twenty miles vanished and the riders became silent. They continually looked to the right and to the left, then back over their shoulders to see who was behind. Paranoia crept in (who is going to catch me) and adrenaline pumped stronger (maybe nobody). They lost track of onlookers and instructions in the ear and concentrated only on the route and the plastic flag rope that outlined the course.

Cody was behind two riders when they hit the twenty four-mile mark. He made his move just before a sharp left-hand turn. He downshifted and jumped out of his saddle, sprinting wide right and passing them at the curve. If he calculated right, the other riders may not have seen his burst. He quickly surged ahead by ten yards before the other two riders reacted. Now all three were sprinting and as the rest of the group rounded the turn, they all jumped and pumped. It was a frenzy to the finish line!

Cody had a fifteen-yard lead and tried to concentrate on pedal stroke and form, pull up and push down, pull up and push down, breathe, don't sway back and forth, stay down close to the saddle, breathe, pull up and push down.

As they rounded the last turn, two hundred yards straight to the finish line, the lead held. Cody's form was perfect, his breath solid, his strokes strong. Could he win it? Could he push across the line?

In the last hundred yards, six riders passed him. He was stunned. He finished seventh.

As the riders coasted down the Embarcadero, he hung his head and tried to regain his composure. A small crowd of people now filled the street and he had to weave his way through. Finally it became too crowded and he stopped. Strangers patted him on the back and looked for the winner. He felt terrible - a combination of losing, the exertion of the ride, the crowd of strangers. He almost threw up but managed to keep it down. He reached for his water bottle but couldn't drink. He drifted to the side of the road before he recognized a familiar voice.

"Brilliant, brilliant!" said Lionel almost at the top of his lungs as he hugged Cody hard. "One hell of a race, one h – e –

double hell of a race!"

"In case you missed it, I lost," Cody managed through gritted teeth.

"But you were right there, dude, a few yards away, just a few measly yards away."

"A miss is as good as a mile," again Cody said with dejection.

"Not quite," Mitchell Burke corrected, his face all smiles. Denny jogged up, too, and gave him a big hug and kiss, patting the sweat on his face with a towel. His mom had to fight through the others for a hug and a high five.

Burke got close to his face and the others gathered in tight, too. "You rode a great race, Cody," he said, holding both shoulders and looking directly into his eyes. "We're all very, very proud of you. Actually, you did much better than I ever thought possible. These guys are close to world-class status for their age and you held your own. You took it to them, never backed down, pushed the pace. You only lost it in the last sprint, and that's certainly nothing to be ashamed of. We can work on sprints. But today, young man, you showed the heart – and legs - of a champion."

Cody breathed deep and his chest swelled a little as he tried to take in the accolades. But somewhere deep down, beneath a smile that gradually crept onto his face, he knew seventh place didn't feel anywhere as good as first place. He looked over at the young man who won the race. A throng of well-wishers and a horde of cameraman surrounded him. Even in a preliminary race like this, the crowd loves a winner, Cody thought. He wanted to remember how he felt at this moment, because he didn't want to feel this way again.

After the commotion of the post-race hoopla calmed down, they all headed back to pack their gear in Burke's SUV. Cody snacked on sandwiches Denny made. Don't ask what else was in them, but the turkey was recognizable. He slipped inside the SUV and changed from his cycling gear, emerging in sweatpants and a new, hooded red Stanford sweatshirt his mother had given him to celebrate the race. Deep down she was still hoping he'd go there someday.

Burke was parked close to the action surrounding the starting line, having moved the SUV the night before. He was adjacent to the truck talking to several men Cody didn't recognize.

"Cody, come over here for a second," Burke asked, motioning him over to the small group.

"I'd like you to meet Mack McClelland, head of the U.S. Cycling team. Mack, this is Cody Calhoun."

"Nice to meet you, sir," Cody said, sticking out his hand.

"Son, the pleasure is all mine. And might I add, that was one fine race you rode today. Thought for a minute you might pull off the upset."

"Me, too."

"I suppose Burkie will have you working on sprints before the day's out."

Burkie? Everyone thought, Burkie?

"Maybe tomorrow," Cody countered.

"Son, I'd like to extend an invitation to you. There's a qualifying race in Las Cruces, New Mexico in three weeks. A two-day race to determine the junior national team. Now, I gotta admit, most of the slots are penciled in and you sure are long shot at this point. Not even on the radar screen before today. But you turned some heads. And Burkie here says you got what it takes. And I trust his judgement. So if you're willing to come to New Mexico, no guarantees mind you, we'll let you race for a spot on next year's team. Whatya say?

Cody looked to his mom for a split second for verification that he could go.

"Go for it," she mouthed to him.

"Absolutely!" Cody beamed.

High fives, hugs and kisses all around. McClelland gave Burke the details and some paperwork to fill out, while the others pulled lawn chairs from the SUV, sat down and started to plan the trip. Cody was adamant that his mom, Lionel and Denny join him. Denny popped open a chilled bottle of Martinelli's apple juice and little plastic champagne glasses to celebrate.

Four days in Las Cruces to make the junior national team. Maybe I'd better work on those sprints this afternoon after all,

Cody thought. Sprints and maybe a few hills, too.

SANSKRIT

After the excitement of the San Francisco Grand Prix wore off, Team Calhoun, as Lionel christened it, got down to work.

Burke upped Cody's training schedule and luckily, Cody was given special permission from the principal at his high school to begin his training day during sixth period, which would have been his regular physical education class. Sarah Calhoun and Mitchell Burke met with the principal to explain the once in a lifetime opportunity for Cody and when she understood that Cody's training was about a hundred times more physical than any high school gym class, not surprisingly, she agreed and let him leave school at 1:45 in the afternoon.

Cody's training was packed with endurance, distance and sprinting work, not necessarily in that order. He tackled it with gusto. His taste of competition in San Francisco whetted his appetite for more and he literally exuded excitement. It was contagious. Lionel began his quest to lighten the Cannondale for the Las Cruces race and he scrubbed down the bike every evening after Cody rode. Denny carefully measured Cody's calorie intake three times a day. Her goal was to drop Cody's weight by two pounds by race day without any effect on his performance. The laptop hummed continuously, updating everything from length of training rides to heartbeat and weight. Sarah Calhoun became the travel agent, booking flights, a rental van, and hotel arrangements.

Although Mitchell Burke was an integral part of the team, he felt somewhat distant from the enthusiasm that engulfed everyone else. He talked with Cody each evening after the ride, working on strategy and giving Cody as much background on the race and the riders as he could. But he knew the disappointment firsthand of failure at such a high level – and the competition was stiff – so he tried to downplay expectations. Stay steady, work hard, put yourself in a good position to succeed were his buzzwords, nothing about winning the race and securing a spot on the team.

There would only be twenty racers traveling to Las Cruces. The Junior National Bicycling Team had twelve slots to fill, so eight riders would go home without an invitation to the team. Burke figured out who most of the riders were through web site information, race results, and conversations with Mack McClelland. The head of the U.S. Cycling team was candid with Burke and the chances Cody had to make the team. They were slim but not zero. McClelland liked what he saw in San Francisco and was always on the lookout for untapped, raw talent. He had requested Cody's training logs and studied them with a trained eye. He knew Burke's regimen of aerobic and anaerobic training and his skill at molding young riders.

But McClelland also saw the real disgust and dismay Cody displayed at losing the preliminary Grand Prix. His keen eye saw a determination in the young cyclist that couldn't always be traced back to training logs and single race results.

Burke had determined that Cody and the crew should spend at least two days before the race training in Las Cruces. He knew that all the racers would be riding the same model bike, Trek 5200's, so Cody would need a day or two to get used to the bike – and it wouldn't hurt to train in the altitude and atmosphere of New Mexico. Just being there would elevate the excitement for Cody and motivate him even more, if that was possible.

As the excitement grew for the team, Mitchell Burke slid further into a funk. He became more critical of Cody's riding performances and his unwillingness to stay strictly to schedule, even if Cody missed a heart rate goal in an afternoon ride. He asked Lionel to turn the music down almost constantly and seemed to snap back at all the novice questions Denny asked about the race. He was affecting the usually upbeat, vibrant mood of the team. Sarah Calhoun finally approached him.

She asked for him to go for a walk with her a week before the team was to leave for New Mexico.

"Mitchell, is there something bothering you?" she asked

as they strolled.

"What do you mean?" he responded defensively.

"I mean just that. You almost bit my head off earlier for asking you a simple question. And you've been really irritable for the past week."

"I'm sorry," he said as he stopped walking, grabbed her hand (she had noticed they weren't holding hands from the beginning of the walk), and looked directly in her eyes. "You're right, I'm sure. I guess I'm just nervous for Cody, that's all."

"But you're the coach, you can't let it show. I'm sure he's nervous enough for all of us, but don't you think it's up to us to try to make this as fun as possible?"

"I don't want his expectations to be so high, that if he's not chosen, he'll come crashing down to earth."

"Mitchell Burke, you know Cody better than that. He won't crash. He'll be disappointed but goodness, he's not even 17 yet, he'll get over it, probably in a day or two. He's the most resilient boy I've ever known."

"You're right, you're right, absolutely," he said.

They walked on in silence, still holding hands, but Burke still seemed distant.

After another block or so, she asked again, "There's something more, isn't there?"

After a deep breath, he responded, "I haven't treated you very well lately, have I, Sarah?"

"We've both been busy, lots of things on our plates…" her voice trailed off.

"I'm sorry, I should have treated you better than that. You deserve better than that. Maybe you deserve better than me."

A tear came to her eye, "I never really felt I had you, Mitchell. You always seemed just close enough to touch, but never close enough to grab hold of."

He nodded his agreement, but said nothing, like it was a foregone conclusion.

"Now you're supposed to say," she sniffled, "how different it will be and how you'll do better and how you're sure we'll continue to grow closer as time goes by."

He turned and looked at her again, stunned that he hadn't

even noticed that she was crying. "Oh, Sarah, I didn't know, I thought, well, I didn't know what to think."

"Me neither, Mitchell. I didn't know if I was just leaning on you for support, especially when it came to Cody, or whether it was growing into something much more."

"I'm a little hard to read, aren't I?"

"Sometimes like Sanskrit." She managed a smile and wiped away another tear.

"I didn't know if you wanted to get close, Sarah. You seemed to be handling your life so well on your own, you're so independent and you do such a good job raising Cody. You just always seemed to have it all together. Sometimes I felt like I was intruding on the two of you."

Now Sarah nodded, "You're probably right. I'm very protective. Of him, and of me. It's only been the two of us for so long."

And it's only been the one of me for so long, Burke thought.

"But I never knew what you were thinking, Mitchell, I mean about you and me."

"I guess I didn't want to get carried away and start thinking that there was something possible for us."

"Why?"

He wanted to tell her everything, but something held him back. He shrugged his shoulders. "I guess I was afraid."

"Of what?"

"Of having it go wrong."

"There aren't any certainties in the world, especially when it comes to people and feelings and emotion. But you never know the possibilities unless you try. Sorry…that sounded too much…like a bad TV movie script."

They had stopped walking and found themselves in the park near Burke's home. They found a bench and sat down, both looking out at the park. Burke was quiet, introspective.

"There you go with that whole Sanskrit thing again," Sarah said, waving her hand in front of his vacant eyes.

"I really do think Cody has all the potential in the world to be a phenomenal racer, I really do."

"I know that, but you haven't told him in a while."

"I don't want him to be disappointed."

"I think he'd be disappointed if you didn't tell him. If he loses, he'll deal with that. But he trusts you a lot. More than anyone in a long time. He needs to hear that you trust him, too. He needs to hear that you care, Mitchell."

"Oh, Sarah, I do, you know that."

"Do I? Does he? People can't read minds, you know, Mitchell."

"Which means you can't read minds, either, can you?"

She shook her head, thinking she'd almost given up trying.

As a cool breeze snuck up on them, Sarah shivered. Burke put his arm around her to keep her warm.

"There's a lot about me you don't know, Sarah."

"I'm willing to learn."

"Some of it you may not like."

"Why don't you let me be the judge of that."

He nodded, "OK, I suppose we'd better start with my medical history." She inched closer, all ears.

Burke had called a team meeting for later that evening at his home. Sarah planned to provide dinner after Cody's training ride and go over their itinerary. Burke wanted to emphasize each team member's role during the trip.

They all gathered in Burke's dining room over spaghetti and meatballs, a pasta feed pre-approved by Denny for its high carbohydrate mix. Lionel had selected a Sammy Hagar album, *Red*, for the pre-dinner soundtrack, but Sarah Calhoun asked him to tone it down a bit over the meal. After Led Zeppelin and The J. Geils Band were rejected by almost everyone except Burke, Sarah stepped in and selected Three Dog Night's *Suitable for Framing*.

> *How can people be so heartless?*
> *How can people be so cruel?*
> *Easy to be hard*
> *Easy to say no.*

Sarah began with the flight times, "OK, so we all are leaving Tuesday afternoon from Oakland on Southwest at 4:50, which means you three will be in school on Tuesday."

Groans all around.

"We'll pick you up at school at 2:30, the bags will already be in Mitchell's SUV. That will get us into Las Cruces at 10:34, find the hotel, get a good night's sleep. Then training starts the next morning, right?" she said looking toward Burke.

"Right, we'll train long and hard on Wednesday, much lighter on Thursday, then race on Friday and Saturday. Fly home on Sunday. Everyone's job revolves around Cody this trip. You get to be the star, man," he said, pointing at Cody with a smile on his face. "We make sure he gets enough sleep – right, Lionel, no late night movies, OK? – gets enough good food to eat, and gets plenty of enthusiasm and support." The last statement he looked directly at Sarah with a wink of the eye only the two of them could see.

Again, directly at Cody, "Nervous?"

"Yeah, a little," Cody admitted.

"Good, you should be, a little I mean. That's normal. You'll be able to use that nervousness and convert it over to adrenaline. Don't worry about it. Do you have any questions about the course?"

"Not really. I think I got it."

But Burke reviewed it one more time for the group's benefit. He and Cody had gone over it at least a half dozen times already. The first day would be long and hard with lots of elevation. The San Andres Mountains east of the city would play a prominent part in the day's ride of 112 miles. The riders would traverse up and down two separate passes in the mountains during the day and finish at the top of a third pass. There was no doubt it would be grueling and deep down Burke figured that at least a couple of riders would not finish the day.

The second day would be split in two, a 20 mile time trial in the morning and a 58 mile trek in the afternoon west of the city that followed the fabled Rio Grande River. The cumulative scores in the three rides would determine the top 12 finishers. After an evaluation period of a few weeks, offers would go out to the riders for the national team.

After he reviewed the ride and spent a half-hour going over the competition from notes he gathered in a spiral notebook, Burke looked up at the faces of Team Calhoun. It looked like they were in a state of shock, all but Cody. Sarah's face expressed the pain she knew Cody would endure. Denny's was all full of sympathy as it often was. Lionel's eyes were wide, like he wasn't quite sure human beings were capable of all this physical torture. Burke knew the time was right.

"Look, all of you, look at me. It will be hard, no doubt about it. But it won't be dangerous. This young man is physically ready to compete at this level. I'm very confident of that. Sure, the competition will be stiff. But you are all looking at a young athlete that is gifted," Burke said as all eyes drifted to Cody, who looked away.

"He's gifted in many ways. He's got the perfect body for a cyclist." Lionel raised one arm, made a fist, and pumped his bicep in a mock pose of strength.

"He is perfectly proportioned, height, weight and strength. He has an amazing capability of converting breath to fuel, the oxygen he needs to run the machine. His knee is 100% - even more, 110% - and his legs are strong. Mentally, he is beyond his years. His concentration, the ability to block out distractions, like pain for instance, is solid. And he's in shape, top shape. And that's not to be taken lightly. There will be riders next weekend that are not ready for this kind of test. They haven't put in the miles, they haven't done the work. They may think they have and their coach may think they have, but trust me, they don't know."

Here Sarah caught Burke's eye and leaned forward with a slight nod of her head, as if to say go ahead, say the rest. Burke hesitated.

"And why is that, Mitchell, that they don't know and you do?" Sarah asked in veiled innocence. Lionel's eyes widened and he took a deep breath in. All eyes shifted to Burke.

"Been there, done that," he mumbled, barely audible.

"No pass, please expound," Sarah retaliated.

Lionel softly hummed the theme song to the TV show

Jeopardy. Da-da-dum-da, da-da-dum, da-da-dum-da, *dum*, da-da-da-da-dum.

"OK, Lionel, go get the scrapbook," Burke relented.

"Allrighty then," Lionel said as he bounded out of his chair and headed to the little white box hidden away in the garage. He returned quickly and laid the book on the dining room table. He flipped open the book to the photograph he had discovered many months ago, the secret he had kept.

Lionel pointed to the photo as he turned the book toward Cody and Denny. "Been there, done that," he said, all proud of himself for knowing the secret and for Burke's accomplishments, too.

"He told me already," Cody said with little emotion.

"He told you?" Lionel asked.

"Told you what?" Denny wondered.

"That he was a pro racer in the Tour de France," Cody answer. "Yeah, he told me." "Am I the only who doesn't know?" Denny asked, looking at Cody, then his mother, then Lionel.

Burke looked around, then nodded.

"Lionel discovered it quite by accident. Actually by sticking his nose where it didn't belong. I swore him to secrecy, but he wasn't able to keep it from Cody. I told Sarah this afternoon."

"I still don't see why it was such a big secret? Why were you hiding it? I would think you'd want to tell the world," Cody asked.

"I wanted to have people know and trust me on what I accomplished day to day, not what I did twenty years ago."

"Yeah...I guess I can understand that, but...why hide it from the people that you're close to?"

"I guess for most of the same reasons. When...you accomplish something...in the past, people want to talk about it even though it's very old news. Like a rock star that has a hit in the 60s and he's still parading around singing it today. People want to hear it, but the song gets old to the singer, so old he can't bear to sing it anymore."

"Like Paul Revere and the Raiders singing Kicks," Lionel

chimed in. "Man, how can they sing that song so many times?"

"Kinda like that. But at least Paul Revere is still a singer. I'm not a biker anymore. I run a business, I heal people and make them better. I want to stand on that, not on something I did in the mountains of France so many years ago. Can you understand that, man?" Burke said to Cody.

"I can understand that part. What I can't understand is the part where you don't tell us..." Cody replied, thinking all the time, do we even know you? Do we know who you are? "I mean I thought we were tight."

"We are."

"I guess not as tight as I thought," Cody said and turned away toward Denny.

Sarah stepped into the conversation. "Cody, he's telling all of us now, you know. It's a step in the right direction. Sometimes it takes a while for people to get to know people. And trust them. Maybe Mitchell's trust had been betrayed in the past, too, just like yours." Here Cody gave her a don't go there look. "And now he knows all of us – and trusts us – with some of the secrets in his life."

Cody softened a bit and looked into his mother's eyes. He saw nothing but honesty and trust there and that she was saying, maybe you need to cut this man a little slack.

"You know," she continued, "men are not particularly known for opening up their hearts and expressing their feelings. Sometimes that's the woman's job, she's built better for that." Sarah snuck a quick look at Denny and smiled.

"Whatever," Cody mumbled.

"Exactly my point," Sarah smiled. She nodded to Mitchell.

He took the prod. "Cody, I never meant to hurt you, or your mom. Or you either, Denny. In hindsight, it was probably a mistake not to tell you all. But you have to realize...I didn't do anything really special. I rode in the Tour de France, sure, but I didn't win it or anything. I won a stage, big deal. Lots of guys won stages and never even finished the race. They are a footnote in the history books. Yesterday's news."

"Besides," he continued, "a coach has to hold something

back to use as motivation just before the big race."

"Like Knute Rockne's win one for the Gipper speech, right?" Lionel blurted.

They all nodded in unison, except for Denny who didn't know the reference. The mood lightened noticeably.

Sarah nodded again to him, giving him encouragement to go on.

"Cody, Springsteen wrote a song called Glory Days, about guys living on what they'd accomplished in the past. I never wanted to be like that. I always set my sights on what I could accomplish in the future. Maybe to a fault. I now know you can have pride in what you've done as long as you're working on something new."

"Makes sense," Cody managed.

"Now it's your time."

Cody looked up, facing him.

"My time is past, but your time is now. Right now. You're ready. It's not like this time will never come again, you'll have tons of opportunities in the future, you're that good. But this time is special. And you're prime for it. You've done the training, the work. You've put in the miles. Now, all that's left is to go for it. Grab hold. Kick some butt. Take no prisoners."

"But enjoy the ride. Don't fear it, win or lose, it can only make you stronger. Be nervous, that's fine, that's normal. But go into the race with a devil may care attitude. Don't let anything stop you. Even when you're body says quit, don't. Push on."

"And remember, we all love you here. One race doesn't make a man. I found that out the hard way in some respects. Come Sunday evening I want us all to say, that was one hell of a weekend. I wouldn't have traded the experience for anything, OK?"

"OK, just no group hugs," Cody said with a slight smile.

Sarah walked over to Burke and grabbed his hand in hers. She leaned close. "That was a good start, Mitchell."

"Meaning…what?…that you're proud of me for letting my feelings out but not quite giving me the Oprah award for sharing every intimate detail?"

"Something like that."

"I didn't think it was the time to tell him everything."

"If not now, when will it be the time?"

He shrugged, "Don't exactly know. Don't know when the time will be right or how to say it."

"Just don't wait too long, it will only make it harder," she said, squeezing his hand before letting go to join the others searching for dessert.

LAS CRUCES, NEW MEXICO

Wednesday morning sped by full of emotion and excitement. Cody, Lionel and Denny went to school only in body, their spirit lost in anticipation of a whirlwind weekend. A small article had appeared in the paper earlier in the week about Cody's chance to make the national team and his morning was a constant stream of well-wishers, back slaps and high fives.

Lionel and Denny were mostly all business. Lionel had a check-off list of everything he needed to take with him to New Mexico that he had checked off at least twenty times. Each time he scanned the list for what he might have missed. After all, he thought, a list was only as good as the person making it. If he forgot to add something to the list, no matter how many times he checked, it wouldn't be there.

Denny was almost giddy. She had accumulated a huge duffel bag full of her special supplements and foods - enough for at least two weeks - that she was planning to carry on the airplane with her. She even packed the blender. Not wanting to trust that she could locate something vital in Las Cruces at the last moment, she stuffed everything imaginable in the bag. But she also knew she would be walking a tightrope in New Mexico. Burke had told her one of her jobs was to help Cody relax, both in mind and body. Not only would her massage skills come to bear, but because of her budding relationship with Cody, she would be called upon to lighten his mood, to take his mind off the pressure of performing. But Burke had also told her that Cody had to focus. Focus on the race and what he had to do, focus on pulling everything out of himself that he could, focus on winning. But too much focus coupled with too much pressure could be tough for any athlete to cope with. It was her job to get him to relax.

Sarah Calhoun spent Tuesday morning at the office tying up loose ends but finding it hard to concentrate on her work. Her

Monday night had been filled with packing suitcases and taking
everything over to Mitchell's house for loading in the SUV. She
had slept little that night, tossing and turning in a state of fog
blurred with excitement, fear, anticipation and uneasiness. She
had always been nervous whenever Cody had to perform –
whether it was soccer, basketball or any sport for that matter –
because she wanted him to do well. She didn't particularly like
to travel and a weekend filled with Cody's race and close
quarters in a room shared with Cody's girlfriend had her mind
skipping from possibility to possibility.

Mitchell Burke woke up that Tuesday morning sluggish
and feeling not at all like himself. Like Sarah Calhoun he slept
fitfully the night before but for different reasons.

Thump-thump, thump-thump, thump-thump.

For the past few weeks he'd felt tired, no energy, like he
had only slept two or three hours a night when actually he'd been
getting more sleep than usual. He hadn't been working
particularly hard, his therapists were doing most of the physical
labor, he'd been concentrating mostly on the high school football
teams in the town and it had been a season, so far cross your
fingers, that had been remarkably injury free. He never looked at
the race coming up in Las Cruces as stress, but he supposed he
was nervous and at least a little stressed. He knew the doors that
would open should Cody do well and turn heads in New Mexico.
He was still a long shot, but the kid had the makings and deep
down, Mitchell Burke knew he'd do well. Maybe better than
anyone expected.

So why did he find it so hard to get out of bed on Tuesday
morning?

After struggling just to take a shower – it didn't help
revive him much – he made an extra strong cup of coffee and
drank it slowly at the kitchen table. He phoned the office to say
he may not make it in at all this morning like he had planned and
gave instructions to the staff in the event that he didn't. Then he
phoned Sarah Calhoun at her office.

"Hi, Mitchell, are we all ready to go?" she said excitedly
when she recognized his voice.

"Well, that's why I called. I'm not feeling well, probably

just the flu bug or something, but I'm thinking of waiting a day or so before I fly over."

"Are you OK?"

"I'll be fine, don't worry about me. Can you drive over and pick up the SUV? Might as well just take it to the airport, it's packed and ready to go. You can leave your car here and when I'm feeling better, I'll just drive it to the airport or get somebody to drop me off."

"Are you sure?" she said, trying to imagine this trip without him.

"Yeah, I wouldn't want Cody to catch whatever's invaded me. I'll get lots of rest, drink lots of liquids, I promise, and see if I can drive the beast out of me in a day or so. I'll fly over Thursday at the latest. You couldn't keep me away from this, not on your life."

"I don't know…how can we manage everything…"

"Sarah, listen. Lionel's got the training routine and he can check with McClelland for routes for tomorrow and Thursday. We've gone over strategy till everyone's blue in the face. Cody's ready to go. Just let him get used to the atmosphere and have a little fun with his training rides. He needs to be fresh and relaxed for Friday and Saturday, so it's no big deal for the next few days. If he's not ready now, no amount of training…what am I saying? He is ready now. Don't worry, he'll be fine."

"It's not him I'm worrying about."

"I'll be OK, I promise."

A cold shiver ran up her spine to the back of her head. She closed her eyes and took a deep breath.

"OK, I'll see you at eleven. Can I bring you something?"

"Nope. I'm going to use some of Miss Clarke's magic potions here in the kitchen and whip myself up a king-sized energy shake. See you soon. Drive carefully."

He hung up and went to lie down on the couch. *Thump-thump, thump-thump, thump-thump.*

The group was more than bummed when Sarah picked them up at school and told them about Burke. Cody seemed like he'd been dealt a deadly blow. His eyes went vacant when he heard the news like he was imagining the world falling around him.

Sarah took Lionel and Denny aside when Cody was loading the car and told them they were both now in charge of turning this situation around. Lionel was in charge of creating the training ride plan and Denny was in charge of lightening the atmosphere.

When they all packed into the SUV for the trip to the airport, Sarah forced upon them her positive spin. She had learned after her divorce that her mood was the single biggest factor in determining how she viewed the future. And she knew that futures usually don't come true unless you have a way to see them in your mind first before you go about making something happen.

"You know, Cody, the last thing Mitchell said to me was that you're ready. These two training rides tomorrow and Thursday, they're just to get you used to the atmosphere, but physically, you're ready to go," Sarah said as they drove through traffic toward the Oakland airport.

"Yeah, sure" was his lethargic answer.

"Look at it this way, man," Lionel chimed in "you're showing up with your mom, your girlfriend and some geek as a mechanic. All those other dudes are seriously going to underestimate you when they see all of us, you know what I'm talking about?"

"Maybe."

"No, really, no way they're going to look at us like professionals. All them other guys probably have coaches, just like you I might add, and we show up without one. Serious underestimation, I'm telling you."

"And the point is?" Cody asked.

"Maybe the point should be that none of these riders are professional," Denny added. "They all are in the same boat you are. Coach or no coach, they all have to ride just as far and just as hard. And the one who rides farther faster and harder faster wins."

Cody looked at her and smiled, "farther faster, harder faster?"

"You know what I mean," she said and punched lightly in

the arm.

"Sometimes you're the bug, sometimes you're the windshield," Lionel said.

Cody scrunched his face and shook his head and said, "Huh?" in mock seriousness.

"When you get lemons, make lemonade," Denny added.

"Oh boy," Cody retaliated.

"If at first you don't succeed, try, try again," Lionel said with a shake of his head.

"Every cloud has a silver lining," his mother offered.

"Stop," Cody smiled.

"When you wish upon a star, makes no difference who you are," his mother sang, sounding not even close to Jiminny Cricket.

"Right off the deep end," Cody said almost under his breath.

"I'm not afraid to die, I just don't want to be there when it happens," Lionel recited.

"Say what?"

"Woody Allen," Lionel clarified.

"Ah, great."

"The only thing we have to fear is fear itself. FDR," his mother added.

Cody looked at Denny like it was her turn to add to all this.

"I'm thinking, I'm thinking," she frowned.

"Ain't no mountain high enough," Lionel sang, "ain't no valley low enough, ain't no river wide enough, to keep me from getting to you babe."

"You're killing me here," Cody said.

"And he's got hi-igh hopes," his mother sang, "he's got hi-igh hopes. He's got, high in the sky, apple pie hopes."

All three of them looked at her like maybe she had slipped off the deep end.

"Sorry," she said, faking like she really was sorry.

"Now I suppose it's time to break into a little BFO?" Cody asked.

Lionel thought for a second and then grinned, "BTO," and

started to sing the Bachman Turner Overdrive song that had
become their theme song,

> *You get up every morning to the alarm clock's warning,*
> *Take the eight fifteen into the city,*
> *There's a whistle up above*
> *People push and people shove,*
> *And all the girls are trying to look pretty.*

Then Denny and Cody chimed in for the chorus.

> *You been takin' care of business, every day,*
> *Takin' care a' business, every way.*
> *You been takin' care a' business, it's all right.*
> *Takin' care a' business and workin' overtime.*
> *Work out!*

Sarah was grateful that the somber mood had been
broken, at least for the timing being, but she knew the kids were
still worried about Mitchell Burke. She was too. He was their
rock, their leader, the one that set the pace. He had always been
steady, never letting his emotions run the circumstances of the
day. He had a plan for Cody and he stuck to it. When the
teenagers got carried away with something – and they always did
– he brought them back to reality. Not in a crashing blow, no
screaming or judging, just in his calm, assertive way.

She had grown very attached to Mitchell Burke. She often
wondered if it was love. It certainly wasn't the type of love that
bowls you over and slams you down. Not the kind that turns you
all gooey inside, all lovey-dovey with stars in your eyes. It had
started out as admiration. She admired the way Mitchell ran his
life. Like many relationships, at first she saw only the good parts.
Looking back now, she realized that that was one sign of being in
love - the filter that shields all the bad qualities of someone from
the person that's doing the looking. Like rose colored glasses.

Then her feelings had turned to friendship, almost like a
partnership. Their cause had been Cody. Mitchell knew that even
though he wouldn't admit it, Cody missed having a father figure

around. And Sarah missed the male perspective in bringing up a young boy. So Mitchell stepped in to fill the void. Again he did it with an almost invisible quality – a little bit of instruction, a little guidance, a good deal of experience and a small amount of vulnerability. Mitchell didn't talk too much about his past life – and that had cost him dearly with Cody – but he wasn't afraid of revealing mistakes he made in his current one. He often would share his indecision about a business issue or a therapy case. Not so much that you doubted his ability to make a decision, but enough to realize that life was a series of them. She now understood that it was his way of sharing himself with her and Cody. He would share an experience in his life and the process of coming to a decision to reveal his softer side to them, to show that he wasn't just training times, heart rate goals and speed workouts. When he talked about the bike, he was solid. When he talked about his life, he was normal. Cracks in his armor appeared, not too noticeable to Cody and at the time only barely visible to Sarah. But as they grew closer together, she discovered that she knew him pretty well after all.

She had seen the chinks in Mitchell Burke and didn't mind them. None were too big to overlook, they were only normal chinks. With her husband she had tried to ignore chinks that had turned into huge holes. At first she had fooled herself into believing that they weren't game breakers. But gradually she knew that she couldn't avoid being swallowed up by the holes, that they would bury her, her marriage and probably her son too. She hadn't seen any holes in Mitchell Burke.

But she had missed one and it was definitely a game breaker.

ONE IS THE LONLIEST NUMBER

That Wednesday Burke stayed on the couch, but he was restless and out of sorts. He tried to sleep but it didn't come. He constantly checked the clock and estimated what Sarah and the kids were doing at that time. He had turned on the weather channel to check the local conditions around Las Cruces and emailed Lionel in hopes that he'd check the laptop for messages. Once they got to the hotel he knew Lionel would plug in and get on-line and he wanted them all to know he was still part of the team.

He didn't go into the office at all that day because he felt so terrible. He couldn't remember the last time he'd missed a day. He didn't turn TV on either. He didn't feel like he could concentrate enough to watch, so he had the radio on, turned down low to an easy listening station.

Burke was feeling guilty about not being with Team Calhoun. It wasn't like him to bail at the last minute when somebody needed and depended on him. It was so out of character he wondered where it had come from.

Certainly he wasn't so afraid of Cody failing that he couldn't bear to watch. In fact he expected Cody to do well, and he wouldn't at all be surprised if he made the team. And he knew that although he'd hurt Cody and the rest by not telling them of his past life as a professional racer, he also knew they forgave him. So he wasn't staying away because he thought they didn't want him there.

He had also looked forward to seeing the competition. It had been a long time since he'd been a vital cog in a racing team, and even though this was a long way from professional racing in Europe, it was still racing. As much as he had tried to hide his feelings for being on a bike, he missed it greatly. As a young man it was what made him vital, it was his passion in life. It defined him. When he gave it up there was a gigantic void and even though his new work had filled that void almost completely, he still longed to be on the bike. His doctors said he could still ride, just not professionally, just take it easy, it will probably be good for you, if you just don't overdo it. But he quickly had found out that once you've been to the mountain, it was hard to hang out in the foothills. Riding for pleasure wasn't pleasure to him. Riding to win was everything to Mitchell Burke and once he was taken out of the race, riding lost all its purpose. The passion was gone, so he had moved on.

He tried to convince himself he was feeling better as the day wore on. He made himself a little dinner, read a little and checked email. Lionel had received his message and written back that all was well, they had made contact with Mack McClelland and he had set Cody up with a training ride with a few other racers the next day. Burke wanted to call and find out exactly what was planned but knew his voice would reveal how ill he felt and he didn't want to disappoint the group. He still planned on flying out tomorrow night to be with them.

He went to bed early that night and slept sporadically. His dreams were vivid and filled with all things imaginable dark and scary. Like dreams invented by Stephen King. He saw blood, red and dripping filling up his vision from the bottom to the top, like a bathtub filling with water. Then he saw the blood overflowing, spilling all around him as he twisted to escape the vision. He saw scary animals with fangs and claws and menacing faces, but he couldn't identify them. At first he thought they were wolves or rats or even mutated cats, but they were somewhere in between all those animals. Then he saw himself falling, the sensation of being in midair when it wasn't possible to be there. No parachute, no plane, no wings. He imagined that he would be drowning next and sure enough he was under water. Searching for the surface, he flapped his arms and kicked his legs but got nowhere.

After each dream he would wake. He was afraid to go back to sleep, but didn't have the energy to get up to stay awake. He'd fall back into another dreamed up hell right here on earth. Spiders and snakes invaded him once, then wind so strong he knew he wasn't in Kansas anymore, Toto. Then water again, waves crashing down on him in such quick succession that as soon as he surfaced, another wave would hit before he had time to catch his breath. Then a man with a knife coming at him, the knife held high, but nothing but goodness and love on the face of the nameless man. Then a woman, a beautiful woman caressing his cheek, finally a respite from the dreamy horrors filling his night. But he couldn't get a look at her face. Who was she? Then she turned and he saw his dead mother staring at him, and her teeth were gone and her face was pockmarked with the decay of death.

He awoke again, drenched in sweat and breathing hard. He prayed for relief. If there was ever a God in heaven, give me relief from this night of blackness, please spare me. He thought of Ebeneezer Scrooge in Dickens' *Christmas Carol* as short, quick glimpses of faces from his past shot by his vision. Dreaming again, he waited for relief. All night long, it never came.

Cody always felt better when he was on the bike and today was no exception. The other two riders that Mack McClelland had introduced him that morning seemed like nice guys, considering in less than 24 hours they would be willing to run you off the side of a mountain just to win a bicycle race. His first couple of days in Las Cruces had been fairly uneventful. After they landed on Tuesday, picked up the rental van and found their hotel, they all let Denny pick a restaurant for dinner. She was downright motherly in what she would let Cody eat, He had to use some serious debating skills to talk her out of bringing her little food scale into the restaurant with her. He was rooming with Lionel and even though he wasn't tired or sleepy, Fitzy turned out the light at ten o'clock. Curfew, he called it. Cody fell right to sleep and never moved until the alarm went off in the morning.

He'd managed to locate Mack McClelland after a short, hard training ride. Cody spent the afternoon with six other riders testing the Treks in the mountains east of town.

He was in a single file draft with the two riders and feeling like a young colt ready to kick up his heels and have a little fun. For the first twenty miles the riders, one from Minnesota (how did he ever get enough training in living there?)

and one from Texas (who worshipped fellow Texan Lance
Armstrong) were riding much too slow for Cody's taste. He
figured they were hesitant to show what they had, wanting to
save any bursts of speed or tactical maneuvers for the actual race
tomorrow or maybe just saving their legs. The three of them had
been content to each take the lead for a quarter mile or so, but not
push the pace.

Since he was mostly on cruise control, Cody had time to
think. At first he had been flattened by the news that Mr. Mitch,
as Lionel always called him, would not be with them for the first
few days in New Mexico. Now he supposed there was a chance
he wouldn't make it at all. Cody had noticed that all the other
riders he saw had some type of coach with them. And, come to
think of it, so do I. I've got Lionel as chief mechanic and he
probably knows as much about my abilities as anybody,
especially since he's been keeper of the training logs.

And I've got Denny. Who else has his own personal
nutritionist and dietician – and girlfriend – all wrapped up into
such a cute package? OK, boy, get your mind out of the gutter
and concentrate on that blue jersey directly in front of you.

Cody also admitted to himself that he was glad his mom
was with him on the trip, too. He supposed not many 16 year old
guys would say that, but he wasn't ashamed of his feelings for his
mother like a lot of kids his age. Most boys were putting down
their moms and complaining how stifling they were to the natural
process of becoming a man, but Cody didn't have a father figure
in his life to balance the scales. Mr. Mitch was always willing to
listen and offer his opinions if asked when it came to those
matters that Cody felt uncomfortable talking with his mother
about. But he'd only known Burke for about a year now and even
though they had spent a great deal of time together, most of it
centered around two wheelers.

Not once in his life could Cody ever remember his mom
letting him down. Just because Burke got sick and didn't make
the trip didn't mean that Burke was letting him down. But if you
got right next to it, he hadn't made the trip, had he? He could see
that his mom was disappointed, too, but she was hiding it well.
She had taken over the mental side of coaching by keeping

everyone up and excited, not letting them dwell on the fact that an important team member was missing.

Texas boy was now in the lead and it seemed to Cody that the boy just didn't want to air it out today. And that Postal Service jersey he had on was just a little too Armstrong if you ask me Cody thought. Plus Texas boy was veering away from the mountains and when did Lance ever steer clear of a challenge?

In every aspect of the logistics of the trip, his mom had taken the lead, but when it came to anything concerning the bike, she purposely kept quiet. Cody really liked that. He and Lionel had mapped out the training rides for the two days when they found out Burke wouldn't be there. They had figured how hard Cody needed to work, for how long and at what speed. Cody liked being in charge. He still knew he had a lot to learn about bike racing but he also figured he was the one on the bike doing most of the work – heck, all of the work – so why shouldn't he take most of the responsibility for leading Team Calhoun. He wasn't so naïve to think he could do it without a coach, but McClelland seemed to have taken a liking to him and helped him check his strategy.

Cody wasn't sure but he also thought that maybe McClelland liked the idea of this kid showing up ready to compete without his coach. Showed some nerve, didn't it? All in all, Cody was ready to make a little lemonade out of this lemon.

And he decided now was the time to start. Minnesota boy had picked up the pace a bit, but not enough for Cody. So he shot around to the left, assumed the front position, and yelled,

"Let's see what these New Mexico roads are made out of, boys!" He sprang out of the saddle and pulled away. Texas boy and Minnesota boy both grinned and gunned it, too.

Mitchell Burke spent half of Thursday on the couch and the other half convincing himself he was going to make that 6:45 flight to New Mexico. He had refused any help from his staff to either take him to the doctor or drop by his home and help him pack. He hadn't eaten much all day but managed to force down a can of chicken soup and a peanut butter sandwich. Sarah had called twice during the day to check up on him and to answer his questions about Cody's preparation for Friday. She had seemed very upbeat to Burke and relayed good news about Wednesday's ride, McClelland's help, the accommodations and most important to Burke, Cody's attitude and demeanor.

Sarah said that Cody was having the time of his life. "He doesn't seem nervous, I'm sure he is a little bit, how could you not be, but he doesn't show it," she said.

Burke took this as wonderful news. He'd seen many an athlete who on the practice field excelled, but really tensed up come game time. The tension and nerves somehow affected the body's performance. The lack of nervousness in Cody showed to Burke that he had confidence in his ability and was ready to prove it. He might have butterflies in flight come race day, but once his well-trained body took over, they would simply flitter away.

Sarah was much more concerned about Mitchell than anything happening in Las Cruces. She urged him to see a doctor, but he had declined, saying he felt OK, it was just that he had no energy, he felt like he was always pushing a wheelbarrow under water, that's the effort it took just to get through the day. Since he had opened up about his medical history to her a few days earlier, she was hesitant to press him to come to New Mexico.

Sarah made sure she told him how much they missed him and how the three kids always quizzed her incessantly about his condition after her phone calls to him. She wanted him to feel needed and still a vital part of Team Calhoun. But she also didn't want him to do anything stupid just to get on that plane. That was the reason she had couched all her comments in a glow of good cheer – she wanted him to see that Cody, and the others to a lesser degree, had taken his lessons over the past year to heart. He had done well in training Cody on the bike, Lionel as the mechanic and Denny as the nutritionist. They were ready to excel with that knowledge.

She also told him that she had noticed something different in Cody this week. He seemed to have grown up almost over night. Maybe it was because Mitchell wasn't here for Cody to lean on, maybe he'd been forced to be his own man. But to Sarah, whatever the reason, Cody had stepped into the role wholeheartedly. He took charge of the group in his quiet, confident way, asking everyone's opinion and getting input, but in the end, he made the final decision. Cody had always been independent, she'd raised him that way, but now she saw him taking another step to being his own man.

Sarah told Mitchell that in a very direct way, he was responsible for Cody's progress. It was important for her to convince Burke that he was needed, loved and an integral part of their lives. Her honesty and sincerity moved Burke. He told her how much it meant to him to hear her say it and he made sure she would tell the kids how proud he was of them. Before they hung up, she urged him to reconsider his decision to fly out later that evening and he said he would, but don't count on it. He wanted with all his heart to see Cody race on Friday.

Burke managed to pack his bag, take a shower and load Sarah's car. He had been buoyed by his talk with her. What a woman he was discovering in Sarah Calhoun. Once he had opened up to her about his past that day in the park, she had opened up to him, too. Funny how that worked with men and women, especially those that had been hurt in the past. They were always so afraid of sharing a small piece of their heart for fear of having it stomped on again. But once one person gave a little, it became easier for the other to give something back. Once a trust was established, it was easier to reveal those feelings of fear or doubt or inadequacy and the vulnerability added to the trust.

It was a new feeling for Burke, too, to share himself with a woman. He had been so fearful of letting somebody get close to him. It seemed much more logical to keep his distance. But now he realized how wonderful it felt to have someone care for him, to express their…go ahead and say it…their love for him.

But although his mood was lifted by his talk with Sarah, his body felt terrible. He had experienced aches and pains during the day in his arms and legs. Not pains usually associated with some virus, where your whole body felt like it had been invaded by a small army of parasites, but rather very specific pains. Earlier in the afternoon he had experienced a sharp pain down his left arm and into his hand.

Now as he gathered his carry-on bag and opened the door

to Sarah's car, that pain flashed again, radiating in his shoulder and up into his neck. He doubled over, slumping against the steering wheel. He hadn't felt this since…since…no, no, it couldn't be, please God, no, not now!

"Damn it, no!" he yelled with all the voice he could muster. He slumped into the driver's seat of the car, gripping his chest, feeling like his heart was ready to explode, which it was.

It seemed like every fiber in his body was on fire with a pain from hell. Burke had only enough wherewithal to try to lie down in the front seat, knowing that if he got horizontal his damaged heart would have to work a little less to pump blood. And he knew the next several moments were critical to life, but he found he had little strength to do much about it.

It was all he could do to try and catch his breath. His breathing was labored and short as his body began to go into shock. He was sweating heavily now and his vision seemed blurred, either by pain or sweat or shock or a combination of all of those, he couldn't tell and didn't bother to analyze it. If he could just relax enough to rest, to get his senses back, a little strength, he might make it. He tried to think, where did I pack the cell phone?

He lay on his right side, slumping toward the passenger door, on top of his carry-on bag. The pain in his free arm, his left, was excruciating, leaving the limb useless. He looked to heaven, and although he wasn't a religious man, he knew God didn't care. If there was a God, and He accepted all comers, anytime and anywhere, as Burke had heard countless times from his church-going friends, maybe He would hear my call now. Please God, help me.

After a short time, the pain subsided just a bit. Burke struggled to push himself up enough to a sitting position to get to the bag and the cell phone inside of it. He nudged the small duffel bag to the floor of the car and managed to open the zippered side pocket and grab the phone. In his shocked state, all he could think to do was hit 911 and wait. The phone connected and rang. Would they come in time, Burke wondered?

WE ALL NEED SOMEONE WE CAN LEAN ON

Sarah Calhoun had been dreaming and she couldn't tell where the buzzing sound was coming from. She slowly came awake and couldn't exactly remember where she was. The buzzing continued and to Sarah it sounded like a woodpecker on amphetamines, tapping away crazily at some distant tree. Then she finally realized it was her cell phone, set on the ring and vibrate mode, on the table next to her bedside. Right, I'm in Las Cruces. Why is the phone ringing at…she looked at the green glow of the hotel clock…1:48 in the morning?

To most people, and especially to a mother, a phone call at this time of night only meant trouble. Mitchell, she thought immediately.

She grabbed the phone quickly, forgetting that she had purposely turned off the option for having the call go to her voicemail if she didn't answer after the third ring.

"Hello, hello, this is Sarah," she said, almost in a panic.

"Mrs. Calhoun," a somber, quiet voice came back to her, "you probably don't remember me, but this is Sheila Graham, from Mr. Burke's office, the receptionist?"

Sheila Graham, Sheila Graham. Sarah couldn't place the face, but vaguely remembered hearing the name someplace before. But it was so out of context, in her sleepy state here in Las Cruces, she hesitated to reply.

"This is Sarah Calhoun, right, Cody's mother?" Sheila asked after a second.

"Yes, yes, I'm sorry…it is… oh, hi, Sheila, now I remember," Sarah said. "Is there anything wrong? What's the matter?"

"Well, yes, it's Mr. Burke," Sheila replied, her voice soft and sincere, but somewhat clinical, Sarah noticed.

No, no, no, not Mitchell. Oh, dear God, not Mitchell.

"He's had a massive heart attack…"

Sarah immediately stopped breathing and her eyes welled with tears. A small cry, not quite a shriek, escaped from her mouth before she could control it.

Denny stirred in the bed next to her and raised her head in alarm. "What?! What?!"

Sarah tried to compose herself and Sheila gave her a second to let the news seep in before she continued. "He's in the best of care right now, at Mercyhurst Hospital, in intensive care, but…it doesn't look good."

"He's going to be all right, isn't he?" Sarah asked, almost not wanting to hear the answer. Denny had gotten out of bed and walked around to Sarah, who was now sitting on the side of the bed. She motioned for the young girl to sit beside and wrapped her right arm around in a half hug. She whispered to Denny, "It's Mitchell."

Denny put her hand to her mouth and a look of grief engulfed her.

"Well, the doctors aren't telling me much, not being family and all," Sheila continued. "I've been trying to get some answers but all they say is that it's touch and go."

Sarah's mind whirled with questions as Sheila described the last few hours, filling in the details that she knew. Burke had been in intensive care since early evening, but she had only been contacted around ten o'clock, since they hadn't been able to contact a family member. Nobody was willing to tell her much over the phone, so she'd driven to the hospital and waited to talk to the attending physician.

As Sheila described the scene back in California, Sarah whispered details to Denny, who seemed to slide closer to Sarah and hug her more tightly with every word.

With each detail, Sarah felt she couldn't keep the emotion in. She began to dab the tears that came and trickled down her cheeks with the bed sheet. Denny found some tissues in the bathroom and quickly returned to Sarah's side. The two women consoled each other without saying a word through their looks, their tears and their touch.

When Sheila had finished, an awkward silence engulfed

the conversation. Sarah took a deep breath to try to calm herself.

Finally, she said, "I'm pretty sure I can get on the first flight home in the morning, but that won't get me to the hospital…before, let's say…well, at least late morning." She began to formulate her plan in her mind as she spoke.

"Sheila, you've got my cell phone number, so can I ask you to call me every hour or so please?"

"Of course, dear."

"And I'll call you when I know our plans, OK?"

"Sure." Sheila gave Sarah her cell number.

"And one more favor? I know this might be difficult, but if you could get word to Mitchell that we, all of us, me especially, love him and that I'm coming…to be with him…as soon as I can get there. Can you somehow get that message to him?"

"I'll find a way, even if I have to push my way right into his room and park myself right by his side, I'll do it," Sheila proclaimed.

Once they hung up Sarah only allowed herself to cry for another minute as she gathered her thoughts. Denny had heard most of the conversation and was lost, too, in a state of shock and sadness.

"I think we have to get the boys up," Sarah finally said, wiping away the final tear.

The three teenagers and Sarah sat around the small table in the boys' adjoining room. When the brief story of Mitchell's attack had been told, the room grew silent. Denny cried almost silently, still clinging closely to Sarah. The boys' faces showed sorrow and confusion as they held their heads low and looked down at nothing in particular. Only Sarah Calhoun seemed to still have a grasp on reality.

"Cody, I know this will be your decision and your decision alone, but since we're a team here and all of us have put a lot of time and effort to get you here, I think you and Lionel should stay and race," Sarah said. "If Denny wants to, I'd love for her to accompany me back to the Bay Area to be with Mitchell."

Denny emphatically nodded yes and hugged Sarah even tighter if that was possible.

Cody was lost. His brow furrowed as if indecision had invaded him and settled in his forehead. He looked to Lionel for help.

"Your call, dude, I'll do whatever you say, but I'm by your side no matter what," Lionel said, anticipating his question.

Cody hesitated. He didn't want to race, all of his emotion had been drained out of him in the last five minutes. But he didn't want to quit either, he'd worked too hard to get here and who knew if he'd ever get another chance like this. He wanted to go with his mother and Denny because he felt he owed Mitchell Burke so much. He wouldn't even be in this position if it weren't for Mr. Mitch. But he didn't want to act like a child who had to cling to his mother when things got tough.

Finally, he shook his head and muttered, "I don't know what to do."

Sarah Calhoun knew her son and knew inherently what he must be going through. She saw the indecision on his face and she could see his eyes shifting to the right and then to the left as he measured both sides of the argument to stay or to go. She let him ponder it a few more moments, not wanting to seem pushy or too motherly.

The four sat there for what seemed like an hour. Sarah noticed that time had almost stopped. She could hear every little sound that seeped through the quiet – Cody's deep breathing, Lionel's nervous finger tapping, Denny's sniffling and the drone of the air conditioner.

Cody finally looked up and to the group, shrugged his shoulders saying without words there's no possible way to make this decision. He sat slumped in the chair.

"If you stay," his mother started, "Denny and I can take a cab to the airport. You two can take the van. We'll make you a reservation to fly back first thing Sunday morning and you'll be home before noon. I've got Lionel's cell number so I can call him with hourly updates starting as soon as we know something. And you know, there's not much you'll be able to do for Mitchell if you're back there."

"And besides," she continued, "this is a chance of a lifetime. You may never get it again. Don't you think Mitchell would want you to race?"

Cody shrugged again, not looking at her, and nodded slightly. "But if I go, I can be there for you," he said, trying to choke back his emotion.

Sarah saw immediately the sacrifice he was willing to make for her and it brought her to tears again. She walked to him and hugged his head tightly to her hip.

"Oh, honey, I appreciate that *so* much. You have no idea how much that means to me," she said as she kneeled down and took his head in both hands. "You've always been there for me – every single minute of every single day since the day you were born. And I know how much Mitchell means to you, I've seen it in your eyes whenever you two are together. He means a lot to me, too." Her tears now came freely, running down her cheeks and landing softly, one by one, on his bare knees.

"But Mitchell isn't dead yet, he's hanging on, and he's strong, amazingly so. He'll probably pull through this just fine. And I think it may even do him good to know you're here racing, putting all his training and teaching together on the course. It may be just the inspiration he needs to get better."

"And I'll be OK. I've got Denny for support. And I'm strong, too," she said hesitating just a moment for effect. "I think maybe it's time you did something for yourself. To race, and to make the team. I think that's the important thing right now."

She patted Cody on the knee, like the decision had been made, subconsciously wiping away her tears from his legs with one hand and from her cheeks with the other. She rose and with a slight nod of her head began in her mind to make plans to pack and get to the airport. She busied herself collecting her things and tossing them onto the bed. Cody drifted back to his room and lay on the bed, knowing that he wouldn't be able to sleep but not knowing what else to do. Lionel helped the girls pack but when it came to emptying out the dresser drawers, he slowly drifted back to the boy's room, too.

Cody was still in a daze. How in the world was he going to get it together enough to race in a little over five hours?

At 5:15 am Sarah and Denny waited in the hotel lobby for

the taxi that would take them to the airport. Cody and Lionel stood beside them looking like lost puppy dogs who couldn't find their master, hands stuffed into their oversized jeans, feet shuffling nervously and eyes fixed on the patterned lobby carpet.

Sarah had made arrangements to get on a 6:30 flight and talked to Mac McClelland in between phone calls to Sheila. McClelland had assured her he would take good care of Cody and even offered to send a van to pick up the boys. She declined the offered for the van but made sure he wrote down her cell phone number in case he had to get in touch with her. Cody was a little embarrassed that she was being so motherly, but he didn't say anything, figuring she had enough on her mind.

After hugs all around, the boys waved stiffly as the taxi pulled away. They stood almost motionless until it finally faded from view as it turned a corner a full three blocks away. Both boys were lost in their thoughts. Neither had been so much on their own in their lives and they were caught somewhere between being boys and becoming men. They were both 16 years old, in a strange town, embarking on a huge journey, with only each other to lean on.

"Is this right, what we're doing? Cody asked.

Lionel shrugged, shaking his head, "No clue."

"Well, if we're going to it, let's go do it," Cody said, finally looking into Lionel's eyes. He wanted to say how much he was depending on Lionel to help him through the next two days. He wanted to say how much he trusted him and valued his friendship. He settled for slipping his arm around Lionel's shoulder and keeping it there for a few seconds. They both nodded and smiled weakly at each other as they turned and headed back to their room to collect their riding gear.

As they checked their duffel bags for the third or fourth time since late yesterday afternoon, Cody couldn't shake the feeling that however much alone he was feeling right now, his mom was probably feeling worse, much worse. She hadn't talked much to him about her relationship with Mitchell Burke, probably because she didn't know how to, Cody figured. He hadn't wanted to talk at all about his father since he'd made the decision to sever his feelings for him, and maybe his mom didn't want him to have to muster up feelings for Burke after what he'd gone through with his dad.

But Cody knew how she felt about Burke, just in the way she looked at him and the way they were with each other. He saw how they held hands when they thought nobody was looking and how they could just talk and talk about almost anything and laugh all the time they were doing it. He knew she loved him. And as he and Lionel drove to the race that morning in the rented van, Cody somewhere down deep inside found that he loved Mitchell Burke, too.

It came upon him as a slow ache right in the middle of his chest. At first he thought it was nerves, but he knew his stomach handled all of those – the butterflies were flapping their wings in a frenzy at the moment. He tried to clear his mind and concentrate on the task right in front of him. He knew the course and had reviewed today's ride several times in his mind. But he couldn't shake the memories that flooded his mind, starting the first time he met Mr. Mitch in his office that day and unfolding in front of him like a virtual scrapbook. Each picture that flipped over in his mind told a part of the story of their relationship.

Lionel kept quiet as they drove, thinking Cody was in his pre-game zone of concentration. Lionel had seen many times before how he went almost to another planet as he prepared to compete. But Cody only thought about Mitchell Burke. Racing was the farthest thing from his mind.

The starting area for today's ride was a beehive of activity as they pulled up. Several riders had arrived early and were going through their pre-ride rituals and warm-ups. As Cody looked around at other arriving competitors, he noticed most had a contingent of people surrounding them. Many were parents, he guessed, and some were coaches, while others more in the background were probably family members there for moral support. Each rider he saw had stern looks of concentration etched into their faces.

Mac McClelland found them quickly and offered his sympathy for Mitchell Burke. Cody was amazed that how in the midst of all the frantic activity surrounding him, McClelland could be so calm and understanding. He told Cody about a time

20 years ago where Burke had ridden and won a race in Scotland with such genuine warmth for Burke that Cody felt tears welling up in his eyes. Then McClelland noticed Cody's blue and white jersey and mentioned it looked almost exactly like the one Burke had worn that particular day in Scotland.

He introduced Cody to a couple of his assistants who had quite a bit less composure than McClelland and instructed them to take care of anything Cody needed. They nodded in compliance but looked like they had a million other things to worry about and this was just one more thing to add to the list.

Cody still couldn't shake the ache in his chest.

After thirty minutes or so, McClelland gathered the riders and gave his last minute instructions. Cody had heard it all the night before at the pasta dinner and his mind drifted. He kept seeing his mother's face, then Burke and his mother together, then Burke lying in a hospital bed hooked up to tubes and machines, then Denny's face with tears sliding down her cheeks.

Lionel had set up his laptop computer in the small section of bleachers McClelland had rented for the race and positioned his sun umbrella for shade. He tested the transmitting device that he would use to talk to Cody during the ride and tested it by playing music from the laptop. Cody nodded with a thumbs up that he could hear. Bachman Turner Overdrive drummed into his head. It brought the first smile in a long time to Cody's face.

Time began to slow down for Cody. As he completed his warm-ups, riders appeared to him almost in slow motion. He could see the shifters move on his bike as he clicked from gear to gear. He was aware of sounds that he usually didn't hear. The hum of his tire on asphalt, the wind whistling through his helmet, his steady breathing. He felt his concentration slowly come back to him as race time approached. He made minor adjustments to his gear – tightening, then loosening his shoes, cleaning his sunglasses, wiping off imaginary dust from his bike – all pre-race habits to try to lock in on the race in front of him.

The sharp blast of a foghorn brought him out of his zone and signaled that the riders should return to the start area. His breathing quickened and the butterflies in his stomach jumped to attention and danced. Cody took deep breaths to try and stem the tide of nerves that engulfed him. He twisted his neck to relieve the stress that had gripped his head and shoulders. He drank desperately from his water bottle to combat his dry mouth. He shook each hand violently to try and exorcise the tension. Nothing worked. Then he remembered one of Burke's nuggets – a little tension is a good thing, make it work to your advantage.

The thought of Burke quieted the butterflies, but brought back that familiar ache to his chest. The riders gathered at the start line and were making final eye contact with their support throngs. Cody found his best friend, smiling, perched on the bleachers. Lionel raised his right hand in a fist, and slowly lowered it to his waist, imitating a trucker shifting gears. It was their silent signal for Cody to shift into race mode. Cody didn't return the signal and the smile drained from Lionel's face.

Cody looked at the digital clock looming over the bleachers. 7:07 it read. Which meant it was 6:07 in California and his mom and Denny were aboard the plane heading home. Cody shook his head, trying to focus on the race.

His gaze shifted back to McClelland who held the starter's gun in his hand, slowly raising it in the air. The tight pack of riders surrounding him dropped their heads, and almost simultaneously locked in one cleat – the sound startled Cody.

He couldn't breathe. Cody tried sucking in air but nothing came. He panicked. He remembered to blow out hard to force air into his lungs. Burke's face appeared in front of him smiling. You remembered what I taught you, didn't you?

The gun cracked and the small pack of riders clicked in their second cleat and slowly pulled away. Cody never moved.

He looked first to McClelland whose face was awash with sympathy, then to Lionel, who was bounding down the bleachers two steps at a time. Tears welled up in Cody's eyes and a lump rose in the back of his throat that almost choked him. He held the bike stoically and straightened his back, throwing back his shoulders. He took another deep breath as McClelland and Lionel converged on him trying without much success to control his emotions. Each looked like they wanted to ask a hundred questions, but neither spoke, waiting for Cody to explain.

"I need to be with my family," Cody croaked, barely able

to get the words out. "I need to be with my coach."

Neither of the three knew what to say next. McClelland looked like he was trying to see inside Cody, to see what he was made of, to see if this was a heartfelt love of his family or a fear of racing. Lionel knew exactly what Cody was feeling, he felt mostly the same way, and he admired Cody for being able to say what they both felt.

Finally McClelland dropped the veneer of being the tough drill sargent he sometimes showed and the look on his face softened. He still couldn't answer the question playing ping pong in his head, but his years of experience had taught him that answers often come in their own time. As quickly as he judged Cody's potential in the San Francisco, he decided not to judge him too quickly here in Las Cruces.

He put his big, bulbous hands on Cody's shoulders and waited for Cody to look him in the eye. "Son, when I heard the news, I was kinda surprised you even showed up this morning. That showed me somethin' in itself. You go be with Mitchell Burke. And when you're ready to show me what you got on that bike, you give me a call. You've got an open invitation to come back."

"Thank you, sir, I appreciate that," Cody managed to reply. He looked at Lionel.

"I already checked. There's another flight out around 8:45. We have to go through Denver, but...we'll make it."

Cody turned to McClelland, "I don't know how to thank you for this chance, Mr. McClelland and I'm real sorry I had to bail on you like this, but this is... just something... I think I gotta do, you know?"

"You just promise to call me tonight and deliver some good news about Mitchell. That'll be enough. We'll talk in a week or so."

"Yes, sir."

"Promise?"

"Yeah, I promise." They shook hands and McClelland looked into Cody's eyes one more time to see if he could detect any relief. Relief that Cody didn't have to race that day. He saw none, only remorse. He smiled at Cody, winked, and walked back toward the starter's table.

"Let's move it," Cody said to Lionel.

"Movin' it here, boss, movin' it," Lionel replied, a smile spreading across his face.

As they headed back to the van, Lionel lugging all his paraphernalia, he asked a question into the air, not wanting to look directly at Cody to hear the answer. "Think you coulda beat those bad boys, Codeman?"

Cody put his arm around Lionel's shoulder. "Someday, we're gonna find out."

I HEARD THE NEWS TODAY, OH BOY

Sarah Calhoun held Denny Clarke's hand tightly as they approached the information desk at Mercyhurst Hospital. "Mitchell Burke's room, please," she asked, a quiver in her voice, barely audible.

Rather remotely, the receptionist answered, "Intensive care, floor two. Take the elevator over there, turn right when you exit on the second floor. You'll have to check in at the nurse's station there." She smiled stoically, Sarah thought, wondering if the computer in front of her had told her anything of Mitchell's condition. They hadn't heard from Sheila since they switched planes in Phoenix and Sarah took that as only bad news.

At the airport in Phoenix, walking between flights, she had also connected with Cody and Lionel. She was a little stunned to find out that they were at the Las Cruces airport heading home. She shook her head in amazement as she heard him describe his decision, realizing the giant leap he was taking into adulthood. She tried to stifle her pride as he detailed their plans to meet her at the hospital, including contacting Lionel's mother so she could pick them up at the airport. He ended the conversation with an I love you, something he didn't say often and that immediately brought tears to her eyes. As she hung up she felt pangs of regret that he would be missing the chance to race, but they were quickly washed away by the strength and energy she drew from the call.

When they found the nurse's station on floor two, they were politely ushered down a carpeted, sterile corridor. On the way they passed what Sarah believed to be the waiting room, filled with anxious loved ones who barely looked up as she, Denny and the nurse passed by. Sarah began to get an ominous, dreadful feeling. Why weren't they going to be waiting with all the other people, why were they so special?

The nurse opened the door to a small room with half a

dozen sitting chairs and two people she didn't recognize at first. Before she realized it, the nurse had vanished and she and Denny were alone in the room with the two strangers.

The middle aged woman with the kindly face approached her, "Mrs. Calhoun, I'm Sheila," she said with outstretched arms.

Sarah felt relief in seeing the friendly face. They hugged warmly and Sheila held the hug just a few moments longer than a first meeting would normally dictate. Sarah felt the dread return.

"I'm so sorry, he passed on just a few hours ago," Sheila said, looking directly into Sarah's eyes.

At first she didn't comprehend. She didn't want to understand. Passed on? Passed on? What was she talking about? Mitchell couldn't be gone, could he? Denny's bursting into tears and almost collapsing brought her out of the confusion and back to the little room.

Denny had settled into one of the chairs and Sarah slumped down to comfort her, hugging her hard, not just in an attempt to comfort the young girl, but also in a futile attempt to find some strength she might draw from her. The two had been virtually inseparable for the past half day, holding each other constantly, always with skin to skin contact, never letting go of each other, each drawing strength from the other. Now they hugged, no strength left between them, only tears, only emptiness.

As Sarah cried for Mitchell Burke, she reminisced about the last year of their lives. She hadn't realized what a solid presence he'd been in her life, how they had blended together so well, especially lately. He wasn't demanding of her time but was always available for her. He'd been a little afraid to open himself up to her, but willing to talk about her life and her problems as long as she needed. As she had vented her frustrations – about work or money or raising a teenager – he often just listened, not offering instant solutions to her problems. They had kissed often, and warmly, even sexually, but he had never forced himself on her, never pushed the envelope to jump in the sack. Now she regretted that they never had.

She was overwhelmed with how much she was going to miss him. The feeling of remorse just kept growing, like a wave in the ocean you see in the distance that swells bigger and bigger as it approaches the shore and you're amazed at how big it is once it hits you.

Denny noticed how Sarah had been hit with the news and began to compose herself. She really hadn't been exposed to death much in her young life, except for a distant aunt that had died when she was only a child, and she hadn't known how to react. Denny's sudden tears had come from almost nowhere, the result of feeling the death of someone she knew well. But as Sarah slumped to the floor and Denny could see the pain on her face, she knew Sarah's tears came from losing someone she had deeply loved.

Sheila retrieved the box of tissues from the end table and handed it to Denny, who managed to sooth Sarah a bit with just the touch of her hand. They both got Sarah up and sitting on the chair.

The man standing against the far wall of the small room looked like he wanted to be anywhere in the world except where he was. Dressed in a dark suit and tie, he looked like a minister bearing bad news. He stoically held his head down toward his chest with his arms behind his back. But he didn't fidget or make a move to escape. He stood waiting.

Finally Sarah noticed him again and dabbing at tears, said, "I'm sorry," knowing she really didn't have to apologize for crying, but not knowing what else to say.

The stranger smiled slowly and shook his head as if to say there is no need in the world to apologize for expressing grief. He took several slow steps to her and knelt down in front of her.

"I'm Tom Rix, a very old and dear friend of Mitch's…and his lawyer. I'm having trouble finding words to express my own grief right now – I've known Mitch for almost thirty years – I can imagine how you must be feeling. I'm just here to help, however I can."

"Thank you," Sarah said, not knowing how he could help and wondering how come Mitchell had never mentioned him.

The next few hours were a blur, a mixture of sadness, nurses, doctors, paperwork and an absolute certainty that the future – at least the immediate future – held only darkness.

Rix began slowly to take charge as Sarah and Sheila found it hard to make decisions. He often gave them choices, do you have a funeral home in mind? I'd either recommend DePaul's or Bindley's. When they were unable to offer even an opinion, he offered a solution, but never acting heavy handed and never without an air of subservience to their feelings and wishes.

Sarah slowly deferred almost all of the work that needed to be accomplished over the next few hours to him. She realized she wasn't a family member, had no real claim to authority for any aspect of Mitchell Burke's life and that saddened her even more. She knew he had loved her, but in the antiseptic world of hospitals and death certificates, her attachment to his heart meant little.

She sat with Denny and Sheila in the small waiting room as Tom Rix worked with the hospital staff.

Sarah had decided not to break the news to the boys until they arrived at the hospital. She hoped that they wouldn't call her again because she didn't know how to tell them Mitchell Burke had died and she certainly didn't want to do it over the phone. Maybe she could find the words if Cody was looking at her, seeing her feelings, knowing her sadness. Maybe Sheila or Tom Rix could help. Maybe Denny. Maybe she wouldn't have to say much at all once the boys saw her face.

Lionel's mother dropped the boys off in front of Mercyhurst Hospital as she went to park the car. They had a relatively smooth trip from Las Cruces, getting seats on the leg to Denver and lucking out by flying standby on the flight from Denver into the Bay Area. They were only about two hours behind the time Sarah and Denny had arrived.

They ambled into the lobby of the hospital and asked for the room of Mitchell Burke. The calm receptionist checked her computer and with no hint of what she found, asked the boys to have a seat and she would call an escort to take them into intensive care. She made it sound like this was routine procedure and the boys were so mentally exhausted from the last 12 hours, they welcomed the chance to sit and wait for someone who might take care of them.

After a few minutes, Sarah and Denny exited the elevator

adjacent to the ground floor reception desk and walked slowly toward the boys. Cody could tell the moment he saw his mother that Mitchell Burke was dead. He saw it in her eyes first, an immense sadness that seemed to flow out of her. He glanced at Denny. Tears welled in her eyes and she couldn't hold his gaze.

His mother hugged them both as did Denny. They sat down in the reception area as Sarah swallowed hard. She grabbed a hand from each boy and looked at them with sorrow and compassion.

"He passed away just a few hours ago. They said once he got to the hospital he probably didn't feel much pain, but there was just too much damage to the heart. He fought hard, but…" her voice trailed off.

The dread that Cody Calhoun fought against for the past half day finally overcame him. The mental roller coaster he'd been on since the news that Mr. Mitch wouldn't be joining them on the trip to Las Cruces, and that led him through the excitement of the upcoming race, the devastating heart attack, the decision to fly home instead of ride and now the final blow were almost too much for Cody to handle. He felt like his chest had been trampled on. His stomach rolled, his breathing became labored and his throat choked. He fought back tears.

Lionel sat stunned, just shaking his head back and forth as if he couldn't believe what he'd just heard.

Cody hugged his mother and tried to express his feelings for her. He'd thought a lot on the plane how she must be dealing with this, another sad chapter in her life. But words didn't come easily. Sarah simply whispered in his ear, "I know, I know" assuring him she knew how he felt and that she felt the same way.

Denny stood close by and when Cody separated from his mother, he motioned for her to come closer. Her face was filled with empathy and like a sponge trying to soak up his sadness, she embraced him. Cody felt the connection, he saw her compassion, and he knew she'd do anything in her power to ease his pain. It was the first time in his entire life he'd felt that from anyone other than his mother. His breath came back again and the tightness in his chest faded ever so slightly. But the changes were noticeable to Cody and he knew they happened because of the young woman by his side. He vowed to himself to keep her close.

Sarah Calhoun saw the subtle change in her son, too, as the two clung to each other. She saw more than a teenage infatuation. She saw for the first time that a second woman had entered his life. Although she didn't have time to dwell on it at the moment, it was a scene she didn't take lightly. She liked Denny Clarke and the two women had become closer over the past few days than either could have imagined or expected. Tragedy can bond people so closely that you can see the flaws in their fabric. Sarah hadn't seen any in the young girl.

As the four huddled in the lobby of the hospital in a quiet haze of what could have been and what do we do now, Tom Rix once again took charge.

He introduced himself to Cody and Lionel and after a proper time of condolence, gave the group an update on the situation at the hospital. He mentioned that Mitchell Burke didn't have much family and in any conversation he'd had with him lately, Burke has spoken of the four of them as if they were his family. Rix asked if they could all get together the next day for lunch to make a few decisions on the final arrangements that still needed to be decided. Sarah offered her home and Rix said he'd have the lunch delivered, to not worry about preparing it. She thanked him again for being so considerate.

He shook the boys' hands again and gave Sarah and Denny a hug before he left.

LAST WILL AND TESTAMENT

"Mr. Rix, there's enough food here to feed a small army for a week, you really shouldn't have," Sarah said, looking at the four large platters of food that had been delivered late that morning.

Rix waved his hand as if saying please don't mention it. "But please, Mr. Rix is my father, call me Tom, OK?"

"All right," Sarah said.

Everyone had gathered at Sarah's apartment and the mood was dull and full of ache, the emotion of the past few days having drained them all of feelings except for a deep sense of loss. Rix had requested, without giving a reason, that Denny and Lionel invite one or both of their parents and both kids were accompanied by their mothers.

Sarah hadn't slept much the night before and was running on pure determination and grit. She had tidied up the house that morning and enlisted Cody to pick up his room and at least vacuum the living and dining rooms. He didn't have the strength to resist or complain.

Lionel had arrived by himself at ten o'clock, a full two hours before the lunch was to begin, just to lend a hand. He had turned on the stereo and searched for a CD that could lighten the mood, but nothing seemed to fit. He finally settled on a local radio station that featured easy listening, hoping it might please Cody's mom. She never noticed. After a few minutes helping Cody, he retreated to the garage and started to unpack the gear they had taken to Las Cruces.

The rest of the gathering arrived shortly before noon. After a lunch filled with mostly small talk and getting to know you chatter, Rix began to speak about the arrangements for Mitchell Burke's funeral and burial. He walked through the details quickly enough to avoid as much sadness as possible but slowly enough for the group to voice their opinions and concerns.

Nobody had any, except for Sarah who objected to the word funeral. They all agreed that it should be renamed a memorial service and should be an uplifting time of remembrance of what Mitchell had meant to the community.

After coffee was served, Rix asked them all to be seated in the living room, he wanted to deliver some good news.

"I knew Mitchell Burke for almost 30 years and as open and honest as he could be, he also had a bit of mystery about him," he began. Several heads nodded slightly in agreement.

"I remember once in college asking him where he always disappeared to on Saturday mornings when most of the rest of us in the fraternity were trying to recover from Friday night. I didn't find out till years later that after he'd lost his grandmother as a teenager he liked to spend time just reading to folks at the convalescent home down the street. He never let anyone know because, I guess he figured, nobody would think it too cool just to read to old people."

"And true to his nature, in his will, he left that same home, which I'm sure he hadn't visited in twenty years…well, at least I don't think he did, you never know with Mitchell…anyway he left them a sizable sum with the expressed wish to install CD players in every room and begin a small library of audio books."

That brought a warm smile to everyone in the room. Rix looked pleased that he'd been able to change the mood even slightly.

"That brings me to the reason I asked you all here this morning. Typically, the reading of the will happens at a more formal meeting, usually in my office. And I'd recommend that we do that. Probably late next week sometime."

"But I thought you all might like to hear some of the details of Mitchell's will before his service." Rix sat down on the couch and Sarah expected him to pull a copy of the will out right there and start reading, but he didn't. He'd had it all committed to memory.

With a faraway look in his eyes, like he'd been transformed back in time to happier days, Rix started up again. "A man of mystery indeed."

"Mitchell had a knack with money. Incredible actually, I've really never seen someone with such an astute awareness of how monetary systems worked. Of course, he was an economics major in school." A look of wonder passed through the crowd like a welcomed cool breeze on a hot, muggy day.

"And he had a sense…of…boldness…courage you might say, when it came to investing. I suppose he got that from his racing days. Maybe it was just in his blood, who he was. It was almost a sense of recklessness, like he didn't have anything to lose, but not quite. He seemed to teeter on that edge, that edge between bold and visionary and reckless and dangerous. And most of the time, not all, but most, it served him well."

Rix had a flair for the dramatic, like a trial lawyer in a stirring closing argument. His audience was caught up in his storytelling, eager to learn more about Mitchell Burke.

"I suppose you all know that Mitchell had little extended family. He was an only child and his parents died young, when Mitchell was in his late twenties. He never married." Rix looked up to his left toward nowhere in particular, and a smile crossed his face slowly.

"He often said if he had a wife and children, he probably would have been much more conservative with his money."

Then he looked directly at Sarah and held his gaze, then to Cody and did the same to him. He wanted to say that his good friend considered Sarah and Cody his family, but it wasn't his place. He hoped Mitchell had the chance to do that himself. He smiled again at both of them hoping they knew what he was trying to say without actually saying it.

"So…I digress. Let me give you the gist of the details. To Lionel K. Fitzhugh he leaves his entire music collection, his entire inventory of bicycle tools, parts and accessories, four first class round trip tickets to Cleveland, Ohio and four, three-day passes to the Rock 'n Roll Hall of Fame. And a $25,000 educational scholarship to be administered by his parents."

Lionel and his mother sat stunned. Lionel's mouth hung open and his eyes were open wide in amazement.

Finally, Lionel said, "Out–rage-ee-ous, totally righteous," slowly shaking his head in wonder.

Rix continued, "To Denise Clarke, he leaves tuition for a six week course at the San Francisco Culinary Academy. He also arranged for you to do a stint as an apprentice to Dr. Arthur Ting, the famed sports doctor in San Jose, and he leaves a $25,000 educational scholarship to be administered by your parents."

Denny's face looked like she was given the most wonderful gift in the world. She started to cry.

"To Cody Calhoun, he leaves his SUV, his bicycles, a cash fund of $50,000 to be yours at your 18th birthday and only to be used for the purchase of racing bicycles and traveling expense money for races, and a $25,000 educational scholarship to be administered by your mother."

Cody was silent, caught between the generosity of Mitchell Burke and the sadness he felt that he'd never be able to thank him.

"And to Sarah Calhoun…he leaves his business…his home…and the remainder of his holdings, which after estate taxes and fees, should total close…to three million dollars."

Sarah closed her eyes, put her hands to her face, and whispered, "Oh, Mitchell, Mitchell."

After Rix left and the kitchen was cleaned up, Sarah made coffee for the adults and Denny made frappachinos for Lionel, Cody and herself. The mood in the small apartment was still somber and the conversation was mostly about anything other than Mitchell Burke and his generosity. They talked about senior year in high school, how the football team struggled this fall and the basketball team would too. The adults mentioned how the holiday season would be here before you know it and the kids were already thinking they would look forward to the break from school that Thanksgiving and Christmas would bring.

A silence covered the group as they sipped their coffee drinks. It was a silence born out of respect for Mitchell Burke. A time for them to reflect, to think about his life, to think about what he had meant to them.

Finally, Lionel broke the quiet. "Mr. Mitch… he treated me like an adult, never a kid. Like how he taught me things about bikes and stuff, but he also let me discover cool things, too. He gave me a challenge, like tracking Cody's training, but he never told me exactly how to do it. He let me figure it out. It was my...I dunno... my victory, my success, not his, when I did. I never thought about that before, but that was pretty cool."

Lionel smiled to himself, like he'd discovered something hidden inside him, a gem. "He made me feel like I really fit in, like I was really a using my talents to be a part of the team."

It was another few minutes before anyone spoke.

Denny said, "To me, he was a great teacher. He encouraged me to look at things that interested me, not just textbook stuff. He let me see that working with nutrition and the body could help make Cody, or anybody for that matter, a better athlete. And he let me experiment and make mistakes, and never made me feel like a fool. He just listened...and understood."

"He was the most gentle person I think I ever knew," Sarah said after a few seconds. "He treated everyone he knew with dignity and respect. He made you laugh. And it was OK in front of him if you cried. He never lost his temper. And he was willing to stretch, learn new things, learn new ways to say what he felt."

"And probably the one thing I'll remember about him is how he made you feel special. I saw it with the way he worked with Cody, with you, Lionel, and you too, Denny. When he was with either of you...and me included...he seemed not be thinking about anything else in the world except you and what you needed. He was probably the most unselfish man I've ever met in this entire world," she concluded.

"If he was so unselfish, how come he never told you he loved you," Cody's voice shot out of him so unexpectedly, so foreign. "How come he never told us he was a racer? That he was so rich? That he was so sick? That he could die any minute?"

Everyone sat looking at Cody, who looked only at his mother. "How come he never told us any of that stuff...and how come we never said any of this stuff to him when he was alive and could hear it?"

It was finally out – all of Mitchell Burke's big, dark secrets – out in the open for all to see. Most eyes in the room diverted away from Cody, not really in embarrassment, more in reflection. Lionel wanted to say something to comfort his buddy, to say, yeah, I was thinking the same thing. But he didn't have the words.

Denny wanted to sit by Cody and hold his hand and maybe hug him, but somehow she couldn't. Maybe it was because her mother was in the room, maybe because on those subjects, she knew she couldn't offer much comfort. She didn't have any answers for those questions.

Sarah Calhoun could see the hurt in Cody's heart. She knew how he'd felt about Mitchell Burke – cautious to care so much for Mitchell, like a son might feel for his father, and yet wanting to have a relationship much more than friendship. Much more than pupil and teacher, athlete and coach. But Cody knew the downside of getting hurt, too. He knew how it felt when his father left. Now Sarah saw the same hurt in his eyes. The hurt of being abandoned.

"I don't exactly know the answers to those questions, Cody," she started. "I suppose he had his reasons…some we can guess at, others…well, I guess we'll never know. But one thing I've been thinking about for a while now. Isn't it ironic, that on the one hand, he was an all-out, go-for-the-gold kind of guy? A world class athlete, a great businessman, a terrific coach. But on the other hand, he sort of shut people out in a way. He never went all the way in his relationships. Sort of halfway, never wanting to get to close. Never wanting to hurt others…because of his condition…never wanting to get hurt, maybe."

Sarah thought back on all the times he had almost told her that he loved her. And how she would have readily returned the sentiment. She thought how close he'd come to expressing his love for Cody, and how eager Cody was for that recognition.

"I, for one, think it's kind of sad," she continued. "Here he was, so close to letting us all in, so close to having it all in his life…but he hesitated. He drew back. And now look at us. We're sitting here saying how much he meant to us, but knowing he could have meant even more. We're saying, really, how much we loved him, but deep down, even though we hope and pray that we're wrong, we don't really know if he loved us back, not all the way like it could have been. We think he did, we pray he did.

And maybe someday, if there's a God in heaven and a heaven above, we'll know. But for now, it's kind of hard not knowing exactly."

"At first I thought it was only his loss. His loss for not letting us in. His loss for not loving us. But now, I think, it's our loss, too. Not just because he's gone, but because of what we never had. We never had all of him. It's sad…really sad."

The mood of the room had returned to a low point. Everyone in the room had finally realized what they had missed. For Lionel and Denny, the pain was bearable. They lost a good friend, but Mitchell Burke would have never replaced their own fathers. They would miss what he brought to their lives, but they'd have other chances to know men who could guide them and teach them.

But for Sarah and Cody, the pain was almost unbearable. Sarah knew that she'd missed a chance at love and that those chances didn't come around every day. She knew that every time you missed a chance that your heart drew back just a little. Every time you were hurt, it took longer to heal. Maybe she'd never have another chance, not at her age.

Cody felt the pain of losing a father all over again. Although he'd never admitted to himself that he loved Burke like a father, he knew he could have. Mitchell Burke had been better to him for the past year or so than he could ever remember his father being. Burke had shown confidence in him, had taught him how to know who he was in the world, had trusted him, had let him grow and become his own man. He had shown all the love of a father, but had never said that he loved him like a son. Cody wondered if he'd ever hear those words.

Sarah flashed back to Mitchell Burke in a teaching moment. She saw him in her mind's eye, a vision came to her of him as a coach. She saw him explaining a situation to Cody and Lionel, like she had so many times in the past. She couldn't hear what he was saying, only the gestures he used. She saw his facial expressions and the way he beamed when one of the kids got what he was trying to say. She saw him clearly and vividly, like he was in the room with her. She also saw the answer she'd been looking for.

"Maybe that was the reason he was in our lives. To show how close we came. To show what we have to do the next time to have it all. Maybe someway God used Mitchell to teach us all a lesson. To not hold back, to not be afraid, no matter what the cost."

Denny walked over to the chair where Cody sat and knelt down beside it. She reached up and took his hand in hers, smiling up at him. It was her gesture, the only one she could think of at the moment, to let him know how much she cared for him.

Cody squeezed her hand and smiled back weakly. It was the best he could do.

Sarah continued, "Maybe there's a bigger lesson there, too. Mitchell had such a can do attitude in everything in life. Always up, always positive, always looking for the best way to succeed. Maybe that's his final legacy. Maybe that's what he taught us all."

"Sort of like the Nike slogan, only with a twist," Lionel said. "Not 'just do it,' but more like 'just go for it.' "

They all nodded in agreement.

As Sarah and the other mothers cleaned up the kitchen, Cody, Lionel and Denny drifted outside to catch a whiff of the fall air. The wind blew a cool breeze and after the heavy air of the cramped apartment, and the heavy conversation within, the teenagers felt relieved. They walked side by side along the pathway that led through the apartment complex. The walkway was surrounded by well-manicured lawns and lined with flowering shrubs and overhanging trees. They strolled almost aimlessly, Cody in the middle, his right hand clutched tightly to Denny's left, with Lionel on his other side.

"You remember when Mr. Mitch made that analogy, about the hard left?" Lionel questioned. "About sometimes in life you come to a crossroads and to go forward, you to have to give up something?"

"Yeah," Cody answered.

"You get the feeling like we're at another crossroad?"

"Yeah, feels just like it."

Denny looked shocked. "You're not thinking about giving up biking, are you? You can't, I mean, you're so good at it, and you've worked so hard. Please tell me you're not thinking about that."

Cody smiled at her, "No way."

"So what do we have to give up?" she asked.

"I'm thinking, maybe, that I need to give up school," Cody replied.

"What?!" Denny exclaimed. "You mean high school?"

"Dude?!" Lionel said, a gleam in his eye.

"No, no, I mean finishing up senior year, but not going straight to college."

Lionel nodded, like he understood where Cody was headed.

"You know," Lionel began, " California's fine most of the time, the weather's great and it's home and everything. But…"

"But what?" Cody played along.

"But I sure would like to experience just once in my life that Colorado Rocky Mountain high!"

"Sounds like a song lyric," Denny said.

Lionel nodded, "John Denver."

"Well, we do need a new coach, don't we?" Cody asked rhetorically. "And I do need to work on my climbing. And what better place to work on your climbing than the Rocky Mountains. Suppose MacClelland would give me another chance? Think my mom would let me move to Colorado if I made that team?"

"Just go for it," Lionel said.

"Hand me your cell phone, Fitzy," Cody asked.

Lionel searched in his jeans and produced the Nokia.

"You got McClelland's number programmed into this thing?"

"Number 8 on your hit parade…and moving up like a bullet," Lionel gushed.

Lionel handed to phone to Cody. As he placed it to his ear, he took a deep breath, punched the number and waited for it to ring.

Songs in the book

About the Author

Bruce Kirkpatrick and his wife and two kids live in Northern
California. He rides a four-year-old Cannondale CAD 7
aluminum road bike. This is his first novel.